GOLIATH AND THE GANG

GOLIATH AND THE GANG

DAVID WHITTET

ISBN 978-1-7386196-2-7 (Paperback – International Edition)

Published by Copy Press Books, Nelson, New Zealand 2023
Copy Press Books, 141 Pascoe Street, Nelson, New Zealand

Cover design by Holly Dunn

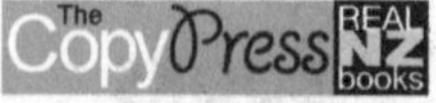

Designed and distributed in New Zealand by CopyPress, Nelson, New Zealand.
www.copypress.co.nz

PART ONE

HALF-BLOOD

CHAPTER ONE

Kaikōura Coast, New Zealand, July 2000

Aaron was just five years old when they took his mother away.

He felt so safe, tucked up in bed with his mother beside him. Her bedtime stories transported him to a world far away from the Gang and scary Uncle Ben. His horrid cousins, too. Nancy, the oldest of the terrible triplets and by far the meanest, had broken the last of his toy soldiers while Tara and Lucy just watched and giggled.

'Serves you right, scumbag.' Nancy raised her fist. 'Don't even think of running to Mummy, or you know what will happen.'

He did. Nancy would tell Uncle Ben, and he'd get a hiding. Why did they hate him so much and treat him like an outcast?

Aaron snuggled up even closer to his mother as she began the story. Nobody could harm him while she was beside him.

'Tonight, I'm going to tell you about David and Goliath,' his mother said, reaching for a book of Bible stories on the shelf. 'It's a story about courage and not giving up.'

Good. Aaron liked those stories best. His mother was a brilliant storyteller, and he loved the grotesque faces she pulled for the villains. Somehow, she always made them look like Nancy or Uncle Ben.

But tonight—tears ran down his mother's cheeks while she read. Why? 'David and Goliath' wasn't a sad story. It was about good triumphing against all odds.

'*David ran fearlessly towards the giant Goliath.*' As she read, his mother pointed to the pictures in the book. 'Look, David put five smooth rocks into his sling. He didn't take any notice of Goliath taunting him. *The giant roared with laughter as the young David took aim carefully. The crowd hushed as David drew back the sling and flung the stones at Goliath. They hit the giant on the forehead. Goliath fell dead to the ground.*'

Why wasn't his mother doing the actions as she read the story? He'd love to have seen her mimic David using the sling and Goliath's fall. And why did she keep losing her place in the story? That wasn't like her. Perhaps Uncle Ben and those wretched cousins had got to her too. Aaron had overheard an argument between his mother and Uncle Ben earlier in the day. It sounded nasty, and Aunt Helena had to break it up as usual.

'Aaron, my darling.' His mother put down the book and wiped her tears on the sleeve of her dressing gown. 'You must be brave like David in the story.'

Aaron stared at his mother. She'd never cried in front of him before. And they'd been through some terrible times together in his short life.

His mother dabbed her eyes and continued, 'If anything happened to me … and I had to go away …' She broke off and flung her arms around him. 'Promise me you'll be strong, and you won't be afraid.'

'Mummy!' Aaron held on to his mother tightly as she clutched him. 'You can't leave me! I won't let you.'

'Darling,' she gasped. 'Mummy can't breathe!'

Aaron's fingers dug into his mother as a loud bang on the front door reverberated through the house.

'Don't worry,' his mother said. 'It'll just be one of Uncle Ben's mates coming to take him down to the tavern.'

That happened most nights, but the men didn't usually bang that fiercely. And if it was just his uncle's mates, why was his mother shaking?

Raised voices in the hallway. Aaron shuddered. They weren't the familiar voices of Uncle Ben's cronies, and they were getting closer. Aaron's eyes met his mother's.

'Remember David in the story,' she said, almost choking on her words, 'and how he defeated Goliath.'

Did she know they were coming for her that night? Is that why she chose to read 'David and Goliath'?

A moment's hush. Aaron glanced over his shoulder at the bedroom door. He heard Aunt Helena's voice in the passage. *Tell them to go away. Please, Aunty.* However much he willed it, Aaron knew the men wouldn't leave. His heart raced as he heard the wood splinter and a massive crash as they burst through the bedroom door. The men towered above Aaron and his mother like hulks, casting dark shadows across the broken door frame and peeling wallpaper. Uncle

     David Whittet

Ben was scary enough, but these ruthless thugs with their cold, menacing eyes and bold facial tattoos, were so terrifying he almost threw up.

Aaron held out a trembling hand against the men. *You're not going to hurt my mother. I won't let you.* He scarcely felt the slap on his face as the men shoved him aside. When the men hauled her off the bed, the terror in his mother's eyes forced him to gasp for air. He knew then that he would never get that image out of his mind.

'Remember what I told you,' his mother cried as they dragged her away. 'Be brave! Don't give up. Your aunt will look after you. I love you, Aaron. With all my heart.'

'Mummy …' Aaron wanted to tell his mother how much he loved her too. But his mouth dried up, and nothing came out. Where were they taking her? What would they do to her?

Uncle Ben followed Aunt Helena into the bedroom and nodded at the men. Had his uncle come to rescue his mother? Uncle Ben always boasted he had the Gang under his thumb. Why wasn't he doing something now? *You can save her! Uncle Ben! Please!*

Aaron felt the bedroom walls close in around him when his uncle turned away and left the room.

If you won't help her, then I will. Aaron staggered to his feet and chased after the men. 'Let go of her!'

That got Aaron another slap from the men, and he fell to the floor. He raised his head to see his mother disappear into the night.

Aunt Helena helped him up off the ground. 'It's all right, Aaron.'

It isn't. Aaron pulled away from his aunt. 'I didn't even get to say goodbye.'

'You'll see your mum again soon, Aaron. I promise.'

Why did that sound so empty? Those gangsters were *mean.* As he sank into his aunt's bosom, Aaron wondered if he would *ever* see his mother again.

Months passed. Aaron's heart still quickened whenever there was a knock at the door. He would jump up and race into the hallway. Could it be his mother? Had she escaped and come back for him? It never was.

By the end of the year, Aaron had given up hope. Now, someone banging on the door just reminded him of the sound of the thugs wrenching his bedroom door off its hinges. He even jumped when his cousins dropped a pencil.

His mother once told him the Gang had stolen her childhood. 'Be strong,' she'd urged him, 'don't let them destroy your life the way they have mine.'

They already had. Taking his mother away so brutally broke his spirit and destroyed his childhood. Aaron's life would never be the same again.

More of his mother's words echoed through his head. *You must be brave like David in the story. Promise me you won't be afraid.* Those parting words remained with him wherever he was and whatever he was doing, from tying up his shoelaces to doing his chores. They gave him the courage to face the world. A fresh wave of determination swept over him each time he heard her speak. Aaron would defeat his two sworn enemies—Goliath and the Gang.

CHAPTER TWO

Parata Peak Power Station, North Otago, New Zealand, March 2022

What's wrong with these people? Why won't they listen to me? Aaron Casper stood at the boardroom window with his back to the rest of the executives. *So what if I'm only twenty-seven? This is 2022, not 1980.* He gazed at the cascading water pounding down the spillway of the mighty Parata Peak Dam. The glacial water was an exquisite shade of turquoise and gravitated like a roaring waterfall. Clean, raw energy. If only there were equal vitality inside the boardroom.

Water had always inspired Aaron. His mind went back to the day he first saw the dam. He'd blown his student allowance on a luxury lodge in the high country to impress Miriama, the love of his life. He'd insisted on stopping when they drove past the Parata Peak Power Station.

'Wow! Look at that!' Aaron was out of the car in a flash and ran up to the observation platform. His eyes had fixed on the floodgates, precisely controlling the flow from the reservoir. 'Hydroelectric power. Harnessing the forces of nature. It's the future!'

He'd told Miriama then that he would run that power station when he finished business school. She'd seemed more interested in finding the luxury lodge, but that didn't stop Aaron from eulogising about pure and renewable energy for the rest of the trip.

Less than a decade on, Aaron was the newly appointed CEO of Parata Peak Power. Success had come at a high price. It wasn't the endless nights of study or the inevitable boardroom backstabbing that brought Aaron out in a sweat. A bitter conflict kept him awake night after night. And it was close to home. Corey O'Connor. His estranged second cousin. Corey would see him finished if Aaron didn't get in first.

Concentrate. I can do this. Aaron took a deep breath and returned to the boardroom table. He immediately caught Margaret Lemming's eye. *Damn.* Margaret had undermined Aaron from the day he joined the company. *Don't let her get you down. She's just sore that you got the CEO job and she didn't.*

Aaron took his seat at the head of the boardroom table. Thank God for an in-person meeting. The last few board meetings had been via Zoom video-conferencing due to the Covid-19 pandemic. When they finally got back to the office, everyone wore face masks. How could Aaron gauge how the board members were really feeling behind their masks? Now he could see their faces and convince them to support his proposal to advance the company by taking over a rival. The pandemic had held back his plans long enough.

The directors certainly knew how to show their frustration, nudging each other and frowning. *Rise above it.* Aaron glanced up at Errol Troy, his late father's business partner. Errol had always backed Aaron, persuading the board that he was the rough diamond the newly privatised company needed to turn the ailing operation into a market leader.

And Aaron *was* a 'rough diamond'. With no time for small talk and niceties, he stood out from the rest of the board. His off-the-peg wardrobe contrasted with the other men's flashy Italian suits and the women's couture outfits. Plus, the battle scar on his chin. Aaron had often considered growing a goatee to conceal it but settled for a day's growth of stubble instead.

Today, Errol's eyes gave nothing away. He scribbled some notes on his agenda papers with his Montblanc fountain pen.

Aaron shifted his gaze to Tony Roche. Sat at his right hand, Tony was his oldest and dearest friend. The man who'd been at his side throughout business school and who always picked up the pieces when things crashed down around him. Surely Aaron could count on Tony's support today for the most crucial motion of Aaron's career to date.

'I'm going to go through the numbers again.' Aaron loosened his tie and undid the top button on his shirt. 'As you can see from the reports in front of you, we've exceeded all our targets, and we must look to new areas if we are going to expand.' He pointed to a pie chart on the whiteboard. 'The figures speak for themselves. We must broaden our base if we are going to increase turnover. And to my mind, there is still only one way to achieve this, the takeover of Jensen Industries.'

Daniel Hayes, a company veteran, looked at his watch and shut down his laptop. 'I've heard enough.'

Steven Salter, another long-serving director, gathered up his board papers. 'Me too.'

　　　　　David Whittet

Aaron jumped to his feet. 'Excuse me. We're not finished.' How dare they pack up before he'd called the meeting to a close! 'Hear me out.' He underlined some key figures on the whiteboard. 'I repeat—Jensen presents the perfect opportunity to broaden our customer base.'

'Bullshit!' Daniel put his laptop away in its bag. 'You won't get away with this. The shareholders will never agree.'

'They will!' Aaron double-underlined the numbers. 'We've done due diligence. The takeover will enable us to expand our turnover and increase revenue—'

Errol cut him off mid-sentence. 'Aaron, we've been through all this before. Jensen has powerful allies. A hostile bid would see us finished.'

Daniel picked up a spiral-bound report and waved it in Aaron's face. 'You call this due diligence? It's pure fantasy!'

Give me strength! Aaron fell back into his chair. 'Our auditors have vetted the numbers. They've cost and analysed every facet of the deal.'

'Creative accounting. That's all this is.' Daniel tossed the file aside. 'We all know why you're hell-bent on pushing this through. Personal grievances have no place in the boardroom.'

'Damn right,' Margaret said. 'Personalities aside, a risk like that is just madness.'

'Couldn't agree more,' Steven added. He picked up his briefcase. 'We agreed at the last board meeting that the Jensen proposal would remain on hold indefinitely.'

Aaron pinched his lips together. 'No. We agreed to progress when the time was right. And that time is now. Jensen is vulnerable. Their stock is down after the Westland scandal. We'll never have a chance like this again.' He drummed his fingers on the table. 'We beat them down. We capitalise on their weakness, and we crush them!'

'I wonder who manipulated the Westland business?' Steven said. 'Very convenient, wasn't it?'

Aaron leant across the table. 'Take that back immediately,' he said, spitting the words at Steven.

'No more,' Margaret interrupted. 'This bickering is unprofessional.' She took a deep breath and faced Aaron. 'This won't do. We are all here for the good of the company. Pull yourself together, Aaron. You may think you're a rising star, but you've a lot to learn about people skills.'

Maybe I have. But I'm right about this. Aaron returned her glare. Margaret cut a formidable figure, power-dressed in a designer suit. *Stay calm. Don't let her get to you.* Aaron straightened his tie and cleared his throat. 'I hear what you say, Margaret, but—'

'But nothing!' Steven leapt to his feet. 'Let's get back to the facts. If we take on Jensen, we take on their lawyers too. Don't forget, they have gang connections. On top of that, raising the capital to buy them out will spread us so thin that we'll be a sitting target for a takeover ourselves.'

Aaron stood up to confront Steven. 'Where's your vision, Steven? If we'd listened to you, this company would be nowhere. Who got us the Southern Power contract? We were an insignificant bit-player in this industry until I got us that business.' His eyes locked on Steven. 'If memory serves me correctly, you voted against it, didn't you, Steven?'

Steven snorted and marched out of the room.

'You'll have to close the meeting now, Aaron,' Margaret said. 'We no longer have a quorum.'

Tony reached out and put his hand on Aaron's arm. 'Listen, Aaron. We all appreciate what you've done for the company. You've been an inspiration, and it's thanks to you we're a force to be reckoned with—the envy of the industry.'

Aaron pulled away. He certainly didn't feel valued.

'You're riding on a high,' Tony continued. 'That's all the more reason to be careful. Why risk everything for a deal that offers us no significant benefits?'

'Exactly!' Errol said.

Backstabbers. Aaron was about to say the word out loud but thought better of it.

'I'm on your side,' Tony said. 'We all are. We don't want to see you ruin your career when you're just starting out.'

Aaron returned to the giant panoramic window and stared at the dam again. The pounding water matched his mood. *This takeover will happen. I just have to find another way to get around those spineless stick-in-the-muds.*

He overheard Errol and Margaret talking.

'He's just like his father,' Errol said.

 David Whittet

'No,' Margaret replied. 'Emir Casper was a pushover. Aaron's something else.'

Aaron remained motionless as the directors filed out of the boardroom. Tony came over and stood behind him.

'This is about Corey O'Connor, isn't it?' Tony said. 'What is it with you and Corey? I thought you'd be mates, not sworn enemies. You were brought up together, weren't you?'

Aaron didn't move his head. 'No. I was raised in exile.'

'But you're cousins—'

Aaron snorted. 'Second cousins. Twice removed.'

Tony put a hand on Aaron's shoulder. 'You could still be business allies. Why can't you two get on?'

Aaron walked away. Why couldn't Tony just piss off? 'Leave it.'

Tony followed him to the boardroom door. 'We need to talk. Please, Aaron. I don't want this to come between us.'

'It already has.' Aaron pushed through the swing doors into reception. 'The moment you sided with gutless morons.'

Tony caught up with him. 'I didn't side with them. I've always fought in your corner.'

Aaron turned to face Tony. 'I didn't hear you stand up for me when Margaret, Steven, and the rest of them shot me down. Call themselves entrepreneurs! What the hell do they know about acquisitions?'

'They're just watching your back,' Tony said. 'And so am I. None of us wants to see you ruined.'

'Balls!' Aaron waved his hands dismissively. 'This takeover will be the making of our company. Exploit Jensen's weaknesses. Seize their assets.'

'No!' Tony put down his board papers on the reception desk and flung his arms in the air. 'There's no business case for the takeover, and you know it.'

Aaron felt his blood pressure rise. Tony had no drive and no imagination. He always played it safe and sided with the majority when it came to the crunch. Aaron was about to say something he might regret, when the receptionist returned from her tea break with the afternoon post in her hands.

'Your mail, Mr Casper,' she said.

'Thanks, Hayley.' Aaron turned back to Tony. 'I expected it from those jerks. But you, Tony. I thought I could trust you. I thought you shared my vision.'

'I do … I …'

'Enough!' Aaron strode off down the corridor. 'Loyalty. That's what I expect from my team. And my friends. You let me down, Tony.'

Aaron was about to close his office door when he heard Tony and Hayley talking in the distance.

'Are you okay, Mr Roche?' Hayley asked.

'I'm fine … It's just …'

'You need to save Aaron from himself.' That was Margaret's voice. 'We're counting on you, Tony. The idiot doesn't seem to realise his job's on the line.'

Aaron slammed his office door. He thumbed through a few executive reports on his desk. None of those proposals would improve the company's outlook. No way should they waste their resources acquiring insignificant players in the industry. *Go for the jugular. Go for Jensen.* Aaron put the papers at the bottom of the pile.

He glanced at his mobile phone. Three missed calls from Miriama. He'd promised to call her the moment the meeting finished. But then he'd been expecting good news. He eyed the call-back button for a couple of minutes, then stuffed the phone in his pocket. It was too soon for comforting words and platitudes.

Miriama had taught him about meditation. *Let go of your anger. Concentrate on what you have. Focus on the positives. Then you will find peace.*

Aaron took some deep breaths. The vendetta with Corey wasn't of his making—at least not at first. Aaron had reached the top through hard work, grit and determination. Corey was only CEO of Jensen Industries because the Gang put him there.

Perhaps Miriama was right. He shouldn't take it all so personally. But the takeover of Jensen was a sound business move. Wasn't it?

What if Tony, Margaret and the rest of the board were right too? Was taking on Jensen a reckless act of vengeance? Aaron felt a weight in his stomach. Was his job genuinely on the line? Steven spoke the truth when he said they'd be taking on Jensen's lawyers and the Gang. Could the deal really bring Parata Peak Power to its knees?

No. Aaron thumped the desk with his fist. The takeover had to go ahead. Whatever the cost.

 David Whittet

CHAPTER THREE

Aaron glanced at his watch. Almost six o'clock. He usually went for drinks at the Bushman's Arms with Tony after work on a Friday. Surely Tony wouldn't expect them to go out tonight after the boardroom debacle that afternoon? Besides, Aaron still needed to clear his mind before seeing Miriama.

Squatted on his office floor in the lotus position, Aaron thought about his mother, Alicia. She'd told him the Bible story about David and Goliath on the very night they took her away. Urged him to be strong, like David.

His mother would have wanted him to fight Jensen—and Corey. Alicia had spent her entire life trying to escape from the Gang. Now it was his turn. Aaron needed all his mother's courage and tenacity to take on Corey and Jensen. Together, they represented one formidable Goliath.

Footsteps. Aaron was about to get up when there was a knock at the door. *Damn.* 'Who is it?'

'Tony.'

Aaron shrugged. 'I suppose you'd better come in.'

Tony opened the door and promptly took a step backwards. 'What the hell are you doing?' He covered his eyes for a moment, then smiled. 'Are you practising voodoo on Jensen?'

Was that meant to be funny? 'No, just meditating,' Aaron said. 'You should try it. Might teach you a thing or two.'

'Maybe I will,' Tony said. 'Listen, about this afternoon—'

'There's nothing more to be said,' Aaron snapped.

'There is. Please, Aaron.'

'No.' Aaron flexed his muscles and drew himself up from the floor. 'You showed your true colours in the boardroom this afternoon.'

Tony rubbed the back of his neck. 'Mate, this obsession with Jensen will be your downfall. I'm sick of covering for you.'

'Then don't. I can look after myself.'

But could he? Aaron had never doubted himself before. He stood in front of his office window. Though not as spectacular as the view from the boardroom, he could still see the dam with the water pounding down the spillway. Returning to his desk, Aaron clung to his mother's words: *Aaron, my darling. You must be brave like David in the story.*

Tony pulled up a chair. 'I know you don't want to hear this, but I'm going to say it. You're a dear friend, and I can't bear to see you throw everything away.'

'Throw everything away?' Aaron settled himself into his black leather executive chair. 'You're such a defeatist, Tony. I'm on the cusp of something great.'

Tony leant forward and tapped his fingers on the desktop. 'This isn't you. I've never known you to let emotion cloud your business decisions. And now—I still don't understand what it is with you and Corey O'Connor, but you're risking everything just to get even with him.'

'I'm not. It's a good deal. How many times do I have to tell you?'

Tony shook his head. 'I can't support you on this, Aaron. Not for an act of vengeance.'

Aaron glared across the desk. 'Don't talk to me about vengeance. Have you any idea what I've been through?' He got up and paced up and down the office. 'If you had, you'd understand. I was just five years old when the Gang took my mother away.'

Tony's face softened. 'I can't begin to imagine what that was like, but—'

'But nothing.' Aaron returned to the window and pressed his forehead against the glass. He could feel the force of the dam pulsate through his body. 'My life was a misery after she'd gone. Brought up as an outcast. Bullied by my cousins, abused by my uncle.'

'But you're a survivor.'

'And I didn't survive to let that son of a bitch Corey take over my industry.' Aaron turned to face Tony, and their eyes locked. 'If the bastard thinks he's going to walk over me again, he's sadly mistaken.'

'But don't you see? If you go on with this madness, you'll be handing it to Corey on a plate.' Tony paused and took a deep breath. 'He'll be the winner when the Jensen takeover collapses. And it will collapse.'

Tony's soulful brown eyes told Aaron that he did genuinely care. But Aaron wasn't ready to listen.

'The deal's rock-solid.' Aaron forced a smile. 'It won't collapse.'

　　　David Whittet

Tony sat up straight. 'I won't let you destroy yourself and everything you've worked so hard to achieve. Even if that means voting against you on the board.'

What? Without Tony's vote, Aaron would lose his majority.

'Tony! You can't do this to me!'

'I don't want to.' Tony swallowed hard. 'But you leave me no choice.'

'And that's your last word, is it?' Aaron pointed to the door. 'You've said your piece. Now leave.'

'We can't part like this.' Tony stood up and hesitated. 'We're still friends, aren't we?'

Aaron didn't answer. He backed away when Tony attempted to pat him on the shoulder. 'Just go. I need to be alone.'

Tony edged towards the door. He paused again before leaving. 'Promise me you'll think about what I've said.'

Aaron buried his head in his arms. Did he have any choice?

❧

Another three missed calls from Miriama. Aaron sat motionless in his office for more than an hour after Tony left. He ought to call Miriama back. Or better still, go and see her. If anyone could understand how he felt, it would be Miriama. So why did he find it so difficult to talk to her? They had so much in common. She'd lost her mother when she was little, too. Adopted by an eccentric Māori diviner, she'd grown up in a caravan, the *Gypsy Rose*. And like Aaron, Miriama was determined to get to the top. After attending a prestigious boarding school in Switzerland, Miriama was a finalist in the New Zealand Young Business Woman of the Year awards. They were the perfect couple. Or were they? Aaron shuddered. Miriama had treated him with such contempt when they first met. Could she really help him now?

It took Aaron another half hour before he picked up his mobile phone. Discussing personal matters was wholly alien to his nature. He'd reached the pinnacle of his career by presenting himself as invincible, and he shunned signs of weakness. His memories of childhood were both vivid and painful. Aunt Helena told him how his mother, Alicia, spent her entire life trying to escape from the Gang. The struggle had almost cost Alicia her life. She'd been pledged to her cousin Mickey in an arranged marriage. And when Aaron's father, Emir, promised her a new life away from the Gang, Mickey put a stop to that. He'd heard many graphic accounts of the shooting at his parents' wedding and how the blood spurted from his mother's gunshot wounds. Aunt Helena said it was a hired assassin, and his father was the real target. Aaron didn't believe that. Not for a minute. Despite a stack of contrary evidence, Aaron remained convinced that Mickey had shot his mother, determined to destroy Alicia's one chance of happiness. And he damn near succeeded.

Aunt Helena had never explained what happened to his father. There'd been a house fire, but she wouldn't say any more. Aaron filled in the gaps in his aunt's story with his imagination. There was no doubt in Aaron's mind that Mickey had set the house on fire. And in doing so, he had murdered Aaron's father.

If Mickey was a ruthless gangster, so was his son Corey. Aaron knew that firsthand. Corey had beaten him in an unprovoked attack the first time they met. Aaron hated them both. Mickey and Corey.

When his mobile started vibrating for the fourth time, Aaron picked up.

'What the hell's going on?' Miriama demanded. 'I called Tony when you didn't answer my calls.'

Aaron almost dropped the phone. What had Tony told her? 'I'm sorry. I just needed some space to get my head around everything.'

'Tony's worried about you. And so am I.' The line went dead for a moment before Miriama continued, 'I didn't realise you were taking quite such a risk with this takeover.'

Damn Tony. 'I'm not.'

'Tony thinks you are. And all to get one over on Corey.'

'He's wrong. The company's on its knees. We need Jensen's business.'

'Yes, but …' Another pause. 'Does it have to be Jensen? There must be other companies you could buy out with much less hassle.'

Why doesn't she trust me? 'Jensen is the perfect acquisition. When have I ever made an ill-considered business decision?'

'Never. But have you ever been this emotionally involved in a deal before?'

Aaron hesitated. Trust Miriama to see right through him. 'Yes, it's personal, but—'

'What is it between you and Corey? Why won't you tell me?'

    David Whittet

'There's nothing to tell.'

'Bollocks!' Miriama's reaction was so explosive that Aaron had to take the phone away from his ear. 'You might get away with that crap with Tony, but don't you bullshit me.'

'I'm not. Honestly …'

'Then get yourself round to my place. I want the truth about you and Corey.'

'Okay.' Aaron shoved some papers in his briefcase and grabbed his car keys. 'I'm on my way.'

'We need to be open with each other if we're going to make this relationship work,' Miriama insisted. 'No secrets.'

'I know. See you in a minute. Love you.'

No secrets. Aaron shuddered as the call ended, and he stuffed his phone into his pocket. His life had been a succession of secrets and uncertainties. How could he make Miriama understand?

Aaron unlocked his car in the parking lot. He glanced across at the reservoir. It looked so tranquil in the twilight. If only Aaron's mind were equally calm. He continued to overanalyse the situation during the twenty-minute drive. To explain how the feud with Corey started, Aaron would have to dredge up childhood memories he desperately wanted to forget. He'd have to live through his beloved mother's kidnapping again.

Twenty-two years on from the night of terror when the thugs took her away, Aaron was no nearer knowing what happened to her. Was her disappearance Mickey's fault too? Aunt Helena insisted that Mickey had supported Alicia through her pregnancy. If he had, which Aaron doubted, why wasn't he there to protect her when the Gang took her away? And if Mickey hadn't been such an incorrigible playboy, Corey wouldn't have been born.

Going through all this again with Miriama would remind her of his gang roots. She had despised him for that when they first met. But that was a lifetime ago and they had both changed so much since then.

Aaron drew up outside Miriama's apartment. She wanted the truth about Corey. Aaron just wanted answers about his mother. Would he ever know the whole story?

CHAPTER FOUR

Roaring Creek, West Coast, New Zealand, 1995

Had Mickey noticed? Alicia lay back in bed and watched him get dressed. She'd thrown up twice already that morning, and her tummy was beginning to show. Alicia covered herself with the sheet. She'd have to tell him soon.

'Mickey …'

He turned towards her, his face covered in shaving cream. 'What?'

Alicia retreated under the bedclothes. 'Nothing.'

Why was life so difficult? Alicia was born into the Gang and had spent her entire life trying to escape. Her father, Reggie, was a notorious gangster and president of the Godzone Gorillas. Mickey's upbringing had been equally brutal. He was groomed to be a future Gang leader, with frequent beatings from his father, Ronnie.

What chance did either of them have coming from such an ignominious family? Ronnie and Reggie were twin brothers, named after the infamous Kray twins and, with their brutality and extortion rackets, despised as much as their legendary namesakes. The family came from generations of gangsters in the East End of London. A failed bank heist before Reggie and Ronnie were born, had forced their parents to leave England. As a result, the family had invaded the sleepy settlement of Roaring Creek on the West Coast of New Zealand's South Island and had since terrorised the once-peaceful locals.

Alicia peeked at Mickey from under the bedclothes. He was shaving with his cut-throat razor. She was always afraid he'd cut himself.

Mickey had been Alicia's one childhood friend, ever since the mischievous rascal had scaled down a tree at the Roaring Creek Falls, pretending to be Tarzan. The cousins had invented a make-believe gang, which Alicia called The Roaring Creek Rescuers. Their gang would be just and undo the evils of the Godzone Gorillas.

Alicia sighed as she pulled back the blankets. Everything had changed when Mickey was chosen as the president-elect of the Godzone Gorillas and became a shameless playboy. Gone was that playful monkey who always put a smile on Alicia's face, replaced by a debauched Lothario with a penthouse pad full of giggling girls.

Worse still, the women of the Gang forced Alicia into an arranged marriage with Mickey. A bitter feud between Ronnie and Reggie had cost everyone dear. The women saw an arranged marriage as a way to unite the divided family. But it hadn't stopped Mickey's wanton behaviour.

Alicia shuddered at the memory and turned her thoughts towards Emir. Unable to tolerate Mickey's hedonistic behaviour any longer, she'd left him and gone back to live with her father. Not that life was any better there. Then Emir burst into her life. The hotshot businessman from the big smoke of Auckland. The man she believed would finally take her away from the Gang. Alicia had met him at the Roaring Creek Falls, too. He was scouting for a possible business venture to bottle mineral water from the falls and exploit their exceptional health-giving properties. Alicia had always known her falls were unique.

Emir *had* enabled Alicia to fulfil her lifelong dream of escaping from the Gang. He'd bought a million-dollar house in the Coromandel for their future together. It was everything she had ever dreamt of. And more.

How quickly it had all fallen apart. Gang reprisals were swift and deadly. Alicia's wedding to Emir was cut short by a barrage of bullets from a masked gunman. She was sure it was an act of vengeance by Mickey. Then, as she recovered from surgery to remove the bullets, their new home was set ablaze, leaving Emir dead and Alicia with severe burns.

Alicia had turned to the only person she could trust—Kāterina, a renowned Māori diviner who lived in a gypsy caravan in the middle of a forest. The caravan was a treasure trove of ornate trinkets, old books, gems and oddities—Kāterina called it an Aladdin's cave. Visits to Kāterina's caravan were a highlight of Alicia's childhood and a heavenly break from the grim reality of life at home.

After the fire, Kāterina had a message Alicia didn't want to hear. At least, not at the time. But Kāterina was a wise soul, and Alicia forced herself to listen. Kāterina unravelled the painful truth of the situation. That the gunman at the wedding was not Mickey but an assassin, and that Emir was the intended target. Likewise, Mickey wasn't responsible for setting fire to the house. It was one of

Emir's enemies, a business partner he'd double-crossed. Mickey had rescued her from the inferno. He was the hero, not the villain.

Four months on from the fire and here she was. Back with Mickey and watching him shave. They'd recommitted to each other at a moving ceremony in front of the Roaring Creek Falls. They were 'blood cousins', just like they'd been in childhood, and Mickey promised he'd be there for her whatever the future brought.

Alicia was happy, blissfully so, except—she held her tummy. She was pregnant, but not with Mickey's child. Alicia was carrying Emir's baby, conceived on the night they had made love before the fire broke out. Mickey had grown up so much. He was a changed man and had put his playboy lifestyle behind him—but would he ever be mature enough to accept another man's child?

Mickey put down his shaving brush and grinned at her. 'You should have seen Edith's face when I called on her last night.' He wiped the remaining shaving cream off his face. 'She thought I'd come back for more of her takings.'

Alicia sat up. Mickey's tattooed face, with 'Godzone Gorillas' branded on his forehead, was enough to scare anyone, never mind a frail old lady like Edith. Thank goodness Mickey was just doing one of what she liked to call his 'mercy runs'. She'd coined the term when they were children to describe Mickey's brave and selfless acts in undoing the misery and injustice perpetrated by the Gang. It was one of the qualities that first attracted her to Mickey.

When he was a boy, Mickey had to accompany his father, Ronnie, to collect protection money for the Gang. Ronnie was determined to bring Mickey up as a ruthless gangster. Mickey hated it and would tell Alicia how much it hurt him to see frail, elderly women bullied and robbed of what meagre savings they had. Mickey felt their pain and was determined to do something about it. After dark, he would climb out of his bedroom window and go around to their houses, giving the money back to them.

Now he was president-elect of the Godzone Gorillas, and the risks were even deadlier. Mickey would be expelled from the Gang and punished severely if he got caught. Undeterred, Mickey continued his mission and delighted in telling Alicia about the 'mercy run' he had just done for Edith.

As president-elect, Mickey had to be seen to be obeying Gang orders. With

     David Whittet

a heavy heart, Mickey had accompanied two brutal gangsters when they raided Edith's grocery store the previous day, demanding protection money.

'Todd and Damon,' Mickey said, 'they're mean as hell. The bastards looted the shop. Damon started kicking cans off the shelves while Todd helped himself to ciggies from behind the counter.'

Alicia shuddered as Mickey went on to describe how Todd threatened Edith with his club.

'The son of a bitch has no heart,' Mickey said. 'He shoved her against the wall and screamed at her. "Open the bloody till and hand over your money. Or else."

'"Please," Edith pleaded. "My protection money's not due till tomorrow."

'Todd just kept laying into her. "Too bad. We've come for it today."'

Alicia had witnessed countless Gang raids and could picture the scene Mickey painted all too clearly. Mickey told her how Edith had fumbled to open the till with her arthritic fingers. Todd got impatient and smashed the cash register open with his club. While Todd and Damon stood laughing at her, Mickey had picked the cans up off the floor and stuffed them in a sack.

Alicia spotted a tear in Mickey's eye when he explained how Edith wept when they left with everything they had collected. To keep up the pretence that he was a heartless gangster, he'd boasted about the amount of food they'd stolen as they left the shop.

'I told them that with this much grub, we wouldn't need to go grocery shopping for months.' Mickey pulled on his T-shirt and smiled at Alicia. 'If only I could have told Edith I'd be back with her money and all the food we'd taken.'

Alicia got out of bed and put on her dressing gown, carefully concealing her tummy. 'I wish I could have been there when you took the money back.'

'It was wicked,' Mickey said. 'She really thought I was going to clean her out again.

'"Please, God, not my life savings," she kept saying. "Anything but that."'

'Poor soul,' Alicia said. 'She's struggled to keep that store afloat since her husband died. And with the Gang taking what little money she earns …'

Mickey beamed. 'Not any more. I told Edith, "Whatever the Gang steals from you during the day, I bring back at night. With interest."'

'Just be careful,' Alicia said. 'If Reggie gets to hear—'

'He won't.' Mickey grinned. 'I'm way smarter than Reggie.'

Alicia shuddered. Her father, Reggie, the Gang leader, had spies everywhere. *Mickey knows that as well as I do. What if …* Alicia stopped herself and cleared her throat. 'Be careful, Mickey. My father's no fool. Just wait till he notices the coffers are down.'

'Chill.' Mickey's grin widened. 'If my old man Ronnie taught me anything, it was how to cook the books.'

Alicia sat on the edge of the bed. 'Mickey …'

'What?'

'There's something I've been wanting to tell you.'

Mickey sat down next to her. 'Spill. Is it about the bathroom? I promise I'll clear up the mess when I get home.'

'No. It's not that.'

'What then?'

'Nothing …' She broke off. 'At least, it can wait.'

Alicia couldn't tell him now. Twenty-seven years of misery, and she'd finally found happiness with Mickey. Admittedly, she hadn't managed her childhood dream of escaping from the Gang. Breaking free wasn't important right now. Righting the wrongs, undoing the damage the Gang had inflicted on the community—that felt even better.

'Okay then.' Mickey stood up. 'Got to go.' He reached for his jacket. 'The more money we collect today, the more I'll have to give back tonight!'

Alicia felt a twinge and held her stomach. They had only been back together for a few weeks, and already they were making a difference. With Mickey at her side, they had the opportunity to change the Gang forever—something they'd plotted so long ago as children. Would her secret put all this at risk?

Five more times over the next couple of days, Alicia sat Mickey down to tell him. Why was it so hard to break the news? And why did she always bottle it? Had he really no idea? Even if Mickey hadn't noticed her tummy or the number of times she disappeared to the bathroom, he must have realised something was up.

Would the moment ever be right? Each night, Mickey crashed out on the bed once he got home from the midnight mercy run. No chance to talk then.

   David Whittet

Not even to ask how much protection money he'd given back to the Gang's victims. Alicia lay awake night after night, his snoring vibrating through the timber framework of their tiny bach. At least there was something useful she could do. Mickey's former bachelor pad definitely needed a feminine touch. Alicia spent the early hours scrubbing the kitchen and throwing out all the rotten food. She'd bought some houseplants and a couple of throw pillows to make it feel more like home.

Exhausted, Alicia sat on the edge of the bed and admired her handiwork. She looked down at her belly and caressed it gently. Despite everything she'd learnt about Emir—Kāterina's revelations and further damning evidence of his shady business dealings—there was still a thrill in her heart that something born of their love lived on in her body. No amount of rationalisation could take that away.

Mickey stirred. 'Hey, babe, what is it?' He wiped the sleep from his eyes. 'Come back to bed.'

Tell him. Tell him now. Alicia got up from the bed. 'Couldn't sleep. I'll boil the jug and make some coffee.'

Mickey was asleep again when Alicia returned to the bedroom with two cups of coffee. *Another opportunity missed.*

Alicia eventually decided on a picnic at the Roaring Creek Falls on Sunday. Since childhood, her beloved waterfalls had been there for her, comforting her darkest moments and sharing her joys. She prayed they'd work their magic for her today. Soften Mickey's heart and help him to understand.

Alicia nibbled at a sandwich. Mickey gobbled a steak and kidney pie and washed it down with a couple of cans of beer. Carloads of day-trippers arrived while they ate. *Damn!* Alicia had pinned her hopes on it being quiet so they could talk in peace.

A group of kids at the riverbank skimmed stones across the water.

'They've no idea,' Mickey said. 'I'm going to show them how it's done.'

Yeah right! Alicia gave Mickey a gentle nudge. 'Go on then. But I seem to remember you always lost when we played that game as kids.'

'Funny. I don't remember that.' Mickey took another swig of beer and went to join the children at the water's edge.

Alicia watched him play with the kids as she cleared up their picnic. He showed them how to take aim and flick the stones. Mickey must have had some practice since they were little—his stones bounced over the river time after time.

One of the kids had a football, and Mickey played with them in the adjacent paddock. Alicia hadn't seen Mickey so carefree since they were children. She ran her fingers through her hair. It seemed like a lifetime since she'd caught sight of that wicked grin from the impish scamp who'd won her heart as a little girl.

'Goal!' Mickey cried as one lad scored the winning shot. He ruffled the boy's hair. 'You'll be the next Maradona.'

Alicia wiped a tear from her eye. *He'll make a wonderful father.*

Sunset and the day-trippers had all left. Alicia and Mickey sat alone on a log in front of the falls.

'Mickey …' Alicia glanced over her shoulder at her beloved falls for courage.

'What is it?'

'I've something to tell you …' She broke off again. *Get a grip, girl. You're not going to bottle it this time.*

Mickey rested his hand on her knee and stroked it gently. Would he still be as affectionate when he knew?

Alicia took a deep breath. 'I'm carrying Emir's child.'

Silence.

Alicia raised her head to meet Mickey's eyes. His face remained expressionless.

'Say something. Micky! Please!'

Mickey pulled back. 'How long have you known?' His eyes widened. 'Did you know when we—'

'No! I'd no idea.' Alicia flinched. Her mind had been all over the place in the lead up to the renewal ceremony with Mickey. Had she really not known? She'd been suspicious, but convinced herself that her missed periods were because of the stress. 'Honestly, Mickey. I just started feeling sick this week. So I got a pregnancy test.'

'And Emir's definitely the father?'

Alicia nodded. 'There hasn't been anyone else.'

          David Whittet

Mickey stood up and walked around in a circle. What was he thinking? Did he believe her about the ceremony? Should she say more, or would that just make things worse?

At last, he sat down again beside her and shuffled on the log.

'Emir's child … *Emir's child* …' Mickey repeated the words under his breath, then glanced up at Alicia. 'Have you any idea what that means?'

'I know this will be difficult for you … accepting someone else's child … but … we can make it work.' Alicia reached out and put her arm around Mickey. 'We'll get through this together.'

'Maybe we could—if it was just us.' Mickey rapped his fingers on the log. 'But Emir was a sworn enemy of the Gang. That means his child will be … a half-blood.'

Alicia clutched her belly. 'A half-blood?'

'To the Gang, yes.' Mickey pulled away. 'Who knows what they'll do to the poor kid—or to us. There'll be a price on all our heads.'

No! Alicia had just made peace with her father. He wouldn't do that—would he? Alicia lowered her head. What if Mickey was right? She knew how much her father despised Emir, but she'd been so worried about what Mickey would think that she'd shut everything else out of her mind.

'We could run away together. Start a new life somewhere else. Unless …' Alicia swallowed hard. 'Unless *you* think my baby will be a half-blood too.'

'No … I don't think that …' Mickey stared down at the ground. 'It's just … you know the Gang. They'd track us down.'

'Not if we play it right.' Alicia gave him a darting gaze. 'You said yourself you're way smarter than Reggie.'

'Who'd look after all the old ladies and take their money back if we disappear?' Mickey jumped back to his feet. 'Besides, there's something else.'

'What?'

Mickey took a step back. 'This isn't easy.'

'Go on.'

Alicia bit her lip as she waited for him to continue. Whatever it was, it couldn't be any harder for Mickey than it had been for her.

'I have a son.' Mickey clasped his hands together. 'At least, I think I have.'

Alicia's jaw dropped. Why was she surprised? Given Mickey's womanising past, he'd probably fathered hosts of children. 'What do you mean? You *think* you have?'

'You remember Tammy? She had a son, Corey. And she claims I'm the father.'

As if Alicia could ever forget. Mickey had a different girl at every party, and his shameful behaviour on the night he seduced Tammy had been the talk of the community for months. Alicia shuddered at the memory. Mickey was the undisputed master of the drinking game, and cheating love rivals at cards was his speciality. He'd got Tammy's boyfriend, Jake, blotto. Once the poor boy was legless, Mickey had made his move on Tammy.

Alicia shrugged. That was Mickey's life back then, and she'd forgiven him. Almost. There was something Alicia found hard to excuse. Mickey and Tammy had gone skinny dipping in the moonlight at the Roaring Creek Falls and had sex under the waterfall. *Gross*. They'd defiled Alicia's spiritual home.

As if that wasn't enough, Mickey couldn't stop himself from boasting down the pub. The cheeky sod claimed Tammy thought he was the Almighty when he screwed her. What was it Tammy was meant to have said? Something about a mythical god filling her insides with a mighty poker. That still made Alicia cringe.

Jake was a decent lad and didn't deserve the humiliation. Nor did his mother, Evie. She was a respected member of the Women's Institute and was horrified by all the gossip. How could Mickey inflict that on a woman who'd been such a good friend to them both?

Alicia steadied herself on the log. 'Please tell me your son wasn't conceived the night of that ghastly party.'

Mickey looked down at his feet. 'It's the only time we made love.'

'Is Tammy sure you're the father? It could be Jake's child.'

'Tammy tried to persuade Jake that he was Corey's father. Seems Jake didn't want to pay child support and got a paternity test.' Mickey returned to the log and shot Alicia a sideways glance. 'Now Tammy wants Corey to come and live with me.'

'How old is he?' Alicia asked.

Mickey paused before answering. 'He's a couple of months. Maybe three, I think.'

Alicia met his eyes head-on. 'How does it feel to be a father? Are you sure you're ready for the responsibility?'

 David Whittet

'I know what you're thinking.' Mickey glanced away, then turned back to her. 'My playboy days are over. I promise. I'm a different man now. You know that.'

Did she? Had Mickey proved himself? Alicia frowned. They'd been through some tough times, and she'd believed him responsible for some terrible things. But he'd done so much good too. The mercy runs. That took guts. And all those acts of kindness he'd done for some of the neediest in the community. Alicia was sure he was as passionate about reforming the Gang as she was. Plus, he'd always been there for her when she'd needed him, since they were little kids.

Alicia felt another quiver in her stomach. Was her unborn child speaking to her? 'We could raise the two children together. Corey and my baby.'

'If only we could.' Mickey tapped his foot on the mud. 'You're forgetting about the Gang.'

Alicia pretended she hadn't heard. 'They'll be cousins. Just like us.'

Mickey dug his heel further into the ground. 'Second cousins.'

'We were blood cousins as kids.' Alicia still wasn't listening and grinned at Mickey. 'You were my one childhood friend. Perhaps they'll be as close as we were back then.'

'Corey's a gang boy.' Mickey paused. 'Gang boys can't associate with … half-bloods.'

Alicia shot Mickey an icy look. 'Please stop using that horrid name for my baby.'

Mickey cringed. 'I'm sorry. I wish it was different, but …' He waved his hands in the air. 'They'll crucify us all.'

Alicia shivered. 'So what are we going to do?'

'You're cold. We ought to get home.' Mickey took off his jacket and wrapped it around Alicia. 'Maybe you should …'

'What?'

Mickey pulled back and took a deep breath. 'My aunt Sonja—'

'No, Mickey!'

'Hear me out. Aunt Sonja's a good woman. She'll look after you. Sort everything out before it's too late.'

'Mickey!' Alicia pulled herself up and glared at him. She'd heard stories about his aunt and her botched terminations. 'I am *not* having an abortion.'

'Think about it. Please. For all our sakes. We're talking about Reggie's bloodline. The honour of the Godzone Gorillas is at stake.'

Alicia wiped away her tears. 'This is my baby. Try to understand how I feel. This child is part of me.'

Mickey hung his head. 'I'm sorry. I shouldn't have said that. It's just … this is doing my head in.' His hands tightened into fists. 'I don't know how I'm going to keep us safe. I want to do my best for my son.' He looked up and placed a hand gently on Alicia's tummy. 'And I'll do what's right by your child, too. Whatever it takes.'

Alicia kissed his cheek. 'Thank you, Mickey.' She kissed him again, full on the lips. 'Thank you from the bottom of my heart.' She held him tight. 'But how are we going to survive?'

Mickey helped her to her feet. 'I won't let them hurt you or the baby. I love you too much for that.'

Could he keep her safe? Alicia's heart beat faster now than it had done when they arrived at the falls earlier in the day. What choice did they have? Stay at Roaring Creek and risk their lives, or disappear and let the Gang continue to terrorise and steal from the vulnerable in the community? Even if they went into hiding, the Gang would find them, as Mickey had pointed out.

Alicia searched for answers as they trudged back to the car in silence. Maybe she should go and see Mickey's aunt. Alicia was born into the Gang and a lifetime of misery. How could she justify bringing her child into such a hostile world?

     David Whittet

CHAPTER FIVE

Mickey's Bach, Later that Afternoon

Life was cruel. Why had Alicia expected anything else? The Gang had stolen her childhood. Savagely ripped away her innocence and youth. She'd vowed they wouldn't claim the rest of her life. But by branding her unborn child a half-blood, they just had. Yes, life was cruel. Bloody cruel, and merciless. Rage boiled through Alicia's veins at the injustice of it all.

'You look knackered,' Mickey said when they returned from the Roaring Creek Falls. 'It can't have been easy talking about the baby. I won't do the mercy run tonight. I'll stay home with you.'

He understands. Alicia hugged him. 'No, Mickey. You go. Those poor old ladies rely on you to give them their money back.'

Mickey gently drew Alicia's hair away from her face. 'Are you sure you're okay?'

'I'll be fine.' Alicia sank onto the bed. 'I just need some sleep.'

'If you're sure.' Mickey picked up the satchel filled with the women's money bags. 'I'll be as quick as I can.'

Alicia *should* have been fine. Talking to Mickey about her pregnancy was meant to make things easier, not turn her life upside down yet again. And sleep—fat chance of that. Alicia gagged on another cup of camp coffee. How long had that half-opened tin been in Mickey's kitchen? She'd meant to go to the grocery for some fresh coffee, but worried someone might notice her bump. How far along was she? Alicia counted the weeks on her fingers. She must be sixteen or seventeen weeks pregnant.

Why was Mickey taking so long? He said he'd be quick. Alicia just wanted him home. To feel safe with his strong arms cuddling and protecting her. She also needed to talk to him about his aunt Sonja. Alicia had made up her mind.

'I'm sorry, bub.' Alicia gently caressed her tummy. 'I love you and I want you … more than anything in my entire life.' Tears streamed down her cheeks as she continued. 'But I can't let the Gang get their hands on you. I won't let them destroy your life the way they've ruined mine.' She kissed her fingers, then rubbed them on her belly. 'This hateful world isn't for you.'

Two in the morning, and Mickey still wasn't back. Had he legged it? Was the news of the pregnancy too much for him? What would she do if he had done a runner?

Alicia gazed at the clock on the bedside table until her eyes smarted. Why did every minute seem like an eternity? She'd got used to the creaking floorboards in Mickey's bach. But tonight, the slightest noise made her jump. Perhaps it was Mickey creeping in so he wouldn't wake her. Or was it the Gang, come for her and her baby?

Pull yourself together, girl. Alicia rolled over and covered her head with her pillow. Another half hour and the bedclothes were almost threadbare. Alicia thought about Kāterina. The wise Māori diviner who lived in a run-down caravan in the middle of the forest. Kāterina's sleuthing had brought Alicia and Mickey back together. Alicia was convinced that Mickey had shot her at her wedding to prevent her from marrying Emir, and that Mickey had started the fire that killed Emir. Alicia wouldn't listen to Kāterina at first. Thank God Alicia had found the truth at last. Mickey was the man who'd been there for her whenever she needed him—her entire life. Like today, when Alicia needed his support for her pregnancy. Mickey had been so understanding and even more supportive than she had dared to imagine.

Our souls belong together. I will always look out for you, Alicia. If you are ever in trouble, I will rescue you. That's what he'd said to her when they'd shared blood.

So, where was he now? Alicia glanced at the clock again. Three a.m. Surely the mercy run couldn't have taken this long?

Alicia could never sleep when she was a little girl. Kāterina had taught her to take deep breaths and relax. The breathing exercises had never worked as a child. Perhaps they would now. Alicia lay flat on her back, inhaled deeply and exhaled slowly. She repeated the process several times and felt just as tense. What else had Kāterina told her? *Focus on your happy place.* Were the Roaring Creek Falls still her safe haven? Alicia closed her eyes and pictured the torrent of water beating down on the rocks. A gentle sound echoed in her ears. Not the thundering waterfall, but a soothing lullaby. Was it Mickey, back at last to comfort her?

     David Whittet

Alicia sat bolt upright. The bedroom was empty, and Mickey wasn't lying beside her. The ethereal voice singing in her ear was her mother, Naomi. Alicia retreated under the bedclothes. It was less than a month since she'd buried her mother and found her long-lost half-sister, Helena.

Don't make the same mistake as me. It was Naomi's voice again. *I tried to sacrifice my baby because I was scared of what the Gang would do to me—and to the child. I was weak. You're stronger than me. Flee the Gang if need be. But bring your child up with love.*

Alicia jumped out of bed and paced around the tiny bedroom. Her mother's untimely death from tuberculosis was still raw. Alicia could still hear the death rattle as Naomi's life ebbed away. She remembered the promise she'd made when she sponged her mother's body for the last time.

'Can you hear me, Mum?' Alicia had said. 'There's something I need to tell you. You've given me courage. You were brave and you got away from Reggie.'

'I wasn't brave,' Naomi had grunted in between gasps for breath. 'I should have taken you with me.'

Alicia had gently stroked her mother's cheeks. 'You did what you thought was right at the time, and you've shown me it is possible to escape from the Gang. That's just the wake-up call I need.'

Alicia collapsed onto the bed. What were her mother's dying words? *I could never give you the life you deserved. Now I can die in peace, knowing you're free. I'm*

so proud of you. Alicia clutched her stomach. Was she any nearer to being free than she'd been as a child? What would her mother think if she knew Alicia was back with Mickey? Naomi had always had it in for the poor boy. She'd probably be turning over in her grave. Still, thinking about Naomi was just the kick up the backside Alicia needed.

Naomi's deathbed confession had deeply unsettled Alicia. Memories of that dreadful day when Naomi almost bled to death in the forest flooded back and brought Alicia out in a cold sweat.

Alicia could better understand her mother's dilemma now. Naomi must have been terrified. Not just pregnant by her brother-in-law, Ronnie, but by Reggie's arch-enemy. No wonder she feared for her life. She must have been desperate when she tried to end the pregnancy herself with a coat hanger in Kāterina's caravan. God bless Kāterina for stopping Naomi. Alicia shuddered. It was a miracle Naomi survived the haemorrhage in the forest and still gave birth to a healthy baby girl.

If Kāterina hadn't intervened—Alicia's half-sister Helena would not have been born. That was too painful to think about. Not that they'd been particularly close. Alicia was desperate to get to know her half-sister better. Having just met her three months ago when their mother was on her deathbed, Alicia had wanted to share a flat with Helena. But Helena was restless and took off with her boyfriend, Ben, and his biking mates.

Alicia hugged herself. *My precious baby. I can't lose you—I won't lose you.* She clasped her hand against her belly. *I'll protect you. Keep you safe.* She raised a fist and waved it at a mental image of her father. *I'm not scared of you, Reggie. Not any more. Do your damnedest. You can't touch me!*

She was about to head back to bed when headlights shone through the window. Alicia peered out. *Thank God.* It was Mickey's car. She raced to the door to greet him.

'Mickey! Where have you been? I've been worried about you …' She broke off as he hobbled towards her with blood pouring from his nose and mouth. 'Speak to me! Who did this to you?'

'You don't want to know.' Mickey gagged on his words and spat a mouthful of blood into a puddle. 'Just a bit of a run-in with one of the men.'

Just a bit of a run-in? Alicia could see he'd lost at least two teeth.

'Come on, let's get you cleaned up.' She helped him into the house and took off his bloodstained jacket and sodden shirt. 'I can't deal with this. You need a doctor.'

Mickey spat yet more blood onto the floor. 'No way. We have to keep this quiet.'

Alicia fetched a towel and sat him in a chair. 'I need to know exactly what happened. No bullshit.'

'Todd.' Mickey wiped his mouth with his hand. 'That son of a bitch has always had it in for me.'

'He did this to you?'

Mickey nodded. 'Todd and his mates. The bastards are onto us.'

'They know about—'

'They were waiting for me outside Edith's place. A bunch of them. I didn't have a chance.'

Alicia gently sponged his face. The last time she tended Mickey's wounds was after his father had beaten him when they were children. Would the vicious circle of violence ever end?

'What are we going to do?' Alicia asked, using a handkerchief to clear the blood from his eyes.

Mickey winced. 'I don't care what they do to me. But the buggers stole the money I was about to give back to Edith and the cash I'd collected for the rest of the women.'

'We can't risk this happening again.' Alicia rinsed the handkerchief under the kitchen tap. 'Who knows what they'll do next time?' Alicia could hardly believe what she was saying. The mercy runs meant everything to her in their constant struggle to combat the Gang's plundering of the neighbourhood. 'We have to stop.'

'No.' Mickey pulled himself upright. 'I can't … I won't … It's the one good thing I've done with my life.'

'But you're president-elect of the Godzone Gorillas. If they find out what you're doing …' Alicia broke off and shook her head. 'Next time, it won't just be a bloody nose.'

Mickey stomped his foot. 'I never asked to be president-elect.'

Alicia fetched a bottle of disinfectant from the bathroom cupboard and dabbed Mickey's face.

'Shit! That bloody hurt!' Mickey recoiled from the sting of the disinfectant on his skin. 'Reggie called me the *chosen one*. I never wanted that either.'

The chosen one. Alicia remembered how Mickey had resented that title. Like everything to do with the Godzone Gorillas, Mickey's elevation to president-elect had been the subject of bitter in-fighting and angst. Reggie reluctantly accepted his twin brother Ronnie's son as his protégé to prevent outside contenders from taking over the Gang. It was the last thing Mickey sought. He just wanted to have fun like other kids. Had Alicia done the right thing to persuade him to take up the challenge and change the Gang for the better? It had cost them both so much.

'Well, your old man got his way, and here I am,' Mickey continued with a mock salute. 'The next president of the Godzone Gorillas.' He leant forward and eyed Alicia determinedly. 'I'm not giving up now. Those old ladies need me.'

They did—the entire community needed Mickey to stamp out the violence, extortion and corruption. Alicia gazed into his bloodshot eyes. She'd never been more proud of him. But what good would he be to anyone if he were dead?

She wrapped him up in a blanket. 'Are you sure? How can we keep you safe?'

'Todd doesn't scare me. Nor do Ed, Joe, or any of his sidekicks.' Mickey clenched a fist. 'I'll be prepared next time.'

Why didn't that reassure her? Alicia squeezed his hand. 'Don't you think we should lie low for a while? Maybe take a trip away—'

Mickey shook his head. 'I'm not going anywhere. In fact, I'm looking forward to rubbing that motherfucker Todd's nose in the shit.'

Alicia used an old scarf as a bandage for Mickey's head. 'That's the best I can do,' she said, wrapping it around his chin and neck. 'At least it'll stop the blood from getting everywhere.'

She sat down beside him. What did this mean for her baby?

'Mickey …' Why did it feel like she was telling him for the first time all over again? 'I've thought about it all night.'

He met her gaze. 'Thought about what?'

'The baby. I'm keeping it.'

CHAPTER SIX

Alicia got used to the catcalls whenever she walked down the street. Hadn't they seen a pregnant woman before? Or did they know?

Mickey had insisted that nobody need find out it was Emir's child.

'There'll be gossip,' Mickey had said. 'But we'll deny it. Claim it's my child.'

'They'll never believe it,' Alicia had replied. 'Everyone knows we weren't together when … you know …'

Mickey had grinned at her. 'I'll tell them I seduced you. We can say I was so shit hot you just had to come back to me.'

Typical male ego. Mickey was almost two years older than Alicia, but with a remark like that, she had to wonder if he had grown up as much as she'd hoped.

Alicia frowned, hiding behind her long dark hair. 'I suppose we could say it was a one-night stand and then we decided to make a go of it for the sake of the child.' Alicia shrugged and fetched her shopping basket. 'But I still don't think they'll buy it. Not with your reputation.'

And Alicia was right. They didn't believe a word of it.

She pushed past the men on her way to the local store.

'Has Mickey lost his balls?'

'Hasn't the bastard kicked you out yet? Bloody disgrace.'

'Up the duff and no father?'

'You're no virgin bride.'

Alicia bolted into the store and shut the door. She took a deep breath and wiped the perspiration off her face with a handkerchief.

'Alicia!' That was Lilly's voice. 'How are you? I haven't seen you since the ceremony at the falls. How's Mickey?'

Alicia looked up. 'Mickey's … fine. We're both fine.'

Lilly beamed at her. 'Why don't you come round for a cup of tea?'

Lovely Lilly. The dear woman who'd been her rock and seen her through so many trials over the years. Thanks to Lilly, Alicia had reunited with her mother,

Naomi, before she passed away. If it wasn't for Lilly, Alicia would never have found her half-sister Helena either.

Alicia had wanted to tell Lilly about her pregnancy before she told Mickey. Since losing her mother, Lilly had been like a beloved aunt. She was a wise and mature woman, maybe a year old two older than Alicia's late mother, who always knew the right thing to do and say. But approaching Lilly about the pregnancy felt awkward. And even more uncomfortable now that Mickey had told her about his son, Corey. Jake—the poor guy Mickey had got drunk and whose partner he had then bonked—was Lilly's friend Evie's son. Evie had also supported Alicia through her darkest moments. It all felt too … complicated.

'I'm sorry, Lilly, but I can't.' Alicia went up to the counter and took out her shopping list. 'Not today.'

'Nonsense,' Lilly said. 'I want to hear all about your pregnancy.'

You don't. Alicia shuffled uneasily. 'Perhaps another time.'

Alicia handed her shopping list to the shopkeeper.

Lilly caught her eye. 'Alicia! You don't fool me. We're friends, aren't we?'

Trust Lilly to see right through her. To realise she was desperate for someone to confide in.

Alicia sighed and packed her groceries in her shopping bag. 'Okay, you win. But I warn you, it's not a very pretty story.'

Lilly shrugged. 'When is it ever in this place?' She turned to the shopkeeper. 'Could you let us out the back door? I don't want those buggers in the street hassling Alicia.'

⁂

Where to start? Alicia sank back into an armchair at Lilly's house. It was all so difficult to explain. Alicia tried to get her head together while Lilly made the tea. Did Lilly know about Corey? And if so, was she angry about it? Was Evie mad with Mickey? How did she explain her mixed-up feelings about Emir's child?

Lilly came in with the tea things on a tray and that reassuring smile which had given Alicia strength during so many crises.

'I'm guessing that's not Mickey's baby,' Lilly said, handing Alicia a cup of tea. 'Is it Emir's?'

     David Whittet

Alicia nodded. She took a sip of tea and burst into tears. 'I don't know what to think. Mickey says he'll pretend it's his child.'

'Well, that's a good thing, isn't it?' Lilly said. 'Mickey's taking some responsibility at last.'

'I suppose …' Alicia dried her eyes on her sleeve. 'Do you know about Corey?'

Lilly nodded. 'I'm pretty sure everyone in Roaring Creek knows. Jake didn't exactly keep the result of his paternity test secret.'

'Is Evie okay with it?'

'I think she's just happy that Mickey's stepping up and is going to be a father to the child.' Lilly put down her teacup. 'How do you feel about having one of Mickey's love children in your home?'

'I'm fine about it. I told Mickey we could bring up Corey and my baby together. It's just …' Alicia felt a pang and clutched her stomach. 'I'm not happy about passing it off as Mickey's baby.'

'I guess you're right.' Lilly frowned, the lines and wrinkles on her face deepening. 'There's been some gossip at the Women's Institute. And while gangsters can be as thick as two short planks, they'll put two and two together and realise it's impossible.'

'They already have. You heard that rabble outside the store.' Alicia cuddled her tummy more securely. 'But it's not that. This is Emir's child. I know Kāterina said all those awful things about him, and maybe she was right. But I loved him and whatever anyone says, I believe he loved me.'

'My poor angel!' Lilly got up from her chair and knelt beside Alicia. 'I'm sure Emir *did* love you. He'd have wanted the best for his child.'

'Exactly.' Alicia kept her hands firmly on her belly. 'He wouldn't have wanted his child brought up by the Gang. Or by Mickey.'

'Yes, but …' Lilly put her arm around Alicia. 'You're with Mickey now. Aren't you thankful he's prepared to treat the child as his own? Not many gangsters would be prepared to do that.'

'I know. Mickey's been amazing.' Alicia took her hand off her tummy and dabbed her eyes. 'It's just … he's not—'

'Emir.' Lilly finished the sentence for her. 'But Emir's gone. You have to think of the future.'

Alicia hesitated before responding. A moment of clarity broke through the confusion and chaos of recent months. Her love for Emir had been a fairy-tale romance. He was the knight in shining armour who had charged in and rescued her from the Gang. But unlike a fairy story, there was no happy ending. Her love for Mickey may not have been perfect—far from it at times—but it was real. Lilly was right. Alicia was with Mickey now, and she had to make it work.

'It *is* the future that matters,' Alicia said at last. 'I just wish everything wasn't so bloody hard.' She looked up and gazed into Lilly's eyes. 'I'm scared. Mickey says the Gang will treat the baby as a half-blood if they find out, and it will put all our lives at risk. I even thought of …' She blinked back another tear. 'I thought it might be best for everyone if I had an abortion.'

'No!' Lilly squeezed Alicia's hand. 'Don't do that. Does Emir's family know?'

'I haven't heard from any of them since the funeral.' Alicia cringed. 'You saw what they were like. They all blamed me for Emir's death, and if they knew I was back with Mickey, the man they accused of killing him …'

'Fonella didn't blame you. She stood up for you at Emir's funeral. I remember.'

Alicia felt a lump in her throat at the mention of Fonella's name. Fonella, Emir's younger sister, was the only one in his family who had defended Alicia after he died. Alicia thought back to Emir's funeral. She'd never forget Fonella's tearful embrace in the church and how cruelly Emir's parents dragged her away.

'Fonella was a darling,' Alicia said, dabbing her eyes. 'I miss her so much.'

'You should write to her,' Lilly said. 'She'd want to know about the baby.'

'And she'd make a wonderful aunty.' Alicia paused. 'But wouldn't that make everything even more complicated?'

Lilly gave Alicia's hand another squeeze. 'I don't see how it could do any harm.'

Alicia frowned. 'I'm not so sure. Mickey made me promise not to tell anyone that Emir was the father.'

'Family's different. Mickey will understand. Fonella could be a terrific support for you. Promise me you'll write to her.'

Lilly had that gleam in her eye that Alicia could never resist.

'Okay. I will.' Alicia looked at her watch. 'I'd better get back. Mickey will be waiting for his dinner.'

'That's blokes for you.' Lilly shrugged. 'Some things never change.'

Alicia sighed. 'Ain't that the truth.'

Lilly got up and helped Alicia out of her chair.

'I don't suppose you've got a midwife?' Lilly asked. 'Or seen a doctor?'

Alicia shook her head.

Lilly sighed. 'I'm taking you to the medical centre tomorrow morning. No excuses.'

The front door was open when Alicia got home. Mickey must have beaten her back. Just as well she'd dropped into the butcher's—he'd be starving as usual. She dumped her shopping bag on the kitchen benchtop.

'I'm back, darling. I've got you a juicy steak for dinner.' Alicia turned to see her father standing at the kitchen door. 'Dad! What are you doing here? Where's—'

'Mickey's doing a job down the valley. He won't be home tonight.'

'But … he …' Alicia dribbled to a standstill. Had Todd been talking? Had her father found out about the mercy runs? She took a sharp intake of breath. 'What's he doing in the valley?'

'No concern of yours.'

It bloody well is! Alicia glared at her father. 'When will he be back?'

Reggie leant against the doorframe. 'When he's finished the job.'

Alicia felt her father's eyes burning down on her. 'I guess this isn't a social call. But I could always cook you that steak.'

Reggie grunted. Alicia unpacked her shopping. She could almost feel her father's mouth watering as she unwrapped the steak.

'Okay.' Reggie sat down at the table. 'But we still have to talk.'

Alicia fetched the frying pan. She'd learnt from bitter experience that the only way to get around her father was through his stomach. Especially now. Cassandra, his current live-in lover, was bone idle and a lousy cook.

'How is Cassie these days?' Alicia asked with a cheeky grin. 'I bet you haven't had a feed as good as this in ages.'

Reggie didn't answer. Typical. He picked up the newspaper off the table and buried his head in it. Alicia turned the steak in the pan and shuddered. What was her old man thinking? What bombshell did he have in store for her?

Alicia *should* have been pleased to see her father. Their relationship had improved enormously since she'd got back together with Mickey. Alicia had even danced with him at the reunion ceremony at the Roaring Creek Falls. But tonight, she was as scared of him as she'd been when she was a little girl.

'Bloody judge!' Reggie threw down the newspaper and slammed a fist on the table. 'That bastard Atkins has sent Marty down for two years.'

Alicia sighed. That wasn't a good start. Her father constantly trolled the court column in the local paper, and he was always in a foul temper when one of his mates got jailed. Why couldn't it have been one of his enemies in the clink? That always put him in a good mood.

'Rare. Just the way you like it.' Alicia handed him the steak. 'Enjoy.'

Reggie picked up the steak off the plate with his hands. Alicia had forgotten his table manners were so gross. Especially when he spat out the gristle and used his fingers as toothpicks. It was as disgusting now as it had been when she was a kid.

He leant back and patted his stomach when he'd got the last morsel of meat off the bone. 'I was so proud of you when you went back to Mickey.' Reggie eyed her across the table. 'I thought that ceremony would be a new beginning.'

It could have been. Alicia thought back to the dance with her father at the renewal celebration in front of the falls. For a moment back then, she'd thought her father was softening. The ugly glare on his face today told her he wasn't.

'You should be proud of me now,' Alicia said. 'I'm giving you a grandchild. An heir for your precious Gang.'

Reggie snorted. 'You're having the bastard child of an enemy of the Gang.'

'No!' Alicia swallowed hard. 'This is Mickey's baby.'

'Don't give me that bullshit.'

'I'm not.' Alicia clutched her tummy. 'This is your grandchild. Mickey's over the moon about it. Why can't you be?'

'Because I know as well as you do that this isn't Mickey's child.' Reggie thumped the table again. 'Do you think I'm stupid?'

'Of course not. But—'

　　　　　David Whittet

'But nothing. Think I can't count? You wouldn't go near Mickey until a month back.' Reggie wagged a finger at Alicia's bump. 'That didn't happen in the last month.'

'No … but …' Alicia scrambled for words. Her father would never buy Mickey's lame explanation, but she had to try it. 'Mickey and I … we had a one-night stand …'

Reggie smirked. 'Crap. That shit-for-brains con artist from Auckland is the father.'

'Emir. He had a name.' Alicia glared at her father. 'Emir wasn't a con man, and he had more brains than you or your mates.'

Reggie rolled his eyes. 'If he had brains, why did he come to such a sticky end? Betrayed by one of his own lackeys, I heard.'

Alicia felt her body tense. *More likely one of your henchmen.* Kāterina had persuaded Alicia that it was a business partner Emir had cheated who had started the fire that killed him. Alicia still had her doubts. She knew Mickey had nothing to do with it. But her father—he was capable of anything.

'It's still your grandchild,' Alicia said. 'Why can't you just be proud of the baby, like Mickey?'

'So Mickey's okay about passing off a bastard half-blood as his own, is he?' Reggie lurched forward across the table. 'I can tell you, the poor sod's shitting himself about the bloody mess you've landed him in.'

Alicia drew back. What if that were true? Had Mickey just been saying the right things to keep her happy? Maybe he really did resent the baby. No. Mickey cared. She'd seen it in his eyes.

'You're a liar. Mickey's happy about the baby. We both are.'

'Mickey's already got a son. Corey—he's a true heir to the Gang.' Reggie flapped his hand at her face. 'I want you to see Mickey's aunt Sonja.'

'Never!' Alicia froze. Had Mickey talked to Reggie about his aunt? Is this what Mickey really wanted? No way. It was her father lying to get his own way, as usual. 'I'm having the baby. *We're* having this baby—Mickey and I agreed.'

'Did you?' Reggie stared her down, the way he'd always done since she was a little girl. 'Well, Mickey's got more important things to think about. Leading the Gang. And he won't do that with this scandal hanging over him.'

Her father wasn't going to get away with it the way he'd done when she was a child. Time for some home truths. 'How is it any different from what you did? You stole Mickey from Ronnie—your sworn enemy.'

'I did what I had to do for the Gang.'

Alicia shook her head. 'I never understood what it was between you and Ronnie. He was your twin brother, and you drove him out of town.'

'It was Ronnie's choice to leave.'

Yeah, right. And your heavies had nothing to do with it. Alicia's fingers curled. She'd wipe that smug grin off her father's face. 'Ronnie got his own back on you, though, didn't he? Slept with your wife behind your back—'

Reggie's face reddened. 'Naomi wouldn't dare—'

'She did. And all because they both wanted to bring you down.'

Alicia watched his neck veins bulge the way they always did when he was mad. She used to think they'd burst if he didn't calm down. Perhaps they would if he knew about Naomi's pregnancy—and Helena. Should she tell him? Maybe it would be safer not to—she hadn't seen his veins that swollen for a long time.

'Liar,' Reggie sneered. 'Naomi didn't have the guts.'

That was it. The words came out before Alicia could stop herself. 'She didn't just sleep with him—she had his baby.'

Alicia bit her tongue. She should have kept her mouth shut. Had she put Helena at risk? Would Reggie try to track her down? Alicia waited for the explosion, but it didn't come. He just glared at her, his mouth opening and closing like a fish.

Reggie eventually got up and pointed a finger at her. 'You'll go and see Mickey's aunt Sonja if you know what's good for you.' He made for the door. 'Otherwise—don't look to me for protection.'

❧

Alicia didn't move for at least an hour after her father left. For the first time in her life, she'd silenced him. But at what cost? Helena had Ben and the bikers to look after her. Ben was every bit as scary as Reggie, perhaps even more so. Alicia was more worried about Mickey. *Doing a job up the valley*—that was a likely story. Had her father's men taken him away to beat him into submission? Would he come back a changed man?

     David Whittet

No way could Alicia spend the night alone. Ten o'clock, and she was round at Lilly's place, hammering on the door.

'I didn't mean to get you out of bed,' Alicia said. 'I'm sorry—but I'm scared. Reggie's sent Mickey on a job in the valley and I don't know when he'll be back. What if Reggie's done something to him?'

'Come here!' Lilly took Alicia into her arms. 'I'm sure Mickey will be okay. He can stand up for himself.'

But could he? Lilly hadn't seen his beaten-up face when he came home after Todd and his mates did him over that night.

'I'm not so sure,' Alicia murmured, snuggling up to Lilly. 'If only Mickey had one of those new mobile phones everyone's raving about. Then I could call him and see if he's alright.'

Lilly stroked Alicia's back. 'I don't think there's any cellular coverage in Roaring Creek. We're the last to get anything new. But remember, whatever happens, I'm here for you.'

Alicia couldn't hold her tears back any longer. 'I know that.'

A cup of hot cocoa and Alicia felt a little calmer. 'You're a lifesaver.'

'I'm not sure about that.' Lilly scratched her head. 'I had hoped life would settle down for you once you were back together with Mickey.'

It would have done if it wasn't for the Gang. Alicia sighed. 'I sometimes think I'm doomed. Destined for a life of misery.'

'Don't talk such nonsense.' Lilly took the empty cups back to the kitchen. 'When we've finished at the doctor's tomorrow, you're going to call Fonella. Talk to her. You need a friend of your own age.'

Perhaps talking to Fonella would help. But even snuggled up in the safety of Lilly's spare room, Alicia couldn't sleep. Would her father poison Mickey against her baby? Did Reggie honestly not care about his grandchild? Was the Gang more important than family? Alicia knew the answer to that one already.

CHAPTER SEVEN

Three days and no sign of Mickey. What had Reggie done to him? Alicia asked herself the same question repeatedly. Was Mickey's disappearance just about the baby? Reggie hadn't said anything about the mercy runs—and he'd have been apoplectic if he'd known.

Todd could have stitched Mickey up *after* Reggie came to the bach the other night. But that didn't make any sense either. Her old man would have been back in an instant with some heinous punishment for her if he knew about the mercy runs. Reggie always insisted she stay out of Gang business and blamed her for giving Mickey a conscience.

Mickey said he wasn't scared of Todd and boasted he would be prepared next time. But what if he wasn't? Alicia shuddered. Todd's men could have attacked Mickey and left him for dead in a ditch.

How Alicia had wished Mickey had been with her when Lilly took her to the doctor. Thank God for Lilly. Alicia comforted herself that it must have been so much harder for her mother, having to go through a troubled pregnancy entirely unsupported.

'Your blood pressure's up,' the doctor said. 'Try to relax while I recheck it.'

Relax! Alicia half-expected her blood pressure to blow the top off the doctor's machine.

'Hmm.' The doctor took the blood pressure cuff off Alicia's arm. 'Still high.'

'Alicia's under a lot of stress,' Lilly said. 'Can you give her something to help?'

'We do need to treat her blood pressure,' the doctor said, 'but we avoid using tranquillisers during pregnancy as they can harm the baby. We'll enrol you with a midwife. She'll teach you some breathing exercises.'

Alicia rolled her eyes. *What good will that do?* She wouldn't feel better until she got Mickey back.

The doctor looked through Alicia's medical file. 'With the scarring from your thoracic surgery and the smoke inhalation, breathing and relaxation are vital for you. Now, jump up on the bed and let me feel your tummy.'

     David Whittet

Alicia squinted at a child's painting stuck to the ceiling while the doctor palpated her abdomen, the bright colours hurting her tired eyes.

'You're further along than we thought,' the doctor said. 'We'll need a scan to confirm, but I'd say you were getting on for thirty weeks.' He took a step back and eyed her intently. 'Surely you must have known you were pregnant before now?'

Alicia turned to avoid his gaze. What could she say?

Lilly jumped in again and saved her. 'Like I said, Alicia's had a lot on her mind. When her periods stopped, she thought it was just through worry.'

Alicia nodded. 'And I haven't been eating. I've lost weight, and I guess that's why the pregnancy didn't show early on.'

The doctor daubed some jelly on his foetal monitor and ran it across her tummy. Alicia blinked back a tear when she heard the heartbeat. *That's my baby!*

Lilly squeezed her hand. 'Your little one's got a strong heart, that's for sure.'

Alicia felt a kick in her tummy. 'And a prizefighter too!'

Would Mickey have been as excited as she was to hear the baby's heartbeat? Was she expecting too much of him? Alicia felt another kick in her stomach and leant her head back on the pillow. What if Mickey had run away because he couldn't face raising Emir's child?

The doctor returned to his desk and scribbled some notes in her case file. 'I'm going to refer you to an obstetrician.'

Alicia slipped as she got off the examination couch. 'Why?'

'Just a precaution with your respiratory history.' He picked up his Dictaphone. 'I want you to see Professor Woodruff. He's the best obstetrician in the South Island. It'll mean a trip to Christchurch, but you'll be in expert hands.'

'Thank you, Doctor,' Lilly said. She helped Alicia to her feet and back into a chair. 'See? Nothing to worry about.'

Alicia straightened her T-shirt. Why didn't she find that reassuring?

'You should get started with some antenatal classes. My nurse will give you the contact details and put you in touch with a midwife.' The doctor got up from behind his desk and showed them out of his consulting room. 'The sooner you get started on your breathing exercises, the better.'

The midwife's relaxation techniques were just as useless as the breathing exercises Kāterina had taught her.

'I'm sorry,' Alicia said. 'This isn't working. I feel even more wound up.'

'You need to take this seriously.' The midwife frowned. 'Stress is harmful to your baby.'

Alicia drew back. Was she hurting her baby? 'You're saying … I'm—'

The midwife smiled reassuringly. 'Sorry. I didn't mean to frighten you. It's just—tranquillity is good for you and the baby.'

Fat chance of that! Alicia eyed the midwife dubiously. 'So what do you suggest?'

'Perhaps we could try yoga. Or meditation.' The midwife put a hand on Alicia's shoulder. 'Don't worry. We'll find what's right for you.'

The only thing that would help would be to have Mickey back and know that he still cared about the baby. Alicia went over what the midwife had said as she walked home with Lilly. Many women in the community had gone into premature labour after being hassled by the Gang when they couldn't afford their protection money. Alicia tried the breathing exercises again as they walked. She had to calm down, or she'd end up losing the baby.

'You're coming home to mine,' Lilly said. 'Don't forget, you need to call Fonella. You can use my phone when we get home.'

Alicia almost missed her step. How did she explain to Fonella that she was back with Mickey? The man Emir's family believed to be responsible for his death. By now, the family had probably brainwashed Fonella into believing that too.

'Are you still sure this is a good idea?' Alicia said. 'I couldn't cope with another disappointment.'

'Would you like me to talk to her first?' Lilly said. 'Test the temperature.'

Alicia sighed. 'No. I need to fight my own battles.'

Maybe she could pretend she'd lost Fonella's phone number. No. Lilly would see straight through that. Alicia sat on the edge of the wicker chair in Lilly's hallway, picking at the straw. Why was this so difficult? Fonella was her friend—at least

David Whittet

she used to be. Alicia lost count of the number of times she dialled Fonella's number and put down the receiver before it rang. *You can do this.*

'Fonella?' Alicia's hand trembled so much she almost dropped the handset. 'Is that you?'

'Alicia! How wonderful to hear from you!'

Alicia gasped. Was Fonella genuinely happy about the call? What should she say? How would Fonella react to her news?

Fonella beat her to it. 'I'm so sorry, Alicia. I've meant to call you so many times. Honestly. I hated the way we left everything after Emir's funeral. I'll never forgive Mum and Dad for the way they treated you.'

'I never meant to set you against your parents.' Alicia paused and swallowed hard. 'Listen, I've got something important to tell you—'

'What is it? Are you alright, Alicia? Are you coping?'

'I'm okay.' Alicia took a deep breath. 'I'm pregnant and Emir's the father.'

A moment's silence. What was Fonella thinking? It was almost as painful as when she told Mickey.

'That's brilliant! I'm going to be an aunty!' Fonella's voice radiated down the phone line. 'I'm going to come and see you. It can't be easy managing a pregnancy on your own.'

Alicia took a moment to prepare herself mentally for the next bombshell. 'Actually, I'm back with Mickey.'

The joy in Fonella's voice disappeared. 'But … I thought it was Mickey who—'

'No. It wasn't Mickey who shot me at the wedding. Nor did he start the fire. It was …' Alicia broke off. How could she explain it to Fonella? That her brother's death was an act of vengeance by someone he'd double-crossed. Perhaps it was best not to try. 'Listen, Fonella. I don't know exactly what went on, but I'm absolutely certain Mickey had nothing to do with it.'

Another agonising silence.

'If you're sure, Alicia. Just be careful. Is Mickey still in with the Gang?'

'Yes—but he's using his influence to change things. We both are.' The line stayed quiet. Was Fonella listening? Did she believe what Alicia was saying? 'Every night, Mickey's out there giving people their protection money back.'

Alicia bit her tongue. Fonella was from another world. She probably didn't even know what protection money was or what life was like in a community ruled by the Gang.

At last, Fonella replied. 'Cool, sis. You know, I've often thought about what happened at the church, and about the fire. My brother made some powerful enemies. It wouldn't have been the first time one of them threatened him. It's just … he was usually at least one step ahead.'

She understands! Alicia could have kissed Fonella down the phone.

'I guess Emir's luck had to run out eventually,' Fonella continued. 'But what a ghastly way to go.'

'Believe me—you can't begin to imagine.' The memory of the fire brought Alicia out in a cold sweat. 'Listen, should we tell your parents about the baby? After all, it's their grandchild.'

'Mum and Dad won't hear a bad word about Emir,' Fonella said. 'Neither will Grace. They'll probably deny that he's the father. Best not to say anything—at least, not yet.'

'Okay. If you think that's for the best.'

'I'm afraid it is.' Fonella's voice picked up. 'But I'm going to be the best aunty in the world. I'll come and see you soon as I can get away. I'm working at Emir's old company. Do you remember Errol Troy? He's my boss.'

Alicia gulped. Errol Troy. Emir's best mate and another smooth operator. He'd been in charge of security at her wedding to Emir. And come to think of it, Errol had been at their house on the day of the fire. Did Errol know more than he ever let on? Was he involved in Emir's demise?

Don't go there. 'Of course I remember Errol. He was always at our place, negotiating some cutting-edge deal with Emir.' Alicia felt an unexpected warmth rise through her body. 'Errol was kind to me at Emir's funeral.'

'When the rest of my family were absolute bastards,' Fonella added. 'I'm afraid I've got to go now. But I'll be on the next flight south when I can get some time off. And that's a promise.'

The best aunty in the world. Alicia repeated the words to herself as she put down the receiver. A cherished aunt. That's precisely what Alicia needed for her baby. That—and for Mickey to return home.

❧

       David Whittet

Alicia couldn't hug Fonella, but she could embrace Lilly. And she did, the moment she ended the phone call.

'Thank you—for everything.' Alicia flung her arms around Lilly. 'You're one in a million.'

'I'm not sure about that,' Lilly said, 'but I knew talking to Fonella would do you good. Will she come to see you?'

Alicia nodded. 'I'd never have had the nerve to call her if you hadn't pushed me.'

'That's what friends are for,' Lilly said. 'Now, I trust you're staying for dinner?'

Alicia hesitated. 'I ought to get back.'

'Nonsense.' Lilly smiled. 'I've got to feed you up. Doctor's orders.'

Alicia sighed. The smell of cooking coming from the kitchen was too tempting to resist. 'Okay, you win.'

They talked non-stop over dinner.

'We must have a baby shower,' Lilly said. 'I'm sure all the women would love to contribute. We could hold it at the Women's Institute.'

Alicia frowned. 'Not so fast. Don't forget my old man. Reggie's still on the warpath.'

'Give him time. He'll adjust to it.' Lilly raised her eyebrows. 'We could still have a baby shower. Just keep it low-key.'

'No.' Alicia put down her knife and fork. 'You know how fast gossip spreads around here.'

'Yes, but—'

'Reggie told me to go and see Mickey's aunty Sonja and get a termination.'

'Bastard.' Lilly almost choked on a mouthful of food. 'His own grandchild!'

Alicia snorted. 'Family means nothing to my old man. The Gang's all he cares about. Look what he did to his twin brother.'

Lilly pushed her plate aside. 'Does Mickey ever hear from his father?'

Alicia shook her head. 'I don't think Mickey even knows where his father is.'

'Patricia says Ronnie's down in Hokitika.'

Patricia. The biggest gossip amongst the women. The mere mention of the woman's name caught Alicia's breath.

'Trust Patricia,' Alicia said. 'It just goes to show what I said about gossip.

If Patricia got wind that we're planning a baby shower, everyone would know in a flash.'

'I guess you're right.' Lilly rolled her shoulders. 'But what about Mickey? Perhaps you should tell him that his father's in Hokitika. He might want to make peace with his old man.'

'I don't think so,' Alicia said. 'You saw how Ronnie treated him, and Mickey never forgave his dad for shagging my mother.'

Lilly shrugged. 'I can't say I blame him.'

'Nor do I. Except …' Alicia played with the last morsel of food on her plate. 'If Ronnie and Naomi hadn't had it off together, I wouldn't have my half-sister, Helena.'

'Does Helena know about the baby?'

If only she did. Alicia looked down. 'I haven't seen her since Mum's funeral. She took off with a bikie gang, remember?'

'She'll be in touch when she's ready. You'll see.' Lilly reached across the table and put her hand on Alicia's. 'Helena will make a fantastic aunty for the baby, too.'

'Maybe.' Alicia stood up and helped Lilly clear the table. 'I sometimes wonder if I'll ever see her again.'

'Of course you will.' Lilly put down the plates and cuddled Alicia. 'Perhaps we get Patricia on the job? She'd soon find Helena.'

'You think so?'

'Well, it was Patricia who gave me the lead to find your mother.'

Alicia followed Lilly into the kitchen. 'Thanks for dinner. That was the best shepherd's pie I've tasted in ages.'

'Glad you enjoyed it.' Lilly made a start on the washing up. 'Come round any time.'

Alicia dried the dishes. 'Why does the Gang have to make everything so bloody difficult? If Reggie's done anything to Mickey, I swear I'll kill him.'

'Mickey can look after himself. You once told me he was like a cat with nine lives.'

Alicia shrugged. 'And he's using them up fast.'

'Maybe he'll settle down now that he's got a son. Corey could be the making of him. And your child too, of course.' Lilly put away the last of the dishes. 'Now, are you sure you won't stay the night?'

'No. I'd best get home. I want to be there for Mickey if …' Alicia broke off for a moment, then stood tall and corrected herself. 'When he comes back.'

Alicia felt less confident when she walked home. What if Reggie had driven him out of town—or worse? Would she really kill her father? She'd been close to it with Cassandra, Reggie's live-in lover. But like Cassandra, Reggie wasn't worth a murder conviction. Besides, vengeance was a Gang trait, not hers.

Was that a light on in the bach? At first, Alicia thought she had imagined it. Was her mind playing tricks on her? Or was it just wishful thinking? Her heartbeat grew faster as she drew closer.

'Mickey! Is that you?' Alicia ran the last few paces to the bach. 'I've been so worried! Why the hell didn't you call me?'

Mickey stood at the open door with a broad grin on his face. He'd have been in a whole lot more trouble if he hadn't been holding an adorable child in his arms.

The pride in Mickey's eyes radiated in the moonlight. 'Meet Corey.'

Alicia stroked Corey's cherub-like face. She'd deal with Mickey in a minute. Right now, she was captivated by the bright sparkle in the little boy's innocent eyes, just as she had been entranced by the charming twinkle on his father's face when they first met.

Corey's eyelids fluttered, and his face scrunched up in an endearing expression of contentment that touched Alicia's heart.

'Oh, Mickey! He's absolutely gorgeous!' Alicia wrapped her arms around both Mickey and Corey. 'But why couldn't you have let me know where you were? I was so scared. I thought my father had done something to you.'

'I couldn't. Reggie sent me on this job up the valley. There weren't any phones up there.' Mickey paused for a moment and shuddered. 'Maybe your old man was trying to finish me off. It was mighty treacherous out there. I nearly lost my foot in an animal trap.'

'What about after that?' Alicia asked. 'There must have been a phone at Tammy's place when you went to pick Corey up.'

Corey sneezed before Mickey could answer.

'Come on, let's get inside and out of the cold,' Alicia said. 'Here, give Corey to me.'

'I tried to call,' Mickey said as Alicia took Corey, and they went indoors. 'Honest, I did. But there was no reply. Where were you?'

Alicia sat down with Corey on her lap. 'I went to stay with Lilly. I couldn't bear it here on my own.'

Mickey squeezed in beside her on the chair. 'I was worried about you too.'

'Just don't let it happen again.'

'I won't. I promise.'

Alicia made cooing noises to Corey. 'Is he ready for a feed?'

'Just about.' Mickey looked at his watch. 'I'll get it ready.'

Mickey got up and fetched a bowl of puree from the fridge.

Alicia pulled a face. 'There's mould in that fridge. Things need to change with a little one in the house.' She bounced Corey up and down on her lap. 'We can't have you getting sick, can we?'

Mickey sighed. 'I know. I'll get a new fridge.'

Alicia kissed Corey on the cheek. 'Just make sure it hasn't fallen off the back of a lorry.'

'Don't worry. It'll be legit.' Mickey heated the bowl in the microwave. 'My mate Jim's got one he's trying to flog.'

Alicia shook her head. 'Why can't we buy a new one? We have to go into Greymouth for my scan on Friday.'

'Okay. You win.'

Mickey lifted Corey off Alicia's lap and cradled him in one arm while he scooped up a spoonful of puree from the bowl with the other hand. He paused to blow on it before feeding Corey. Alicia watched in amazement. Mickey spooned the puree into Corey's mouth with such skill and ease. It was like he was born to be a father. The aroma coming from the bowl was heavenly.

'What's in that puree?' Alicia asked. 'It smells delicious. Did you make it yourself?'

'Mashed sweet potato with chickpeas and cauliflower,' Mickey said proudly. 'Tammy's mother helped me, but I'm learning how to be a good father.'

Alicia blinked back a tear when Corey squealed with delight as the food ended up covering his chin and cheeks.

  David Whittet

'Mickey!' Alicia exclaimed, her arms held out wide. 'He's got your mischievous grin. I bet he will be just as much of a rascal as you!'

CHAPTER EIGHT

Alicia's eyes fixed on the monitor, and her hand grasped Mickey's while the sonographer scanned her abdomen. What did all those wavy black and white lines on the screen mean?

'See that?' The sonographer pointed to a pulsating image on the monitor. 'That's your baby's heart beating.'

Alicia tightened her grip on Mickey's hand. Could that tiny shadow really be her baby's heart? Another thought played on her mind. Had the drinks she'd consumed after the reunion ceremony at the Roaring Creek Falls harmed her baby?

'It doesn't look very strong.' Alicia drew back and met the sonographer's eyes. 'Everything's alright, isn't it?'

'Your baby looks absolutely perfect.' The sonographer continued to run the probe over Alicia's abdomen. 'That curve there, that's the spine. Down here, we have the organs. Do you want to know if you have a girl or boy?'

Alicia glanced up at Mickey. They'd talked about it that morning, and Alicia had made up her mind that she wanted it to be a surprise.

'Go on,' Mickey said. 'You're dying to know. So am I. Will Corey have a brother or sister?'

'Okay.' Alicia took a deep breath and turned to the sonographer. 'Yes. Please, tell us.'

The sonographer beamed. 'You're going to have a boy. And this scan says it's not too far away. You're thirty-four weeks along.'

Alicia sat up and hugged Mickey. 'Corey's going to have a playmate.' She'd been going to say—*they'll be brothers*. But were they? The relationship was complicated. Would they be second cousins? That didn't matter in the excitement of the moment. 'We'll bring them up as brothers. How wonderful.'

The sonographer cleaned the gel off Alicia's tummy. 'I'll send the scan result to your midwife and your obstetrician in Christchurch. You're seeing Professor Woodruff next week, aren't you?'

 David Whittet

Alicia nodded. Mickey helped her climb off the couch.

'I can't wait to tell Lilly,' Alicia said. 'I hope she's coping with Corey.'

'Yeah.' Mickey raised an eyebrow. 'It was kind of Lilly to look after him. Corey can be a right handful.'

Alicia grinned. 'Rubbish. He's an absolute darling.'

Mickey hesitated for a second. 'I think he's got a touch of my rebellious streak in him. I hope he won't be too like me for his own good.'

Alicia had worried about that as well. But today was a day for celebration, not negativity. She pulled down her top and straightened her maternity skirt. 'Then I'll just have to take both of you in hand, won't I?'

'Guess so.' Mickey paused again, resting his hand gently on Alicia's tummy. 'I only hope that Corey will be a good influence on your boy and that they'll get on well together.'

'I'm sure they will.' Alicia grabbed her handbag. 'Remember, we've got to buy a new fridge before we go back to Roaring Creek and rescue Lilly. But I need to pee first, I'm bursting after all that water!'

Alicia froze when they got to Lilly's place. Evie was there, too. She was on the floor with Lilly, playing with Corey. Alicia didn't know where to look. Was Evie still mad at Mickey? The shameless womaniser who had got her son Jake blotto, then seduced his girlfriend and got her pregnant. Yet here Evie was, pulling funny faces to entertain that very baby.

'Evie! I didn't realise you'd be here,' Alicia said. 'Are you sure you're alright with—'

'It's okay.' Evie looked up and smiled at Alicia. 'All that's in the past and none of it was your fault.'

Alicia pushed Mickey back into the hallway. 'No, but …'

'It's alright, Mickey, you can come in,' Evie said. 'All's forgiven. If not entirely forgotten.'

Mickey stepped forward. 'I'm sorry, Evie. I was a bastard back then.'

'You were.' Evie shrugged. 'I hope you've learnt your lesson.' She put her arm around Corey. 'You must set this little one a good example.'

Alicia glanced at Mickey. His face was bright red.

'I will,' Mickey said, 'with Alicia's help. I promise.'

'You'd better.' Evie let go of Corey, and he crawled across the floor to his father.

'He will. He's a new man!' Alicia put her arm around Mickey. 'And guess what? I—we—are going to have a baby boy!'

Lilly rushed over and hugged Alicia. 'I'm so happy for you. And everything's fine with the baby?'

'Yes. At least, the ultrasound lady seemed to think so.' Alicia paused and held her stomach. 'But we've got to see that specialist in Christchurch next week.'

'Do you want me to look after Corey again?' Lilly said. 'Honestly, he's no trouble.'

'You're an angel, Lilly,' Alicia said. 'But we're taking him with us to Christchurch.'

'Are you sure?' Lilly said. 'There's bound to be loads of hanging around in hospital waiting rooms. Corey will get mighty bored.'

Alicia took Corey into her arms. 'We're making a family day of it. As soon as we finish at the hospital, we're off to the park for some fun.'

'You sure deserve some fun,' Lilly said. 'After everything—'

'Let's not think about that.' Alicia held Corey up. 'Now, we've got this little one's first birthday party to organise. Have you booked the Women's Institute?'

'I have,' Lilly said with a wink. 'It's going to be a joint party. Corey's birthday and your baby shower.'

❧

The fridge was new, but the rest of the kitchen was shabby. Alicia's frustration grew when Mickey opened a can of baby food for Corey and carelessly chucked the empty container at the rubbish bin, only to miss and have it land on the floor.

Alicia let out an exasperated sigh. 'Mickey! Pick that up! And the other ones too.'

He sheepishly collected the empty cans and threw them into the trash. 'Sorry.'

     David Whittet

Alicia scowled. 'Sometimes sorry isn't good enough. I've told you before, a bachelor pad is no place to bring up a child. This kitchen was spotless when I cleaned it up a few weeks back. Look at it now!'

Mickey grinned. 'Corey doesn't care what it looks like.'

'But I do.' Alicia crossed her arms. 'And it's unhygienic. The pantry stinks.'

Mickey pulled a face. 'It's not that bad.'

'It damn well is.' Alicia glared at him. 'Seriously, I don't know why I bother trying to clean up after you.'

Mickey finished feeding Corey, and they sat beside her on the sofa. 'Don't be like that. The place has looked amazing since you moved in. What with the house plants and the pillows—'

Alicia stared at him in astonishment. 'You noticed?'

Mickey nodded. 'Sure thing. And I *will* make an effort to be better. I've never had to worry about anyone other than myself before.'

Alisha shrugged. 'Looks like I'll have to start another cleanup operation in the morning.'

'Mind you don't overdo it. You need your rest.' Mickey squeezed her hand. 'I'll get up if Corey wakes in the night.'

'You need sleep too.' Alicia gave him a stern gaze. 'Some nights, you look half-dead when you get back from the mercy runs. I don't want you to burn out.'

Mickey flexed his muscles. 'Sleep is for wimps. I'm strong.'

And I'm not? Alicia couldn't let that go unchallenged. 'I'm just as strong as you. I've had to be to survive. Besides, I beat you at arm-wrestling when we were kids.'

'Yeah.' Mickey ducked as he spoke. 'But only because I let you win.'

Alicia gave him such a dig in the ribs that he almost fell off the chair. If it wasn't for Mickey's bewitching grin, which she never could resist, and the fact she was cuddling his child, the wretch would be flat on his face on the floor.

Corey began to cry and looked at Alisha as if to say, *How could you think of doing that to my father?* Then he promptly spewed his dinner.

Alicia shot up and fetched a tea towel from the kitchen benchtop. 'Let me take him. You didn't wind him after feeding him.'

Mickey scratched his head. 'Tammy's mother did say something about getting his wind up.'

Alicia cradled Corey in her arms and slowly paced around the kitchen while patting his back. 'We're going to show your dad how things are done, aren't we?'

Corey gurgled and then let out a loud burp.

'Good boy!' Alicia said, tickling his tummy with a gentle touch.

Mickey snorted. 'You don't say that when I belch.'

Alicia grinned. 'Corey's burps don't stink of beer.' She gave Corey another pat on the back, and more wind came up. 'I'll put Corey to bed. You get some sleep because tomorrow we're going to have another arm-wrestling competition! And I'm going to win. Again.'

The next few days they felt like they were kids again. After so many disasters and false starts, Alicia's lifelong hopes and aspirations had suddenly come together in one blessed moment. Defying the Gang. How long had she dreamt of that? And she was doing it with Mickey, her childhood companion and sweetheart. He was putting his own future at risk with the mercy runs. She was looking after his child, and her own baby was only a couple of months away.

When Corey woke at three in the morning, Alicia wondered what it would be like to get up for two children. When he returned from his mercy run, Mickey crashed out on the bed and didn't stir until morning. Was she as strong as she made out? Alicia felt puffed when she rocked Corey back to sleep. The doctor had talked about the damage to her lungs. Was her body strong enough to last the rest of the pregnancy and deliver her baby? *Don't even go there.* She sang Corey a gentle lullaby. Alicia was a survivor, and she knew it.

Professor Woodruff was everything Alicia imagined a distinguished obstetrician to be, with his immaculate three-piece suit, balding grey hair and neatly trimmed beard. He looked at her over his thick-rimmed bifocals.

'You're a remarkable woman,' Professor Woodruff said after he finished examining her. 'In thirty years of medical practice, I've never seen anything quite like it. To survive bullet wounds so close to the heart is extraordinary, but then to escape the fire—'

Alicia put a hand on Mickey's arm. 'This man pulled me out of the fire.'

'She certainly is an amazing woman,' Mickey said. 'I'll second that.'

'No question.' Professor Woodruff studied her chest scan on his screen. 'Considering everything, your heart and lungs are in excellent shape. I don't envisage any particular problems with the delivery.'

Alicia wiped a bead of perspiration off her forehead. *Thank God!*

'As a precaution,' the professor continued, 'we'll admit you for an elective Caesarean section. I'll perform the operation myself.'

Alicia squeezed Mickey's hand even tighter. 'A Caesarean section? And I'll have to have the baby in Christchurch?'

'I assure you, it's merely a preventative measure.' Professor Woodruff smiled reassuringly. 'We don't want to take any chances with your baby.'

'Ba-by.' Corey, who had sat quietly on Mickey's lap throughout the consultation, copied the word. 'Ba-by.'

Mickey gave Corey a kiss. 'Mummy's going to have a baby.'

'Ma-ma,' Corey burbled. 'Ma-ma.'

Mummy. Ma-ma, Ma-ma. They were the most beautiful words Alicia had ever heard.

Mickey had the car radio blazing as he drove them to Hagley Park. Alicia was lost in thought. Was it usual for the professor of obstetrics to carry out routine surgery himself? Alicia should have felt reassured, but the consultation left a niggling doubt. Was Professor Woodruff more concerned than he let on?

Alicia dismissed the notion. She was determined not to let anything ruin their picnic in Hadley Park. Mickey parked the car on the grass verge and got Corey out of his child seat in the back. Corey immediately spotted an ice-cream van with its brightly coloured paintwork and the catchy 'Mister Softee' jingle it was chiming.

'Icy cream! Icy cream!' Corey chanted, tugging on his father's arm. 'Icy cream, Da-da!'

Alicia laid a blanket on the ground and opened the picnic hamper while Mickey bought Corey an ice cream. She laughed when Mickey brought Corey across, with both their faces covered in ice cream. That was nothing compared to the mess on Corey's face when Mickey tried to feed him a sandwich. It obviously wasn't as tasty as the ice cream, and the little rascal kept turning his head away. Mickey soon gave up and tucked into a steak and kidney pie that he had smuggled into Alicia's picnic basket.

Priceless. Alicia would have to have her wits about her as Corey grew up. He would definitely be every bit as mischievous as his father.

Alicia laid back on the rug and watched Mickey push Corey on the swing. Mickey looked so happy and relaxed. And he was taking his parental responsibilities seriously, using an infant-safe swing seat. The excitement on Corey's face as he swung backwards and forwards brought tears to her eyes. Her instincts were right. Mickey would be a fabulous father.

Corey groaned when Mickey paused for a rest.

'Ma-ma, Ma-ma.'

Mickey beckoned to Alicia. 'He wants you to give him a push.'

Alicia pulled herself up off the rug. That bump was definitely getting heavier. She summoned all the energy she could muster to gently push the swing and felt a surge of joy when Corey cackled with delight.

'Don't overdo it,' Mickey said. 'You're tired. I'll take over.'

Tired? Alicia hadn't felt so exhilarated in years.

 David Whittet

CHAPTER NINE

Would she finish the cleanup in time? Alicia put down the scrubbing brush and rested on a stool. With just two weeks to go before her admission to Christchurch Hospital, getting Mickey's bach fit for a newborn was an impossible task. She watched Mickey finish his dinner, washing the last of his lamb chop down with a bottle of beer. At least he didn't use his fingers as toothpicks like her father.

'You're president-elect of the Gang,' Alicia moaned, 'so why are we living in such a grotty dump?'

Mickey took another swig of beer. 'I thought you liked my penthouse pad.' He glanced around the room. 'It's got character and these walls have seen some action.'

Alicia stamped her foot on the floor. 'Your playboy days are over. You're a father now.'

'I know.' Mickey patted his full belly. 'It's just …'

'Just nothing.' Alicia threw a duster at him.

Corey smiled and cooed from his high chair.

'See?' Alicia said. 'Even Corey agrees.' She got up from the stool and sat down next to Mickey. 'Seriously, love. Can't we find somewhere better to live with another child coming?'

Mickey grunted. 'I know it's not a palace, but this is our place. It's cool.'

It's tiny and dirty. Alicia put her arm around him. 'What about the empty house on Cliff Road? That would be perfect. It belongs to the Gang, doesn't it?'

Mickey shrugged. 'It's set aside for some big name. They'd never let us have it.'

Alicia shook her head. 'Why not? You're vice president. You should have first dibs.'

'Have you forgotten about your old man? Reggie's still mad as hell about the pregnancy.'

As if Alicia could ever forget about her father. 'I'll talk to him. The old man's softening in his old age.'

Mickey put down the beer bottle. 'Don't fool yourself.'

'I'm not.' Alicia cleared away Mickey's plate and took it to the sink. 'Lilly says Reggie and Cassie split up. He's back with Felicity.'

'What difference does that make?'

Everything. Alicia smiled. 'Felicity is a good influence on him. If I can get her on side—we'll convince Reggie it's a bad look to have the two-I-C living in a hovel.'

'It's not a hovel.'

'Whatever.' Alicia scrubbed the fat off the dish. 'You don't know Felicity. Between the two of us, we'll soon bring Reggie round.'

'I wouldn't be so sure.' Mickey got up from the table. 'Besides, Reggie can't afford to be generous. Not now that I'm giving his precious protection money back to his victims.' Mickey reached for his jacket. 'And talking of that, I'd better get going. Edith and the rest of the old ladies will be waiting for their money.'

❧

Alicia fed Corey and put him to bed after Mickey had left. Since Corey's arrival, Mickey had started doing his mercy runs earlier in the evening. If he got back early enough, he'd read Corey a story. Corey always slept well after his father came in and kissed him goodnight.

What was keeping Mickey tonight? Alicia looked at her watch. Eleven o'clock. Mickey usually tried to get home by half past ten at the latest, and tonight was the first time Alicia couldn't get Corey to settle.

'Hush, my darling,' she said, rocking him in her arms. 'Daddy will be home soon.'

But he wasn't. Alicia read Corey another story. And another. She sang a lullaby, but her mouth was so dry she had to lay Corey down to get a glass of water.

Corey howled. Alicia dropped the glass, and it smashed on the floor. She felt a contraction in her tummy as she slipped on the wet carpet in her rush to comfort Corey.

'There, there, my angel.' Alicia held Corey with one hand and clutched her tummy with the other. 'Daddy's not far away. I promise.'

 David Whittet

Corey screamed louder. Even a baby could tell she wasn't in a position to promise anything. What if she went into labour, alone and looking after another child?

Lilly. Alicia hobbled to the telephone, Corey still in her arms. *I have to call Lilly. She'll know what to do.*

The moment Alicia picked up the receiver, Mickey burst through the door.

'They're onto us!' Mickey panted. 'We have to get out.'

Alicia almost dropped Corey. She'd never seen such terror in Mickey's eyes.

'What is it, Mickey?' She shuddered when he didn't reply immediately. 'Speak to me!'

'It's Todd. He's grassed. Reggie knows everything.'

Alicia froze. 'About returning the protection money?'

Mickey nodded. 'We're dead meat.'

'No.' Alicia paced up and down the tiny room, still clutching Corey. 'You've got mates who can hide you. You've done it before. Me—I'll go and stay with Lilly.'

'Get real!' Mickey threw his arms in the air. 'You're in as much danger as me. Reggie knows it was you who put me up to it. And he's still raging about the baby. The half-blood.'

'I'll take my chances. My father doesn't scare me any longer.' Alicia shivered as she spoke the words. Her old man had done some mighty mean things to her in the past. But surely not even Reggie would kill his own daughter.

Mickey's breath caught in his throat as he answered. He'd always been able to read her innermost thoughts.

'Maybe your father won't kill you, but Todd wouldn't think twice. Nor would Damon or any of his band of thugs.' Mickey clenched his fists, and his body stiffened. 'We've got to get out of here. For your sake and the baby's.'

'About the baby.' Alicia felt another contraction as she clung to Corey. 'I think I'm going into—'

'There's no time to lose.' Mickey cut her off before she could finish the sentence. 'Go to Lilly and she'll be dead, too. Remember what happened to Olivia?'

Alicia did. Olivia—the dear lady who'd done so much for both her and Mickey. Alicia shivered. Olivia had paid for it with her life when Reggie thought she'd betrayed the Gang.

'But Mickey …' Another contraction. 'I'm having the—'

Mickey snatched Corey out of her hands. 'I'm taking Corey back to Tammy. He'll be safe with his mother.'

What? I'm his mother now! Alicia felt Mickey had ripped out her heart. 'I thought Tammy wanted nothing more to do with—'

'There's no time to talk.' Mickey strapped Corey into his car seat. 'Once Corey's safe with Tammy, we're out of here. We'll go underground in Christchurch. A couple of mates up there owe me.' He glanced back at Alicia. 'Then you'll be in Christchurch when the time comes for—'

'Mickey!' Alicia clutched her belly. How could she make him understand? 'The time's here—'

Mickey clearly wasn't listening. 'Once I'm back, we're gone.'

He took a gun out of his jacket pocket and handed it to Alicia. 'Take this. Any trouble before I get back … don't be afraid to use it.'

'Mickey, I can't!'

'Take it!' Mickey thrust the gun in her hand, secured Corey in the ute, and started the engine. 'Don't panic. I'll be back in ten. Max.'

The ute swung out of the yard. Mickey was gone.

Alicia's hand trembled as she held the gun. Was this the same weapon Mickey had used to threaten her when he discovered she was going to marry Emir?

Thank God the contractions slowed down. Alicia went inside and collapsed on a chair. If Mickey got back in ten minutes, she might manage to hold on. Maybe those breathing exercises would buy her some time. What was it the midwife had said? Take a slow, deep breath and then slowly exhale. If it was meant to make her feel calm, it wasn't working.

Surely ten minutes was up. *It must be.* Alicia was too scared to look at her watch. She focused her eyes on the front door. *Where the hell are you, Mickey?* How Alicia longed for the sound of the ute's engine to break the deathly silence of the night. She glanced through the kitchen window, praying she'd see the headlights approaching. Instead, she glimpsed the kitchen clock. Midnight. Perhaps it was wrong, like everything else in that wretched bach.

Another half hour. Still no Mickey. Had the Gang got to him before he had a chance to get back to her? Alicia shuddered. What had they done to him? Was he … dead? No. They were kindred spirits. She'd know if they'd killed him.

     David Whittet

The contractions restarted. *Mickey! You can't leave me! Not like this!* Alicia curled up as she fought off another contraction. As the pain swept through her body like a knife slashing her insides, she cursed Mickey for deserting her. Why hadn't he taken her with him when he took Corey to Tammy? But when the contractions subsided, Alicia's mood changed. Was Mickey hurting too? She could only imagine the agony he'd be in if her father's henchmen had captured and tortured him.

What was she going to do? Would she give birth to her baby all alone in that decrepit bach? Would someone find her and her baby, both dead on the floor days, weeks, or even months later?

Pull yourself together, girl. You won't let that happen. Alicia took another deep breath and crawled on her hands and knees until she reached the telephone. She'd been about to call Lilly before Mickey burst in and took Corey. Alicia's hand shook as she picked up the receiver. She paused for a moment, then dropped it to the floor. *I can't do this. Not if it means the Gang will destroy Lilly the way they did Olivia.*

A chill struck Alicia as violently as any of the contractions. The Gang would punish anyone she asked for help. *I'm on my own. I have to escape. Run away. Disappear.* But how? She'd die if she didn't get medical help fast.

Another wave of pain brought a fresh idea. *Kāterina!* Dear, wise, Kāterina. Maybe Kāterina wasn't a midwife, but she was a Māori health practitioner, and she had friends who were midwives. Better still, Kāterina lived out in the forest—a safe distance from her father's men. At least for tonight.

Reality set in with the next contraction. Mickey had taken the ute, their only vehicle. Alicia was trapped. *Think.* She picked up the telephone again.

'Lilly … I need you to do something for me and not ask any questions. Something's cropped up. I want to borrow your car.'

'Of course,' Lilly replied. 'I'll come right over.'

'No. I don't want you getting into trouble.' Alicia paused and took a deep breath. 'Just go out and put the keys in the car and I'll come and get it.'

'Whatever's the matter? Are you alright? Are you sure you don't want me to come around?'

'Please don't.' Alicia garbled her words. Gang spies could be watching. Lilly would be in danger if she rushed to the bach. 'Just leave the keys in the car and go back inside. I'll sneak over and drive away in it. That way, nobody will know that you helped me.'

'I don't understand. You're my friend, and I don't care what anyone else thinks.'

'Please listen to me, Lilly. Do as I say. Mickey and I—we're in trouble with the Gang. I can't risk you getting involved. Just let me take the car, and if the Gang comes asking questions, tell them your car was stolen.'

Alicia put the phone down before Lilly could protest. *Don't let me down, Lilly.* Alicia breathed the words under her breath. *You're my only hope.* Alicia was sure Lilly would let her have the car. But would Lilly heed the warning and stay home?

With a groan, Alicia pulled herself up off the floor and grabbed her coat. As she made for the front door, she heard a car pull up. Had Mickey come back for her? Or had the Gang come to take her away? Alicia knew the answer before she opened the door.

'Lilly! I told you not to come.'

'Do you think I'd allow you to take off on your own in your condition?' Lilly stamped her foot on the doorstep. 'Wherever you're going, I'm coming with you.'

'If only you could.' Alicia met Lilly's determined gaze. 'But I can't let you. The Gang will crucify you if you do. Like they did to Olivia.'

Lilly flung her arms around Alicia, tears streaming down her cheeks. 'I don't care about the Gang or what they do to me. I care about you!'

'I know.' Alicia felt the tears well up in her eyes, too. Should she relent? Lower her guard and let Lilly drive her into the forest? It could be Alicia and her baby's only chance of staying alive. No. She couldn't have Lilly's demise on her conscience. 'I'm going alone. This is for the best. You know me—I've survived worse than this before.'

Alicia snatched the keys from Lilly's hand.

Lilly tried to get them back. 'Don't do this, Alicia! You've never been in labour before.'

Alicia edged towards the car. Could she get to it before Lilly stopped her? Lilly was about to grab hold of her when the force of Alicia's next contraction took over and propelled her into the car.

Alicia started the engine and put her foot on the gas. She wound down the window and shouted back to Lilly as she accelerated down the street. 'You're my saviour, Lilly. One day, I'll be back to thank you. And remember, you never saw me tonight!'

❧

How many times had Alicia taken that winding road into the forest? When she was a little girl, she looked forward to the visits to Kāterina's caravan. They were her first true escape from the Gang. How Alicia laughed each time her mother swerved to miss a pothole. Tonight, the car veered all over the unmade track with each of Alicia's contractions.

Rain pelted against the windscreen. Thunder rumbled in the distance. In her manic flight, Alicia had scarcely noticed the storm clouds descend. And if she had, they simply felt like a reflection of her dark mood. She glanced out of the side window and wished she hadn't. The Roaring Creek River had swollen and would soon break its banks. Did nature have it in for her, too? Alicia hit the accelerator. *Don't panic.* She'd made her way to the *Gypsy Rose* before in some pretty wild weather. But she wasn't in labour then.

Alicia cried out as each contraction ripped through her body, a searing pain that made it almost impossible to breathe. With each passing second, the pain intensified. She grabbed her stomach, gritted her teeth and balled her fists while holding on to the steering wheel with one hand and desperately trying to keep her eyes on the road.

A bolt of lightning struck Alicia's heart as violently as it lit the sky. What if Mickey had deserted her deliberately? Maybe the Gang hadn't taken him—he could have planned it all along. So much didn't add up. How come Tammy was so ready to take Corey back? Had Mickey been in touch with her before tonight? If he had, it meant everything Mickey had told her was a lie.

Don't even think that. Alicia gripped the steering wheel even tighter as the car's wheels churned through the mud. *Mickey loves me!* He did—he'd risked everything to help her reform the Gang, and she'd seen the terror in his eyes when he left with Corey. Terror so extreme Mickey couldn't possibly have faked it.

Another flash of lightning almost blinded Alicia. Was she still on the right track? She looked for familiar landmarks, but branches swirled in the wind and brushed against the windscreen, further obscuring her view. At last, she recognised the clearing where her mother used to park their vehicle. Should Alicia leave the car here and go on foot as they had done when she was a kid? No. Alicia drove on down the path. She had to get to the *Gypsy Rose* before she gave birth.

The track narrowed. Alicia hit a shrub, and the side-view mirror snapped off. She jumped and the car swung, almost destroying the other side mirror. *Keep going. You can do this*. How much further was it? The car skidded in the sodden undergrowth. The engine spluttered as the car sunk further into the mud. *Don't give up on me now! Please!* Alicia revved the engine and the car jolted forward. Trees bent over in the gale-force wind. Were they going to land on top of her? A sudden blast brought a tree down across the track. Alicia pumped the brake, but the car jackknifed and hurtled forward. She squeezed her eyes shut as the car crashed into the tree.

Was she still alive? Another contraction told her she was. It was several minutes before Alicia dared open her eyes. The front of the car was smashed in and smouldering. Could she get out? Alicia felt something trickle down her legs as she forced the door open. She persuaded herself it was just the rain until she put her hand on her crotch. Blood. The trickle had become a torrent.

Alicia dragged herself out of the car, her bump catching on the twisted doorframe. The rain beat against her so forcibly she could hardly stand up. She grasped a tree for support when another contraction struck. *You can do this*. Her mother had haemorrhaged in the forest when she was pregnant with Helena, but both Naomi and her baby had survived.

Alicia drove herself forward through the howling wind and the maelstrom of foliage that blew into her face. Her foot caught in a tangle of scrub, and she stumbled to the ground. Voices. Were the branches talking to her, urging her not to give up? Or was it her unborn baby speaking to her?

Not much further.
Not much further.
Look up, Alicia, look up!
What do you see?

 David Whittet

Alicia raised her head. Was that glimmer of light in the distance just moonlight breaking through the fast-moving clouds? Alicia struggled to her feet. Please, God, let that light be Kāterina's caravan.

She caught her hand on a jagged thorn. The sharp prick eased the pain of the next contraction and propelled her further down the track. The voices in her head grew louder.

Keep going.
Keep going.
Never give up.
Never give up.
Nearly there.

Alicia paused for breath and pricked her ears. Was that just the wind echoing through the trees? Or was it—dared she hope? There it was again, a horse neighing. Alicia would recognise that horse's cry anywhere in the world—it was Cleo, Kāterina's horse.

'Cleo! I'm coming!'

Alicia hardly noticed the next contraction. Or the one after that. If she could just reach the caravan—nothing else mattered.

'Kāterina!' Alicia cried out as another contraction, even more intense than the last, doubled her over. 'Kāterina! Help me!'

Could the old woman hear her? Was Kāterina asleep?

Cleo neighed even louder.

Again, Cleo, again! Alicia willed Cleo to rouse Kāterina. 'Wake up your mistress! Kick the caravan! Rock it! I need her. Now!'

Alicia managed another couple of paces forward before she collapsed. She could see the *Gypsy Rose* just a few metres away. So near—but still so far.

'Kāterina!' Alicia's voice was breaking and barely audible. 'Kāterina! Can you hear me?'

Submerged in dense thicket, Alicia tried to crawl along the path, but her legs were trapped in the undergrowth. That was it—she was stuck and would never make it to the *Gypsy Rose*. She'd failed. Another flurry of foliage blew over her prostrate body. Her mind drifted and the pain eased. This would be her—and her baby's—leafy grave.

'Tāku tamaiti! My poor child! Push, Alicia! Push!'

Alicia opened her eyes. She was flat on her back on the floor of the *Gypsy Rose*. Kāterina hovered over her, a towel in one hand and a bowl of soap and water in the other.

Alicia raised her head and gazed at Kāterina's beaming face. 'Am I … alive?'

'You most certainly are.' Kāterina wiped the perspiration off Alicia's face. 'Now, I'm no midwife, but I'd say your baby's almost out.'

Alicia glanced down at her belly. An intense contraction confirmed that she was very much alive.

'One more push,' Kāterina cried. 'One more push and you're there.'

Alicia grunted and pushed with what little energy she had left.

'Harder,' Kāterina urged. 'Don't give up now! I can see the baby's head!'

Alicia's moans and cries of effort echoed around the caravan as she pushed for what felt like an eternity, feeling that her insides were being ripped apart. But then, amidst the chaos, there was a sound more beautiful than anything she'd ever heard before. Her newborn baby crying.

Kāterina lifted the baby off the floor and placed him in Alicia's arms. 'You have a baby boy. A beautiful baby boy.'

Had she truly made it? Alicia held the tiny shred of humanity close to her bosom. 'My darling Aaron. I've been waiting so long to meet you.'

CHAPTER TEN

Miriama's Apartment, North Otago, New Zealand, March 2022

Aaron rose and paced up and down the room. 'So there you have it. Born on the floor of your foster mother's caravan.' His eyes met Miriama's. 'Sometimes, I think I was cursed from birth.'

'You haven't done too badly for yourself,' Miriama said. 'CEO of Parata Peak Power at twenty-seven.'

Yes, but at what cost? Aaron grunted. 'And that bastard Corey is determined to take it all away from me.'

Miriama frowned. 'You still haven't told me what it is between you and Corey. At least, not everything. And what about your mother? Did she ever get back together with Mickey?'

Questions, questions. Why couldn't Miriama just let go of the past?

Aaron sat down again, next to Miriama on the sofa. 'I was only five when my mother disappeared. I don't think she saw Mickey again, but I'm not sure.'

'It must have been tough for Alicia,' Miriama said. 'Have you any idea what happened after she gave birth to you in the caravan?'

'My aunt Helena said my mother got an infection and went into septic shock. We had to be airlifted to Auckland Hospital.'

'Your poor mother. But she made a full recovery?'

Aaron nodded. 'After that, we went to live with my aunt Fonella.'

'Fonella?' Miriama looked blank. 'Who was she?'

'Fonella was Emir's sister.' Aaron lowered his head. 'She was the only one of my father's family prepared to accept that Alicia had nothing to do with his death.'

Miriama sighed. 'I don't suppose anyone will ever know the whole truth about that fire.'

Aaron stared at his feet. 'The Gang killed my father and they kidnapped my mother.'

'You don't know that.' Miriama put a hand on his shoulder. 'At least …
not for certain.'

Aaron pulled away. 'I bloody well do. God knows what they've done to my
mother.'

Miriama put an arm around him again. 'Have you no idea what happened
to your mother?'

Aaron shook his head.

'Are you sure it was the Gang that took her?' Miriama said. 'Why would
they?'

'They've had it in for my mother ever since she married my father.' Aaron
knew that wasn't the real reason—or at least, it wasn't the whole story. 'I'm sorry.
I don't want to talk about it.'

Miriama got up. 'I'll make some more coffee. You *are* going to talk to me,
Aaron. Even if we're up all night.'

Aaron followed her into the kitchen. 'I want to talk. It's just …'

Miriama turned to face him. 'What?'

Aaron took a step back. Why couldn't he talk to the woman he loved about
his mother's disappearance? He'd feel better if he did. So what was stopping
him? 'I'm sorry, Miriama. It's still too raw.'

Aaron *was* still hurting. Twenty-two years on, and he still had no idea what
had happened to his mother. He'd hired a private detective as soon as he'd got
a job and could afford it.

Miriama fired up her state-of-the-art espresso machine and made two
more cappuccinos. Aaron's mind went back to a day seven years earlier when
he entered the offices of the Sullivan Detective Agency. Back then, he was full
of hope that after a string of false leads, they might finally be onto something.
Rodney Sullivan had at last located a disaffected ex-member of the Godzone
Gorillas who was willing to talk …

Sullivan pulled down the blinds in his dingy office.

Aaron leant across the desk. 'Are you sure this dude's on the level? If this is
another dead end—'

     David Whittet

'It won't be.' Sullivan sat down on his swivel chair and turned to face Aaron. 'Remember, this man is frightened. Let me do all the talking.' He pressed the intercom on his desk. 'Bring Gerry in, Mildred.'

Gerry was a tall man, standing at just over 1.8 metres, with a fading full-facial tattoo and the words 'Godzone Gorillas' still visible across his forehead.

'Thank you for coming, Gerry,' Sullivan said. 'This is Aaron Casper. Rest assured, anything said in this office stays—'

Gerry drew a knife from his pocket and pointed it at Aaron. 'Swear on your life you won't grass …'

Aaron pulled back. What had he got himself into? 'Of course I won't. Like Mr Sullivan said, anything we say in here is entirely confidential.'

Gerry brandished the knife even closer to Aaron's face. 'Swear it!'

'Alright.' Aaron lifted his hands defensively. 'I swear!'

'Okay.' Gerry put the knife away and sat down next to Aaron. 'It's just … they treat you harshly if you grass on the Gang.' He unbuttoned his shirt to reveal a mesh of battle scars on his chest. 'When you've been double-crossed as often as I have, you don't take any chances.'

Aaron wasn't sure how he was supposed to react. He'd got enough scars of his own from skirmishes with the Gang during childhood. He shot Sullivan an icy stare. This was going to be as useless as the rest of Sullivan's so-called leads, and his bill would be as exorbitant as ever.

Sullivan cleared his throat and addressed Gerry. 'Aaron is naturally eager to hear what you know about his mother. Tell him exactly what you told me.'

Gerry did up his shirt. 'About the mock trial?'

'Everything,' Sullivan prompted.

Aaron's heart missed a beat. *Mock trial?* The mere sound of the words breathed terror.

'What they did to Mickey was cruel, but the way they treated Alicia …' Gerry broke off and flapped his hands. 'And her being Reggie's daughter and all. It wasn't right.'

Aaron focused on a mole on Gerry's neck. Fifteen years of pent-up rage boiled over. Aaron leapt up and grabbed Gerry. 'You were one of the bastards who took my mother away that night.' Aaron continued to shake Gerry violently. 'Go on! Admit it, you son of a bitch!'

'Alright. Yes.' Gerry wrestled free. 'I was there, and I wish to God I'd had nothing to do with it.'

'Calm down, both of you.' Sullivan glared at Aaron and rapped his fingers on the desk. 'I said I'd do all the talking.'

Aaron glared back at Sullivan. 'You weren't there. I was five years old, and I watched this bastard and his mates manhandle my mother and drag her out of my bedroom.'

'They weren't my mates.' Gerry clasped his hands together. 'I had no choice. They'd have killed me if I'd refused. I told you, I didn't want any part of it.'

Aaron wasn't listening to any excuses. He lurched at Gerry again. The bastard could brandish his knife again for all Aaron cared. 'I should wring your bloody neck.'

Sullivan sprang to his feet and pulled Aaron back. 'Enough. Do you want to hear what Gerry has to say or not?'

Aaron let go of Gerry and sank back into his seat. It was all very well for the bastard to show a modicum of remorse now. Even if he had been press-ganged into it, he did nothing to stop the assault. Aaron couldn't look at him. But if this man knew anything about his mother … if she was still alive … her whereabouts even …

'I'm sorry.' Aaron forced himself to take a deep breath and control his voice. 'Please, tell me all you know about my mother.'

'It ain't pretty,' Gerry said. 'Your mother … she'd been on the hit list for years. Ever since Mickey went down.'

Aaron lowered his head. 'Because of me?'

'No.' Gerry's chin quivered as he spoke. 'Alicia and Mickey … they'd been giving folk their protection money back … the Gang was nigh on broke by the time Reggie found out.'

That was his mother. Helping others. Aaron felt a momentary flutter in his stomach. Alicia always stuck her neck out to do the right thing. But Mickey— the man Aaron still held responsible for his father's death—was he capable of such selfless acts of kindness?

Aaron eyed Gerry. Was this dude a reliable witness? 'Why should I believe a word you say?'

Gerry returned Aaron's stare. 'Because I'm telling the truth. Honest, guv.'

          David Whittet

And doubtless because Sullivan is paying you a fortune. With my money. Aaron gave Sullivan a darting glance and then turned back to Gerry. 'So what did you do to my mother when you took her away?'

'Reggie never did his own work. That was left to his minions. We took her to an old warehouse. Tied her to a post. Todd and Dylan kept smacking her face.'

'And you?' Aaron said. 'Did you join in?'

'No!' Gerry's voice trembled as he continued. 'I went to see Reggie. Tried to talk him out of it. I told him straight. What he was doing was wrong. Surely no one, not even a powerful gang leader, could be so heartless as to punish his own daughter so severely …'

Gerry shifted his weight from one foot to the other as he stood facing Reggie. The darkness of Reggie's office gave way to a flickering light—the glow from a broken, spluttering fluorescent bulb hanging from the ceiling, casting long shadows across the walls. Wood-panelled walls that were covered with gang trophies, each representing some poor sod's misfortune. The air was stale, like death. Reggie leant forward and glared at Gerry with his menacing eyes. Eyes that could kill.

'If I wanted your opinion, I would ask for it.' Reggie spat the words in Gerry's face. 'Now piss off.'

'She's your daughter,' Gerry pleaded. '*Your daughter.*'

Reggie grunted and sat down at his desk. 'She ceased to be my daughter when she betrayed the Gang. Have you any idea what her treachery has cost us?'

'She's still your daughter.' Gerry's voice wavered as he edged closer. 'Your own flesh and blood.'

'I've washed my hands of her, dammit!' Reggie slammed his fist on the desk. 'She made a laughing stock of all of us.'

'Can't you forgive her?' Gerry took another hesitant step forward. 'Showing mercy isn't a sign of weakness.' The stony face before him showed no signs of yielding. 'Showing the Gang has a human face might even strengthen your position.'

'Alicia made her own choices. Now she has to live with the consequences.' Reggie gave Gerry the finger. 'Get the hell out of here. Can't you see I'm busy?'

Aaron spotted a tear in the corner of Gerry's eye—at least, he thought he did. Maybe this guy could be trusted after all.

'So …' Aaron paused. Did he really want to know? 'What did you—they—do to my mother in that warehouse?'

Aaron closed his eyes as Gerry painted a bleak picture of Alicia's mock trial at the hands of her father's men. Gerry didn't spare any of the gory details as he described how they tied Alicia to that post in the deserted warehouse …

The rope dug into Alicia's skin and bound her so tightly she could hardly breathe. Gerry winced each time the gangsters slapped her face. Blood poured from her nose, mouth and cheeks.

Gerry looked away in horror. At the opposite end of the vast warehouse, a group of gangsters were playing snooker at an enormous pool table. Laughing and joking and drinking beer as if nothing was happening. Callous bastards.

Everyone hushed when Kaine, Reggie's right-hand man, arrived and took charge of the mock trial. He stood more than 1.8 metres tall in his black leather boots, striding with grim confidence. His dark hair was tied back in a ponytail that emphasised his coarse, tattooed face and unflinching determination.

'You have been tried and found guilty,' Kaine said, his fingers tucked into his sturdy leather belt, engraved with the insignia of the Godzone Gorillas. 'You have brought shame and ruin on the Gang.'

'No!' Alicia ducked to avoid yet another slap. 'I was just trying to do what was right. Make the Gang more just.'

'Bitch!' Cassandra, Reggie's ex-lover, let out a feral scream, her hand pulling back before launching forward with all her might, delivering a decisive blow to Alicia's stomach. 'Take that! You always thought you were above everyone else.

 David Whittet

Well, you're not!' Another punch came flying through the air, which connected with a sickening thud against Alicia's body. 'You're just a stuck-up pig!'

Alicia gasped. 'At least I'm not a gangster's whore.'

That got Alicia yet another hearty punch in the guts from Cassandra.

Todd pushed forward. 'If you were a man, you'd be shot.' He bared his teeth and raised his fist to Alicia's head. 'You're the bitch that got Mickey lynched. Teaching the bastard to give folk their money back.'

'What have you done to Mickey?' Alicia screamed in desperation. 'Have you … killed him?'

'Wouldn't you like to know?' Todd's eyes narrowed with contempt. 'Well, here's a taste of what we did to him.'

Gerry raised his arm to shield his face. He couldn't bear to watch another brutal assault on an innocent woman.

'Enough!' Kaine's shrill word of command echoed around the warehouse. 'I want this done properly.'

Silence. Even the snooker players laid down their cues.

Kaine stood facing Alicia, his black eyes glaring as he said each word slowly and precisely. 'There is only one punishment for betraying the Gang.' He looked over his shoulder and nodded to his minions. 'Take her away.'

Stop! I can't take any more! Aaron lost count of how often he muttered these words under his breath and covered his ears when Gerry described the mock trial. At one point, Aaron thought he might pass out, but he had to hear the truth after so many years of imagining the worst. Assuming, of course, that this was the truth. And even if it wasn't—sharing his mother's pain proved strangely cathartic.

'Just tell me one thing.' Aaron stared at Gerry with his eyes wide, studying every line in the man's face for clues as to his trustworthiness. 'Is my mother still alive?'

Gerry shrugged. 'They took her away. I don't know any more.'

Aaron continued to eyeball him. 'You must do.'

Gerry shook his head. 'I was so cut up about what they did to your mother that I got out of the Godzone Gorillas soon after that.'

I didn't think you ever escaped the Gang. 'And you haven't heard anything since?'

'Nothing.'

Aaron refused to let Gerry break eye contact. 'You must have heard rumours.'

'I don't think they've killed her if that's what you mean.' Gerry shuffled in his chair. 'She is probably rotting away in some Gang hideout. Along with all the others who've got on the wrong side of Reggie.'

'Bloody Gang!' Aaron wrung his hands. 'If I could get my hands on Reggie or Kaine, I swear I'd crucify both of them.'

Sullivan got up from behind his desk. 'Well, thank you for coming in, Gerry. That's been most … useful.'

Gerry extended a hand towards Aaron. 'It wasn't all the Gang's doing.'

Aaron glared at him. 'What do you mean?'

'Your mother moved to Auckland after you were born, didn't she?'

Aaron nodded. 'She was sick. They took her to Auckland Hospital in a helicopter.'

'And after that, you went to live with your aunt. What was her name? Yes, Fonella.'

Aaron sat bolt upright. How the hell did Gerry know all this? 'What has that to do with anything? We were safe up there.'

'So why did you leave Auckland and go to the Kaikōura Coast?'

Aaron paused for a moment. 'We went to live with my aunt Helena.'

Gerry scratched the mole on his neck. 'Bad move.'

Aaron had never been sure why they'd risked leaving the relative safety of Auckland. 'My mother must have had her reasons.'

'She did.' Gerry gave his mole another rub. 'Emir's folks. That was the reason.'

'What?'

'When Emir's old man—what was his name? Yes, William.' Gerry edged his chair towards Aaron. 'When William and his missus found out Alicia and her baby were living with their daughter, they went ballistic and demanded you and your mother get out at once. They threatened to cut Fonella off if you didn't leave.' Gerry got so close the smell of tobacco, alcohol and stale sweat

     David Whittet

almost made Aaron retch. 'They even accused Alicia of pretending you were Emir's child just to get her grubby hands on their son's money.'

Aaron pulled back. 'And you know this how?'

'Because it was William who grassed on Alicia. He found out where you were living. Guess he dragged it out of Fonella. He tipped off the Gang. Told them where to find you. Reggie was rubbing his hands together for days.'

Aaron buried his head in his hands. *Betrayed by my own grandfather! Betrayed by both my grandfathers!*

Sullivan still hovered behind his desk. 'Thank you again, Gerry, for being so … candid.' He turned to Aaron. 'This can't be easy for you. But at least you have some answers.'

Answers? All Aaron could think of was more questions. He peeked through his fingers. Watched Sullivan escort Gerry to the door and discreetly hand him an envelope. How much was the wretch getting paid for piling so much misery on him?

Gerry turned back. 'Mate, I don't know where you're going on this, but you be careful.'

Aaron raised his head. Who the hell was this ex-gangster to give him advice?

'I get that you want to find out about your mother,' Gerry continued, 'and good luck to you. But if you're thinking of taking on the Gang, watch your back.'

What did this jerk know about anything? Aaron had been fighting the Gang his entire life.

Gerry took a step towards him. 'And if you're thinking about vengeance—don't. They treated your mother rough. But they treat men worse. I was there when they took Mickey down.'

Aaron sat up. Perhaps there'd be some justice if Mickey had suffered an even worse fate than his mother. 'What did they do to him?'

Gerry grimaced. 'You really want to know?'

Aaron nodded.

'By the time they caught him,' Gerry said, 'Mickey had given almost a hundred grand back to its rightful owners. Reggie went raving mad.'

A hundred grand! Aaron's mouth fell open. Maybe Mickey wasn't the villain he'd always believed his so-called stepfather to be. But he was still Corey's father.

Gerry sat down again, opposite Aaron. 'Mickey had a heap of enemies, all biding their time. Todd had been onto him for months. Caught him giving protection money back to old ladies. But that was small fry. Todd was set on nailing Mickey for good. So he set up a sting. We got a tip-off. Mickey was giving cash to a penniless farmer up the valley. So we set up a stakeout at the farmhouse.' Gerry shivered. 'That must have been getting on for thirty years ago, but I remember it clear as day. We all got soaked to the skin. It was the night the Roaring Creek River broke its banks.'

The night of the great storm. Aaron's mind went into overdrive. Was this the night he was born? Aunt Helena had told him how his mother battled her way through the forest to Kāterina's caravan.

Aaron bit a nail. 'Go on.'

'We caught Mickey in the act. He had a backpack full of dough.' Gerry pressed a hand to his throat. 'We tied the poor bastard up and shoved him in the back of our van. He kept going on about having a child in his ute. Begged us to take the kid to his mother. We thought he was lying at first. But sure enough, a kid was bawling his eyes out in the ute.'

Corey! Aaron cringed. 'And did you … take the kid to its mother?'

Gerry nodded. 'Mickey kept pleading that this was the last time he'd ever go against the Gang. That he was going away with Alicia that night, and he'd be out of everyone's hair. Todd wasn't having a bar of it. He didn't waste a minute getting Reggie out of bed to deal with Mickey.'

Aaron shuddered as Gerry described the lynch mob. Mickey may have been a lowlife, but did he deserve this?

⁂

The gangsters dragged Mickey into the wrecker's yard and dumped his bruised and battered body at Reggie's feet.

'I should have you shot, Mickey!' Reggie roared. 'Who the hell do you think you are? Robin bleeding Hood?'

'Kill him! Kill him!' Todd led the gangsters' chorus. 'Kill him! Kill him! Kill the son of a bitch!'

Reggie spat on Mickey. 'I chose you as my successor, and this is how you repay me? You're a traitor, Mickey. You stole from the Gang.'

'No.' Mickey raised his head, then dropped back to the ground. 'I was just trying to do the right thing. Giving back the money *we* had stolen.'

'You've been listening to my daughter. Didn't I tell you women must be kept in their place?' Reggie spat on him again. 'You're unworthy of office, you fucking moron.'

'Kill him! Kill him!' The gangsters stomped on Mickey with their jackboots. 'Kill the motherfucker!'

'De-patch him,' Reggie ordered. 'You betrayed us, Mickey. There's no place for traitors in the Gang.'

The gangsters ripped off Mickey's jacket with its vice president's patch. They continued to tear off his clothes, their fists smashing into his body until he was left naked on the ground, blood streaming from wounds all over his body.

Todd picked up a bowl of steaming hot tar.

'Do it,' Reggie commanded.

Todd poured the tar over Mickey's face, scalding him as the boiling black liquid obliterated the words 'Godzone Gorillas' tattooed on his forehead.

Mickey writhed in agony. 'Mercy! Please! Mercy!'

Todd drew a pistol and aimed it at Mickey's head.

'No!' Mickey's voice rose in an agonising crescendo, tears streaming down his face. 'I'm a father. My boy needs me.'

Todd's finger hovered over the trigger.

'Stop.' Reggie stepped forward. 'Let him go.'

'*What?*' Todd kept his pistol aimed at Mickey's forehead. 'This isn't right. Mickey betrayed the Gang. He should die.'

'I said leave him,' Reggie repeated.

'Betraying the Gang means death,' Todd glared at Reggie, his face twisted in fury and disbelief. 'How many times have you told us that?' He gave Mickey's bloodied body another kick with his jackboot. 'Why is this motherfucker any different?'

Reggie returned Todd's furious stare. 'Are you questioning my authority?'

'No.' Todd reluctantly dropped the pistol. 'But if it was any of us, you'd have had us shot without a second thought.'

'Maybe I would.' Reggie clenched his fists and spat on Mickey one last time before turning on the gangsters. 'So you better watch yourselves.'

Gerry drew back and breathed a sigh of relief when he finished the story. The room fell silent as the grizzly details of Mickey's demise sank in.

'Why did Reggie let Mickey go?' Aaron asked eventually.

Gerry shrugged. 'Probably thought shooting the poor bugger was too quick. Wanted him to suffer. And by all accounts, he did.'

'What do you mean?' Aaron said.

'Mickey turned to booze. Last I heard, he was with his father in Hokitika. A couple of drunken sods living together.' Gerry got up again and headed to the door for the second time. He turned back before leaving. 'Watch yourself, Aaron. You don't mess with the Godzone Gorillas. I wouldn't like you to end up tarred and beaten like Mickey.'

Miriama put the two cappuccinos on the table. 'I understand if you don't want to talk about your mother. But I have to know what's going on between you and Corey.'

Aaron looked up, his mind still immersed in that disturbing meeting at the private detective's office. Sullivan had tracked down more ex-gangsters, but none of them knew or were willing to say anything more than Gerry.

'Don't lose heart,' Sullivan kept saying. 'This time, we're onto something.'

Fat chance. Sullivan's bills were as big as his promises.

'What I don't understand,' Miriama continued, 'is that if you and Corey weren't brought up together, what started the feud?'

Aaron glanced at his watch. Three a.m. He stifled a yawn and took a sip of coffee. The last thing he wanted was to talk about Corey, but he knew Miriama wouldn't back off.

'Corey blamed me for what happened to his father,' Aaron said.

Miriama frowned. 'That had nothing to do with you.'

'That's not how Corey saw it. He was convinced I was the reason he was sent back to live with Tammy and a stepfather who didn't want him.'

'That wasn't your fault.'

 David Whittet

Aaron shrugged. 'I was the scapegoat. The half-caste. Corey believed what the Gang told him. That it was my mother who'd talked Mickey into giving protection money back to folk and who got him de-patched.'

'That's so unfair.' Miriama moved closer and put her arm around Aaron. 'But isn't it time to put all this behind you?'

Aaron pulled away. 'I didn't start the fight. Corey attacked me the moment he set eyes on me. The bastard damn near killed me.'

'You were kids then. You're both grown men now. Surely you can reach some kind of agreement?'

Aaron snorted. *Agreement?* What planet was Miriama on? 'That son of a bitch will regret the day he got his sorry arse into my business.'

Miriama shook her head. 'That kind of attitude will get you nowhere.'

'I refuse to let the bastard trample over me yet again.' Aaron clenched his fists. 'I won't let him destroy everything I've slogged my guts out to achieve.'

'Heading a rival company doesn't mean he's out to get you.'

'You don't know Corey like I do.'

Miriama put an arm on his shoulder again. 'We didn't get off to a good start, you and I, but we're okay now. I was mean to you when we first met at the caravan. Remember?'

As if he'd ever forget. Miriama had made Aaron as miserable as Corey had by constantly putting him down.

Aaron gave her a frosty look. 'You were a bitch.'

'I was.' Miriama lowered her head. 'I might have been kinder to you if I knew what you'd been through.' She raised her eyes to meet Aaron's. 'But don't you see? If you can forgive me, you can forgive Corey.'

I can't. 'You've changed. Corey hasn't.'

'Are you sure?' Miriama continued to eye Aaron. 'When did you last see him? Have you thought about mediation?'

Mediation! The mere mention of the word sent Aaron's blood pressure sky high. 'You're as bad as Tony and the rest of them. You don't negotiate with the Gang.'

Miriama frowned. 'Corey's not the Gang. He's CEO of Jensen Industries.'

'He's a puppet. Reggie put him there to get control of the power industry.'

Miriama raised an eyebrow. 'That's not what Tony says. You should talk to him. He's worried about you.'

Aaron shrugged. Perhaps if Tony knew what Corey was really like, he would agree the bastard needed to be put in his place.

'Maybe I will. But right now, I need to get back. I'm meeting Alan Fitzpatrick'—Aaron looked at his watch again—'in about three hours' time.'

'Alan Fitzpatrick?' Miriama drew back. 'The head of the Emporium Group?'

Aaron nodded. 'Maybe if I can get him on side, Tony and the rest of the board will sit up and take some notice.'

❀

Miriama followed Aaron onto the street.

'Promise me you'll think about what I've said?' She gave him a kiss as he got into his car. 'And that you'll talk to Tony.'

'I will.' Aaron started the engine. 'But I won't change my mind about Corey.'

He drove off before Miriama had a chance to reply. What had Tony said to her? Could he really lose his job if the takeover collapsed?

Damn it! Aaron accelerated down the highway. He ought to be mentally preparing himself for the meeting with Alan Fitzpatrick, but his mind was still all over the place.

Dawn broke as Aaron approached his flat, the reservoir glistening in the early morning sun. The water appeared as calm as it had when he set out for Miriama's apartment the previous evening. Aaron sighed. Would he ever find peace of mind?

Time for a quick shower and a change of clothes, then back to the office. That would give him a couple of hours at least to go through some figures before Mr Fitzpatrick arrived.

Concentrate! Aaron cursed himself as the spreadsheets confounded his addled brain. He cursed Miriama, too, for dredging up all those horrid memories.

Aaron got up from his desk and stared out of the window. The Parata Peak Power Station with its raw energy always invigorated him. But this morning, he didn't see the cascading torrent of water. He didn't see the dam at all. Aaron was back at his aunt Helena's house, and his three wretched cousins were still tormenting him.

 David Whittet

PART TWO

GREAT EXPECTATIONS

CHAPTER ELEVEN

Aunt Helena's House, Kaikōura Coast, August 2005

You must be brave like David in the story. Five years on from his mother's disappearance and the words still rang in Aaron's ears. They helped—but they were just words. Aaron needed his mother here to defend him from his cousins' constant taunting and Uncle Ben's bullying. At home and at school, every day it was the same gruelling battleground. Today was no exception. Aaron had to stay behind after school when the rest of the kids went home. An hour's detention—and as usual, it was all his cousin Nancy's fault.

Aaron was used to staying in after school. Nancy regularly spilt paint from the art room on his homework and scribbled on his exercise books.

'You must take care of your work,' Miss Randall, their teacher, would say. 'Honestly, Aaron. You'll have to write it all out again.'

Nancy was the teacher's pet. Aaron couldn't think why. Nancy was always talking in class, but Miss Randall never heard her. Was Miss Randall deaf or something? She was quick enough to pounce on anyone else who made a noise.

Nancy's harassment had become more vicious recently. It started with a frog in his locker and today culminated with a stink bomb in his desk.

'Aaron!' Miss Randall glared at him. 'You should be ashamed of yourself.'

'But Miss Randal—it wasn't me! It was …' Aaron stopped. What was the use? She'd never believe him over Nancy.

'There's nobody to blame except yourself.' Miss Randall rapped her fingers on the desk. 'Go on like this, and you'll get yourself expelled.'

Would that be such a bad thing? Aaron pondered as he wrote 'I must not disrupt class and disrespect my teacher' for the two hundredth time.

The class had been evacuated, but he had to stay in that stinking room to write his lines.

Not that Aaron was in any hurry to get home. Uncle Ben had been trying to lure Aaron into his shed with the promise of a new bicycle.

'You need to learn about blokes and their sheds,' his uncle kept saying. 'And learn to ride a bike. That is if you want to be a real man.'

Yeah, right. Aaron had squinted through the shed window, and there wasn't a bike in sight. His mother had told him never to go inside Uncle Ben's shed alone. Aaron shuddered. What would his uncle do to him if he did go in? Why wasn't his mother still there to protect him?

Aaron asked Aunt Helena about his mother whenever he got the chance.

'Please, Aunty.' Aaron held onto Helena's arms as she kissed him goodnight. 'What's happened to my mummy? You know, don't you?'

'She's um …' Helena hesitated, then gave Aaron a reassuring smile. 'I'm sure she'll come back someday soon.'

Aaron sat up in bed. 'Really? Are you sure? When?'

'Soon. Just hold in there.'

His cousins screaming in the next bedroom drowned Aunt Helena's voice.

'Sorry. I have to go.' Aunt Helena quickly tucked Aaron in, then made for the door. 'Nancy and Lucy are at each other's throats again.'

Typical. If it wasn't his cousins fighting, it would be Uncle Ben demanding his supper. Just when Aaron thought he was getting somewhere with his aunt, one of them would cut off the conversation. Aaron covered his head with the pillow. Did Helena really believe his mother would be home soon? Or was she just trying to cheer him up and give him some hope?

At least Aunt Helena was kind to him and was fair. Nancy may have been Miss Randall's pet, but her mother didn't let her get away with anything. The cousins were painting on the kitchen table when Aaron had got home from school that afternoon.

Nancy had smirked at him. 'Shucks, Aaron. In detention *again*. Do you know what he did this time, Mummy? Stank the classroom out.'

Helena shot Nancy an icy stare. 'Don't tell tales.'

Nancy held up her picture and snorted at Aaron. 'Too late to join in now.'

As if you'd let me anyway, Aaron had thought.

Nancy promptly knocked over the jar with the paintbrushes in it and made a mess all over the floor.

Aunt Helena had wagged a finger at Nancy. 'Clean that up, Nancy.'

Nancy had pulled a face. 'Aaron did it. He pushed me.'

　　　　　David Whittet

'He did not. Now get out the mop and clean it up.'

Aaron rolled over in bed and allowed himself a chuckle. Nancy's face had been an absolute picture when she'd mopped the kitchen floor.

Ten o'clock and Aaron still couldn't sleep. Rain pelted against his bedroom window. He got out of bed and drew back the threadbare curtain. The miserable night outside reflected the misery he felt inside.

He was about to get back into bed when he spotted a hooded figure on the footpath. It was probably just another of Uncle Ben's mates, come for some free beer or to get away from the police. That happened all the time. But the hooded figure made for the front door. Ben's mates usually snuck in around the back.

Aaron pressed his nose against the window and strained his eyes to catch a glimpse of the mysterious stranger. It was a grey-haired woman—he could see that as she pulled back her hood and hammered on the door. His breath fogged up the glass, and he wiped it clean. The woman's face looked worn out—and not just from fighting the storm. Was it—could it be—his mother?

'Let me in!' the woman cried. 'Please let me in!'

Was that his mother's voice? Aaron ran from his bedroom and into the hallway. Uncle Ben's Rottweiler barked outside.

'Alright, I'm coming.' That was Aunt Helena's voice. She always answered the door in case it was the police coming to get Uncle Ben.

The Rottweiler barked even louder. Aaron clenched his fist. If that dog harmed his mother—Aaron swore he'd kill the beast.

'It's a wicked night out there,' the woman continued. 'Please let me take shelter.'

It didn't sound like his mother—but then it was five years since Aaron had heard her voice.

'Ben!' That was Aunt Helena's voice again. 'Come here! There's a strange woman at the door.'

Aaron retreated to his bedroom when Uncle Ben appeared.

'Filthy gypsy,' Uncle Ben bellowed. 'Get out of my house!'

'Wait a minute.' Aunt Helena's voice. 'I've seen you before. You were at my mother's funeral.'

Aaron peered around the bedroom door. He had to get a good look.

'Your mother was a dear friend,' the woman said. 'Your half-sister, too. And Aaron was born in my caravan.'

'You must be Kāterina,' Aunt Helena said. 'I've heard so much about you.'

'I don't care who she is,' Uncle Ben said. 'I want her out of the house. We don't have gypsies in here.'

Aaron slumped to the floor. He could almost feel his heart shrinking. That wasn't his mother—just some distant relative, an old woman who lived in a caravan in the middle of nowhere.

The old woman had woken his cousins up too. Aaron could hear their voices on the other side of their bedroom door.

'Is it the cops?' Lucy asked. 'Come for Dad?'

'No,' Nancy said. 'It's some old woman. Looks like she's come to take Aaron away.'

'Yay!' Tara squawked. 'Aaron's going away!'

'Shut up!' Nancy said. 'I'm trying to listen.'

Aaron pulled himself up off the floor. Had this woman really come to take him away? Then he'd be rid of Uncle Ben and his cousins once and for all. Maybe this old woman also knew what had happened to his mother.

Kāterina's voice boomed through the passage. 'I need to see Aaron. Please, take me to him.'

Aaron didn't wait. He shot into the hallway and flung his arms around Kāterina. 'Take me to my mother,' he said. 'I know you've come to take me to my mother.'

Kāterina stroked his hair. 'Aroha mai! Aroha mai! If only I could.'

Aaron thought his heart would shrivel up for the second time that night. He let go of Kāterina, and his hands fell limp at his side.

'But I promise I'll help you find her,' Kāterina continued. 'If you'll do something for me.'

Aaron stared at her. 'What?'

'I want you to read to me.'

Aaron scratched his head. Had this old woman really braved the storm just to ask him to read to her?

'My eyes are getting tired,' Kāterina said, 'and I can't read my beloved books

David Whittet

any longer.' She grasped Aaron's hand. 'Come to my caravan after school and read for me.'

'Your caravan?'

Kāterina reached out and held his other hand. 'You'll love the *Gypsy Rose*. It's been my home for many a year and it's an Aladdin's cave of beautiful things.'

An Aladdin's cave. That rang a bell. Aaron remembered his mother telling him about the treasure trove of trinkets and curiosities in Kāterina's caravan. His mother had often promised to take him to the *Gypsy Rose*. Aaron brushed a tear away with his hand as he thought back. She would have done so—if the Gang hadn't taken her away.

'I'll fetch you after school,' Kāterina said, 'and take you to the *Gypsy Rose*.'

'I don't know about that,' Aunt Helena said. 'Anyway, I thought your caravan was stuck in the ditch in the middle of a faraway forest.'

'Not any more,' Kāterina said. 'I've had the old girl fixed. We've travelled the length and breadth of the country together, my caravan and I.'

'Are you going away soon?' Aaron tugged on Kāterina's arm. 'Take me with you. Please!'

'Do us all a favour,' Uncle Ben said, 'and take the half-blood away for good.'

'Ben!' Aunt Helena pulled Aaron back. 'Not so fast. You're not taking him anywhere.'

'Don't worry,' Kāterina said. 'I'm not going anywhere. Not now. My caravan's parked at the domain. I'll bring him home safe. I promise.'

Aaron turned to face his aunt. 'Please.'

Aunt Helena hesitated for a moment. 'I suppose it'll be okay.'

Uncle Ben shook his head. 'Hell's teeth. A gypsy and a half-blood. Frigging unbelievable.'

'That's enough, Ben,' Aunt Helena said. 'Aaron's not a half-blood. He's our nephew.'

'He is a goddamn half-blood. And he's *your* nephew. Not mine.' Uncle Ben turned on Kāterina. 'Just get out of my house. Bloody gypsy.'

'I'm going.' Kāterina pulled the hood back up over her head. 'But I'll be at the school tomorrow for Aaron.'

What if Aunt Helena changed her mind and wouldn't let him go to the caravan? Aaron made a dash for the door as Kāterina left. 'Wait! I'm coming with you.'

Aunt Helena pulled him back. 'No, Aaron. We'll talk about this in the morning. Now off you go back to bed.'

Aaron flung himself on his bed. *We'll talk about this in the morning.* That sounded like his aunt *was* going to change her mind. If she did, he'd run away. It couldn't be hard to find a gypsy caravan in the domain.

Aaron overheard his cousins gossiping in the next bedroom.

'Maybe the gypsy will kidnap him,' Lucy said, 'and we'll be rid of him for good.'

'She's not a gypsy,' Tara said. 'She's a witch.'

'Even better,' Nancy said. 'Maybe she'll cast a spell and boil Aaron up for her supper.'

Aaron rolled over in bed. Witch or no witch, the extraordinary old woman had promised to help him find his mother, and all he had to do was read a few old books.

      David Whittet

CHAPTER TWELVE

Aaron eyed his aunt at breakfast the following morning. Was she in a good mood? Would she let him go?

'About last night … I want to go to the caravan … please, Aunty.' Aaron paused and took a deep breath. Had she any idea how much this meant to him? 'Kāterina promised she'd help me find my mother.'

Aunt Helena frowned. 'I don't want you to get your hopes up about your mother. Maybe it would be better if you didn't—'

Before Aunt Helena could finish, Nancy jumped in. 'Let him go to the caravan.'

What? Was Aaron hearing things? Nancy was on his side?

'Then,' Nancy continued, 'at least we'll have a couple of hours to ourselves after school.'

That didn't make sense either. Nancy was always getting him into detention, so he was always late home. Perhaps she really believed Kāterina would gobble him up for her dinner.

'I don't see why he should get a treat after school,' Lucy said. 'The caravan sounds cool. Can't we go as well?'

You're not invited. Aaron wished he had the nerve to say the words out loud.

'Don't be so selfish!' Aunt Helena glared at Lucy, then turned to Aaron. 'Alright, you can go. But I want you home before dark.'

'Bags we get an ice cream after school to make up for it,' Tara said.

Aaron gulped down the rest of his cereal and got ready for school before his aunt could change her mind.

Getting around his aunt was just the first step. Aaron couldn't afford to be in detention today. He glanced at Nancy across the classroom. What was she up to? Why had she stood up for him? Was she planning to get him kept in after school to embarrass him when Kāterina came to fetch him? That wouldn't happen. Aaron turned his head back to his school books and concentrated. *Up yours, Nancy. You're not getting me into trouble today.*

Aaron was first out of the classroom when the final bell rang. Both Kāterina and Aunt Helena were waiting for him at the school gate.

'Be good for Kāterina,' Aunt Helena said. 'And remember, I want you back before eight.'

'Don't worry,' Kāterina said. 'I'll look after him. We're going to have some fun, aren't we, Aaron? You'll love the *Gypsy Rose*.'

Aaron nodded and blinked back a tear. He hadn't had fun since his mother disappeared.

Kāterina led him through the township to the domain. They stopped at the roadside to cross the highway. A line of motor homes sped past them. Aaron had always envied tourists and their freedom to go where they pleased.

'Nearly there,' Kāterina said.

Aaron stared across the domain. Surely that faceless caravan parked on the verge couldn't be the *Gypsy Rose*. His mother had told him about a magical caravan full of treasures, not an ugly, mass-produced job.

'Is that ...' Aaron hesitated and pointed to the caravan. 'Is that the *Gypsy Rose?*'

'Good heavens, no,' Kāterina said. 'I wouldn't be seen dead in anything as hideous as that.' She raised her arm towards the far side of the domain. 'That's the *Gypsy Rose*.'

Aaron turned his head and ran across the domain. 'Wow! That's a real caravan!'

It was everything his mother had said and more. From the brightly painted crimson panels to the ornate wooden carvings, the *Gypsy Rose* could have come straight out of a fairy tale. And beside the caravan stood the most beautiful white horse Aaron had ever seen.

Kāterina caught up with him. 'Meet Cleo. My trusty steed.'

Aaron stroked the horse's head. 'She's beautiful! Can we ride her?'

'One day, perhaps.' Kāterina climbed the rickety wooden steps into the caravan and came out with a copper kettle. 'But first, I need a cup of tea, and then you must read to me.'

     David Whittet

Aaron continued to pet Cleo while Kāterina boiled the kettle on a rusty old gas stove outside the caravan.

'Come inside,' Kāterina said. 'Welcome to my whāre!'

The inside of the *Gypsy Rose* was even more breathtaking. Aaron stared at the mass of ornate trinkets, paintings and oddities that filled every inch of the caravan. Baubles hung from the ceiling. Leather-bound books stacked on shelves that were positively overflowing. He could scarcely believe how Kāterina had packed so much into such a small place.

Kāterina finished making the tea. 'Everything's better with a good brew.' She poured herself a cup. 'Don't worry. There's lemonade for you.'

Lemonade! The cousins always boasted about having fancy soft drinks when they went to a party. Another way they made Aaron feel left out. But today, he was one up on those miserable cousins and not just the lemonade. *I bet they've never seen anything like Kāterina's caravan.*

Kāterina handed him a glass and sat down beside him. 'I knew you'd love the *Gypsy Rose*.'

'It's so cool.' Aaron continued to gaze around the caravan. 'But where do you sleep?'

Kāterina pointed to a bunk underneath a pile of cushions and washing.

Aaron shook his head. 'You sleep there?'

Kāterina nodded. 'It's mighty cosy. Even on cold winter nights.'

Aaron pointed to a pair of model hands on a small circular table draped with a purple cloth. 'What are they?'

Kāterina reached over and picked up the model hands. 'I use them for my palmistry.'

Aaron screwed up his face. 'Palmistry? What's that?' He ran his fingers over the hands. 'What are all those lines for?'

'I examine people's hands and compare them to the markings on the model.'

'Why?'

'So I can look into the future and help people plan for the future.'

Aaron jumped up. 'Can you tell my future?'

'All in good time.' Kāterina put the model hands back on the table. 'You're just like your mother. She always wanted to see into the future.'

Aaron felt another tear well up and looked down at the floor. Had Kāterina foreseen his mother's disappearance? Did his mother know she was going to be taken away? Was that why she read him 'David and Goliath' from the book of Bible stories on that awful night?

Kāterina stood up and fetched her crystal ball from its plinth. 'Your mother loved looking into my crystal ball.'

Aaron looked up. The dazzling reflections in the crystal ball appeared more threatening than promising.

'Kāterina …' Aaron stumbled on his words. 'You said you'd help me find my mother.'

'I will. But remember, you've got to do something for me first.' Kāterina took a dusty old volume off her bookshelf. 'This is *Great Expectations*. One of my favourite books. I want you to read it to me.'

With its antique leather binding and gilt edges, the book looked formidable. Aaron ran his fingers over the gold embossed title on the maroon cover. *Great Expectations by Charles Dickens*. It was sure to be full of words that were impossible to pronounce.

Aaron hesitated before opening the book. 'You don't think …' He swallowed hard. 'You don't think my mother's dead do you?'

'No!' Kāterina put her arm around Aaron. 'Don't even think that. Your mother's alive.'

Aaron met Kāterina's eyes. 'Are you sure?'

'Certain. I've seen it in my crystal ball.' Kāterina gave his hand a squeeze. 'Now, let's make a start on *Great Expectations*.'

Aaron turned to the first page and began reading, running his finger along the page to help him keep his place. '*Chapter One. My father's family name being Pirrip, and my Christian name Philip, my infant tongue could make of both names nothing more explicit than Pip.*' Aaron glanced up at Kāterina then back to the page. Why had she chosen a book with such tongue-twisting words? '*So, I called myself Pip, and came to be called Pip.*'

The next bit was creepy. In the story, Pip had never seen his parents, and there were no photographs back in the time when the book was set. So the young Pip imagined what his parents looked like by studying their tombstone. Aaron scratched his head and read on. '*The shape of the letters on my father's gravestone*

 David Whittet

gave me an odd idea that he was a square, stout, dark man with curly black hair. From the character turn of the inscription, "Also Georgiana Wife of the Above", I drew a childish conclusion that my mother was freckled and sickly.'

How weird was that? Aaron could sympathise with Pip losing his parents. But at least Pip knew where his mother was. Aaron glanced up at Kāterina. When would this curious old lady tell him about his mother?

The following paragraph was even more difficult to read. Long, wordy descriptions of the graveyard. Aaron stumbled over the words.

'You can skip that bit,' Kāterina said. 'Go to the top of page three. That's where it gets exciting.'

And it did. Aaron found the place and cleared his throat. '*"Hold your noise!" cried a terrible voice as a man started up from among the graves at the side of the church porch. "Keep still, you little devil, or I'll cut your throat!"'*

Wow! Aaron almost dropped the book as he pictured the scene. Impossible words or not, he had to find out what happened next. Would this awful man really kill Pip? Aaron raced through the chapter.

'*"Now look here," the man said, "the question being whether you're to be let to live. You know what a file is?"*

'*"Yes, sir."*

'*"And you know what wittles is?"*

'*"Yes, sir."'*

Aaron broke off and turned to Kāterina. 'What are wittles?'

'Food,' Kāterina said. 'The man's an escaped convict and he's starving. He needs the file to get the irons off his legs.'

Aaron's imagination ran wild as he finished the chapter. 'Will that horrid man really take Pip's heart and liver out?' he asked Kāterina with a shiver. 'Then roast and eat them? Gross!'

'You'll find out next time.' Kāterina took the book off Aaron. 'That's enough for today. I'll get you another glass of lemonade. Your mouth must be dry after all that reading.'

Aaron took another look around the caravan while Kāterina fetched the lemonade. Amongst the collection of oddities on the dresser, some battered old binoculars caught his eye. He picked them up for a closer look. Would they still work with all those dents?

Kāterina returned with the lemonade and a plate of biscuits. 'Your mother loved those binoculars, too. I told her they belonged to a great Māori warrior called Kamaka, and he used them to spy on the enemy in the great Māori Land Wars.'

With the metal casing peeling off, the binoculars certainly looked like they'd been in a war.

'They must be precious,' Aaron said.

'Not really.' Kāterina sighed and put the refreshments down on the table. 'I don't think they had binoculars back in the Land Wars. Your mother was heartbroken when I admitted they didn't belong to a great warrior.'

'They're still cool.' Aaron put the glasses up to his eyes. 'Wow! The bubbles in my lemonade look massive through the binoculars.'

'I want you to have the binoculars,' Kāterina said.

'You mean I can keep them? Seriously?'

'Ka pai, Aaron. You've earned them.' Kāterina took a sip of tea. 'You read well today and made me happy.'

'Thank you.' Aaron put down the binoculars and hugged Kāterina. 'I'll treasure them, always.'

And he would. Owning something that had been dear to his mother meant so much.

'I'm sure you will,' Kāterina said. 'Now, drink up your lemonade. It's time I got you back to your aunt.'

'Can't I stay a bit longer?' Aaron felt at home with Kāterina and the magical world of her gypsy caravan. Did he really have to go back to his miserable cousins? 'I could always read you another chapter.'

'You can come again after school tomorrow.' Kāterina finished her cup of tea and cleared up. 'If your aunt will let you.'

Aaron made his glass of lemonade last for as long as possible.

'Come on.' Kāterina fetched his jacket and helped him into it. 'It'll be dark soon.'

Aaron sighed and followed Kāterina out of the caravan. He didn't take much notice of a bunch of kids at the other end of the domain. At least not at first. But as they got closer, it was clear the kids had their eyes on him. They looked mean. Real mean.

 David Whittet

Aaron clutched the binoculars with one hand and held on to Kāterina with the other.

'What is it?' Kāterina said. 'They're just kids.'

Before Aaron could answer, the mob was on top of them. The boys dragged him away from Kāterina and held him down, while the ringleader punched him in the stomach.

'Take that!' The ringleader landed him another punch. 'Half-blood!'

Aaron fell to the ground and held his stomach. The boys' taunts continued. Why did they call him a half-blood? What the hell did these boys have against him?

'Stop that at once,' Kāterina shouted. 'I mean it! Get out of here!'

The ringleader hauled Aaron up off the ground and punched his face. 'You even fight like a girl. Nancy said you were a wimp and you need an old woman to protect you.'

Nancy! Had she set him up? Got some of her mates to beat him up? No wonder she hadn't wanted to get him in detention that day.

Kāterina bent down and picked the binoculars up off the ground. 'Get off him! I'm warning you. Bugger off.'

'Shut it, old bag.' The ringleader snatched the binoculars from her hand. 'You'll stay out of this if you know what's good for you.'

'Give that back,' Kāterina demanded. 'You don't frighten me, Corey!'

Corey. Aaron had heard that name before. Weren't they related somehow? So why did this boy have it in for him? It was all too much. Aaron's head swooned, and he collapsed back onto the ground.

'Go!' Kāterina's voice again. 'Pōkokohua!'

Aaron looked up. Kāterina's eyes were on fire as she glared at the boys.

'She's a witch!' one of the boys screamed. 'I'm out of here!'

Aaron could scarcely believe what he saw. The boys backed off. Corey dropped the binoculars as Kāterina continued to stare at him. Did she really have some magical powers?

'You'll pay for this, half-blood.' Corey spat on Aaron and then made off with the rest of the gang. 'I haven't finished with you.'

Kāterina shook her fist in the air. 'Don't you dare come near him again. Or you'll regret it.'

The boys ran away even faster. Unbelievable—and proof positive that Kāterina had magical powers.

Aaron sank back into a pool of blood. Kāterina wouldn't always be there to protect him and Corey would be back. Aaron was sure of that.

David Whittet

CHAPTER THIRTEEN

The next thing Aaron knew, he was back in the *Gypsy Rose* with Kāterina sponging his face. He must have passed out in the domain.

'We can't have you going back to your aunt's house covered in blood,' Kāterina said. 'She'll never let you come and visit me again if she sees you like this.'

Aaron sat upright, overtaken by a sudden and overwhelming sensation of dread. 'I can't come back. Please don't make me.'

Kāterina frowned. 'Why not? Don't you want to know what happens to Pip in *Great Expectations*?'

'Yes, but …' Aaron raised his head and met Kāterina's eyes. 'You heard what Corey said. 'He'll be back, and he'll kill me next time. I know he will.'

'Not if I'm there to protect you.'

'But you're just—'

'An old woman?' Kāterina grinned knowingly. 'Didn't you see how quickly those boys disappeared when I gave them a hard stare?'

'What was it you shouted at them?' Aaron asked. 'Poko something.'

'Pōkokohua. It's a Māori swear word.'

'What does it mean?'

'Literally, it just means a boiled head.' Kāterina got up to fetch a bottle off a shelf. 'To Māori, the head is tapu. That's why it's offensive.' She opened the bottle and daubed some liquid on a cloth. 'And it worked, didn't it? They soon buggered off.'

Aaron nodded. It was true—Kāterina had scared them off with her evil eye. Perhaps he would be safe with her.

Kāterina wiped the abrasions on Aaron's face with the cloth. 'This may sting.'

It did. It hurt as much as Corey's punch. 'Ow! Stop. Please. Ow! What is that?'

'Disinfectant,' Kāterina said. 'I have to get these wounds clean. Otherwise, they'll get infected, and we don't want that. You must be brave.'

Aaron squirmed as Kāterina continued to tend his wounds. His mother had told him to be brave on that awful night before they took her away. Her voice still echoed in his head: *You must be brave like David in the story. Promise me you'll be strong, and you won't be afraid.*

'I wasn't very brave today,' Aaron said. 'I let my mother down.'

'Nonsense!' Kāterina said. 'Corey and his mates were the cowards. Half a dozen of them against one of you.'

Maybe Corey was a coward. But the thought of disappointing his mother hurt far more than the pain of Corey's punches or the sting of Kāterina's disinfectant.

'Ka pai,' Kāterina said when she finished cleaning his face. 'I'm going to make you a cup of hot cocoa, then we really must get you back to your aunty.'

Aaron breathed a sigh of relief when Kāterina put the bottle of disinfectant back on the shelf and went outside to boil the kettle on the stove. He gazed into the rusty old mirror on Kāterina's dresser. His heart missed a beat when he saw his bruised face. What would his aunt say? Maybe it was just the old mirror, but his entire face looked distorted.

Kāterina returned with a mug of cocoa. 'Here you are,' she said. 'Get this down you and you'll feel better.'

Aaron took a sip. 'Who is Corey? Am I really related to him?'

Kāterina sat down on her bench. 'He's your second cousin.'

Aaron took another sip of cocoa. 'What does that mean?'

'Your mother, Alicia, and Mickey, Corey's father, were first cousins. Their fathers, Reggie and Ronnie, were brothers.'

'Reggie and Ronnie were sworn enemies, weren't they?' Aaron asked. 'At least, that's what Aunt Helena said.'

Kāterina sighed. 'They both wanted to lead the Gang. Their wretched fight ruined countless lives.'

They sure ruined my mother's life. And mine. Aaron eyed Kāterina. 'Is that why Corey hates me? Because of a Gang feud?'

'Mickey was a shameless playboy before he settled down with your mother, and he had a string of girlfriends.' Kāterina shook her head. 'Then the inevitable happened. He got one of his girls pregnant.'

Aaron had worked that much out from snippets of conversation he'd

     David Whittet

overheard at his aunt's house. But that still didn't explain why Corey hated him with such a vengeance.

'Alicia forgave Mickey,' Kāterina continued, settling herself on the bench, 'and as an infant, Corey came to live with them. Then when she found out she was pregnant with you, they planned to bring you two up together, like brothers.'

Aaron stared back at her. 'So, what went wrong?'

'They tried to do the right thing. Mickey started doing mercy runs, giving back the protection money the Gang had stolen. When the Gang found out— well, you can imagine what happened.'

Aaron didn't need to use his imagination. 'I was there when they came for my mother. But what happened to Mickey and Corey?'

'Corey went back to live with his mother. Mickey was lucky to get away with his life. Last I heard, he'd turned to the bottle and gone to live with his father in Hokitika.'

Aaron scratched the back of his neck. The only bit of his head that didn't hurt. 'So Corey's fight is with the Gang, not me.'

Kāterina shrugged. 'I don't understand it either. I guess he thinks your mother put Mickey up to doing the mercy runs, and it was her fault that his father got thrown out of the Gang. But it's not fair of him to blame you.'

Aaron's wounds still stung like hell. Damn right, it wasn't fair.

'I feel sorry for Corey's mother,' Kāterina continued. 'Poor Tammy. Corey was nothing but trouble after his father went away. No wonder she had to send him to a special school.'

'What's a special school?' Aaron asked. 'I'm guessing Corey didn't like it.'

'They used to call them borstals. Not that anything's changed. They're just a breeding ground for criminals, if you ask me. Corey didn't have a chance. His school, Moreton Hall, is the worst of the lot. Full of the most hardened offenders in the country.' Kāterina stood up and glanced out of the window. 'It's dark outside. We need to get going. I've a good mind to call the principal of Moreton Hall when we get back to your aunt's house. They shouldn't let him out of the school if he's going to terrorise you like that.'

Aaron froze. 'Don't do that. It'll just make him madder than ever.'

'Well, we'll see.' Kāterina wrapped Aaron in a shawl. 'There's a nip in the air, and we can't have you catching a chill.' She took his hand and led him out of the caravan. 'Come on.'

Aaron took a last look around the *Gypsy Rose*. 'Was I really born here in the caravan? I heard you talking to Aunt Helena.'

'You were,' Kāterina said, 'and I was your impromptu midwife.'

Aaron suddenly tugged on Kāterina's arm. 'The binoculars! What happened to the binoculars? Did Corey get away with them?'

Kāterina pulled the binoculars out of her pocket. 'I picked them up when Corey dropped them.' She handed them to Aaron. 'Take care of them, mind.'

Aaron clutched the binoculars against his chest. 'I will.'

'Your mother almost lost them too, and it brought her a heap of grief.' Kāterina hesitated before continuing. 'That was Mickey's fault. Sometimes I think Corey has inherited all of Mickey's vices and none of his virtues.'

Kāterina continued to chatter all the way back to Aunt Helena's house, but Aaron had something else on his mind. He didn't want Nancy to see his battered face and give her the satisfaction of knowing her treachery had worked. Just what had she told Corey? Would he be safe in the house if Corey knew where he lived?

Aaron's heart beat faster with each footstep. Perhaps Nancy would be in bed, and he wouldn't have to face her until the morning. No such luck. Aaron squinted through the kitchen window when Kāterina knocked on the front door. The family were just finishing their dinner. He was sure he saw Nancy wink at her father.

Aunt Helena came to the door and flung her arms around him. 'Aaron, my darling. What's happened to you? Are you alright?' She turned to Kāterina. 'Who did this to him?'

Kāterina looked down at her feet. 'Corey and a bunch of his mates.'

Aunt Helena glared at Kāterina. 'And you stood by and let it happen?'

'No,' Aaron said. 'Kāterina saved me. I don't know how she did it, but they all ran away when she stared at them.'

'We'll talk about this later.' Aunt Helena gave Kāterina another dubious look then turned to Aaron. 'You're shivering. Let's get you inside and warmed up.'

 David Whittet

Aaron pulled the shawl over his face as Aunt Helena led him into the kitchen.

Lucy giggled. 'Look! Aaron's dressed like a woman!'

'What have you done to your face?' Nancy said with a smirk. 'Bang your head on the caravan, did you?'

As if you didn't know. Aaron drew himself up. 'What's it to you?'

'We were worried about you,' Nancy said, barely managing to keep a straight face. 'Weren't we?'

Like hell you were. Aaron watched his cousins put their heads together in a huddle. Were they all in on it?

'Nancy,' Aunt Helena said. 'Do you know something about this?'

Nancy shrugged.

Aunt Helena continued to eye Nancy. 'Have you been talking to Corey?'

'What if she has?' Uncle Ben said. 'Good on Corey. Bash the half-blood. I've a good mind to give him another one.'

Uncle Ben clenched his fist and waved it in Aaron's direction.

'Don't you dare!' Aunt Helena shot across the kitchen to confront Ben. 'You lay a finger on Aaron and I swear I'll kill you.' She turned to the cousins. 'And you three can go to bed. I'm going to make Aaron some supper.'

Aaron smiled to himself. Aunt Helena was magnificent when she was angry. But why did she stay with Uncle Ben when she was so lovely and he was horrid? Aaron had heard children at school talking about their parents being divorced. Why didn't Aunt Helena divorce Uncle Ben? She'd be much happier without him. Maybe the triplets would be kinder, too, if their father wasn't there encouraging them to be cruel.

Aunt Helena brought him his supper. 'I've made you some soup,' she said. 'It'll be easier for you to eat with your sore mouth.'

'Thank you, Aunty.' Aaron picked up the soup spoon. Dare he say anything to her about divorcing Ben? He took a mouthful of soup while he thought about it. Maybe he wouldn't get another chance. He seldom had time alone with her.

'Aunty …' Aaron cleared his throat and started again. 'I was wondering … I mean … have you ever thought of divorcing Uncle Ben?'

Aunt Helena swung round from the kitchen sink where she was washing the soup pan and smiled. 'Every day. But it's not that easy. Ben's high up in the Gang and you don't divorce the Gang.' She sat down at the table next to Aaron. 'I know he's a miserable sod now, but I loved him once. He was part of a biking gang. We used to take off together on his Harley Davidson with his biking mates. I lived for the thrill of the open road. Wind in my hair. We would drive for days along winding highways, soaring through hills and valleys, feeling like nothing could slow us down. I've never felt so alive.' Aunt Helena broke off and sighed wistfully. 'But that was all so long ago.'

Aaron couldn't imagine Uncle Ben ever being the least bit lovable. But he had heard his mother say that once you married into the Gang, there was no way out.

He overheard his aunt talking to Kāterina after he'd gone to bed.

'You expect me to let him go with you again?' That was his aunt's voice. 'No way.'

'Please, Helena.' Kāterina's voice. 'Aaron needs time away from his cousins. One-to-one time with an adult. It's what his mother would have wanted.'

Aaron *did* need to get away from his cousins. Kāterina was right about that. But his aunt was also right when she went on about the risk of Corey attacking again. Perhaps with a bigger bunch of thugs.

Aaron rolled over in bed. He wasn't sure if he wanted to go back to the *Gypsy Rose* or not. The caravan was magical, and Kāterina had promised to help him find his mother. But would she still be able to scare off Corey if he came back with reinforcements?

'Okay.' Aunt Helena's voice again. 'But I'm coming with you when you walk Aaron to and from the caravan, and I'm bringing Ben with me.'

'What?' Aaron could picture the expression on Kāterina's face when she replied. 'If Corey attacks us again, Ben will join in.'

'No, he won't,' Aunt Helena said. 'Not if he knows what's good for him. Like it or not, the old bastard will protect us.'

Yes, Aunt Helena *was* magnificent when she was all fired up.

Would Uncle Ben really escort them to the *Gypsy Rose?* He was mighty quiet over breakfast the following morning. Nor did he stick up for Nancy when Aunt

     David Whittet

Helena gave her a rollicking for ganging up with Corey. Aaron did his best to hide the gleeful smile he felt inside. Nancy would have extra chores to do when she got home from school.

'As for you, Ben,' Aunt Helena said, 'don't forget what I told you. You'll be at the school gate at four, or else.'

Uncle Ben just sat there with his head ducked. Nancy didn't say anything, either. That was a first. She even kept her head down at school. Unbelievable.

Aaron couldn't concentrate on his lessons. As the final bell got closer, he tried to work out if he was more excited than anxious. Would Corey be back? Would his uncle defend him? Aaron thought his head would explode as he kept going over it in his mind.

Four o'clock at last, and sure enough, Aunt Helena and Kāterina were waiting for him. And beside them, Ben on his motorbike in his full gang regalia. Was he there to protect Aaron or frighten him?

Aaron held on to Aunt Helena with one hand and Kāterina with the other as they walked through the township and onto the domain. Uncle Ben coasted behind them on his motorbike, revving his engine and honking his horn when he passed a mate.

Cleo was happily grazing beside the *Gypsy Rose* as they approached. She reared and backed into the caravan when Uncle Ben got close.

'Do you have to make that much noise?' Kāterina shouted at Uncle Ben. 'You're frightening my horse.'

Ben gave his horn an extra loud blast. 'I thought you wanted us to frighten everyone off.'

Typical Uncle Ben. Aaron gave him a dirty look then helped Kāterina to comfort Cleo.

'There, there, my steed,' Kāterina said, stroking Cleo's mane. 'That's just an ignorant man making all that noise.'

Aaron patted Cleo's head. 'Kāterina,' he said, 'I've had an idea. Next time we could ride to the caravan on Cleo.'

'Maybe,' Kāterina said. 'If your aunt will let us.'

Aaron looked across the domain. Ben had rounded up some of his mates, and they started playing football. 'Cleo would be more use than Uncle Ben. If Corey shows up, I bet Cleo can gallop faster than Corey can run.'

Kāterina fed Cleo some hay. 'We'll talk to your aunt later. Now, I want to hear the next chapter of *Great Expectations*.'

Aaron sat on the edge of the stool as he read how Pip took food to the escaped convict. He knew exactly how Pip felt, always on the lookout and constantly afraid of getting caught. Would Corey and his mates turn up? And if they did, would Uncle Ben protect them? Aaron glanced out of the tiny caravan window. He blinked and took another look. Maybe it was just the stained glass of the window. Or was he imagining it? No. This was no illusion. Corey was playing football with Uncle Ben and his mates.

'Whatever's the matter?' Kāterina said. 'You look like you've seen a ghost.'

If only it was a ghost. Aaron began to shake. 'It's Corey. He's out there, playing with Uncle Ben.'

Kāterina took the book out of his hands before he dropped it. 'I've had enough of this,' she said, marching out of the caravan. 'It's got to stop. Right now.'

Aaron stayed inside, sat on the floor with his head down. He heard Kāterina shouting.

'Get out of here, Corey. Haere atu i konei! Pirau i roto i te reinga! Kanga koe! Kanga koe!'

'You don't scare me,' Corey said. 'I'm not frightened of your Māori curses.'

'You should be,' Kāterina said.

A moment's silence, then Corey's voice: 'You're a witch! A witch! Don't come near me!'

What had Kāterina done to turn Corey into a gibbering wreck? Was it the fire in her eyes again? Or had she put a gypsy spell on him? Aaron peeked through the window. Corey was across at the other side of the domain. He couldn't have run any faster if a bull was chasing him.

Kāterina strode back inside the *Gypsy Rose* and rubbed her hands together. 'He won't give you any more trouble, and we won't need your Uncle Ben to escort us any more.' She handed the book back to Aaron. 'Now, let's get on with *Great Expectations*.'

Aaron stumbled through the next chapter. He kept glancing up at Kāterina in wonder and losing his place. This seemingly frail old lady had seen Corey off. For that, Aaron was eternally grateful.

     David Whittet

Over the next few weeks, *Great Expectations* took on a whole new significance. Aaron enjoyed it much more than he thought he would. After a month of reading to Kāterina, he began to get his tongue around those long and old-fashioned words. He looked forward to their regular sessions. Most days, they walked to the caravan. But sometimes, as a treat, Kāterina would bring Cleo, and they would ride to the *Gypsy Rose* in style.

As Pip's story unfolded in the book, Aaron saw more of his own life reflected in the story. Pip was sent for by a rich but eccentric hermit called Miss Havisham to 'play' in her run-down old house, full of dust and decay. While the *Gypsy Rose* seemed much more inviting than Miss Havisham's mausoleum, like Pip, Aaron made regular visits to entertain a weird old woman.

Miss Havisham had an adopted daughter called Estella, whom she brought up to wreak revenge on the male sex. Estella treated Pip with contempt. She despised him for being a common labouring boy. At least Kāterina didn't have a daughter. Or did she?

'Ka pai, Aaron,' Kāterina said one day when he'd finished reading. 'We're almost halfway through *Great Expectations*, and you've improved so much since the first time you read to me.'

'Thank you,' Aaron said. 'I just don't know why Dickens has to use such difficult words.'

'You must remember, *Great Expectations* is almost a hundred and fifty years old. People spoke differently back then.' Kāterina got up to make the cocoa, then sat next to Aaron. 'But next week, we'll take a break from reading.'

What? Aaron couldn't afford a break. Kāterina had promised to help him find his mother when he finished reading *Great Expectations*. They *had* to complete the book.

He raised his eyes to meet Kāterina's. 'Why? It's just getting interesting.'

Kāterina grinned, her eyes twinkling. 'Miriama, my foster daughter, is coming home from boarding school in Switzerland at the weekend.'

Aaron stared at her. 'I didn't know you had children.'

'I don't have any children of my own,' Kāterina replied. 'Miriama is my foster daughter.'

Aaron scratched his head. 'What does that mean?'

'I took Miriama in when she had nobody else to look after her.' Kāterina paused for a moment to reflect. 'Like your aunt Helena took you in when you lost your mother.'

Aaron held his breath. So he had something in common with this girl. Perhaps Miriama would understand how he felt if she'd been abandoned by her parents. They could be best friends. Maybe not. Aaron's confidence rapidly disappeared when he remembered what he had learnt about Switzerland at school. His teacher had said it was one of the richest countries in the world. Aaron lowered his head. Would Miriama be stuck-up like the kids from the nearby private school?

'I'm so proud of Miriama.' Kāterina's eyes shone even brighter as she spoke. 'She's so clever. Top grades in all her exams.'

Aaron shuffled uncomfortably. That meant he would never be good enough for Miriama.

Kāterina leant forward. 'I want you to play with her.'

'Play?' Aaron almost fell off the bench. This was too weird for words. 'You mean like Pip and Estella in *Great Expectations*?'

'Not exactly.' Kāterina pursed her lips with a rather curious expression. 'I just want you to get to know each other.' Her face brightened, and she raised an eyebrow. 'But who knows? Maybe you'll steal her heart.'

Aaron couldn't sleep that night. Would Miriama be hostile like Estella in *Great Expectations*? Would she look down on him as a gangland boy? That had to be just as bad as 'a common labouring boy' in Dickens' book.

     David Whittet

CHAPTER FOURTEEN

Aaron paused on the steps outside the *Gypsy Rose*. A glance back across the domain and no sign of Corey or his mates. It was the first time he'd walked to the caravan alone. He tried to persuade himself he wasn't scared—but his heart still raced. Today he would meet Miriama.

Would she really look down on him? Aunt Helena had ironed his best shirt for the occasion and told him to relax and be himself. That wouldn't be easy. He wasn't at some posh boarding school in Switzerland like Miriama. Hers was the best school in the world if Kāterina was to be believed. Aaron shrugged. Maybe he would have gone to a classy school if the Gang hadn't killed his father. Besides, if he had made it to a decent school, he would have got top grades in all his exams, too.

Aaron wondered how Kāterina could afford to send Miriama to an expensive school. Kāterina never looked like she had any money. Then Aaron remembered what Aunt Helena had said when he first went to the caravan. Something about Kāterina having once been a Māori rights activist and receiving compensation from a land settlement. Aaron wasn't sure what that meant, but Aunt Helena made it clear that Kāterina lived as a hermit in a run-down caravan through choice.

Aaron held up his head. He wasn't just a gang boy—so why was he putting himself down? *I'm going to be—what's that word? An entrepreneur. Like my father.* Aaron took a deep breath and knocked on the door of the *Gypsy Rose*.

A stunning Māori girl, who must have been a year or two older than him, opened the door. Her dark flowing hair hung about her shoulders, and her entire face glowed with life. And those mesmerising eyes! To Aaron, they gleamed azure, far brighter than any of the trinkets that adorned the *Gypsy Rose*. Her elegant black dress, embroidered with a traditional Māori motif that sparkled in the sunlight, swirled around as she took him inside.

Kāterina nudged Aaron, a wry smile on her lips. 'I told you she was beautiful.'

Aaron reluctantly looked away from Miriama and towards Kāterina. 'She's the prettiest girl I've ever seen.'

Kāterina beckoned him to come closer and whispered in his ear. 'Remember what I told you? You can steal her heart.'

Miriama pulled a face. 'I heard that. I'm not your plaything, you know.'

Kāterina lowered her head. 'I didn't mean that.'

Miriama snorted. 'If I ever lose my heart to anyone, it'll be to someone with a future.'

I've got a future! Aaron blinked back a tear. If only he dared say that out loud.

Kāterina answered for him. 'Aaron's determined to make a success of his life. One day, you'll be proud to say you know him.'

Miriama shrugged. 'Whatever. I thought you said he was a gang boy.'

'His mother was born into the Gang,' Kāterina said. 'But Aaron can't help that'—she leant forward and eyed Miriama—'any more than you can help your parentage.'

Miriama scowled. 'Don't start that again.'

Aaron still couldn't take his eyes off Miriama. He hadn't understood why Pip was so captivated by Estella—until now. Miriama was just as entrancing, whatever she said about him.

'Perhaps you'll like Aaron better when you get to know him.' Kāterina stood up and walked to the door. 'I'm going to leave you two together while I plant my vegetable garden.'

Miriama raised her eyebrows. 'What? You're going to dig up the domain?'

'No, silly,' Kāterina said. 'I've got an allotment in the paddock.' She put a hand on Miriama's shoulder as she left. 'Be kind to him.'

What could he do or say that would impress Miriama? Aaron scanned the caravan. The model hands. Of course. Kāterina had explained how the intricate markings on the replica foretold the future through a pattern of sacred lines. That had to win Miriama over.

'I can tell you your fortune,' Aaron said, his hand shaking as he picked up Kāterina's giant magnifying glass. 'I know all about the circles of life.'

'Do you indeed?' Miriama said. 'My foster mother's rammed that rubbish down my throat since I was a little girl.'

'It's not rubbish,' Aaron said. 'What was the word Kāterina used? Palmistry. That's right. And she said it was … er … scientific.'

'As if you know what that means.'

'I do!' Aaron caught her eye. 'Kāterina told me how this Māori healer—'

'You're so gullible,' Miriama said. 'You can't believe everything my foster mother tells you.'

'It true!' Aaron shot back. 'Kāterina got me to read about it in the newspaper.'

'Alright!' Miriama held out her hands. 'Give it a go.'

Aaron examined her hands with the magnifying glass. 'For a girl, the right hand represents what you have when you are born, and your left hand shows what you'll get during your life.' He glanced up at Miriama's face and then back to the magnifying glass. 'Your life line is long. That's good.' He ran a finger over Miriama's palm. 'This is your heart line—'

Miriama shook her head. 'What does it mean?'

Aaron held Miriama's hand alongside the palmistry replica and compared their markings. What had Kāterina told him about the heart line? It was something to do with love and romance.

'Your heart line starts here.' Aaron pointed to her index finger. 'And it goes right across your hand.'

Miriama rolled her eyes. 'So?'

'It means …' Aaron paused. 'It means one day you will meet a handsome prince and get married.'

How could he have said something so soppy? Aaron bit his tongue the moment the words left his mouth and braced himself for the inevitable tongue-lashing.

Miriama didn't answer straight away. She just looked down at him with those penetrating eyes.

'Maybe I will,' she said. 'I'm spoilt for choice at school in Switzerland. The boys I hang out with are the sons of counts, presidents and important people.' She stood up and towered over Aaron. 'One thing I can tell you for certain. If I do get married, it won't be to a lowlife like you.'

I'm not a lowlife. Aaron opened his mouth, but nothing came out. He wanted to tell her that he was going to be a success. Carry on his father's work and change the world. Instead, he lowered his head. He couldn't let Miriama see him cry.

'I'm going to help Mum,' Miriama said.

'No. Wait.' Aaron scrambled to his feet, and the model hand crashed onto the floor.

'You clumsy boy!' Miriama picked the hand up off the floor. 'Mum will kill you for this!'

'Is it broken?'

Too late. Miriama was out the door and took the model hand with her. Had he just destroyed one of Kāterina's most prized possessions? Aaron slumped back onto the bench. Would she ever forgive him?

Voices outside. 'I'm not surprised he dropped it with you hounding him.' That was Kāterina. And she wasn't mad with him. 'Still, there's no harm done. At least, nothing a bit of glue won't fix.'

Aaron still wished he could disappear when Kāterina came back into the caravan with the damaged model in her hand.

'I'm sorry, Kāterina,' he said. 'I didn't mean to—'

'Of course you didn't. It was an accident.' Kāterina put the model hand down on the table and smiled at Aaron. 'Your mother knocked it over once. Broke off the thumb. We fixed it then and we'll fix it again now.'

Miriama glared at Aaron. 'You wouldn't have to if he hadn't been so careless.'

'We'll have no more of that,' Kāterina said.

'It won't happen again,' Aaron said. 'I'll take care.'

'I know you will.' Kāterina reached for the kettle. 'Now, I'm going to make some cocoa. Then it's time for you to go home.' She turned to Miriama. 'And we're going to walk back with Aaron.'

Miriama followed Kāterina to the outside stove. 'Must we?'

'Yes.'

Aaron got up to join them but stopped on the steps when Kāterina began cursing in Māori.

'He kotiro kino koe! Kaua e tino kino!'

Aaron didn't know what the Māori words meant, but he could guess. He'd never seen Kāterina so angry before as she laid into Miriama.

'You're no better than him. Your birth parents weren't exactly saints.'

Miriama waved her hands defiantly. 'But I'm going to be a lady. He'll never be a gentleman.'

Aaron didn't want to hear more. He ran back inside the caravan and crouched on the bench.

❧

Kāterina broke the silence as they drank their cocoa. 'Aaron's been reading to me. We've made a start on *Great Expectations*.'

'Bully for you,' Miriama muttered through clenched teeth.

'Don't be like that.' Kāterina reached for another book off her shelf. 'This is another of my favourites. *Little Women* by Louisa May Alcott.' She handed the book to Miriama. 'I'd like you to read this to me.'

Miriama turned up her nose. '*Little Women*. Why don't you just buy the audiobook?'

'I don't think so,' Kāterina said. 'Can you imagine me with one of those new-fangled gadgets? What is it they call them?'

'A Walkman,' Miriama said. 'You should get one.'

Kāterina threw her head back. 'With headphones, I'd be like a fish out of water.'

Aaron smiled to himself. He could just picture Kāterina wired up for sound.

'You could always get an iPod,' Miriama said. 'They have cool white earphones. You can buy one for me, for that matter.'

Kāterina took *Little Women* back from Miriama. 'I want *you* to read it to me. Is that too much to ask?'

Miriama pulled another of her faces. 'I have to read all the time at school. This is my holiday.'

Kāterina sighed and put the book back on the shelf. 'Fetch your coats, both of you. Time to take Aaron home.'

Aaron glanced at Miriama's sulky face as they walked home in silence. Why did she delight in putting him down? Was she really a cut above him? Aaron looked down at his muddy feet and shabby shoes. He shuddered when they reached Aunt Helena's house with its broken-down motorbikes piled across the front garden and paint peeling off the weatherboards. That would doubly convince Miriama of his gang background.

Aaron's mental turmoil continued in bed that night. So Miriama was going to be a lady. Then he was going to be a gentleman. And he would steal her heart—whatever the cost.

     David Whittet

CHAPTER FIFTEEN

A month passed and Aaron was still under Miriama's spell. Why had he let her entrance him? The more she belittled him, the more he worshipped her.

His life sucked. It was so unfair—he'd never be Miriama's equal if he continued at his miserable run-down rural school. If only *he* could go to a flash school in Switzerland. He would have done if the Gang hadn't killed his father. Aaron made up his mind. He needed to get a scholarship and go to college. Then he could look Miriama in the eye.

Perhaps Aunt Helena could help. He rehearsed what he wanted to say a thousand times in his head. Pip had come straight out with it in *Great Expectations* and said, *I want to be a gentleman.* Would Aunt Helena buy that? Probably not. Pip had then explained why he wanted to be a gentleman, and his friend Biddy told him that was absurd. Aaron was afraid Aunt Helena would give him a similar answer.

After putting it off for days, Aaron told himself he had to talk to his aunt that weekend. He followed her around all Saturday morning, desperate to catch her alone. Why did his cousins always get in the way? First, it was Nancy. She couldn't find her kit for her netball match that afternoon.

'How many times have I told you to look after it?' Aunt Helena said. 'I expect you've left it at school.'

Nancy pulled a face. 'I haven't. I brought it home yesterday.'

Aunt Helena shook her head. 'Then go back to your room and look.'

'Oh, alright.' Nancy stamped her foot and headed for the door. 'But you're much better at finding things than me.'

Next, it was Lucy's turn. She hadn't lost her netball kit but wanted it ironed.

'Can't you do it yourself?' Aunt Helena said. 'I'm busy.'

'S'pose,' Lucy groaned. 'But I'll probably end up burning it.'

'Not if you're careful,' Aunt Helena said.

Lucy scowled and went to fetch the iron. Tara caught her arm.

'Any chance you could do mine while you're at it?' Tara asked.

Lucy slammed the kitchen door. 'Bugger off.'

At last, Aunt Helena was alone in the kitchen. Aaron hesitated. Perhaps now wasn't the right moment. His aunt was busy, and his cousins had wound her up. But she might not be alone for the rest of the weekend.

Aaron took a deep breath. 'Aunty … can I talk to you?'

Aunt Helena turned around from the kitchen sink with a warm smile. 'Of course you can. What is it?'

'Since I've been going to see Kāterina in the caravan …' Aaron faltered as he tried to find words that expressed how he felt. 'What I mean is …'

'Aren't you happy going to the caravan?' Aunt Helena said. 'You don't have to go any more if you don't want to.'

'No!' Aaron bit his tongue. Why was everything coming out wrong? He cleared his throat and started again. 'I have to keep reading to Kāterina. She promised she'd help find my mother when we finished *Great Expectations*.'

Aunt Helena sighed. 'You can't believe everything Kāterina tells you. I don't want her giving you false hope. Perhaps I should stop you going to the caravan.'

'No, please! I have to keep going.' Aaron wiped a bead of sweat off his forehead. Why had he opened up to Aunt Helena? 'There's something else.'

'What?'

Would Aunt Helena laugh if he said he'd fallen in love? 'You see … these last few weeks, Kāterina has had her foster daughter, Miriama, staying with her—'

'Has she been mean to you?' Aunt Helena rapped the kitchen benchtop with her fingers. 'I've heard Miriama is a spiteful little madam.'

'No, it's not that. Miriama … she's …' Aaron shuffled his feet. 'From the moment I saw her, I knew …'

Aaron was about to open his heart when Uncle Ben came in and fetched a beer from the fridge.

'Go on,' Aunt Helena said. 'Don't take any notice of your uncle.'

Aaron made a dash for the door. 'It's nothing. Just don't stop me from going to the caravan.'

Damn Uncle Ben! Why did he have to choose that moment to come in?

     David Whittet

Aaron sank onto his bed. He was mad with himself, too, for bottling it. Nancy and Lucy were arguing in the next bedroom.

'That's my top,' Nancy screamed. 'Give it here!'

'No, it's not.'

'It is so!'

And so it went on. The fighting didn't stop until they heard the jingle of the ice-cream van outside. Typical.

'I want one!' Lucy shouted at the top of her voice. 'Can we, Mum? Can we? Can we? Can we?'

'Bags I'm first,' Nancy butted in.

'Why do you always have to be first?' Tara said.

Aunt Helena put her head around Aaron's bedroom door. 'Would you like an ice cream, Aaron?'

He wanted to say yes, but he didn't want to come out of his bedroom. 'No, thank you, Aunty.'

'Are you alright?' Aunt Helena asked.

'I'm okay. I'm just not hungry.'

It was true. He wasn't. But Aaron had to show his face for lunch, and then the regular Saturday afternoon trip to the school to watch his cousins' netball match. Aaron ducked when Nancy started arguing with the referee. *Not again.*

'She knocked the ball out of my hand,' Nancy insisted.

'She did not,' the referee shot back.

Aaron wandered across the playing fields and watched the boys' rugby match. Maybe he should sign up for the team. Their sports master insisted rugby was a gentlemen's game. That should impress Miriama. Not that there was anything gentlemanly about all the scrums and tackles. Also, Uncle Ben played for the Golden Oldies, and he was no gentleman. Aaron sighed. At least joining the team would show Miriama he was a man.

The whistle blew for half-time. Aaron felt his stomach flutter as he approached Mr Higham, the team coach.

'Sir, I um …' Aaron hesitated. Did he really want to do this?

Mr Higham got in first. 'Aaron! You want to join the team?'

Aaron nodded.

'Well,' Mr Higham said, 'there's no time like the present. Jason's twisted his ankle, and we're a player down. Go and get changed. There's a spare set of kit in the changing room.'

'What, now?' Aaron gripped his hands together. 'But I haven't been to practice. I'll be useless.'

'You'll be fine,' Mr Higham said. 'We need all hands on board if we're going to beat Moreton Hall.'

Aaron froze. *Moreton Hall.* He squinted across to the away team, huddled around their coach. And there was Corey with his shoulders back and chest out and looking as mean as ever.

'Are you alright, Aaron?' Mr Higham said. 'You're as white as a sheet.'

Should he make a run for it now, while he still had a chance? Aaron closed his eyes for a moment. If he ran away, Corey would have won again.

Aaron stood tall. 'I'm okay. I'll go and get changed.'

Mr Higham patted him on the back. 'Good on you.'

The changing room smelt of sweaty bodies, and the kit was far too big for him. None of that mattered. Aaron had only one thing on his mind. Today the stakes were even. Corey didn't have his army of thugs with him, and they would face each other on a level playing field. Aaron pulled the rugby shirt over his head. He was determined to win.

The whistle blew and Aaron wasn't so sure of himself. Two minutes into the second half and he found himself opposite Corey in a scrum.

'Half-blood! Half-blood!' Corey taunted as they jostled into position.

As soon as the scrum broke up, Corey kicked him in the balls.

'Take that, half-blood.'

Aaron bent over in pain. Hadn't the referee seen it? Why hadn't he sent Corey off? By the time Aaron got his breath back, Corey was up the other end of the field with the ball. The bastard was about to score a try.

Aaron barely felt the pain as he tore after Corey. He just prayed his legs wouldn't give out until after he'd caught up with the bully. *Faster, faster. Don't let him get to the line.*

Corey was almost there when Aaron lunged at him. *Take that, you loser!* Corey didn't look nearly so cocky with his head buried in the mud.

Aaron scarcely heard the crowd cheering.

     David Whittet

'Bravo! Brilliant tackle! Bravo!'

Corey staggered to his feet. 'You'll pay for this.'

Maybe he would. Aaron's heart missed a beat at the hatred in Corey's eyes. But Aaron had won this round and prevented Corey from scoring a try.

Full time and they'd beaten Moreton Hall thirty-five to thirty-two.

'Man of the match!' Mr Higham ran across the field and embraced Aaron. 'That tackle saved the game.'

The team exchanged their muddy rugby shirts. Aaron held his breath and put his head into a particularly sweaty top. *Gross!* But when his head came out the other end of the shirt, he saw something even more important to him than the admiration of his teammates. Corey was in trouble with his team coach. It sounded like he was getting a right rollicking.

Aaron cocked his ears to hear what they were saying.

'How many times have I told you about playing dirty?' The coach waved a fist at Corey. 'You need to control your temper. I saw you kick that boy in the balls. You're dropped for the next three matches.'

Corey stared at his coach. 'You can't do that!'

'I can and I will. You're a disgrace, Corey.'

Aaron wanted to hear more, but his teammates hoisted him onto their shoulders.

'We are the champions!' they chorused. 'Hurray for the man of the match!'

Yes. Aaron had well and truly won that round.

After the third lap of the field on his teammates' shoulders, Aaron spotted his Aunt Helena talking to Mr Higham.

'Your nephew's a star,' Mr Higham said. 'He's going to join the team.'

'That's wonderful,' Aunt Helena said. 'Aaron needs to make new friends and feel he belongs.'

The team put Aaron down beside his aunt.

'It's great to have you on board, Aaron,' Mr Higham said. 'We practise for a couple of hours each afternoon after school.'

Aaron lowered his head and kicked the ground. 'I can't do that.'

Mr Higham stared at him. 'Why ever not?'

Aaron shuffled his feet. 'After school, I have to read to an old lady in her caravan.'

Mr Higham scratched his head. 'Surely being part of the team is more important than that?'

'It would be, but …' Aaron's voice trailed off. How could he explain that this old lady would help him find his mother? 'You see, she promised she'd do something for me if I read to her.'

Mr Higham continued to stare at him. 'What?'

Aaron hesitated. 'It's hard to explain …' Why couldn't he just spit it out?

Aunt Helena rescued him. 'It's such a shame about the team. But Aaron's made a commitment to this lady. She's very lonely in her caravan, and she looks forward to Aaron reading to her. It would break his heart to disappoint her.'

Mr Higham raised an eyebrow. 'Is this the gypsy who's parked her caravan on the domain?'

Aaron nodded. What could he say? Mr Higham had that pinched look grown-ups had when they were getting angry.

Aunt Helena took over again. 'She's not a gypsy. Kāterina's a wise woman. And Aaron's a boy of his word.'

'Alright, alright,' Mr Higham said. 'Maybe next season then?'

'Can I? That would be awesome.' Aaron jumped from one foot to the other. 'We'll have finished *Great Expectations* by then.'

'We'll see,' Aunt Helena said. 'Now, you'd better go and get changed. I'll go and fetch the girls. I left them to get changed after their netball match finished.'

The friendly mobbing of Aaron's teammates continued in the changing room.

'That was a hell of a tackle,' one of the boys said. 'Did you see the look on that bastard's face?'

'First time we've beaten those punks from Moreton Hall,' another boy chipped in. 'We'll need you next week when we play Kaikōura Intermediate.'

Aaron put on his shirt and fumbled with the buttons. 'I won't be joining the team until next season.'

'Why not? We need you now!'

'I'm sorry.' Aaron pulled on his pants. 'But there's something I have to do after school this term.'

Aaron couldn't look at the boys' disappointed faces or listen to their groans. Perhaps it was just as well that he wasn't joining them straight away. After all, he'd only made that victorious tackle because he was driven by the overwhelming

     David Whittet

desire to get even with Corey. Playing against a different opposition next week, he'd probably be rubbish.

'Good luck against Kaikōura Intermediate.' Aaron grabbed his jacket and made for the door. 'I've got to go.'

His legs shook as he walked across the field to meet his aunt and the cousins. Nancy ran towards him. Why did she look so pleased with herself?

'I hear you've chickened out of joining the team,' she said. 'You're such a sissy, Aaron. Reading fairy tales to an old gypsy when you could be playing rugby like a man.'

Aunt Helena caught up with them. 'Don't be mean to him, Nancy, just because you lost at netball.'

Nancy could laugh all she liked. For a glorious moment that afternoon, Aaron had felt like a winner. People had looked up to him. Showered him with praise. Aaron was more determined than ever to turn his life around and make Miriama proud of him.

CHAPTER SIXTEEN

Sunday afternoon, and Aaron still hadn't had that all-important heart-to-heart talk with his aunt. After yesterday afternoon, he needed it more than ever. He'd got close to it last night when she came into his bedroom to say goodnight. She was about to sit down on his bed when Lucy and Tara began fighting, and she had to leave to break it up.

Aaron sat on the back doorstep after Sunday lunch and thought. Would he have been so driven if he hadn't met Miriama? His mother had told him to be brave and urged him to make something of his life. What would his mother have thought of Miriama? She'd probably side with his aunt and say Miriama was just a spoilt child. They'd both be wrong.

Aaron watched his cousins play tag in the backyard.

'You're it!' Nancy screeched at Lucy. 'Bet you can't catch me.'

Nancy, Lucy and Tara. Aaron sighed. They *were* spoilt. Spiteful too. Didn't they want to make something of their lives? Or would they just end up as gangsters' wives?

Aaron glanced across at Uncle Ben. Slouched on a deck chair with a beer can in his hand, his uncle's belching was as ugly as the cousin's screaming. Perhaps they wouldn't notice if he snuck across and talked to his aunt.

Aunt Helena was at the other end of the garden, hanging the washing on the line. Aaron took a deep breath, stood up and strode up to his aunt.

'Have you come to help me?' Aunt Helena said. 'You're a good boy.'

'Actually …' Aaron paused to pick a shirt out of the washing basket and peg it on the line. 'I was hoping we could talk.'

'Great,' Aunt Helena said. 'I get bored hanging the washing out on my own.'

Aaron hung another shirt on the line. 'You see, Aunty, I've been thinking about what I want to do when I grow up.'

Aunt Helena smiled. 'After yesterday afternoon, I wouldn't be surprised if you're not an All Black one day.'

'It's not that.' Aaron shuffled from one foot to the other. 'I want to get a scholarship and go to university.'

Uncle Ben's voice boomed across the garden. 'University, my arse! Aren't you the high and mighty?'

Aunt Helena turned to face Uncle Ben. 'Shut up, you moron. What do you know about anything?' She turned back to Aaron. 'University? That's a lot of hard work. And a scholarship?'

Aaron felt his cheeks flush. 'My father got a scholarship and went to business school.'

'Yes, but …' Aunt Helena shook her head. 'I don't think anyone from our little school has ever got a scholarship.'

'I could be the first,' Aaron said.

'Listen, Aaron.' Aunt Helena stopped hanging out the clothes and eyed him intently. 'I don't want to see you get hurt. Has Miriama put you up to this?'

Uncle Ben roared with laughter. 'The half-blood's got a crush on that bit of gypsy skirt.'

Aunt Helena shot him an evil look and then put her arm around Aaron. 'Don't take any notice of your uncle. But don't set your hopes too high. Be yourself. You don't have to go to university to make something of your life. And you definitely don't have to suck up to Miriama.'

Aaron pulled away. *I'll never be anything unless I get away from this place.* He watched his uncle take another swig of beer and then throw the can onto the pile at his feet. *Just you wait. I swear I'm going to university, and you'll still be here, drinking your life away.* If only he dared say it to his uncle's face. Aaron turned back to his aunt. Was there any point in carrying on with the conversation? She didn't understand how he felt.

Aunt Helena picked up the empty clothes basket. 'Come on. Let's go inside and get tea ready.'

Nancy caught Aaron's arm as he followed his aunt into the house.

'You think you're a cut above the rest of us, don't you?' Nancy spat the words in his face. 'Don't make me laugh. You'll never go to university. You can't even do your sums. I've seen you counting on your fingers.'

Damn Nancy. Trust her to have listened to his private conversation.

'You can laugh all you like,' Aaron said, 'but I'm going to get that scholarship and one day, you'll look up to me.'

But was he kidding himself? Aaron knew he was hopeless at maths. Was university just a childhood dream?

'Look up to you?' Nancy scoffed. 'Never. You're a loser!'

'I'm not!' Aaron couldn't afford to let Nancy see that he had doubts. 'Just you wait and see.'

Aaron marched into the kitchen before she had the chance to say anything else.

'There you are,' Aunt Helena said. 'I wondered where you'd got to.' She reached out and took Aaron's hand. 'Hold your head up high. Be strong—and don't you change for anyone.'

❧

Why had he confided in his aunt? He'd just given Nancy more ammunition to use against him. She'd tell everyone, and it would be all around the school in the morning.

And it was—morning break brought a barrage of teasing and mockery. They even gave him a new nickname.

'He thinks he'll be a great businessman,' Nancy announced to her friends. She turned to Aaron. 'Well, I've got news for you, moron. You have to be able to count to get on in business.'

'I *can* count,' Aaron hit back.

Nancy giggled. 'Yes, but only on your fingers!'

The crowd burst into fits of laughter.

'Fingers! Fingers! Let's call him Fingers!'

'Hey, Fingers. Are you going to be the next prime minister?'

'Nah! More likely a dustman.'

And so it went on. Aaron's self-esteem couldn't have been lower when he arrived at the caravan after school. How could he face Miriama with his dream of success shattered? And there she was, sitting on the steps outside the *Gypsy Rose*, waiting for him. She'd never done that before. Maybe she'd heard the school gossip and couldn't wait to rub his nose in it.

    David Whittet

Miriama jumped up and ran to greet him. 'I heard how you tackled a cheating brat at rugby on Saturday and saved the match.'

After such a ghastly day, Aaron had almost forgotten his victory on the sports field.

'Yes, I um …'

Before he could get any further, Miriama kissed him on the cheek.

'Good on you. Bad sports deserve to be taken down a peg or two.'

Aaron felt the warmth of Miriama's kiss radiate through his entire body. Never had she shown him affection before. What did it matter if his schoolmates called him names? Today, Miriama was proud of him. And she'd kissed him!

That evening, Miriama helped him read the next chapter of *Great Expectations*. Aaron read Pip's lines and Miriama, Estella's.

Kāterina sighed and put the book back on the shelf when they were finished. 'I enjoyed that. You both brought the story to life. Pity we won't be able to do it again for a while.'

What did Kāterina mean? Why did she have a tear in the corner of her eye when she made the cocoa?

'You'll have to say goodbye to Miriama tonight,' Kāterina said. 'So will I. Miriama's going back to school in Switzerland tomorrow.'

What? Just when Miriama was starting to show him some respect. How could life be so cruel? Back in Switzerland, Miriama would be mixing with all those swanky rich boys from Europe's elite. Aaron didn't stand a chance against such opposition. She was bound to fall for one of those high-class boys.

'Don't look so sad,' Kāterina said. 'She'll be back for the summer holidays, won't you, my dear?'

Miriama nodded.

Kāterina cleared up the cocoa cups when they finished. 'I'm planning on taking us all on a road trip for the summer.' She glanced around the *Gypsy Rose*. 'That is if I can get this old girl roadworthy again.'

'What?' Miriama raised her eyes. 'All three of us cooped up in this tiny caravan?'

'It'll be cosy,' Kāterina said, 'and fun.'

It would be an incredible adventure, but the look on Miriama's face made

Aaron wonder if she would come home for the summer. Maybe she'd make an excuse and go and stay with some wealthy Swiss boy and his family.

Aaron couldn't sleep that night. Would Miriama forget about him? She'd kissed him again when they parted. So why was the thought of the three of them going away together on a road trip so terrible?

Kāterina said they'd finish *Great Expectations* before Miriama returned for the summer holiday. That meant Kāterina would have to keep her promise and find his mother. Aaron would try to read faster. He missed his mother so much.

There was another reason why Aaron needed to finish *Great Expectations*. He had to find out if Pip and Estella got married.

❦

Parata Peak Power Station, March 2022

Aaron paced up and down in his office. He ought to be preparing for his meeting with Alan Fitzpatrick, not living in the past. Why had Miriama forced him to dredge up all these memories?

He sat down at his desk and took another look at the spreadsheet on his computer screen. The figures remained an unintelligible blur.

Aaron glanced at his watch. *You've got half an hour to pull yourself together. Don't waste it obsessing over the numbers.* After all, he'd paid his accountant to work around the clock to ensure the financials stacked up. Aaron turned off his computer and rehearsed his pitch. *With our combined resources, Jensen doesn't stand a chance. Parata Peak Power will be the largest player in the industry. You'll see a return on your investment within a year. Eighteen months max.* But would he? The New Zealand stock market was volatile, given growing inflation, the global pandemic and war in Europe. Increasing government regulation, supply chain issues and staff shortages, also negatively impacted the power industry.

Aaron thumped his desk. This was no time to doubt himself, not before such a high-stakes meeting. He *had* to impress Alan Fitzpatrick. Without the backing of the Emporium Group, the takeover of Jensen would be dead. That couldn't happen. Because if it did, Corey would be the winner.

   David Whittet

Come on! You can do better than this! Aaron stood up again and gazed out of the window. *Sock it to Fitzpatrick! Present him with a case he can't possibly refuse!*

The minutes ticked past. Aaron cursed himself. *Focus on the presentation, damn you!* Alan Fitzpatrick was moments away, and Aaron still couldn't stop his mind drifting back to Miriama and the summer that changed everything.

Tony put his head around the door. 'Mr Fitzpatrick's in reception. Shall I bring him in?'

Aaron straightened his tie. 'Give me a minute.'

'Are you alright?' Tony asked. 'Have you been up all night preparing for the meeting?'

Aaron shook his head. 'I've spent the entire night talking to Miriama about things that are best forgotten.'

Tony frowned. 'I don't want to rush you, but it's not a good look to keep Mr Fitzpatrick waiting.'

Aaron buttoned up his jacket and closed his eyes for a moment. 'Okay. Bring him in.'

Immaculately dressed in a Savile Row suit and slicked-back hair, Alan Fitzpatrick cut an impressive figure. He must have been in his mid-forties. His impeccable appearance reminded Aaron of one of the dragons on the *Dragons' Den* television show. On top of that, his handshake almost cut off Aaron's circulation.

'Pleased to meet you, Mr Casper.'

Aaron retrieved his hand. 'Call me Aaron, please.'

Aaron hadn't expected him to be a pushover but didn't bargain for the raised eyebrows during the presentation. Alan Fitzpatrick had a reputation for sniffing out a lucrative deal, so why wasn't he lapping up the figures? Aaron reached for a folder on his desk and pulled out a page of figures. This *had* to impress him—didn't it?

The numbers had made perfect sense when the accountant presented them to Aaron. So why couldn't Aaron make the numbers add up now when it really mattered?

Tony nudged Aaron and passed him another paper. 'You're on the wrong page.'

Alan Fitzpatrick stood up. 'I've heard enough. I'm sorry, Aaron. Your head's all over the place. I can't invest in you.'

Aaron stumbled to his feet and pointed to the pie chart on the whiteboard. 'Perhaps I didn't make it clear. Just look at the numbers. With the combined might of the Emporium Group and Parata Peak Power—'

Alan Fitzpatrick cut him off. 'It's not the numbers I'm worried about. It's you.' He picked up his briefcase and gave Aaron a cold stare. 'As I said, you're uninvestable.'

Aaron and Tony sat in silence for several minutes after Alan Fitzpatrick left.

'Don't take it to heart,' Tony said at last. 'There'll be other opportunities.'

Aaron had been dreading one of Tony's empty platitudes. 'Didn't you hear what he said? I'm *uninvestable*.'

Another silence.

'What were you and Miriama talking about all night?' Tony asked. 'Did you fight? I've never seen you like this before.'

Aaron shrugged. 'We didn't fight. It might have been easier if we did.'

'What then?'

'You don't want to know.'

Tony pulled his chair closer. 'I do.'

Aaron tilted his head back. 'She wanted to know what started the bad blood with Corey.'

Tony shook his head. 'I wish I understood that one, too.'

'It got me thinking …' Aaron broke off and stared into the distance.

'About Corey?'

'Miriama, mostly.' Aaron almost forgot Tony was there as he rambled on. 'When I first met her, Miriama acted like she was a princess. She convinced me that she was the daughter of some noble aristocratic family. Years later, Kāterina told me the truth. She picked Miriama up from a children's home. Miriama's mother was a prostitute. She had postnatal depression after Miriama was born and abandoned her baby.'

'Poor Miriama,' Tony said.

Aaron hunched over the desktop. 'You wouldn't say that if you knew how she treated me when we were kids.'

'It can't have been easy for Miriama,' Tony said. 'Being brought up like a

     David Whittet

gypsy in a caravan, then sent off to an elite school in Switzerland. I guess she had to pretend about her ancestry to fit in with all those movers and shakers.'

'You're probably right.' Aaron raised his head. 'It still hurts, though.'

Tony stood up. 'Do you fancy going for a coffee?'

'No. I'm going home to sleep.' Aaron stifled a yawn. 'I need to clear my head of all these wretched memories.'

But the memories refused to go away. Aaron couldn't stop thinking about Miriama and that road trip in the *Gypsy Rose*. Miriama had returned from Switzerland even more full of herself. There were no more kisses for Aaron but plenty more put-downs.

CHAPTER SEVENTEEN

Kaikōura Coast, January 2006

Aaron had worried about losing Miriama to some smooth-talking, well-bred boy from Switzerland. She'd boasted about joint parties with the local boys' boarding school, and the exploits they got up to afterwards. However, shortly after Miriama returned to New Zealand, Aaron overheard a conversation that told him the real threat was closer to home. Kāterina had sent him outside to pick some vegetables from her allotment. Aaron knew that wasn't the real reason. He waited outside the *Gypsy Rose* and listened to their conversation.

'I want the truth'—that was Kāterina's voice—'about you and Travis.'

Silence. Aaron stood on tiptoes and looked through the caravan window. Miriama's face was even meaner than when she rebuked him—if that were possible.

'I've heard he's a bad lot,' Kāterina said, 'and he's in the Gang.'

Miriama rolled her eyes. 'So what if he is?'

Kāterina shook her head. 'You make poor Aaron's life hell because his mother was born into the Gang.'

Another scowl from Miriama. 'That's different.'

'No, it's not.' Kāterina shook her head. 'Please tell me you haven't slept with Travis.'

Aaron lost his footing and fell to the ground. He'd heard boys at school talking about 'sleeping around' but wasn't entirely sure what it meant. With his father dead and his mother gone, there'd been nobody to explain these things to him. How old was Miriama, anyway? Aaron had always assumed she was about his age or perhaps a year or two older. Maybe she was much more.

Raised voices continued from inside the caravan, but Aaron couldn't bear to listen any more. He ran off to the allotment and pulled some vegetables out of the ground. Would Kāterina and Miriama still be arguing when he got back to the *Gypsy Rose?* What would he do if they were? He could always leave the vegetables at the caravan door and leg it back to Aunt Helena's house.

 David Whittet

Kāterina was alone when Aaron crept up the steps to the *Gypsy Rose* and peered through the door. She sat cross-legged on the floor with her crystal ball on her lap.

'I've brought you the vegetables,' Aaron said.

Had Kāterina heard him? She continued to caress the crystal ball and chant to herself.

'Tēnā koa te Atua, korerotia mai ki ahau he aha te mahi.'

Aaron placed the vegetables on the benchtop and turned to leave.

'Don't go.' Kāterina put the crystal ball down on its plinth and picked up the vegetables. 'Stay for supper. I could do with the company.'

'Where's Miriama?' Aaron asked.

Kāterina shrugged. 'Out at a party.'

'You're cross with her, aren't you?'

Kāterina nodded. 'How do you know?'

'I … um …' Aaron quickly changed the subject. 'Those words you were singing when I came in. What do they mean?'

'I was chanting in Māori, asking God to tell me what to do.' Kāterina sighed and began peeling the potatoes. 'Now, how do you fancy a bowl of homemade leek and potato soup?'

Kāterina insisted you couldn't beat soup made with freshly picked vegetables. Aaron wasn't so sure. How would he survive the road trip with no meat and Kāterina and Miriama constantly at each other's throats?

'Get that down you,' Kāterina said, handing him a bowl of soup. 'Food for the soul.'

Aaron took a sip. 'This is yum!'

'Don't look so surprised,' Kāterina said.

Aaron played with his spoon when he finished. 'How old is Miriama?'

Kāterina put down her bowl on the benchtop and sighed. 'She's at a difficult age.'

'Is that why you argue so much?' Aaron asked.

Kāterina shrugged. 'It's been tough for Miriama. You have to understand, her life has been hard. Try to forgive her when she's nasty to you. She doesn't really mean it.'

Aaron thought about Kāterina's words as he walked home. So Miriama's life had been difficult. What about his? Aaron's entire life had been a disaster—his father killed before he was born, and his mother kidnapped by the Gang, never to be seen again. Even now, brought up with three cousins who resented him, Aaron would never be as mean as Miriama had been to him.

Kāterina hadn't answered Aaron's question. He still didn't know Miriama's age, and there was that other question he couldn't bring himself to ask Kāterina. What did Kāterina mean when she asked Miriama if she'd slept with that boy—what did she call him? Travis.

Aaron had to know. Even if it meant a conversation with Aunt Helena that was every bit as difficult as talking to her about his dream of going to university. He seized the moment when his aunt came to say goodnight, praying that the cousins wouldn't interrupt him.

'Aunty,' Aaron began, 'I need to ask you about …'

Aunt Helena sat on the edge of the bed. 'About what?'

Aaron shuffled with the bedclothes. How could he put it? What was that phrase he'd heard at school? 'Aunty, I want to know about the birds and the bees.'

Aunt Helena blushed. 'Haven't they taught you about that at school?'

Aaron shook his head. 'I need to know because …' He paused and took a deep breath. 'Kāterina asked Miriama if she was sleeping with a boy. What did she mean?'

Aunt Helena's jaw dropped. Her face turned even redder. 'So, Miriama's sleeping around, is she? I told you she was no good for you. I've a good mind to tell Kāterina you're not going on that trip in the caravan.'

'No! Please, Aunty!' Aaron bit his lip. Why hadn't he kept his mouth shut? 'I've been looking forward to going away for so long.'

Aunt Helena frowned. 'I know you have. But with you and Miriama cooped up in that tiny caravan, who knows what could happen?'

Aaron sank back on the pillow. He just wanted to know the facts of life. Why couldn't he get a straight answer to a question? Aunt Helena was as bad as Kāterina. They both twisted his questions into something else.

'Nothing's going to happen, Aunty,' Aaron said. 'Miriama hates me, and Kāterina will be with us the whole time.'

'I'll have to think about it,' Aunt Helena said, 'and talk to Kāterina. Now, off you go to sleep.'

Aaron rolled over in bed. Would his aunt let him go? Had she any idea how much that road trip meant to him? The summer holidays might be his last chance to win Miriama's heart before she went back to all those upper-class, well-educated boys in Switzerland.

Three days later and they were on the road.

'Giddy-up!' Kāterina cried, pulling on Cleo's reins. 'The open road lies ahead. Let the adventure begin!'

With a lurch, Cleo dragged the *Gypsy Rose* off the domain and onto the highway. The wheels creaked, the chassis shook, and the caravan swayed from side to side. Aaron wondered if they'd make it out of the township, never mind the campsite where they were to spend the night.

When they turned a corner, Aaron almost landed on Miriama's lap.

'Watch it!' Miriama pushed him away. 'Get off me, you idiot.'

'I'm sorry,' Aaron said. 'I couldn't help it.'

Miriama scowled. 'Of course you could.'

Kāterina looked over her shoulder. 'Come and sit next to me, Aaron. You can help me with Cleo's reins.'

Aaron clambered across to the front of the caravan and sat beside Kāterina.

'Remember what I told you,' Kāterina said. 'Miriama doesn't mean to be nasty.'

Doesn't she? Aaron glanced back at Miriama. *It sounds like she does to me.* Still, it was more fun up at the front, holding on to the reins and helping Kāterina to steer Cleo along the road.

After a few exaggerated yawns, Miriama turned on her portable ghetto blaster. The music blazed out across the country lanes.

Kāterina turned and glared at her. 'Turn that wretched noise down. Or better still, turn it off.'

Miriama reduced the volume by a fraction. 'I said you should have bought me an iPod.'

'And you're going to torture me with this racket until I do,' Kāterina muttered.

Cleo slowed down as the shadows grew longer.

'Just a little bit further!' Kāterina pulled harder on Cleo's reins. 'I want to get to the campsite before dark.'

Aaron helped Kāterina pitch the tent in the dusk when they finally reached the campsite.

'Just one night here,' Kāterina said. 'Tomorrow, we're going to a holiday park further down the coast. You'll love it.'

Miriama sauntered across when they'd finished erecting the tent. 'This is cool,' she said. 'Dibs I get the sleeping bag and not that grotty mattress!'

It was the first time Aaron had seen Miriama smile since she'd come back from Switzerland.

❧

After another long day on the road, Aaron wondered if they'd ever reach the holiday park. The *Gypsy Rose* grew less stable with each corner they turned. The erratic motion and Miriama's music gave Aaron an almighty headache.

'I can see you're bushed,' Kāterina said when they drew up at the park. 'We'll get something to eat before putting up the tent.'

'Actually,' Aaron said, 'I'm feeling a bit sick.'

'You're looking a little peaky.' Kāterina put her hand on his forehead. 'No fever. It's probably travel sickness. A mug of soup and you'll soon feel better.'

If I don't throw up. Aaron watched Kāterina drag the gas stove out of the caravan and heat the soup. Miriama had dropped off to sleep. At least that gave them a rest from her endless music.

The soup smelt good, and Aaron began to feel better.

Kāterina smiled at him. 'I told you this would work wonders.'

Miriama emerged from the caravan rubbing her eyes. 'Not vegetable soup *again.*'

'You don't have to have it,' Kāterina said. 'There are some sandwiches in the chilly bin.'

Miriama turned up her nose. 'I've had enough sandwiches in the past couple of days to last me a lifetime.' She took a spoon and tasted a sample of the soup from the pot. 'It's not that bad.'

Kāterina continued stirring the pot. 'Not bad, indeed. It's good wholesome nutrition.' She glanced up at Miriama. 'Tomorrow, I want you to take Aaron to the beach. You could collect some seashells.'

'What?' Miriama pulled a face. 'Collecting shells? You've got to be kidding!'

'No, Miriama,' Kāterina said, grinding her teeth. 'It *will* be fun.'

Miriama rolled her eyes. 'Then why don't you take him.'

Kāterina shook her head. 'Tomorrow, I'm going to be busy.'

Aaron crouched on the ground while Kāterina and Miriama argued. Collecting seashells would be fun, but not if Miriama was in one of her moods. Miriama was still arguing with Kāterina when he finished his soup.

Aaron stood up. 'Shall I help you put up the tent, Kāterina?'

'You're a good boy,' Kāterina said. She glared at Miriama. 'You can wash the dishes while we fix the tent.'

Aaron and Kāterina pulled the tent base across the tarpaulin.

'I think Miriama does mean what she says,' Aaron said. 'She really does hate me.'

'Nonsense.' Kāterina drove the stakes into the ground with a rubber mallet. 'Just give her time. By the end of this trip, you'll be the best of friends. I promise.'

Aaron gazed up at her. 'Really?'

'Yes.' Kāterina winked at him. 'I've seen it in my crystal ball.'

Would Miriama ever be his friend? Could Kāterina's crystal ball really see into the future? It didn't feel much like it when Aaron woke the following morning. He rubbed the sleep from his eyes and glanced around the empty tent. No sign of Miriama. He yawned and stepped out of the tent. Kāterina was feeding Cleo outside the *Gypsy Rose*.

'Help yourself to some cereal for breakfast,' Kāterina said. 'Then you'll have to spend the day with me, I'm afraid.'

Aaron climbed into the caravan and fetched a bowl of corn flakes. 'Where's Miriama?'

Kāterina shrugged. 'She's gone for a walk. Said she needed to be alone.'

Aaron sat on the step and ate his cereal. Miriama must have been older than he thought if she was allowed to go out walking on her own. Come to think of it, he'd heard Kāterina telling Miriama to act her age. What was it she'd said? *You should be setting Aaron an example, not gallivanting all over the place.* He hadn't understood what 'gallivanting' meant at the time, but it began to make sense now.

Aaron finished his cereal and took his bowl back into the caravan.

'You look disappointed,' Kāterina said. 'Is it because Miriama's taken off?'

Aaron shuffled awkwardly and washed his bowl in the tiny sink.

'Never mind,' Kāterina said. 'We'll have fun together, and you'll see my crystal ball in action.'

What did she mean by that? Aaron dried his bowl with a tea towel and stared at the crystal ball, sparkling in the early morning sun. Did it really have magical powers? Or was it more of the nonsense grown-ups expected children to believe?

'Time for work,' Kāterina said, sniffing the air. 'Today, the spirits are with us.'

She bustled into the caravan and took a small bottle off a shelf.

'What's that?' Aaron asked.

'Incense,' Kāterina said. 'It's—beautiful. Intoxicating. Exhilarating.' She stuffed the bottle in her pocket, lifted the crystal ball off its plinth and polished it with her shawl. 'My precious!'

Aaron stared as Kāterina held the crystal ball high above her head and began to chant.

'Korero pono, e taku utu nui! Korero pono!'

Aaron stepped back a pace or two. Was he seeing things? Kāterina's grey hair stood on end as she continued chanting.

'Korero pono, e taku utu nui! Korero pono!'

Aaron didn't know what to do. Should he wait outside the caravan until she'd finished? She didn't seem to realise he was there. Aunt Helena had warned him that Kāterina was eccentric. That was another new word. Aaron continued to gaze at Kāterina. Whatever 'eccentric' meant, it suited her perfectly.

As he edged towards the door, Kāterina lowered her arms and stopped chanting.

'Are you okay?' Aaron asked.

'Fine.' Kāterina put the crystal ball in a pouch and hung it around her neck. 'Are you ready to go?'

Aaron nodded. 'What were you singing about?'

'I was talking to my crystal ball—my precious,' Kāterina said. 'Urging it to tell the truth.'

'The truth about what?'

Kāterina took his hand. 'You'll see.'

She led him to a neighbouring caravan in the holiday park and knocked on the door. What on earth was she up to? The woman who opened the door looked as bewildered as he was.

'Good morning,' Kāterina announced. 'My name is Kāterina Kururangi. I am a matakite.'

The woman, dressed in a tank top and knickers, scratched her head. 'A what?'

'A matakite,' Kāterina repeated. 'A Māori diviner.'

The woman still looked confused. Kāterina reached under her shawl and pulled her crystal ball out of its pouch.

'Are you some kind of fortune teller?' the woman asked.

Kāterina pulled a face. 'That term is an abomination.'

'What then?' The woman tapped her foot on the step. 'A clairvoyant? Or an astrologer?'

'Even worse!' Kāterina shook her head and took a sharp intake of breath. 'I believe in what I do. Not like those charlatans. I've advised many a Māori leader in my time. And for a small koha, I can give you insight into your life.'

The woman raised her eyebrows. 'A small what?'

'A koha,' Kāterina said. 'A donation.'

A male voice boomed from inside. 'Who is it?'

'Some crazy fortune teller,' the woman shouted back.

Aaron watched Kāterina shudder when the woman used those words again.

The woman turned back to Kāterina. 'You'd better push off before my husband comes out. He's not into that sort of thing.'

The man emerged in a T-shirt and boxers and glared at Kāterina. 'You heard what she said. Bugger off.'

Kāterina stared into his eyes. 'Something is worrying you. Tell me about it. I can help you.'

Aaron blinked. Was this for real? It was as if Kāterina had put a spell on him. The man's face softened, and without another word, he beckoned them inside.

Kāterina sat cross-legged on the floor and the couple squatted beside her. Aaron hovered by the door. Should he come in or wait outside? Kāterina took the bottle out of her pocket and sprinkled the contents in the air. What was it she called it? Incense. Aaron felt goosebumps on his neck, and the potent smell made him positively lightheaded.

Aaron didn't fully understand what they were talking about. It had something to do with money, and they used lots of words he hadn't heard of before. Foreclosure. Repossession. Mortgagee sale. But whatever Kāterina told them, it made the couple very happy.

Before leaving, Kāterina put her hands together with the couple's and prayed.

'Kia ata noho. Kia mau te rongo. Be still. Be at peace.'

Aaron traipsed behind Kāterina as they went from caravan to caravan. He still couldn't decide if she was just tricking them or if she really could see into their future. But Kāterina knew what was on their minds before they said anything, and they were all much happier by the time she left. Was she just telling them what they wanted to hear? Aaron shrugged. If all these people trusted Kāterina, perhaps he should too. Maybe he would be best friends with Miriama by the end of the trip, however unlikely that seemed.

Some of the caravans they visited were really smart. And as for the motor homes, Aaron could scarcely believe how much they fitted into such a small space. Comfy beds, electric heater, a proper kitchen and a fridge. An American family had a camper van that looked bigger inside than outside. Three children, and it didn't feel crowded. It even had a television and a gaming console! A road trip in a camper van like that would be awesome.

The children let Aaron play on the gaming console while Kāterina read the parents' palms.

'Can I really?' Aaron's hand trembled as he held the joystick. Kids at school boasted about having PlayStations, but he'd never had a chance to use one before. 'Wow! Did I really slay the dragon?'

It was like David and Goliath for the twenty-first century. Aaron was in the middle of a battle when Kāterina finished with the parents.

'Time to go, Aaron,' Kāterina said. She turned to the children. 'Thank you for letting him play.'

'That was brilliant,' Aaron said as they left. 'Why don't you buy a motor home, Kāterina?'

'A motor home?' Kāterina almost dropped her crystal ball. 'That would be the end of everything! *Everything!*'

Aaron shook his head. 'Why? It would be much more comfortable for you, and Miriama's always moaning about not having enough space.'

Kāterina snorted. 'A traveller and their chariot can never be separated. Their bond is irrevocable. The *Gypsy Rose* will be my home till the day I die!'

Dusk and still no sign of Miriama. Aaron helped Kāterina clear up after supper. They were stacking the dishes on a shelf inside the *Gypsy Rose* when Miriama finally showed up.

'Where've you been?' Kāterina demanded. 'And where did you get those sunglasses?'

Miriama chewed on some gum. 'Hanging out.' She took off her purple-rimmed sunglasses. 'I didn't nick them if that's what you're thinking.'

'I should hope not,' Kāterina said. 'Hanging out with who?'

Miriama shrugged. 'Some mates. Nobody you'd know.'

Kāterina eyeballed Miriama. 'Tell me it wasn't Travis. And take that chewing gum out of your mouth when you're talking to me.'

Miriama spat out the gum. 'Travis is history.'

Kāterina tapped her foot. 'Why don't I believe that?'

'Believe what you like.' Miriama raised her eyes to the ceiling. 'See if I care.'

Crouched on a stool in the corner, Aaron couldn't bear to listen to more of their quarrelling. He hid his face and covered his ears, but the raised voices didn't go away. Kāterina got up and poured herself a glass of water. Was this his chance to sneak out and wait in the tent? Too late. They were at it again before he could move.

'Now, you listen to me, Miriama,' Kāterina said. 'You're not going out alone again until I know who you've been with—and what you've been up to.'

Aaron peaked through his fingers to see Miriama pull another of her faces.

'I'm not spending all day cooped up in here,' Miriama said. 'That's for sure. Anyway, what's for supper?'

'There's some soup left in the pot,' Kāterina said. 'You'll have to make do with that.'

Aaron jumped up. 'I'll get it for you.'

'Good boy,' Kāterina said.

He grabbed a bowl and ran out to the stove. What a relief to get outside. They were still arguing when he went back in with the soup.

Miriama glared at Kāterina. 'Just try and stop me.'

'I will.' Kāterina rapped her fingers on the benchtop. 'Tomorrow, you *will* take Aaron out for the day.'

'What?' Miriama rolled her eyes. 'Picking seashells? Give me a break!'

Aaron handed Miriama the bowl of soup and retreated to the stool in the corner again.

'You don't have to do that,' Kāterina said. 'Take him for a hike over the cliffs. There are some lovely nature rambles around the bay.'

'Nature walks?' Miriama almost choked on her soup. 'You've got to be kidding.'

      David Whittet

Kāterina frowned. 'You might even enjoy yourself.'

'Yes, Miriama,' Aaron chipped in. 'It'll be fun.' Perhaps Miriama would lighten up with the beautiful view and the sea breeze on her face. Or was that too much to hope for?

'I'd take him myself,' Kāterina said, 'but I've work to do.'

Miriama scowled. 'I thought we were meant to be on holiday.'

'We are,' Kāterina said, 'but some more holidaymakers arrived this evening, and I sense they need my help. I need to get around to them before they move on.'

'Oh my God!' Miriama put down her soup bowl and flung her arms in the air. 'You're not starting that witchcraft again, are you?'

Kāterina glared at Miriama. 'How dare you talk to me like that? It's not witchcraft.'

Miriama raised her eyebrows. 'It bloody well is!'

Aaron saw the hurt in Kāterina's eyes and wished he'd escaped to the tent when he had the chance.

'I am a professional,' Kāterina shot back. 'Our whānau has a strong tradition in the healing arts. You'd do well to appreciate your heritage.'

Miriama stuck a piece of chewing gum in her mouth. 'Whatever.'

Kāterina continued to eyeball Miriama. 'And may I remind you, young lady, that my *witchcraft* pays your tuition fees?'

Miriama scoffed. 'Balls. I heard about the massive payout you got from working on that treaty settlement, and the compensation from that land covenant. I never understood why we had to live in this crappy caravan when you had all that money.'

Kāterina gritted her teeth and balled her hands into fists. Her voice rose as she spat out each word. 'If you can't show me some respect, maybe I'm wasting my money sending you to an exclusive school in Switzerland.'

Aaron pressed his hands to his cheeks. If Kāterina didn't let Miriama go back to Switzerland, did that mean she'd be going to his school? Was that what Kāterina had seen in her crystal ball?

'Don't give me that,' Miriama said. 'I've heard you boasting to your cronies about how well your foster daughter is doing at school in Switzerland.'

Kāterina gritted her teeth. 'I'm not too proud to cancel your place.'

'You wouldn't.'

'Just you try me, Miriama!'

Aaron shielded his face. The fire in Kāterina's eyes was so fierce he thought it might blind him. He peeked at Miriama's sulky face. That told her.

'Enough,' Kāterina continued. 'Time for bed, both of you.' She turned on Miriama. 'And I'll expect you to be in a better mood when you wake up in the morning.'

❧

The early morning sun shone through the tent. Aaron wiped the sleep from his eyes. Had Miriama got up early and taken off to avoid spending the day with him? He peered over his shoulder. No, she was still curled up in her sleeping bag.

Kāterina put her head inside the tent. 'Breakfast time. Up you get, you two.'

Miriama rolled over and groaned. 'Must we? Can't Aaron go for a walk on his own?'

'Don't start,' Kāterina said. 'I'm in no mood for a repeat of last night.'

Miriama had a face on her at the breakfast table. 'This milk's off!'

'It is not!' Kāterina turned to Aaron. 'You'll find some beautiful pāua shells on the beach and some rare native birds if you go up on the cliffs.'

Miriama pushed her cereal bowl away. 'Maybe I'll take Aaron to see the mad hatter in his castle.'

Kāterina started to clear up. 'The *what*?'

'There's a psycho who lives in that old castle up on the hill,' Miriama said.

Kāterina rubbed her chin. 'Yes. Come to think of it, one of the locals I talked to yesterday said something about a hermit buying that mansion.'

'And he's a raving looney.' Miriama grinned mischievously. 'Perhaps he's the bogeyman. Come to take Aaron away.'

'Stop that,' Kāterina said. 'I won't have you frightening Aaron.'

She's not. At least, not much. Aaron looked up. 'We won't be going anywhere near the castle, will we?'

'Of course not.' Kāterina eyed Miriama. 'You're to stick to the beach or one of the official nature walks. Understand?'

Miriama made a mock salute. 'Understood.'

 David Whittet

Half an hour later, Miriama and Aaron set out. Aaron held on to the picnic basket and looked over his shoulder at Kāterina.

'Is she out of sight?' Miriama asked.

Aaron took another look back and nodded.

Miriama smiled. 'Good. We're going to explore the castle.'

Aaron froze. 'No. You promised.'

'So?' Miriama bent down to Aaron's eye level. 'Don't tell me. You're afraid the psycho will get you and carry you off to his dungeon.'

Aaron pulled himself up. 'I am not!'

Miriama scoffed. 'You are so!'

Aaron *was* scared. Both of the mad hermit and of what Kāterina would say if she found out.

Miriama stamped her foot. 'Time to make up your mind. Are you coming with me, or are you running back to Kāterina?'

Aaron looked down at his feet. Whatever he chose, there'd be consequences, and all of them disastrous—he was sure of that.

'I'll take that as a no.' Miriama gave him the finger and headed up the winding path toward the castle.

'Wait!' Aaron couldn't have her think he was spineless. He took a deep breath and followed her up the path. 'I'm coming with you.'

Miriama already had a head start on him. 'Get a move on then.'

After twenty minutes of strenuous climbing, Aaron lagged even further behind. His feet ached, and he stopped to catch his breath. How much further was this wretched castle, anyway?

'Come on, slowcoach,' Miriama shouted. 'Don't tell me you're knackered already. I thought you were training for the rugby team.'

Aaron clasped his chest and pushed himself up the path. Miriama had reached the top by the time he caught her up.

She pointed to the castle. 'Wow, look at that!'

Wow indeed. Aaron almost tripped on the gravel. The fairy-tale castle looked like something out of one of Kāterina's picture books. Perched on the top of the cliffs and guarded by massive stone lions in the grounds, it was something else. Intricately carved giant wooden eagles stood sentry above the entrance. Grander by far than anything he'd seen before.

Miriama gazed at the castle. 'Imagine living in a house like that. Cocktail parties on the patio. Garden parties in the summer. Playing croquet on the lawn. How awesome would that be?'

Aaron wasn't sure if she was talking to him or herself but decided to answer. 'Kind of spooky, isn't it? One lonely man living in such a huge place.'

Miriama's eyes remained fixed on the castle. 'Why can't I live here? All my friends at school live in chalets and palaces. Lucky sods. And what do I come home to? That grotty old caravan, and we're always on the move. I hate it.'

Aaron still couldn't work out if she was talking to him, and this time, he decided to stay quiet.

'I've always wanted to live in a proper house,' Miriama continued. 'Whenever I come home, I pray that wretched caravan will have fallen to pieces.'

'That would break Kāterina's heart,' Aaron said.

'I'd be over the moon. Then we'd have to get a real home.' Miriama sighed. 'If only I had a Prince Charming to whisk me off to their castle.'

Aaron's heart missed a beat. That meant she hadn't lost her heart to one of those boys in Switzerland—at least, not yet. Was there anything he could say that would endear him to her? A sudden thought came into his mind.

'Remember when I read your palm?' He paused for a moment and cleared his throat. 'I said you'd meet a handsome prince and get married—'

'And I said it wouldn't be you,' Miriama snapped. 'Perhaps this is my Prince Charming, right here. I shall march up to the door, announce myself to the owner, and ask him to marry me.'

That wasn't the reaction Aaron intended. And as for going up to the front door—was she for real, or was she just winding him up?

'You can't do that,' Aaron said. 'You said the owner was a mad recluse.'

Miriama shrugged. 'Well, at least he's rich. He must be to buy such a gigantic castle.' She eyed Aaron with a twinkle in her eye. 'I can do mad recluse if he's rich and lives in a castle!'

She must be kidding. Or was she serious? Aaron still wasn't sure. 'You're not really going to knock on the door, are you? He might have an army of bodyguards.'

     David Whittet

'You're such a wimp!' Miriama pushed Aaron aside and climbed across the cliff towards the castle. 'You're afraid of everything.'

'No, I'm not!' Aaron followed her into the castle grounds. 'Stop! You don't know what you're getting yourself into.'

Miriama continued to stride across the lawn. 'Sometimes you have to take chances to get what you want.'

Aaron's heart beat faster as he struggled to keep up with her. 'Come back, Miriama! It's not safe!'

'It's worth the risk. I need to find my prince.'

Aaron caught up and grabbed her arm. 'Please, Miriama.'

'Jealous are you?' She turned to face him. 'Kāterina hopes I'll fall for you. Fat chance of that.'

Aaron blinked back a tear. 'Don't say that.'

'Well, you're going nowhere, are you?' Miriama pinned him with her eyes. 'You'll never be able to buy a girl a house like this place, will you?'

I am going somewhere. Just you wait. Aaron stared back at her. 'One day, I will buy you a house just like this. I promise!'

'In your dreams.' Miriama strode off towards the castle entrance.

Aaron stared after her. If this was a joke to make him feel small, it had gone too far.

A Rottweiler barked as Miriama approached the imposing timber door with cast-iron hinges and latches. *She's going to do it. She's really going to do it.* When Miriama hammered the ornate brass door knocker, Aaron could scarcely bear to look. More dogs joined in, their ferocious howling echoing around the stone walls. Had Miriama a death wish? Or had she spent too much time listening to Kāterina's predictions and staring into the crystal ball? Maybe, like her foster mother, Miriama was finding it difficult to distinguish between fairy tales and reality.

Aaron glimpsed a shadowy figure in a window on the top floor. Was this the mad recluse? Aaron blinked and looked again. Grotesque with his scarred face and bulging eyes, this monster of a man resembled something out of one of Nancy's comics. The man had seen them. He waved his fist so frantically that Aaron thought he would break the glass.

'Run, Miriama!' Aaron cried out. 'It's the Incredible Hulk!'

Miriama didn't move. *I have to get her out of here.* Aaron ran towards her but tripped on a paving stone on the patio and grazed his arm. *Damn!* He scrambled to his feet. Too late. The giant oak door opened with a loud lurch, and the Hulk appeared.

Miriama screamed. 'Get away from me, you freak!'

The man stepped forward. The Rottweilers roared and strained on their leashes.

'Help!' Miriama tore down the path and into Aaron's arms. 'He's going to kill us!'

Aaron grabbed her hand. 'Hold on to me, and don't let go.' He glanced over his shoulder as they fled across the lawn. The man's piercing eyes cut right through him. 'Faster, Miriama! He's catching us up.'

Miriama gasped for air. 'It's no good. I'm finished.'

Another glimpse over the shoulder. Aaron saw the man set the Rottweilers free. What could he do? The dogs would be at their heels in moments and tear them to pieces. His heart pounded against his chest, but he had to stay strong for Miriama.

'Jump up. Quick! Trust me.' Aaron carried Miriama piggyback as they veered off the path and down the bank. He stumbled on the undergrowth, and they rolled down the cliff in each other's arms.

Was Miriama hurt? Was she still alive? What if she'd broken a bone? How would he get her back to the caravan?

'Miriama,' he whispered in her ear, 'are you okay?'

Miriama stirred. 'I'm fine.'

She sat up and kissed him on the cheek. For a moment, Aaron didn't feel the pain in his grazed arm or the fear in his heart. It was only the third time she'd kissed him, and he wanted it to last forever.

Miriama jumped to her feet. 'We should get going. That psycho might still be following us.' She helped Aaron up and gave him another kiss. 'Thank you.'

CHAPTER NINETEEN

A freight train rattled along the coastal railway line. Aaron stood with Miriama at the level crossing, waiting for the train to pass. Were they safe? He looked over his shoulder for the zillionth time. No sign of the Rottweilers—he hadn't heard them bark since they rolled down the cliff. Did that mean they were safe or was the madman still chasing them? Aaron watched Miriama lean against a signpost and pant. He had a stitch. Neither of them could run much further.

How would they get back to the caravan? With their frenzied escape from the castle, Aaron had lost all sense of direction. He couldn't even remember the name of their holiday park.

The last of the freight trucks rolled past. Aaron took Miriama's hand. 'Have you any idea where we are?'

Miriama shook her head. 'Not a clue.'

Aaron looked around. 'There's a dairy over there. Let's go and ask.'

He took Miriama's hand and they crossed the train track.

A gang of skinheads loitered on a bench outside the store. A boy with a baseball cap whistled a catcall. 'Nice bit of skirt.'

Miriama hid behind Aaron and he felt her hand tense.

'Don't take any notice of them,' Aaron said. 'We'll just go inside and find the way home, then we're out of here.'

The boy with the baseball cap blew his cigarette smoke in Aaron's face. 'Why don't you push off home and leave the chick with us?'

Aaron fanned the smoke away from his face and spluttered. 'No way.'

The boy took another drag and blew more smoke onto Aaron. 'And you're going to stop us, are you, young'un?'

Aaron pulled himself up to full height. 'I am.'

The mob jeered. 'Let him have it, Spike!'

Miriama pulled Aaron away. 'Forget it! We're going.'

'Not so fast.' Spike stubbed out his cigarette and pumped a fist. 'Bloody hell! I thought as much. It's the gypsy girl!'

Aaron spun around to face Miriama. 'You know these boys?'

Miriama nodded. 'And they're mean as hell.'

Aaron stared at her. 'What do they want with you?'

Spike pushed Aaron aside and lunged at Miriama. 'Nobody makes a fool of me and gets away with it.'

Aaron fell and gashed his knee on a broken beer bottle on the ground. How the hell had Miriama got herself mixed up with a bunch of skinheads? And what could he do? A lone schoolboy against an army of thugs.

Two skinheads held Miriama down while Spike taunted her.

'It's payback time, gypsy girl.' Spike brandished a knife. 'You humiliated me in front of the entire gang.'

Aaron closed his eyes for a second. He had to do something—and fast.

'Help!' Aaron scrambled to his feet and tore into the dairy. 'They're going to kill my friend!'

The shopkeeper grabbed a baseball bat from behind the counter. 'Not Spike and his mates again.' He called his assistant. 'Come on, Marty, let's break this up.'

Aaron limped behind, holding his throbbing knee as the shopkeeper and his assistant ran onto the street.

'Let the girl go,' the shopkeeper shouted, 'and get the hell out of here before I call the police.'

The jeering stopped for a moment. Aaron willed Miriama to run for it while there was a diversion.

'You heard what I said.' The shopkeeper raised his bat. 'Clear off, or I call the cops.'

What was Miriama waiting for? Aaron caught her eye and mouthed the words. 'Run, run for your life.'

The mob began to split up. Miriama broke free and flew down the street.

Spike charged after her. 'Come back here, you bitch! I haven't finished with you.'

He was going to catch her—and he still had the knife.

'Stop!' Aaron bolted down the street in pursuit. 'I won't let you hurt her.'

Would his injured knee give way before he caught up with Spike? He thought his heart would explode, but with a final surge of adrenaline, Aaron pounced

 David Whittet

on Spike, grabbing hold of his legs and bringing him down in a rugby tackle. It felt as good as when he felled Corey on the rugby field.

Spike rolled over and gave Aaron the finger. 'You little shit!'

Up yours too, you bastard. Aaron let go of Spike's legs and helped Miriama to her feet. This was even sweeter than getting one over on Corey.

The mob laughed raucously—except Spike.

One of the skinheads gave Miriama a mock salute. 'He packs quite a punch, your new bodyguard. Or is he your new boyfriend?'

The young men continued to pour scorn on Spike.

'Do you need a hand up? Never thought I'd see the great Spike flattened by a snot-nosed kiddie!'

'That little squirt too much for you, Spike?'

'You didn't even fight back. If a babyface did that to me, they wouldn't get away alive.'

'Shut up!' Spike's face turned bright red, and his veins bulged. 'Get out of here. The lot of you.' He waved a fist at Miriama. 'You'll pay for this. Just wait till I tell Rita. This isn't over yet.'

Had they really gone? Aaron remained motionless after the mob left.

Miriama knelt beside him. 'You saved me.'

Aaron frowned. 'How did you get mixed up with a load of skinheads?'

Miriama looked away. 'You don't want to know.'

'I do,' Aaron said. 'And who's Rita? Will I have to save you again?'

The shopkeeper came over before she could answer.

'That's a nasty gash on your knee, young man,' he said. 'Come inside, and we'll clean it up. Then I'll drive you home.'

Aaron took a step towards the dairy and fell back to the ground, cradling his knee.

Miriama bent over him. 'Here, let me help you.'

Aaron held his breath, frightened his leg would fall off if he stood on it again.

Miriama held his arm and lifted him up. 'Don't worry. I've got you.'

Aaron braced himself for a fresh burst of pain when his foot touched the ground. He couldn't let Miriama see how much it hurt and pinched himself as the stabbing fire shot up his leg.

The shopkeeper took his other arm, and they helped him hobble to the back room at the dairy.

'I'll fetch some disinfectant and bandages,' the shopkeeper said.

The disinfectant ought to have stung, but Aaron hardly felt it. The agony eased to a gentle throb with Miriama's gentle nursing. When she wrapped his knee in a bandage, he felt almost whole again.

The shopkeeper went to serve some customers and left them alone at the back.

'Why did those thugs have it in for you?' Aaron asked. 'And what about Rita? Do we need to be scared?'

Miriama hung her head. 'It's best you don't get involved.'

Aaron pointed to his knee. 'I'm already involved.'

'I know. I'm sorry.' Miriama burst into tears. 'But if I tell you, you'll think I'm a horrible person.'

Aaron put an arm on her shoulder. 'I won't. But I have to know what's going on.'

Miriama dried her eyes and took a deep breath. 'I've been seeing this boy, Travis.'

Aaron frowned. 'I heard you tell Kāterina that Travis was history.'

'I had to say that to get her off my case.' Miriama played with her hair and hid behind a lock. 'I was ropable when Kāterina said we were taking off in the caravan. So I asked Travis to follow us on his motorbike.'

'Is that where you were yesterday?' Aaron asked. 'With Travis?'

Miriama nodded. 'Kāterina told me Travis was bad news, but I wouldn't listen.'

Aaron hesitated for a moment, trying to piece things together. 'So was Travis one of those skinheads?'

Miriama shook her head. 'Travis got wind of a big party and said we should gatecrash. A rave-up in some dude's penthouse pad. I thought it would be a hoot.'

Aaron drew back. 'And that's where you met the skinheads?'

 David Whittet

'Turned out the party was a birthday bash for a local gangster, and the place was full of skinheads.'

Aaron stared at her. 'So why didn't you do a runner?'

'Wish I had. But Travis kept giving me drinks. Everything was a blur after that.'

Aaron stared at her. 'You got drunk?'

Miriama buried her face in her arms. 'I don't know what they put in the drinks, but it went to my head. Next thing I knew, this skinhead had his arms around me.'

Aaron's jaw tightened. 'It was Spike, wasn't it?'

Miriama kept her face hidden. 'I wish I'd never set eyes on the bastard. He started touching me—'

'Stop!' Aaron held up his hands. 'Miriama! Please tell me you didn't'—what was that word Kāterina had used?—'you didn't *sleep* with him, did you?'

'Hell no.' Miriama raised her head. 'When he came on to me, I gave him a kick where it hurts most, and all his mates were watching and jeering.'

'So that's why he's got it in for you?'

'Too right.' Miriama's cheeks flushed, and she hid her face again. 'I humiliated him in front of his mates. You should have heard them. Mocking him for letting a gypsy girl get the better of him and kick him in the balls. Bloody cheek. Calling me a gypsy girl. And just when I thought it couldn't get worse, Spike's girlfriend, Rita, turned up and accused me of stealing her man. Now she's after my blood too.'

Aaron put his arm around her. 'You're safe now. They'll soon forget about you.'

Miriama raised her eyes. 'And if they don't?'

Aaron shrugged. 'The shopkeeper promised us a ride home. They won't dare come after you at the *Gypsy Rose*. Kāterina would scare them to death with her crystal ball.'

Miriama grinned. 'Oh, Aaron. You're one in a million.'

'No. I'm a half-caste.' Aaron gave her a gentle nudge, and they both giggled. 'And you're a gypsy girl.'

❧

Aaron glanced at the clock on the back room wall. Almost six o'clock.

'We ought to be getting back,' he said. 'Kāterina will be worried about us.' Poor Kāterina. She'd be beside herself if she knew what happened that afternoon. 'I'll see if the shopkeeper's ready to run us home.'

'Wait.' Miriama caught Aaron's arm. 'What's that noise?'

Shouting and banging rebounded from the shop. Were the skinheads back? Or was it—

Miriama completed Aaron's train of thought. 'It's Rita.'

'You stay here.' Aaron stood up and hobbled towards the door. 'I'm going to see what's going on.'

'No. You've done enough.' Miriama pulled Aaron back. 'It's me they want. I have to face up to it.'

The door burst open before Aaron could reply, and a giant hulk of a woman appeared. Her violent smile made Aaron shiver. She was standing by the door and already invading their space. From the devil tattoos on her arms to the menace in her eyes, this woman was trouble. Behind her, a mob of a dozen equally intimidating youths wearing 'Girl Power' T-shirts began trashing the store.

'Stop that,' the woman shouted at the mob. 'I want this done properly.'

Aaron glanced at Miriama. A terrified nod confirmed that this was Rita.

'Thought you could mess with me, did you?' Rita spat in Miriama's face. 'Maybe you can get away with it with your poncy friends in Switzerland. Well, the rules are different here.'

'Yeah!' Another girl spat at Miriama. 'You're not in the playground of your fancy school now.'

Rita turned to the mob. 'Get her.'

'Leave her alone!' Aaron cried.

He tried to push them back, but the mob pushed him aside and surrounded Miriama.

'Can we strip her?' one of the girls asked.

'Strip her! Strip her!' they all chorused, lunging at Miriama.

The shopkeeper pushed his way forward. 'Not in here, you don't!'

A girl landed him a punch in the guts. 'Shut up, grandad!'

'Shut it, all of you!' Rita glared at the mob. 'I said I wanted this done properly.' She signalled to the girl next to her. 'Give it to me, Bella.'

     David Whittet

Aaron's heart raced as the girl handed Rita a pair of shears. What were they going to do to her? Had Miriama told him everything? The hatred in Rita's eyes suggested it was more than just Miriama being caught with her boyfriend.

Rita pointed the sheers at Miriama. 'You've been tried and found guilty. I can't think what Spike saw in you. You're a miserable cow.'

The mob held Miriama down as Rita opened the shears.

Aaron gasped for breath once he realised what Rita was going to do. Trampled underfoot by the mob, he was helpless to stop her. Aaron squeezed his eyes shut. When he opened them, Rita had already cut off a lock of Miriama's hair.

Rita held up the shorn lock of hair. 'Not so high and mighty now, are you, cocky bitch?'

The rest of the girls joined in the taunting.

'Think you're so much better than everyone else? Just because you go to school in Switzerland. Well, you're nothing but a common gypsy girl.'

'Gypsy! Gypsy!'

'Slut!'

'Slapper!'

Rita triumphantly held up another lock of Miriama's hair like a trophy.

Aaron's head pounded, his arms shook, and his knee throbbed, but an overwhelming rage surged through his body.

'Let her go!' Aaron pushed through the mob to confront Rita. 'Why are you doing this to her?'

Rita glared at Aaron and pushed him aside. 'Stay out of this if you know what's good for you.'

'Don't hurt him,' Miriama cried. 'He's got nothing to do with this!'

Rita took the shears to Miriama's hair again.

'No! I won't let you!' Aaron lunged at Rita, and the shears gashed his chin. He fell to the ground, blood gushing from the wound. He ought to have been writhing on the floor in pain. Instead, an unexpected calm spread through his battered body. Rita had dropped the shears. Then moments later, sirens blazed, followed by a blue and red flashing light shining through the window.

'It's the cops!' Rita screamed. 'Get out! All of you!'

'Too late.' The shopkeeper blocked the doorway. 'There's nowhere to run. I've got it all captured on CCTV.'

Aaron sank back to the floor. The scene blurred to a haze as the police rounded up the mob and took them away in an armoured van.

'You'll need some stitches on your chin,' the police officer said, 'and there's blood coming from the bandage on your knee. We'll have to take you to the hospital.'

'Please, Kāterina will be worried to death,' Aaron stammered. 'We have to let her know we're safe.'

'I'll run the girl home,' the shopkeeper said.

'No.' Miriama scrambled to her feet. 'I'm staying with Aaron.'

'Perhaps we could call her,' the police officer said.

'She doesn't have a phone,' Miriama said.

'We'll send an officer round to the campsite,' the police officer said. 'But we need to get the boy to the hospital quickly before he loses any more blood.'

Miriama held on to Aaron's hand as the police car sped along the country lanes to the hospital. Aaron gazed at her face in the twilight, the occasional street lamp highlighting the mess Rita had made of her hair. What had Miriama done to make Rita so angry? Should he ask her? Demand to know the truth? Aaron leant back on the headrest. No. He didn't want to know.

⚘

Aaron's Flat, Parata Peak, March 2022

Aaron dragged himself out of bed and rubbed the scar on his chin. Why was he still lost in the past? His future at Parata Peak Power was on the line. If he didn't find a backer to replace Alan Fitzpatrick, the takeover of Jensen would collapse. Unthinkable. Aaron had staked everything on the deal going through. He pressed the button on his automatic coffee machine. A caffeine fix usually concentrated his mind.

Not today. Aaron's mind remained fixed on that dreadful day when the mob attacked Miriama. He still wasn't sure what she'd done to provoke such a violent reaction. The mystery made her all the more captivating. Aaron put his coffee cup down on the kitchen benchtop. If Miriama was allowed to have secrets, why did she have to know everything about him and Corey? How would

Miriama feel if Rita reappeared and threatened to turn her life upside down? Then she'd know how he felt.

A second coffee. Aaron fired up his computer and scanned through his contacts. There *had* to be one of them he could persuade to invest. *Make them an offer they can't refuse.* Aaron shot off some emails and shut down his computer. He'd been to a course on Zen meditation and squatted on the floor to put it into practice. But when he closed his eyes, all he could see was the emergency room at the hospital and the doctor stitching his chin.

The stitches had hurt like hell. Why did they bother with the local anaesthetic when it stung more than the stitches? Still, Miriama held his hand throughout the procedure, which was better than any painkiller.

Perhaps it wasn't such a bad day after all. It wasn't long after that incident that he came into his good fortune. Kāterina had set up a trust fund to pay for his education to reward him for saving Miriama from the thugs. Seventeen years on, and Aaron wasn't sure if that was the only reason for Kāterina's generosity. Maybe Kāterina felt guilty because she hadn't found his mother. Not that she'd broken her promise—they never got to finish *Great Expectations*.

Aaron had just cleared his mind when his mobile phone rang. Damn Tony. Why did he always interrupt Aaron's meditation?

'I hope this isn't a difficult time,' Tony said, 'but I thought you'd want to know straight away. Dame Cynthia has vetoed the takeover of Jensen.'

It was all Aaron could do not to throw the phone across the room. He took a deep breath. 'She can't do that.'

'I'm afraid she can,' Tony said. 'She's the company president. You're just the hired hand.'

Aaron hung up without another word. How dare Dame Cynthia Forbes-Hamilton interfere with the company's operational matters? That was *his* responsibility as CEO. He'd worked his butt off at business school—and for what? To let some out-of-touch socialite walk all over him and destroy everything he'd achieved? Well, if she didn't appreciate what he's done for the company, she could bugger off. He practised his resignation speech and was halfway through dialling Dame Cynthia's number when a voice in his head told him to cancel the call. It was Miriama. She always insisted he slept on it before making an irreversible decision.

How would he get through the day? He remembered how excited he'd been when the lawyer had called at Aunt Helena's house with the news of his scholarship. At last, he would be Miriama's equal. Today—Aaron felt it was all a waste of time and effort. If only he'd known what lay ahead when that smooth-talking lawyer turned up, he could have refused the offer and saved himself a heap of grief.

     David Whittet

CHAPTER TWENTY

Life was never quite the same after the road trip. Aaron's street cred skyrocketed once word got out that he'd taken on two notorious young gangsters and won. He had the battle scar on his chin to prove it. Praised at home and cheered on at school, even Nancy had to show him respect. That was sweet revenge.

But all this meant nothing to Aaron without Miriama. They had just one precious week together following the attacks before Miriama went back to school in Switzerland. She'd opened up to him like never before. Told him she'd never meant to be so mean to him. After a course in psychology at school, she'd practised self-analysis.

'It wasn't really about you,' she told him, 'I was hitting back at Kāterina. I hated the caravan and the nomadic lifestyle. And when she kept trying to pair me off with you, I rebelled. I'm sorry. It was unkind.'

Damn right! But Aaron kind of understood. What would a girl who had the pick of Europe's most eligible men want with him?

Miriama kissed him on the lips before she left in a taxi for the airport.

'Forever friends,' she whispered in his ear.

She looked more radiant than ever. Kāterina had done a brilliant job with Miriama's hair, restyling it so that Rita's assault with the shears didn't show.

Would Miriama forget him once she was back with her wealthy classmates? She would return from school—or the Academy for Young Ladies, as she liked to call it—as a true lady. He was no nearer being a gentleman. If anything, his fight with Spike, Rita and the mob merely emphasised his position as a gang boy.

Aaron had long since given up hope of getting a scholarship and going to university. His aunt was right. Nobody from their school had ever won a scholarship or distinguished themselves. It still hurt. Aaron had let his father's legacy down.

Going back to his old routine was hard. Aaron remained restless. There had to be more to life than chores, school and listening to his cousins' squabbling. He glanced out of the kitchen window while helping his aunt dry the dishes after lunch. A smartly dressed man with grey hair and a leather briefcase walked down the street. Aaron had hoped that he would one day wear an expensive suit and strut down the street with an attaché case.

What was this man up to anyway? Businessmen never came calling in their street. He was looking at the numbers on the gateposts.

'Aunty,' Aaron said, 'there's a man in a suit outside, and he's coming to our door.'

Aunt Helena peered outside. 'What on earth does he want with us?'

Uncle Ben came in from the yard and grabbed a beer from the fridge. 'I bet it's the cops. You know the drill. Get rid of him.'

'He doesn't look like a cop,' Aunt Helena said. 'He's got a nice suit and a snazzy tie.'

'Don't let that fool you,' Uncle Ben said, disappearing out the back. 'You heard me. Get rid of the bastard.'

The doorbell rang. Aunt Helena glanced in a mirror and tidied her hair. She didn't usually bother with that before answering the door. Aaron stayed in the kitchen and listened.

'Good morning,' the man said. 'My name is Anton Le Squillier.'

Aaron heard his aunt mutter something in reply, but he couldn't make out what she said.

'I'm a lawyer,' the man continued. 'Here is my business card. You are Helena Samuels, are you not?'

Another mumble from his aunt.

'I act on behalf of a benefactor,' the man said. 'A benefactor for Aaron Casper. You are the legal guardian of Aaron Casper, I believe.'

A pause and then his aunt's stumbling voice. 'Well, he lives with us since his mother had to go away, but I'm not exactly his … Well, actually … I'm not his *legal* guardian …'

'Quite.' The man's voice. 'Don't worry. Your domestic arrangements are

      David Whittet

not my concern. But I have splendid news for Aaron. His life is going to change.'

'That's wonderful,' his aunt said. 'Aaron needs some good news.'

'May I come in?' the man asked. 'I need to meet Aaron and tell him the news in person. There are also some conditions we need to go through.'

He's come to see me? With good news? Aaron quickly wiped a stain off his T-shirt. It had to be important if such a distinguished-looking man had come just to see him.

Aunt Helena ushered the man into the kitchen. 'Aaron, this is Mr Le Squillier. He has something to say to you.'

Aaron shook his hand. 'I'm pleased to meet you, Mr Le Squillier,' he said, copying how he'd heard Miriama address an elder. 'Very pleased indeed.'

Uncle Ben roared from the back room. 'Bloody hell! Haven't you got rid of the bastard yet?'

'It's Mr Le Squillier,' Aunt Helena shouted back. 'He's a lawyer. And he's here to see Aaron.'

'Lawyer?' Uncle Ben's voice blazed. 'We don't have lawyers in this house. And what would a lawyer want with that half-blood?'

'Calm down, and we'll find out.' Aunt Helena turned to the man. 'I do apologise, Mr Le Squillier. Won't you take a seat?'

Uncle Ben burst into the kitchen, glaring at Aunt Helena. 'Are you sure he's not an undercover cop?' He raised a fist at Le Squillier. 'Get the hell out of here!'

Mr Le Squillier sat up straight. 'Not until I have talked to Aaron.'

That told Uncle Ben! Aaron still couldn't work out who Mr Le Squillier was or why he was there, but anyone who could put Uncle Ben in his place was a hero.

The three cousins raced in from the garden.

'What's going on?' Nancy said.

'This is Mr Le Squillier,' Aunt Helena said. 'He's a lawyer, and he's come to see Aaron.'

'What's a lawyer?' Lucy asked. 'And why has he come to see Aaron?'

'They're the ones that stick up for you when you've done something wrong,' Nancy said. 'Aaron must be in trouble.'

Aaron sighed. At this rate, he would never find out the reason for Mr Le Squillier's visit.

'Children!' Aunt Helena said. 'Sit quietly or go to your room and play.'

Mr Le Squillier cleared his throat. 'Aaron Casper, I act for a benefactor. Do you understand what that means?'

Aaron shook his head. He'd heard Mr Le Squillier use the word 'benefactor' on the doorstep. Although he'd not come across the term before, it sounded like it ought to be something good.

'How shall I put it?' Mr Le Squillier continued. 'A certain person, who must remain anonymous, has set up an endowment on your behalf.'

That made even less sense than the single word 'benefactor'. Aaron waited for Mr Le Squillier to explain.

'It is the particular wish of your benefactor that you go to business school.' Mr Le Squillier opened his briefcase and took out some papers. 'Now, there are a few formalities we must go through.'

Business school! Aaron pinched himself to make sure he wasn't dreaming. He *would* be Miriama's equal after all, and he would uphold his father's legacy.

'Business school, my arse!' Uncle Ben bellowed. 'And an endowment for a half-blood! Don't make me laugh.'

Aunt Helena glared at Ben. 'Can't you be happy for him for once?'

'What's an endowment?' Nancy said. 'Can I have one too?'

Lucy and Tara jumped up and down in front of Mr Le Squillier. 'We want one too! Please! Please!'

'Behave yourselves, kids,' Aunt Helena said. 'This is important.'

'My goodness!' Mr Le Squillier smoothed down his suit. 'You certainly have some lively children, Mrs Samuels. Coming back to the matter at hand, my client, Aaron's benefactor, naturally expects him to live in a manner appropriate to an up-and-coming businessman.' Le Squillier turned to Aaron. 'You will receive an allowance and money to buy new clothes befitting your situation. Do you understand?'

Aaron nodded. Could he have wished for anything better? Miriama had constantly mocked his ragged working-class clothes.

Nancy stomped her foot. 'That's not fair. I haven't had any new clothes in ages.'

'It's perfectly fair,' Aunt Helena said. 'Aaron deserves this.'

Nancy glared back. 'And I don't?'

    David Whittet

Aaron felt a warm glow inside. Good on Aunt Helena for sticking up for him.

Mr Le Squillier coughed to regain attention. 'Now, Aaron, your benefactor will naturally want you to mix in appropriate circles. Of course, that means cutting all contacts with gangs.'

Aaron saw him look at Uncle Ben and the gang tattoos on his arms and the patch on his jacket.

Mr Le Squillier turned to Aunt Helena. 'Regrettably, this will require Aaron to leave your care. I will assume guardianship of Aaron until such time as his benefactor chooses to reveal their identity. Are you in agreement with this?'

Aunt Helena blinked back a tear. 'I suppose so. If it's the right thing for Aaron.' She lifted her gaze to Mr Le Squillier. 'This is … I mean … it is all above board, isn't it?'

Mr Le Squillier bowed his head slightly. 'My dear Mrs Samuels. It is entirely legitimate.' He straightened his gold tie pin and brushed a piece of fluff off his jacket. 'You have my business card. Feel free to check my credentials. I assure you, this will all be done through the Family Court. So everything will be above board, as you put it.'

'Good.' Aunt Helena wrapped her arms around Aaron. 'We can't let just anyone take you away.' She held him tightly. 'It's what your mother would have wanted for you. But I'm going to miss you, Aaron.'

Aaron shed a tear of his own. 'I'm going to miss you, too.' Aunt Helena was the *only* thing he'd miss from staying at that house.

'Miss him?' Uncle Ben sneered. 'Miss a half-caste?' He glared at Le Squillier. 'You're welcome to the bastard. Take him away.'

'Enough!' Aunt Helena eyeballed Uncle Ben and then turned to Aaron. 'Don't listen to him. We *will* miss you. I'll come and see you whenever I can, and you'll always be welcome here.'

Mr Le Squillier shook Aaron's hand. 'With that, I will take my leave and wish you good luck.' He turned to face Aunt Helena. 'I will now apply to the Family Court for a custody order. Once the formalities are settled, I will arrange suitable accommodation and enrol Aaron in a private school until he is old enough for business school.'

'So you're not taking him today?' Ben said. 'Are you sure you're not a cop?'

Tara tugged on Aunt Helena's arms as she showed Mr Le Squillier out. 'Can I have Aaron's bedroom when he leaves? I'm sick of sharing with Lucy.'

Aaron stopped Mr Le Squillier at the front door. 'Can't you tell me the name of my benefactor?'

Mr Le Squillier hesitated. 'All I can say is that it's someone who holds you close to their heart and wants to make up for your difficult start in life.'

Of course! Kāterina. Who else could it be? The more Aaron thought about it, the more certain he became. Kāterina had the money to send Miriama to school in Switzerland, so she must be able to pay for him to go to business school. Had Kāterina always planned for him to be together with Miriama?

⚜

Aaron couldn't wait for his next visit to the *Gypsy Rose* and the chance to thank Kāterina. But Mr Le Squillier had said his benefactor wished to remain secret. Would she be upset if he told her he knew it was her? Aaron went through several different scenarios on his walk to the caravan.

When he arrived, Kāterina made it easy for him.

'I've heard your news,' she said. 'So you go to a private school in Christchurch next term and then business school when you're eighteen?'

Aaron nodded. 'I'm so grateful for the opportunity.'

Kāterina eyed him. 'Then you must make full use of it.'

'I will!' Aaron rushed his words. 'I'll work hard. I won't let you down.'

Kāterina smiled. 'I know you'll do your best. You put your heart into everything you do.'

'I'm going to make you proud of me.'

Kāterina blinked back a tear. 'I'm proud of you already. I'm going to miss your visits so much. How am I going to manage without you reading to me?'

Aaron frowned. 'I guess I'll never know how *Great Expectations* ends now.'

Kāterina reached for the book and took it off the shelf. 'Actually, Dickens wrote two endings for the book. One happy and one sad.'

Aaron shook his head. How did that work? Either Pip and Estella got together and lived happily ever after, or they didn't.

'Don't look so confused,' Kāterina said. 'I'm sure *your* story will have a happy ending.' She handed the book to Aaron. 'I want you to have the book. You'll think of me whenever you look at it.'

'Thank you!' Aaron grasped the book. 'Thank you! For everything.'

'Don't thank me too much,' Kāterina said. 'I haven't found your mother yet. But I will. I promise you.'

Aaron met her eyes. 'Are you sure? I'd almost given up—'

'Never lose hope. When I promise something, I mean it. Now, I'm dying for a cup of tea.' Kāterina had a twinkle in her eye as she boiled the kettle on the stove. 'Miriama's coming home next week for her mid-semester break. You'll be able to tell her your good news.'

It had to be perfect. Aaron spent the entire week deciding how he'd tell Miriama. Mr Le Squillier had been back and had taken him to a menswear shop in Kaikōura. As well as a few suits, he'd bought some smart casual wear. That would be perfect for the picnic Aaron was planning. He chose the spot carefully. A secluded beach with a panoramic view of the ocean. They might even spot a dolphin. He arranged for a picnic basket from the local delicatessen—only the best for such an auspicious occasion.

The moment he'd been waiting for had arrived. He laid out a blanket on the cliff and opened the picnic basket. Had Kāterina told her already? It didn't matter. This was *his* moment, and he would enjoy every minute of it.

He waited patiently until Miriama had finished the last sandwich, and they both lay back, basking in the autumn sun.

'Finally, my life is going somewhere,' Aaron began. 'I'm going to St Andrew's College in Christchurch next year. And then Victoria University Business School in Wellington when I'm old enough. St Andrew's! The Victoria Business School! I'm going to be a success!'

'What an incredible opportunity!' Miriama put an arm on his shoulder. 'I'm so happy for you, Aaron.'

'I've always wanted to go to Wellington,' Aaron said, 'and Victoria is the best business school in the country.'

'I know. You're going places—and you deserve it.'

Aaron sat up. 'One day, I'll own my own company. Just like my father.'

'You've never told me about your father.'

'He died before I was born.' Aaron stared out to sea. 'He was on the brink of a great discovery when he was killed. He'd discovered some precious rocks under a waterfall. In the end, it cost him his life.'

'I never knew my parents either,' Miriama said. 'Kāterina's my foster mother. You knew that, didn't you?'

Aaron nodded. 'You're lucky to have such an amazing mother figure.'

'Guess I am.' Miriama rolled over and gave Aaron a gentle poke. 'Look at you, going to business school!' She grinned. 'I won't be able to call you a gang boy any longer.'

Aaron smiled back. 'And when you're finished in Switzerland, I won't be able to call you a gypsy girl.'

'No.' Miriama laid back on the blanket. 'I'll be a lady and you'll be a gentleman. Or at least a businessman. A gentleman and a businessman. If that's not mutually exclusive.'

Aaron had no idea what she meant but laughed with her.

Miriama sighed. 'Who'd have thought it? We've both come so far since you read my palm the day we met.'

Aaron stiffened. He didn't want to remember that awful afternoon. 'Guess we have.'

Miriama dabbed her eyes with a napkin. 'Can you ever forgive me for the way I treated you?'

Aaron stroked her hand. 'I already have.'

'You risked everything for me, and I gave you nothing but abuse in return. I should never have said all those nasty things. I could see how much they hurt you.'

Aaron shook his head. 'That's all in the past.'

'I've done a lot of thinking this past term. When I went back, you know … after Spike, Rita and everything …' Miriama dried her eyes on the napkin again. 'My friends in Switzerland … they all seemed so shallow. My friend Sabrina wanted me to spend the half-term break with her at her parents' château on the banks of Lake Lucerne. But I said no. I wanted to come home to see you.'

Aaron felt he'd been waiting for those words his entire life. 'Oh, Miriama!' He flung his arms around her and hugged her for dear life.

CHAPTER TWENTY-ONE

Victoria University Business School, Wellington, August 2013

Aaron clutched the letter in his hand. *Miriama's coming home!* He danced around his tiny student room. *Brilliant!* Business school hadn't been quite as glamorous as he'd anticipated. He'd worked his butt off that term and needed a break. Aaron was a plodder. Nothing came easily. He'd written to Kāterina and told her he spent every hour God gave him studying. And it was true. He had his nose in his textbooks while his fellow students partied. Not that it worried him—he would get a first-class degree and make it to the top. That was never in doubt.

But a few precious days with Miriama! Everything else paled into insignificance. Aaron was determined it would be as magical an experience as the day he told Miriama about his change in fortune. How could he make this an idyllic tryst she'd never forget?

Aaron searched the internet for the perfect location. After half an hour of browsing, one picture leapt at him from his laptop screen. A magnificent luxury lodge overlooking Lake Aviemore in the Waitaki Valley. That would put even the most opulent château on the banks of Lake Lucerne to shame. He scrolled down the webpage and gulped when he saw the price. Could he afford it? Only just, and it would blow the remainder of his student allowance. There'd be no more takeaways when the student hall meals were inedible. What did that matter? It was worth the sacrifice—for Miriama.

Aaron crossed off the days on the calendar on his bedroom wall. He printed the photo of the lodge and stuck it next to the calendar. Saturday couldn't come fast enough.

Where was she? Crowds flocked through the arrivals gate at Wellington Airport, but no Miriama. Aaron's heart beat faster. Had she missed her flight? Or had she changed her mind? Aaron fiddled with the keys to his hired car. The last stragglers appeared, and there at the very back was Miriama.

Aaron flung his arms around her. 'I thought you weren't coming.'

'What? Miss a long weekend at a luxury resort?' Miriama raised an eyebrow. 'Sometimes, I think you don't know me at all.'

Miriama was full of gossip about her rich friends' antics as they drove to the Interislander ferry terminal. All Aaron could talk about were his business studies, and that would bore Miriama to tears.

They stood on deck during the crossing to the South Island. The wind blew through their hair as they sailed through the beautiful Marlborough Sounds.

'You should come to Europe,' Miriama said. 'The opportunities there for high-flyers are amazing.'

'I'm not sure I'm a high-flyer,' Aaron said. 'Besides, does Europe have anything like this?'

He pointed to the myriad of tiny islands scattered across the sea like a giant mosaic.

'You'd love Switzerland,' Miriama said. 'It's beautiful too, in a different way.'

'Switzerland is a landlocked country, isn't it?' Aaron continued to stare out across the sounds. 'I've always loved the sea. It asks nothing of you.' He paused for a moment and sighed. 'I could watch it for hours. Eventually, your heart beats in sympathy with the pounding waves.'

Miriama gave him a playful dig in the ribs. 'You should be a poet, not a businessman.'

Miriama fell asleep during the long drive south to the lakes. Jet lag must have caught up with her. Aaron admired the majestic terrain. The route took them along the rugged coast, through tunnels hewn out of rock, over rivers and streams and through mountain passes. Aaron could never leave New Zealand.

Miriama stirred when they neared the lakes and rubbed her eyes. 'What time is it? Where are we?'

'It's four o'clock, and we're nearly there,' Aaron said. 'You've missed some spectacular scenery. Snow on the hills. Icicles on the trees. What's not to love?'

          David Whittet

'Icicles?' Miriama pulled a face. 'It was summer when I left Europe.'

Aaron suddenly pulled onto the side of the road and parked the car. He'd spotted the mighty Parata Peak Dam.

'What is it?' Miriama asked.

Aaron stared through the windscreen. 'Hydroelectric power. Come on, let's get a closer look.'

He jumped out of the car in a flash and climbed up to the observation platform.

Miriama followed several paces behind. 'I thought we were going to a luxury lodge. Not a power station.'

'We are, soon. I promise.' Aaron pointed to the torrent of water cascading down the spillway. 'Isn't it fantastic?'

Miriama zipped up her jacket. 'It's mighty cold.'

Aaron continued to gaze in awe at the dam, mesmerised by its power and strength.

'This is the future, Miriama,' he said. 'Look. It's clean, raw energy.'

Miriama sighed. 'Yes, well, it's not actually raw. We learnt about harnessing energy at school. The water flow causes a turbine to rotate, which in turn drives an electric generator.'

What? Aaron was unimpressed by such an unemotional and technical explanation. How come Miriama was unmoved by something so incredible? She *definitely* wouldn't make a poet.

'It's more than that,' Aaron said. 'Can't you see? Like I said, it's the future!'

Miriama wrapped her arms around herself. 'Whatever.'

Aaron continued to gaze at the deluge of water and saw a vision of his future. Half to himself, he made a determined resolution. 'One day, when I get through business school, I will run that power station!'

PART THREE

BLOOD MONEY

CHAPTER TWENTY-TWO

Parata Peak Power Station, April 2022

Aaron gazed out of his office window. Nine years ago, as an impressionable student, he promised himself he would run the Parata Peak Power Station. Now here he was, and in danger of losing everything.

How had it come to this? Aaron's rise to the top had been meteoric. Perhaps that was the problem. He hadn't had time to think. Or grow up.

When he got back to the university after that trip to the lakes with Miriama, he'd embarked on a research paper on optimising natural resources in power generation. When an eminent business journal agreed to publish his work, he couldn't wait to tell Miriama.

'You are going places,' Miriama said when he called her. 'Who knows, one day you might run that power station we stopped at, where I almost froze to death.'

She remembered! Aaron wasn't sure if she'd even heard his whispered declaration on that momentous day.

A year later, he rang to tell her about a job offer. 'I've been headhunted. Can you believe it, Miriama? Headhunted!'

Impressed by his paper and his first-class honours, senior civil servants at the Ministry of Economic Development recruited him for a junior post in a government-sponsored think tank on restructuring the power industry. With his ability to think outside the box and develop innovative solutions, Aaron soon found himself in demand as a business advisor. When a leading recruitment agency set out to find a dynamic junior executive to grow and strengthen a former state-owned power company, Aaron was the ideal candidate. A struggling company in need of fresh blood—just the challenge Aaron needed. Six years in senior management, and then appointed CEO. Aaron couldn't conceal his pride when the business press ran with the story. *Parata Peak Power appoints New Zealand's youngest CEO. Aaron Casper is a rising star and the sole topic of conversation around the water coolers for the nation's leading industrialists.*

Miriama had also made a name for herself. To Aaron's surprise, she began by canvassing Māori leaders, promoting herself as Kāterina Kururangi's protégé. The daughter of the once-renowned Māori advisor. Aaron had feared this would take her away from him. But Miriama turned down a position in Rotorua, instead settling for a business consultancy in the South Island to be close to him.

Life couldn't be better. Or could it? There was just one black cloud on Aaron's horizon. Corey. The media had a new story now. *Gang boy makes good. Charismatic leader Corey O'Connor appointed CEO of Jensen Industries.* Charismatic indeed! Aaron wanted to spit. And it wasn't just the business press. Were they trying to rub Aaron's nose in it? Corey's picture was plastered on the front page of the nation's newspapers, and his story was on billboards on every street corner.

Tony banged on about how tough it must have been for Corey. 'He didn't have a benefactor to put him through business school, did he?'

'No,' Aaron had hit back. 'Corey had the Gang propping him up.'

Aaron glanced at his watch. It was almost time for a briefing with Tony. Would he have to sit through another hour or two of Tony making excuses for Corey?

'Mediation?' Aaron thumped the desk with his fist. 'You've got to be joking.'

'I'm not.' Tony handed him a file. 'Take a look at this.'

Aaron read the first paragraph and almost choked. 'A counterproposal? Who the hell does Corey think he is?'

'He thinks he's the CEO of Jensen,' Tony said, 'which he is.'

Aaron flicked through a few more pages. 'A joint venture between Jensen Industries and Parata Peak Power. Damn Corey! He cannot be serious.'

'I'm afraid he is.' Tony took a deep breath. 'So is Dame Cynthia. Plus Margaret, Daniel, Steven and the rest of the board.'

Aaron threw the file onto the desk. He might have known Corey would pull a stunt after the takeover bid collapsed. There had to be a way to stop him. Would Tony help? Or had Margaret and the others got to him already?

     David Whittet

'A joint venture with Jensen?' Aaron said as calmly as he could. 'That's never going to work. Our companies—they've nothing in common.'

Tony gave him a hard stare. 'That's not what you said when you pushed for the takeover.'

'That was different.' Aaron flung his arms in the air. 'What I mean is … their culture is entirely different to ours.'

'Maybe it is,' Tony said, 'but the numbers stack up. I also seem to remember you insisted numbers didn't lie when we were discussing the takeover.'

Trust Tony to dredge that up. Aaron bit his tongue. He had to keep a level head. 'Corey is a puppet of the Gang. If we go into partnership with Jensen, the Godzone Gorillas will have us by the short and curlies.'

Tony scratched his head. 'I don't think Corey's a puppet of the Gang. At least, not any longer.'

Give me strength! Aaron could feel his blood pressure rise. 'Of course he is. How else do you think he got to be CEO? The Godzone Gorillas bought out Jensen with gang money. Blood money.'

Tony leant forward. 'Are you sure? I've heard Corey's cleaning up Jensen.'

'Balls!' Aaron spat the word in Tony's face.

'My mate Frank,' Tony said, 'overheard something when he was walking home from the pub late one night.'

'What?'

'Corey's voice screaming for dear life.'

'So? I bet he's always fighting with his gangster mates.'

'No.' Tony edged even closer to Aaron. 'That's not what Frank thought. Corey was terrified.'

'He was probably just getting what he deserved.'

'Hear me out,' Tony said. 'Frank caught a glimpse of them down the alley. Two thugs had Corey pinned against the wall, and they kept slapping his face.

'"Don't forget who put you here, Corey," one of them said. "Don't forget where your loyalties lie!"

'Then Corey answered, "With Jensen Industries."

'That got him a kneeing in the groin.

'"No, my friend," the thug hit back. "Your loyalties lie with the Gang!"'

Aaron drew back. 'I don't believe it. I know Frank. He's full of crap.'

'Margaret believes it,' Tony said, 'and she's determined to push it through at the board meeting.'

Aaron hit his desk again. 'Margaret's just after my job. She's been trying to get me kicked out since I got the top job.' He stood up and paced around the office. 'Well, if Margaret gets her way with this, she's welcome to my job. Because there'll be nothing left of the company for her to take charge of.' Aaron turned to face Tony. 'What about you, Tony? Are you for me or against me?'

Tony sighed. 'It doesn't matter what I think.'

Aaron stared at him. 'It does. We have to stop this before it's too late.'

'It's too late already.' Tony got up and walked towards the door. 'I'm sorry, Aaron. But everyone on the board's made up their mind already.'

'They can't have!' Aaron loosened his tie. 'We haven't even discussed it at the board yet.'

'I know.' Tony grabbed the door handle. 'It's the first item on the agenda for tomorrow's meeting. Haven't you looked at your board papers yet?'

Tony was out the door before Aaron could answer. *Bloody typical.*

Aaron grabbed the file on the proposed merger and threw it against the door. It gave him immense pleasure to see the papers scatter across the floor. *I've slogged and made sacrifices to get where I am. As for Corey, the son of a bitch thinks he can do as he likes just because he's got the Gang behind him.*

The Gang had killed his father, taken away his mother, and now it threatened to destroy his career. Before they took his mother away, she told Aaron how she loved going to the Roaring Creek Falls as a little girl to gaze at the cascading water. Aaron used to feel like that about the Parata Peak Dam and spent hours watching the endless torrent of water. Not now—one glance at the window and Aaron pulled down the blind. Today, he couldn't bear to look at the dam.

After sitting in silence for half an hour, Aaron picked up the merger papers off the floor. He felt his blood pressure rise further as he read through the proposals. Between them, Margaret and Corey had well and truly stitched him up. *Damn them both.* Aaron raised a fist to Margaret's smiling face on a photo of the Parata Peak Power board of directors on his office wall. *I'm not giving up now. I've come too far to let this go.*

❧

Takeaway sushi usually lifted Aaron's spirits. But would it help him prepare for the board meeting in the morning? Miriama called him while he was at the sushi bar and invited him to her apartment.

Aaron joined the end of the queue as he answered his mobile. 'I can't, Miriama. I have to get my head together for tomorrow's board meeting. My life depends on it.'

'Then perhaps I can help you,' Miriama replied. 'I'm a good sounding board.'

'I know you are, but …' Aaron shuffled a few paces forward in the queue. 'Thanks for the offer, but I have to do this on my own.'

Miriama paused on the line. 'Are you sure that's a good idea?'

'I am.' Aaron knew Miriama would push him to compromise, and that wasn't going to happen. 'This way, if I stuff up, I've only myself to blame.'

'That's what I'm afraid of,' Miriama said. 'The worst thing you could possibly do is to lose your cool in front of the board.'

'I won't. Hang on a moment.' Aaron reached the front of the queue and paid for the sushi. 'Thank you.' He took the bowl of sushi and headed for his car. 'Are you still there, Miriama? Can you believe it? I had Corey over a barrel. Now Margaret wants to go into partnership with him.'

'Is that such a bad thing?' Miriama harrumphed down the phone. 'Then you and Corey would have to sort your differences and get on with each other.'

Aaron almost dropped his phone. That was precisely why he didn't want to see Miriama that night. He bit his lip and did his best to sound conciliatory. 'If only we could. But if we go into partnership with Corey and Jensen, we're joining the Gang too. Is that what our shareholders want?'

Silence. Aaron was tempted to say more. That he refused to let Corey trample over him again, and Corey's aggressive tactics made it clear he wasn't ready for a truce, either.

Aaron sighed. Time to end the call before they got into an argument. 'Listen, I've got to go. Love you, Miriama.'

'Love you too. Remember what I said. Stay calm. You're better than this crazy vendetta.'

Aaron put his mobile in his pocket and got into his car. Was Miriama right? Would the feud with Corey destroy both their lives? Aaron sat in the car for a few minutes before starting the engine. Should he step back and let the joint venture go through? He could always abstain from the vote—that way he could avoid jeopardising his position as CEO, but still not condone the deal. What was he thinking? Aaron shook his head and grabbed the steering wheel. He could never do business with the Gang—the Gang that had killed his father and kidnapped his mother.

The flat felt especially cold and empty when Aaron turned on the light. Where to start? The more he read the proposal document, the lower his spirits sank. This wasn't a joint venture. It was a sellout. How could Dame Cynthia, Margaret, and the rest of the board possibly sanction such a deal? Parata Peak Power would become a virtual subsidiary of Jensen Industries. Bad enough, the board hadn't supported his bid for Jensen, and now they were handing Corey their company on a plate. Aaron could just picture Corey's smug face.

Unthinkable. Aaron fired up his laptop and began to work on his rebuttal speech for the board meeting. Miriama had urged him to be open-minded and amenable. But how could he remain composed while the board took the company—*his* company—on the road to inevitable destruction?

What could he say to change their minds? Aaron typed out a few lines: *As Chief Executive Officer of Parata Peak Power, I must ask you to stand behind me on this matter. We must stand firm and united.* That was how he always started meetings, and bugger all good it did him. He deleted his introduction and started again.

A disturbing thought came to him while he struggled to find the right words. He constantly accused Corey of being a puppet of the Gang. Was Aaron just a puppet of Dame Cynthia Forbes-Hamilton and her entourage? Maybe Dame Cynthia was getting a massive payout from the Gang for selling out to Jensen. Perhaps the entire board was in on it for a backhander. But surely not Tony. His best friend could be a pain in the butt, but he had integrity. In fact, Tony was the most trustworthy and genuine person Aaron had ever met.

Two hours later, and with nothing achieved, Aaron shut down his computer and threw the uneaten sushi in the garbage. Tomorrow's performance in the boardroom would be impromptu. He would fight to the death not only for the

 David Whittet

company but also for his honour and his career. Aaron poured himself a stiff whisky before retiring to bed. He held the glass in the air and made a promise to himself. By taking on Jensen and the Gang, he would avenge his mother and father. And he would win. Aaron was in no doubt whatsoever about that.

CHAPTER TWENTY-THREE

Aaron felt like an intruder in his own company when he arrived at work the following morning. Dressed in an overcoat with an upturned collar and a scarf covering his face, he parked his car around the back and went in the trade entrance. He wanted an hour alone in his office before the board meeting to give himself a pep talk. A bold approach. That's what he needed. Remind the board of his achievements. Aaron mentally rehearsed his opening gambit.

When I joined Parata Peak Power two years ago, we were inefficient, losing money and laying off staff. All that changed when I got us the Southern Power contract. Did that sound too presumptuous? Maybe he should have asked Miriama to help him with his presentation after all. Too late now. *Since the Southern Power contract, the company has reached new heights, with increased productivity, solid investments, and profits we could only dream of a couple of years back.*

How should he address the failed Jensen takeover? The fact that the board was hell-bent on the joint venture must mean they saw his plan's potential. Aaron continued practising his pitch. *Following the success of the Southern Power deal, I proposed a takeover of Jensen Industries in an attempt to raise our revenue even further. My plan met with resistance from this board, and yet now you wish to go into partnership with them on terms that are much less favourable.*

A knock at the door interrupted Aaron's train of thought. *Damn.* It would be Tony. Well-meaning, dependable Tony, here to give him some words of encouragement before the meeting. But Aaron needed more time on his own to prepare himself.

'Go away, Tony,' Aaron shouted without getting up from his desk.

'It's not Tony. It's me. Errol Troy.'

What the hell did Errol want? Aaron had mixed feelings about Errol, his late father's business partner. They'd been close when Aaron first joined the company. Errol had championed Aaron's bid to be CEO. But since then, they'd grown apart. Aaron didn't fully trust him. Errol hadn't supported him on the Jensen takeover, but it ran deeper than that. Aaron had so many questions about his

     David Whittet

father, and as his business partner, Errol must have known the answers. But for whatever reason, Errol invariably deflected the questions. Had he something to hide?

Aaron sighed. So why was Errol at his office this morning, an hour before the board meeting? Had he come to sabotage everything?

'Come in, Errol.'

Aaron sank back in his chair as Errol entered his office with a flourish. Power-dressed in an immaculate Versace suit, Aaron was acutely aware that Errol looked more the part of a CEO than he did.

Errol settled himself into a chair. 'I just wanted you to know that I'm on your side. Whatever happens in the boardroom, I've got your back.'

Like you had when you stabbed me in the back over the Jensen takeover. Aaron forced a smile. 'Well, that's good to hear. I've got a feeling I will need all the help I can get.'

'Flexibility,' Errol said. 'That's the key to survival. Adapt to the circumstances. Reaching the top's one thing. Staying there is something quite different.'

'Can't argue with that.' Aaron ran his fingers through his hair. What was Errol after?

Errol waved a hand. 'I've lost count of how many times I've reinvented myself. That's how I've stayed at the top of my game.'

And doubtless fleeced a load of investors in the process. Aaron resisted the temptation to say the words out loud. But surely Errol hadn't come in early just to give him business advice.

Errol rubbed his hands together. 'Keep your friends close—'

Aaron finished the sentence for him. 'And your enemies closer?'

Errol nodded. 'It's the only way to survive in a cut-throat world.' He raised his head and eyeballed Aaron. 'It's what your father did, too.'

Aaron returned the hard stare. 'You've never told me about my father. Why? You must know who killed him. It was the Gang, wasn't it? The Godzone Gorillas.'

Errol paused before answering. 'I told you about the water bottling factory your father wanted to build next to the Roaring Creek Falls. He was convinced the water had unique health-giving properties and would make us a truckload of money—'

'You're wrong!' Aaron shot back. Why was Errol playing games with him? They'd been through all this before. 'I still don't believe you. My father wasn't in it for the money. He was on the verge of discovering something that would benefit all humanity.'

Errol shrugged. 'Your friend Kāterina didn't think so. She was the one that got the locals all fired up about an industrial development at the Roaring Creek Falls. Kāterina led the protest marches.'

Aaron shook his head. 'It wasn't just Kāterina. You said it was the Gang.'

'The Godzone Gorillas claimed ownership of the land. Insisted all the profits were theirs.' Errol leant forward. 'And that was your father's undoing. He got in the way of the Gang.'

Aaron kept his eyes fixed on Errol. 'So you admit it at last. The Godzone Gorillas did kill my father.'

'Your father had many enemies. Who knows which one pulled the trigger?'

Aaron snorted. 'More like who lit the fuse. My father died in an arson attack.'

Errol waved a hand. 'I used the term metaphorically.'

Aaron pulled back. What was the point of talking to Errol? He wasn't going to learn anything he didn't know already. And it was wasting vital time he should have been using to rehearse his speech to the board. Aaron had abandoned all hope of getting anything meaningful from Errol years ago.

'But someone pulled the trigger at your parents' wedding,' Errol continued. 'I know you don't believe—'

'That was Mickey,' Aaron interrupted. 'He tried to kill my mother in a fit of jealousy. He couldn't bear her marrying someone else.'

'That's what the police thought—at first. But they couldn't pin it on Mickey or anyone else in the Gang.'

Aaron tapped his fingers on the desktop. 'I bet it was one of their bent lawyers who got them off.'

'Maybe.' Errol edged closer to Aaron. 'Is there still no news of your mother?'

'No.' Aaron sighed. 'I've spent a fortune on private detectives. I don't suppose I'll ever know the truth.'

'Don't give up hope.' Errol extended a hand across the desk. 'I was very fond of your mother.'

 David Whittet

'I know. You were good to her after my father was killed.' Whatever Troy's recent transgressions, Aaron was thankful to him for being there for his mother. 'I'll always be grateful for that.'

'I wish I could have done more.'

Aaron hesitated, inwardly regretting allowing Errol to drag him back into painful memories. 'When I was little, Kāterina promised she'd find my mother. I used to read to her when I was a boy. She said we'd start the search when I finished reading *Great Expectations* to her. But we never got to the end.'

Errol leant back. 'Kāterina Kururangi. She was a thorn in your father's side. Mine too. Used her influence to block some of our best business deals.'

Aaron frowned. 'She's a wise woman. She wouldn't have done that without good reason.'

Errol's expression dulled. 'She cost me dear, that's for sure. Thank goodness she's not on those government think tanks any longer.'

Aaron glared back at him. 'She's been a good friend to me.'

Errol rubbed his chin. 'I grant you, she was good in a crisis. She was at your parents' wedding. She called the ambulance while everyone else was panicking.'

A warm feeling spread through Aaron's body. That was so typical of Kāterina. Always calm and composed while everyone else fell apart. 'Kāterina put up the money for me to go to university. I owe everything to her.'

Errol caught his breath. 'Kāterina? You never told me she was your sponsor. I thought—'

Aaron cut him off. 'She's been my guardian angel.'

Before Errol could reply, there was another knock at the door, and a voice boomed from the other side.

'Hi, Aaron. It's Tony here. Margaret and Steven have arrived and they're heading for the boardroom. We should get in there too.'

'Okay, Tony,' Aaron shouted back. 'We're coming.'

Aaron picked up his board papers and laptop and made for the door.

Errol followed and put a hand on Aaron's shoulder. 'I met this guy at the Rotary Club the other week. He's an ace private eye with a fantastic reputation. Solved that notorious missing person case in Blenheim last year. Why don't we get him to find your mother?'

Aaron kept walking. 'I've had it with private detectives. They're all full of empty promises. I don't want any more false hope.'

Errol chased after him. 'Think about it. The offer's open.'

Aaron still wasn't sure if he trusted Errol. Did that matter anyway? What if Errol could succeed where he'd failed and find his mother? But Errol was always full of himself—and full of shit. If he'd been that close to Alicia, how come he didn't know about her disappearance?

One thing was sure—Errol's visit had sabotaged his preparation for the board meeting. Maybe that was his plan all along.

Aaron felt everyone's eyes close in on him when he took his seat at the head of the boardroom table. Without a doubt, this was the most crucial meeting of his career to date. From their smug looks, it appeared the board knew it as much as he did. Aaron didn't bother to fire up his laptop or refer to his notes. He'd no intention of *reinventing* himself, but today he would be spontaneous and speak from the heart.

'Parata Peak Power stands at a crossroads,' Aaron began, eyeing each board member in turn. 'We have a stark choice ahead of us. Either we remain an independent company and keep our integrity, or we get into bed with the Gang. It's as simple as that. Honesty versus corruption. Make no mistake, we cannot reverse this decision once made.'

'We're not getting into bed with the Gang,' Steven said. 'We're planning a joint venture.'

Aaron glared at Steven. 'You know as well as I do that the Godzone Gorillas bankroll Jensen Industries. With blood money. If we go into partnership with them, we're tarred with the same brush.'

'Have you even read the proposal?' Margaret snapped. 'The joint venture will be ring-fenced.'

Aaron waved the file in the air. 'Of course I've read it. But if you think you can distance yourself from the Godzone Gorillas with a few exclusion clauses in the contract, you don't know the Gang.'

 David Whittet

'Our legal counsel has gone through this proposal with a fine-tooth comb,' Steven said. 'He's assured us there'll be no repercussions.'

Then our legal counsel's as stupid as the rest of you. Aaron bit his tongue. 'A legal opinion is one thing. But when have the Godzone Gorillas ever cared about the law? Go ahead with this deal, and they'll walk right over us.'

Margaret raised an eyebrow. 'Really? Are you sure you're not just upset that you'll have to work with your old rival, Corey O'Connor?'

Damn you, Margaret. Aaron took a moment to compose himself. 'That's not it at all … but you must understand … Corey is nothing but a stooge for the Godzone Gorillas.'

'Nonsense,' Margaret said. 'I've met Corey O'Connor, and he's a decent young man. You could learn a thing or two from him.'

Aaron gulped. Margaret had met with Corey behind his back? Aaron opened his mouth, but nothing came out.

'Can't you see, Aaron?' Margaret continued. 'We're getting everything you wanted from the takeover with none of the financial risks. How many times have you told us that Jensen offers us a tremendous opportunity to expand our client base? With a carefully structured agreement defining clear lines of responsibility and providing appropriate safeguards, we get all those benefits without fighting the Gang in a hostile takeover.'

Aaron shook his head. 'It'll destroy us.'

Margaret glared at him through her thick-rimmed glasses. 'Then please explain how your takeover plan would have been any different. We'd have been in open warfare with the Gang.'

Aaron felt his throat close up. *Stay calm. Think before you speak.*

'Well?' Margaret tapped her fingers on the table. 'Nothing to say, Aaron?'

'My proposal …' Aaron cleared his throat. 'A takeover would have seen Jensen cut all its ties with the Godzone Gorillas. Jensen would have been entirely under our control. If we go ahead with the joint venture, the Gang will infiltrate our company and before we know it, the Godzone Gorillas will take full control of Parata Peak Power. Then we'll all be out of a job.'

Margaret sighed. 'Do I have to repeat myself?' She held up the proposal document. 'We have checks and balances in place.'

Aaron couldn't hold back. 'And how many times do I have to tell you that means nothing to the Gang?'

'You may be CEO of this company,' Margaret said, 'but you do not have the power of veto. Now I suggest we continue and appoint our observer to the Jensen board.'

An observer? Aaron shook his head. That wasn't in the proposal. How dare they go behind his back?

'I'd like to put myself forward for the role,' Errol said.

So Errol Troy was in on this too. Aaron drew back. He was right not to trust him.

'Are you sure you have the diplomacy for the task?' Steven said.

'Wait a minute,' Aaron interrupted. 'Have we stooped so low that we have to spy on our competitors?'

'It's part of due diligence,' Margaret said. 'We appoint an observer to their board, and they will do the same.'

Aaron flung his hands in the air. 'So you're giving Jensen free rein to spy on us?'

'No,' Margaret said. 'We're allowing them an observer on our board.'

Aaron closed his eyes and lowered his head. *How naïve can you get?* The board was playing into the Gang's hands. 'Believe me. This won't end well. They'll trample all over us.'

Margaret rapped the table again. 'What did I say about checks and balances?'

'Aaron's got a point,' Tony said. 'If Jensen are privy to all our deliberations, they'll be at a competitive advantage.'

Thank God for Tony. At least someone else on the board had a modicum of sense.

'Whenever we have sensitive issues to discuss,' Margaret said, 'we will ask the observer to leave and wait outside. Now, Tony, I think you are the ideal candidate for our observer on the Jensen board.'

Aaron watched Tony squirm. 'I'm not sure ...'

'Of course you are,' Margaret said. 'Everyone trusts you.'

'I appreciate your faith in me ...' Tony's voice petered out. 'I'm just ... not sure I'd be right for this.'

     David Whittet

Aaron caught his eye. 'Go for it, Tony. If we must have someone spying on Jensen, I want it to be you.'

Aaron closed the meeting and disappeared as surreptitiously as he'd arrived that morning. At least it hadn't come to a vote of no confidence in his leadership. And Tony with a place on the Jensen board! Aaron felt a sudden flutter in his heart. Tony would be his very own undercover agent in his enemy's camp. Armed with inside knowledge, Aaron would expose Corey's crooked dealings and prove he was nothing but a puppet of the Gang.

Sweet revenge! Aaron couldn't resist calling Miriama the moment he was out of the building. 'The buggers think they've got one over on me. Big mistake. They'll be laughing on the other side of their faces when I've finished with them.'

CHAPTER TWENTY-FOUR

Where the hell was Tony? Aaron had been awake most of the night, desperate to get the lowdown on Tony's first board meeting at Jensen Industries. Tony wouldn't give anything away when Aaron rang him last night.

'Mate, I'm dead on my feet,' Tony had said. 'We'll talk in the morning.'

'You can't do this to me,' Aaron had groaned. 'At least tell me you've got something on Corey.'

'Tomorrow,' Tony had insisted.

'My office. Nine tomorrow. No excuses.'

Nine thirty and still no sign of him. Trust Tony to be late today of all days.

Aaron checked his mobile for messages. Nothing. He picked up the office phone and buzzed his secretary. 'Any sign of Tony? He was supposed to be here at nine sharp.'

'No,' his secretary replied. 'I haven't seen Mr Roche this morning.'

Damn. 'Okay. Thank you, Sandy. Send him through as soon as he arrives. Then see to it that we're not disturbed.'

The minutes dragged past on the office clock. Had Tony slept in? Or broken down on the way to work? Aaron flicked him a text: *WTF Tony! Get your arse in here!*

Aaron fiddled with a paperclip while he waited for a reply.

SRY M8 Held up. ETA 15 min.

Aaron sighed. At least that meant Tony was on his way. Aaron went through the emails on his computer and shook his head. They were all about the partnership with Jensen. He could only hope that Tony had got him some ammunition. Bored with the emails, Aaron gazed at the Parata Peak Dam through the window. *Clean, raw energy.* Hydroelectric power, with its pounding water, still cast a spell on him, and no way would he let Corey take that away from him. *Please let Tony have found some dirt on the bastard.*

Nine forty-five, and at last, Tony bustled into the office.

'About bloody time,' Aaron said. 'I've been sweating buckets waiting for you.'

　　　　David Whittet

'Sorry, but … I'm a bit uneasy about this meeting.' Tony pulled up a chair and sat down on the edge of the seat. 'I'm not sure I should discuss this with you before talking to Margaret.'

Aaron leant forward. 'I am the CEO of Parata Peak Power. Not Margaret. Now spill, Tony.'

'Okay. I suppose.' Tony cleared his throat. 'You probably don't want to hear this, but Jensen's board meeting was like a rerun of our last one.'

Aaron pulled back. 'What?'

Tony settled into his chair. 'Same old arguments about which company will come out on top, Jensen or Parata Peak Power. Corey put forward exactly the same arguments as you did—and got the same response from the board. In fact, I could have closed my eyes and believed it was you talking, not Corey.' Tony raised his head and met Aaron's eyes. 'You're so alike. It's uncanny.'

'Bullshit!' Aaron flapped his hand. 'I want to know exactly what he said.'

'He said you have a price—'

Aaron jolted upright. 'Corey's put a price on my head? I told you the bastard was after my blood!'

Tony shook his head. 'Why do you always jump to conclusions? Corey wanted Jensen to raise the money to buy you out.'

'A likely story.' Aaron felt his muscles tense. 'Anyway, I'm not for sale. No amount of blood money from the Gang will see me back down.'

Tony shrugged. 'The Jensen board didn't like the idea either. One of the women, Amanda, I think they called her, said the feud was bleeding the company dry. "I urge you to make your peace with Aaron without delay," she said. "Before you bankrupt us all."'

'Fat chance of that,' Aaron shot back.

Tony sighed. 'That's exactly what Corey said. But Amanda didn't let it go. "Why can't you just put the squabble behind you and put this sorry business to rest once and for all?" she said. "Just pick up the phone and talk to Aaron."'

Aaron felt his cheeks burn. 'I'd have given the bastard a piece of my mind if he had.'

Tony gave him a stern look. 'Calm down!'

How can I, with Corey and the Gang out to ruin me? Aaron took a sharp breath. 'There are Gang members on the Jensen board. I know that for a fact. You must have seen them.'

Tony paused for a moment. 'There was one bloke. Tattoos all over his face and neck, and a voice as loud as his shirt.'

'That sounds like the Godzone Gorillas. What is his name?'

Tony rubbed his chin. 'Kaine, I think they called him.'

'Kaine!' Aaron leapt out of his chair. 'That's the bastard who had my mother put away.'

'How do you know that?'

Aaron paced around the office. 'A couple of years back, I hired a truckload of private detectives to try and find my mother. Most of them were useless. One guy, Sullivan, was the best of the bunch. Sullivan dredged up an ex-gangster called Gerry, who'd belonged to the Godzone Gorillas. Gerry said Kaine was judge and jury at my mother's trial.'

'Oh, Aaron, mate, I'm sorry!'

Aaron clenched a fist. 'I could kill Kaine for what he did to my mother, and now he's in league with Corey.'

'I don't think there was any love lost between them,' Tony said. 'Kaine gave Corey a rough ride.'

Aaron sat down again. 'Tell me more.'

Tony frowned. 'I overheard them after the meeting. Kaine laid into Corey. I didn't catch it all, but it went something like this,' he began.

'"The Gang means more than your petty vendetta," Kaine said. "Aaron's a jumped-up half-blood. Forget about the bastard."

'Next thing, I heard Corey groaning. "Get off me! You don't understand …"

'"You understand this, Corey," Kaine said. "Nothing stops the Godzone Gorillas. *Nothing*. Not you, Corey. Not that miserable half-blood either. Nobody stops us."'

'That proves my point. The Godzone Gorillas control Jensen Industries.' Aaron waved a hand at Tony. 'And we want to go into partnership with them. It beggars belief.'

Tony drew back. 'Corey clearly wants Kaine out. Actually, I think Corey's trying to clean up the board. You should work together instead of fighting each other.'

        David Whittet

Aaron felt his blood pressure skyrocket. He counted to ten before replying. 'Me? Work with the thug who tried to punch my lights out when we were kids? You've got to be kidding.'

Tony rubbed his chin. 'But that was ages ago. Can't you forgive and forget? What if he's changed since then?'

'Gangsters don't change.' Aaron glared at Tony. 'Corey even tried to steal my place at business school. The bastard badmouthed me to the university, then tried to bribe them to take him instead of me. Damn near stitched me up.'

'Don't forget, Corey didn't have a fairy godmother like you did. There was no Kāterina to pay for him to get a university education.'

Aaron snorted. 'Corey didn't need to go to university. Not with the Gang bankrolling him and buying his place at Jensen.'

'I still think you should put your differences behind you for the company's good.' Tony looked at his watch and stood up. 'You'll have to excuse me. I've got a meeting with Margaret at eleven, and I'll be recommending that you and Corey go to mediation.'

Tony was out of the door before Aaron could reply. *Mediation!* What planet was Tony on?

An hour later, Tony was back in his office with Margaret at his side. What had they been plotting?

'Tony has briefed me on the Jensen board meeting,' Margaret said. 'It is clear that our two companies have the potential to work together on a profitable joint venture.'

Aaron shook his head. 'I can't believe you're suggesting we partner with the Godzone Gorillas.'

'We are not doing business with the Gang,' Margaret said. 'We're negotiating a deal with Jensen Industries.'

Aaron scowled. 'Same thing.'

'That's not true,' Margaret said. 'Thanks to Tony, we have firsthand intelligence. The only Gang member on the board is Kaine, and Corey is as keen to get rid of him as you are.'

'Nonsense!' Aaron protested. 'They're all puppets of the Godzone Gorillas.'

'They are not!' Margaret waved a hand in Aaron's face. 'Corey is determined to clean up Jensen's image. You should support him. That's why I'm taking up Tony's suggestion of mediation between the two of you.'

Judas! Aaron glared at Tony. 'I will not mediate with a gangster.'

'Come on, Aaron,' Tony said. 'Corey's trying to do the right thing. You should too.'

Aaron flinched. 'Cosying up with the Godzone Gorillas is *not* doing the right thing. I can't believe either of you are hell-bent on doing business with the most vicious gang in New Zealand. Believe me, it won't end well.' He eyeballed Tony. 'You heard Kaine ranting. He'll never relinquish control of Jensen. Don't forget either, it was Gang money that bought Corey his place as CEO.'

Margaret returned his glare. 'We won't take any nonsense from them. You may let the Gang walk all over you, but not me.'

'That was unkind, Margaret,' Tony said.

'Maybe it was,' Margaret replied. 'But I've stood up to lowlifes before and won.' She turned to Aaron. 'Which is why you *will* go to mediation.'

Aaron felt his chest tighten. 'What if I won't?'

Margaret shrugged. 'Then you'll force me to recommend a vote of no confidence in you as CEO of Parata Peak Power.'

A vote of no confidence. Aaron had dreaded the words for so long that they took a moment to sink in. He could scarcely bear to listen to Tony's platitudes.

'Listen, mate.' Tony edged towards him. 'Trust me. It won't be that bad. I'll be with you as your support person.'

'Miles Mayhew, our legal counsel, will be with you too,' Margaret said. 'And believe me, he won't stand for any of the Gang's antics.'

Miles Mayhew. He was an old fart, and Corey would have him under his thumb in no time.

Aaron had started the day with such hope. Now he just wanted it to end. He couldn't bring himself to speak to anyone—not even Miriama. Aaron sent her a text: *Working late tonight. Talk tomorrow.* As he pressed the send button, a message arrived from Margaret: *Mediation fixed for next Thursday in Wellington.*

How had it come to this? Had Corey really changed? Or was Margaret setting him up to fail? Maybe she knew the joint venture would end in disaster, and he

     David Whittet

would cop the blame as CEO. Was Margaret that devious? Aaron shuddered. Of course she was—she'd do anything to get his job. Aaron was equally determined she wouldn't have it. He pumped his fist. *Bring on the mediation! I'll show the bastards what I'm made of!*

CHAPTER TWENTY-FIVE

A blast of wind buffeted the Air New Zealand A320 aircraft on its approach to Wellington Airport. Aaron glanced out of the window at the forbidding grey sky, the wild sea and the bleak Wellington landscape. Squashed between Tony and Miles Mayhew on the packed flight, Aaron could scarcely breathe. An inauspicious start to what threatened to be an even more depressing day. Corey had won round one when they were kids and round two when he thwarted the takeover bid. Aaron shuddered. Would Corey win the next round at mediation today?

Aaron's sense of foreboding continued when the taxi pulled up at the stark, faceless building that housed the mediation service. His heart pounded faster by the minute as the mediation staff led them through the maze of corridors.

'Chin up,' Tony said. 'I've got your back.'

Why wasn't that reassuring?

'Don't forget what I told you,' Miles said. 'Whatever happens, don't rise to the bait.'

Miles had banged on about not letting Corey goad him and get the upper hand.

Aaron sighed. 'I won't.'

But would he? Aaron had no idea how he'd react when he set eyes on his nemesis. In fact, Aaron kept expecting to bump into Corey each time they turned a corner in the labyrinthine building.

Half an hour in the waiting room at the mediation offices listening to Tony's small talk, and Aaron was beside himself. Where the hell was Corey?

'Tactics,' Miles said, thumbing through his papers for the umpteenth time. 'It's a well-known ploy. Arrive late and make your opponent sweat. But we're wise to their tricks, aren't we?'

Aaron shuffled in his chair. What could he say? He knew how he felt. *If I sit here much longer, I'll explode. And when the bastard finally shows up, I'll wring his bloody neck.*

Tony put a hand on Aaron's shoulder and answered for him. 'Corey can try it on, but he won't rattle us.'

He already has. Aaron pulled away. *Can't you see?* But then again, Tony never was much good at reading body language.

Voices echoed through the corridors.

'I'm sorry, sir, but we do not permit gang patches on our premises. I must ask you to leave.'

'Going to make me, are you? You and whose army?'

A giant of a man with a full-facial tattoo and a patched jacket burst into the waiting room, followed by two men in suits and a frustrated mediation staff member.

Tony pointed to the tattooed man and whispered in Aaron's ear. 'That's Kaine.'

The bastard who put my mother away. Aaron fought the temptation to get up and throttle Kaine. As he struggled to control himself, Aaron caught the eye of the second man in the Jensen entourage. *Corey. I'd know the smug bastard's face anywhere*. Aaron had to admit that Corey had cleaned up well since they last met face-to-face as kids. With a trendy suit and a floral silk tie, Corey appeared super smooth. Aaron straightened his tie and buttoned his jacket. He'd never done cool. Or smart.

The mediation staffer tried to block Kaine from getting any further. 'I asked you to leave. Do I have to call security?'

'Kaine has every right to be here,' Corey said. 'He's my right-hand man.'

Aaron glared at Tony and hissed in his ear. 'I thought you said Corey wanted Kaine out. The two of them are in it together. Up to their necks.'

A smartly dressed woman emerged from the conference room. 'What's going on out here?' she asked.

The staffer pointed to Kaine. 'This man is a gang member. I have asked him to leave.'

The third man in the Jensen team stepped forward. 'Good morning, madam. I am Lance Everson, the legal counsel for Jensen Industries. I must insist that Kaine stays. He is the vice president of Jensen Industries.'

'And vice president of the Godzone Gorillas, I believe,' Miles said.

Aaron sprang to his feet and glared at Tony and Miles. 'I told you this was just an attempt by the Gang to take over our company. We're leaving now.'

'Hold on,' Miles said. 'We have to see this through. Margaret gave me strict instructions—'

'Damn Margaret!' Aaron shook his head. 'We do not do business with the Gang.'

Miles scowled back. 'We are here to do business with Jensen Industries, not the Godzone Gorillas.'

It's the same thing, and you know it. Aaron wanted to say it out loud, but Miles gave him a firm nudge. Why was Margaret so hell-bent on this joint venture? Was she beholden to the Gang too?

The woman clapped her hands to get everyone's attention. 'My name is Valerie Goodman and I will be your mediator.' She turned to Kaine and eyed his Gang patches. 'Very well. But if you are to stay, I must insist you remove your jacket. Gang regalia is strictly forbidden in this building.'

Kaine took off his jacket and handed it to the staffer.

'He can't take the Godzone Gorillas tattoo off his face,' Aaron muttered as he followed the rest of them into the conference room.

Aaron sat on the edge of his seat as they gathered around the mediation table. Corey leant back in his chair and crossed his legs. He was also chewing gum. Aaron almost dropped his laptop as he pulled it out of his briefcase. Why couldn't he relax like his adversary?

Valerie Goodman cleared her throat. 'As I said, I will be your facilitator for the mediation. I would like to begin with a short mihi—'

'Cut the crap,' Corey interrupted. 'I don't need this. The sooner we finish this pantomime and get out of here, the better.'

Valerie tapped her fingers on the table. 'This may be a waste of time for you, Mr O'Connor, but in my experience, taking a few moments to clear our heads before starting is time well spent.'

Aaron couldn't resist a grin and a sideways glance at Corey. *That put you in your place, you ignorant bastard.*

Corey didn't answer. He spat out his chewing gum and opened a new packet.

Valerie lowered her head and closed her eyes. 'May our deliberations be wise and our decisions fair and just. Let us put all our prejudices and preconceived ideas behind us as we strive to reach a solution that meets all our needs.'

 David Whittet

Fine words, Aaron thought, but how could he possibly reach an agreement with the Godzone Gorillas—the Gang that had taken both his parents away from him?

Valerie looked up and opened a file. 'Let me begin by outlining the problem as I see it. We have two companies that wish to partner in a joint venture. Parata Peak Power hopes to grow its operation and expand its customer base. Jensen Industries, on the other hand, has a diverse portfolio. They are keen to raise their profile in the power industry.'

Aaron shook his head. *No. Corey just wants to use Jensen Industries to destroy me.*

'So what is stopping the partnership?' Valerie continued. 'On paper, the deal makes sense for both parties.' She eyed Aaron and Corey in turn. 'All that stands in the way is a longstanding conflict between the CEOs of the two companies.'

Corey snorted. 'A conflict? More like a duel to the death.'

Valerie gritted her teeth. 'That kind of talk is not helpful, Mr O'Connor.'

'Isn't it?' Corey lunged across the table at Aaron. 'This little shit tried to take over my company and have me thrown out. Now the son of a bitch will get what's coming to him when I control his company.'

Valerie glared at Corey. 'I will not have that language in my offices. And I repeat, such talk is counterproductive.'

Corey smirked. 'Good. I told you this whole charade was a waste of time.'

Valerie's jaw dropped. 'Mr O'Connor! I must—'

'Let's get this over with.' Corey stood up and eyeballed Aaron. 'Are you a man? Dare you meet me in private?'

Aaron shrank back. 'In private? Why? What have you got to hide?'

'Too chicken to come and find out, are you?' Corey rolled his eyes. 'You're still that scared little boy, clinging to an old gypsy woman for protection. I taught you a lesson then. You're about to get another one now.'

'I'm not afraid of you, Corey,' Aaron said. 'Tony said you were trying to clean things up. He was wrong. You're still a shameless gangster.'

Corey sneered and held up a piece of paper. 'And you'll always be a half-blood.'

Aaron had watched Corey doodling on his notepad. His fists clenched when he saw the caricature Corey had sketched. Aaron was on a cross, crucified by the

Gang. *Bastard! Who the hell does he think he is?* Aaron closed his eyes and covered them with his hands. His mind went back to the night the men took his mother away. She'd read him the story about David and Goliath and had told him to be brave like David. Now Aaron was facing his own enemy, his own Goliath. He took a deep breath and then unmasked his face. 'Okay, Corey. We meet alone.'

Miles raised a hand. 'I strongly advise against this.' He turned to Lance Everson. 'Mr Casper will not countenance such an irregular request. Nor will he take part in any meeting without my presence.'

'He's got a point,' Lance said to Corey. 'Best to keep everything out in the open.'

'No, wait,' Aaron said. 'Corey and I have issues to sort out. The mediation will go much better if we get them out of the way.'

Miles shook his head and caught Valerie's eye. 'Would you mind if I had a few words with my client?'

'Please do,' Valerie said. 'I would be most uncomfortable about those two—'

'Bullshit!' Corey interrupted. 'Is the mighty Aaron Casper incapable of making up his own mind? Bunch of tossers, the lot of you!'

'I've warned you about your language, Mr O'Connor,' Valerie said. 'Your behaviour is wholly inappropriate. Any more, and I'll ask you to leave.'

'Then you'll have failed at your job.' Corey gave her the finger. 'I saw the paparazzi waiting outside. You're dying to make a statement about how you negotiated a landmark deal in the power industry.'

Lance pulled Corey back. 'This isn't helping.'

'It certainly is not,' Valerie said. 'We'll adjourn for half an hour to give Mr Mayhew a chance to talk with his client.'

Aaron scanned the street when they stepped out of the building to have a coffee at a nearby café. No sign of the paparazzi. What was Corey on about? Aaron shrugged. *More of Corey's lies.*

'Listen, Aaron,' Miles said, 'I can see how Corey winds you up. But meeting with him in private. That's asking for trouble.'

Aaron took a sip of coffee. 'I'm not going to have fisticuffs with him, if that's what you're thinking.'

'I should hope not,' Miles said. 'But things could get mighty ugly.'

'At least let me come with you,' Tony said.

     David Whittet

'You?' Aaron spluttered on a mouthful of coffee. 'Remind me, Tony. What did you say about Corey? How he'd changed. How he'd turned over a new leaf—'

'I thought he had,' Tony said.

'Well, he hasn't. He's the same bastard who beat me up when we were kids.' Aaron slurped the last of his coffee. 'Besides, if you come with me, Tony, he'll insist on bringing Kaine. Then there *will* be fisticuffs. I promise you.'

Miles sighed. 'Is there anything I can say that'll make you change your mind?'

'No.' Aaron moved towards the door. 'Let's get this over and done with.'

Aaron led the way back into the conference room. *Game on, Corey! I've waited long enough for revenge!*

Valerie raised her eyebrows at Miles. 'Have you dissuaded your client from such a foolish course of action?'

Miles shrugged. 'I'm afraid not. Once Aaron makes up his mind—'

Damn right! Aaron was fed up with Miles making apologies for him.

Corey grinned at Miles. 'Well, Mr Mayhew. It appears your client has some balls even if you haven't!'

'I think you need to find our clients a private room,' Lance said. 'Now, if you'll excuse me, I need another drink. And this time, it won't be coffee.'

'You and me both,' Kaine said. 'I need a beer and another fag.' He turned to Corey. 'Remember what I told you? We don't want any cock-ups.'

What did that mean? Aaron shuddered. Maybe this private meeting wasn't as spontaneous as Corey made out. Was there a hidden agenda that was not being revealed?

'Are you sure you're alright?' Tony asked. 'You've gone quite pale.'

'Don't worry about me,' Aaron said. 'I can look after myself.'

The staffer arrived to escort Aaron and Corey to a private meeting room. Miles and Valerie followed them down the corridor. Aaron strained his ears to hear what they were saying.

'I fear we're in for a long wait,' Miles said. 'Where do you recommend we go for some lunch?'

'You won't go wrong with any of the eateries around here,' Valerie said. 'Let's hope they won't be too long. I was hoping to wrap this up by the end of the day.'

'I wouldn't be too sure of that,' Miles said. 'Sometimes I despair of my client.'

'The two of them behave like spoilt children,' Valerie said. 'I could bang their frigging heads together!'

Bloody cheek! Aaron turned back and scowled at both of them.

❧

Aaron shuddered as the assistant led them to what must have been the dingiest room in the building. He wasn't usually claustrophobic, but being confined in this windowless cell with his arch-enemy brought him out in a cold sweat. His heart missed a beat when the assistant left and closed the door behind her.

Corey slouched into his chair and put his feet on the table. 'So we meet again after all these years. You haven't changed. You'll always be a half-cast. And a loser.'

You haven't changed either. You're still a cold-blooded bully. Aaron sat down opposite him and bit his tongue before replying. 'Is this why you've got me here, Corey? To trade insults?'

'Fancy yourself as a business leader, do you?' Corey spat out yet another piece of chewing gum. 'Just look at you. Dressed in your Sunday best, and you can't even get your tie right!'

Aaron clenched his fists under the table. It was true—for all his success, Aaron had never mastered the art of knotting his tie. He wanted to hit back with a one-liner. *You may wear a designer suit, Corey, but you're still a gangster.* Better not to inflame things. Tony and Miles had implored him to stay calm. 'Listen, Corey. This kind of talk is getting us nowhere—'

Before he could finish, Corey jumped up and grabbed Aaron's tie.

'Allow me,' Corey said. 'I'll show you how to knot your tie.'

Aaron shoved Corey away. 'Get off me, you bastard.'

Corey sat down again with a snigger and put his feet back on the table. 'Perhaps you still need that old gypsy woman to help get you dressed.'

Aaron seethed. 'How dare you? Kāterina is an exceptional woman—'

'Really?' Corey rolled his eyes. 'I heard she was a useless has-been and as mad as a hatter.'

 David Whittet

Aaron thumped the table. Any pretence of keeping his cool had just disappeared. 'Then you thought wrong. She's been a force for good for her people. But of course, that wouldn't mean anything to you.'

'So what?' Corey shot back. 'She bent a few politician's ears. That doesn't make her exceptional.'

Aaron shook his head. 'She's done far more than that. She's fought for Māori women's rights and made a difference to countless lives.'

Corey leant forward. 'You didn't do too badly out of her either, did you?'

How did he know that? Aaron glared back at Corey. 'Yes, Kāterina put me through business school. At least I didn't use gang money to get where I am.'

Corey tipped his head back. 'And I did? What makes you think I needed the Gang to back me?'

'Come off it, Corey. We all know you're just a puppet of the Godzone Gorillas.'

Corey scoffed. 'You really believe that shit, don't you? Well, hear this. I'm my own man.'

'Like hell!' Aaron gave him the finger. 'I should have gobbled you up when I had the chance. Gobbled you up and spat you out.'

'But your miserable takeover plan failed, didn't it? What went wrong? Board didn't support you? Perhaps you are the puppet, my friend.'

Corey's self-satisfied smile drove Aaron to distraction.

'Damn you, Corey!'

'Now I'm about to take over your company.' Corey chuckled and rubbed his hands together. 'Make no mistake. Once this deal goes through, I *will* control both our companies. Perhaps I should gobble *you* up and spit *you* out.'

'In your dreams! The Gang will control both companies—not you.' Aaron held up his hands. 'Can't you see? The moment we sign the contract, the Godzone Gorillas with take over the entire operation, and we'll both be history.'

'You, maybe,' Corey said. 'But not me. I'm far too valuable for that.'

Aaron leapt to his feet. 'So you admit it? You *are* the Gang's stooge.'

Corey shrugged.

'Blood money! That's what's behind this deal! Blood money! The Gang murdered my father! Kidnapped my mother! Blood money!' Aaron stormed out of the room and slammed the door. He continued shouting as he bolted down the corridor. 'Blood money! BLOOD MONEY!'

CHAPTER TWENTY-SIX

This time, the paparazzi were lying in wait when Aaron tore out onto the street. Camera lenses and pulsating flashlights almost blinded him. Reporters fired a barrage of questions at him.

'In a hurry to leave, Mr Casper? Have negotiations broken down?'

'Why the rush? Not getting your own way this time, Mr Casper?'

'Will this deal mean higher power costs for consumers? What have you to say to your customers?'

'Are you just lining the pockets of your shareholders?'

'Or maybe filling the Gang's coffers. We saw a patched member of the Godzone Gorillas arrive with Mr O'Connor.'

'Is it true that Jensen has gang affiliations?'

Aaron pushed his way through the media scrum. 'I will not be making a statement until the deal is finalised.'

'When will that be?'

Never, if I had my way. Aaron ducked his head and kept walking. 'You'll just have to wait.'

So even the reporters had worked out that he was about to make a pact with the devil. Aaron cursed himself for making such a dramatic exit after his showdown with Corey. The press would have a field day. Aaron pictured tomorrow's headlines: *Aaron Casper storms out of mediation. Do the Godzone Gorillas have the upper hand in power industry negotiations?*

Aaron shook off the last of the reporters and made for the waterfront. What did it matter? If they went with a story like that, at least it would bring Jensen's gang connections out into the open. Maybe that would be enough to make Dame Cynthia and Margaret reconsider. Unless they were both beholden to the Gang.

What would Miles and Tony say when he didn't return? How would they explain his absence to the mediator? What would Corey say about their confrontation?

Aaron smiled to himself. Miles would find a way of putting a positive spin on it. He always did.

The smile disappeared when his mobile rang.

'Hello, Miles.'

'Where the hell are you?' Miles hissed down the phone line.

'Sorry. I just needed to get some air.'

'You left me in an impossible situation. Corey looked like he'd just won the lotto. And I had to grovel to Valerie Goodman. You can't imagine what it was like.'

I can. 'I didn't mean to land you in it.' Aaron's smile crept back. 'But I'm sure you handled it perfectly, Miles.'

'Tony's freaking out. He's scared you might top yourself.'

Dear Tony. A good friend and always so earnest. 'Tell Tony I'm fine.' Aaron waited for the pedestrian light to turn green before crossing the road. 'Don't worry, I won't do anything stupid. I wouldn't give Corey the satisfaction.'

'We've adjourned until ten tomorrow morning,' Miles said. 'Promise me you'll be there.'

'I promise.' Aaron reached the waterfront. 'Now, if you'll excuse me, I'm going to meet Miriama. She's flying into Wellington this afternoon to provide moral support. You sound like you need a drink. Get one for Tony from me while you're at it.'

❧

There she was. Sat on a bench at the quay, reading a book.

Aaron ran towards her. 'Miriama!'

She looked up from her book. 'You're early! I wasn't expecting you for another couple of hours.'

Aaron hugged her. 'I know. Things got a bit … heated. I left before we'd finished.'

Miriama pulled back. 'You mean you walked out of the meeting? What did I tell you about keeping a level head?'

'I know. I know.' Aaron held out a hand defensively. If it wasn't Tony telling him to stay calm, it was Miriama. 'It's not how it sounds. Corey insisted on meeting me in private.'

Miriama raised an eyebrow. 'And you agreed?'

'I had to. Otherwise, Corey would have thought I was chicken.'

Miriama shook her head. 'You men and your egos.'

Aaron glanced out over the harbour. How could he make Miriama understand? 'Kaine was there. The gangster who put my mother away.'

'Oh, Aaron. I'm sorry.' Miriama put an arm on his shoulder. 'But what was a member of the Godzone Gorillas doing at the mediation?'

Aaron sighed. 'The Gang controls Jensen. How many times do I have to tell you that?'

'I know you have, but … I mean … I thought …' Miriama dribbled to a standstill.

You didn't believe me until today. Aaron pinned her with his eyes. 'Kaine is vice president of both the Godzone Gorillas and Jensen Industries. What more proof could you have?'

Miriama hesitated. 'If that's true … I think you should …'

'What?'

Miriama took a long, harsh breath. 'Maybe you should get out of Parata Peak Power.'

You've got to be kidding. Aaron threw his arms in the air. 'Leave the company I've built up from nothing? And just when I've reached the top.'

'I don't want you tarred with the Gang's brush.'

'Don't worry. I won't be.' Aaron stood up and walked across the quay. 'The Gang will be history when I've finished with them.'

Miriama followed him to the shoreline. 'Get real. You can't take on the Godzone Gorillas single-handedly.'

Want to bet? I can and I will. Aaron met her eyes. 'I've got a plan. Corey brought Kaine with him to freak me out. But I'm smarter than them. I'll wipe the smirk off their faces. Just you wait and see.'

'What if it's a trap?' Miriama grabbed his arm. 'You've fought so hard for your reputation. I won't let you throw it away just to get one up on Corey.'

Aaron cursed under his breath. Why had he told Miriama he was plotting something? Whose side was she on, anyway? 'Listen, Miriama. It isn't just about Corey and the Gang. Sure, I could kill Kaine for what he did to my mother—'

'I understand why you hate him. Of course I do.' Miriama tightened her grip on his arm. 'I'm just scared you're going to get hurt all over again.'

'I was about to say I'm not doing this out of vengeance.' Aaron broke eye contact. What was he saying? He was determined Kaine and Corey would pay for what they had done. 'But Kaine turning up to mediation—I can turn that to my advantage.'

Miriama sighed. 'I hope you know what you're doing. I don't want us to spend the rest of our lives waiting for the night the Gang kills us in our bed.'

'That's not going to happen.' Aaron looked up and made eye contact with Miriama again. 'I'll keep you safe. I promise.'

She'd said *kill us in our bed*—did that mean she *was* serious about a long-term relationship?

Even a bottle of fine wine over dinner at the hotel didn't seem to relax Miriama. Aaron sighed. She'd barely said a word since they'd left the waterfront. What could he do to lift her spirits?

'Why don't we go for a walk?' Aaron said. 'It's a beautiful evening.'

Miriama wiped her mouth with a napkin. 'Why not? The spring flowers will be out in the botanic gardens. I'll fetch my coat.'

The winding path up the hill to the botanic gardens reminded Aaron of the fateful day when they'd climbed up to the castle as kids. Aaron had struggled to keep up with Miriama then, and it was the same today. Out of breath, he followed Miriama as she admired the trees and shrubs and sniffed the flowers' nectar. Suggesting a walk had definitely proved a wise move.

Aaron stared across the horizon. The sun's fading rays cast an almost ethereal glow over the Wellington skyline.

'It's going to be a glorious sunset,' he said. 'Just look at the symphony of colours and those magical reflections on the sea.'

Miriama smiled. 'You're still a poet at heart, aren't you?'

'Guess so,' Aaron said. 'How could you not be with such a magnificent view?'

Miriama tilted her head to one side. 'I remember the first time you set eyes on that wretched power station. I was quietly freezing to death while you waxed lyrical about hydroelectric energy.'

Aaron would never forget that day either—it was a defining moment in his life. 'There was I, admiring the extraordinary power of the clean, raw energy'—he gave Miriama a gentle prod—'and you tried to burst my bubble with some unimaginative and technical explanation about harnessing energy.'

Miriama nudged him back. 'Well, I just couldn't understand how anyone could be so starry-eyed about a power station. But then, like you've always said, I'm no poet.'

'Maybe not.' Aaron beckoned her across to a park bench overlooking the city. 'But you don't need to be a poet to enjoy such a beautiful sunset.'

They sat down and watched the sun sink lower in the sky.

Miriama fidgeted with an earring for a couple of minutes, then turned to face Aaron. 'I still think you should consider quitting Parata Peak Power. It's brought you nothing but grief. In fact, why don't you get out of the power industry altogether? It's changed you, and not for the better.'

Aaron flinched. *So you liked me more when I was poor and unsuccessful? That's not what you said when we were kids.* He counted to ten before replying. 'You used to delight in telling me I was useless and going nowhere. Now I've made something of my life, and you want me to throw it away?'

'Of course not. I want the best for you, and us.' Miriama gazed across the city and pointed to a grand manor house nestled on a cliff overlooking the harbour. 'Imagine living in a house like that. Cocktail parties on the patio. Garden parties in the summer. Playing croquet on the lawn. How awesome would that be?'

Aaron gulped. Those were the exact words Miriama had used when they saw the hermit's castle as kids. So she was thinking back to that day, too. He forced a smile. 'So, are you going to march up to the door, announce yourself to the owner, and ask him to marry you?'

Miriama giggled. 'You remembered! God, I was a pretentious brat back then.'

Bloody right! That had been another defining day in Aaron's life. He instinctively rubbed the scar on his chin. What happened after they fled from the castle had left its mark on both his mind and body.

Miriama dabbed her eyes with a handkerchief. 'You were so brave. I'll never forget how you stood up to those thugs.' She blinked back another tear, then

     David Whittet

grinned at Aaron. 'Something else I haven't forgotten. Remember what else you promised me that day? You swore you'd buy me a castle, just like the one where that mad recluse lived.'

'And to do that, I need a well-paid job,' Aaron shot back. 'So it looks like I'll have to stay on at Parata Peak Power. Poets can't afford houses like that.'

Miriama sighed. 'Suppose not. But you'd get to the top in another industry.'

'Not if I stuff up at Parata Peak. Nobody will touch me with a barge pole.' Aaron stood up and took Miriama's hand. 'We'd better make a move. It's getting late, and I have to prepare myself for the onslaught in the morning.'

Aaron wasn't focused on the mediation as he walked back to the hotel with Miriama. Something far more important occupied his mind. Earlier that day, he'd spotted a jeweller in the city, and an exquisite moonstone ring in the window had caught his eye. He'd read in a women's magazine that a moonstone engagement ring was said to represent new beginnings. That was just what he and Miriama needed. The article had gone on to say that moonstones brought inner calm and compassion. Even better, the ring in the jeweller's window was set with a cluster of sparkling diamonds encircling the large oval moonstone. Perfect.

Maybe Miriama would have to wait for that castle, but tomorrow she would have the best engagement ring money could buy.

CHAPTER TWENTY-SEVEN

Would Miriama say yes? And would she approve of the bold coup he was about to execute? Aaron didn't have time to stop and think. He could still make the mediation offices by ten if he got a move on. Maybe not. The elderly jeweller took forever to get the ring out of the cabinet and insisted on polishing it to perfection.

It was five past ten when Aaron burst into the mediation offices. Miles' twitching lip told him he was in for a rough ride. Aaron was dying to show Tony the ring, but sat in the waiting room with his arms crossed instead. His old mate looked as tense as Miles.

'What time do you call this?' Miles pointed at the clock on the wall. 'I asked you to be here early for a briefing before the meeting.'

'I know,' Aaron said. 'I'm sorry.'

Miles shook his head. 'Now we have to go into the meeting cold. I wanted us to be clear on our strategy.'

'Don't worry,' Aaron said. 'I've got our plan of action worked out. This is going to be fun.'

'Fun?' Miles shuddered, holding on to the back of a chair for support. 'Please, Aaron. Listen to me. This is no place for payback or settling old scores. Promise me you won't do anything foolish.'

Why don't you trust me? Aaron stood tall with his head tilted back. 'Don't worry, I've got the board's backing on this one.'

'You can't have—'

The arrival of a mediation staffer cut Miles off mid-sentence.

'Ms Goodman is waiting for you in the conference room,' the staffer said. 'Follow me, please.'

Miles almost tripped over his feet as they followed the staffer. His quivering lip now almost out of control.

'Good morning,' Valerie Goodman said as they entered the conference room. 'I trust you are all in a better frame of mind today after taking time out and sleeping on the matter. We need to move on from past differences and reach an agreement.'

Aaron pulled up a chair. 'Indeed, we do.' He glared at Corey. The bastard still had that smug look on his face. Kaine too. Neither of them knew what was coming to them. Aaron shifted his gaze to the mediator. 'I apologise for my absence yesterday afternoon. Like you said, I needed some time out.'

Valerie raised an eyebrow. 'I hope you used the time wisely.'

'I did.' Aaron opened his briefcase and pulled out his laptop. 'Earlier this morning, I convened a breakfast meeting with the Parata Peak board. We met via Zoom and agreed unanimously—'

Miles cut him off. 'I need some time with my client before we proceed.'

Lance Everson threw his arms in the air. 'I object. We'll be here till Christmas if these clowns get their way.' He leant forward and glared at Miles. 'I briefed my client before the meeting. A pity you didn't do the same and come prepared.'

Valerie frowned. 'I'm inclined to agree. We've lost enough time already, and you've had plenty of time to confer with your client.'

Miles took a sharp intake of breath. 'I just need a few minutes with Aaron.'

Corey rolled his eyes. 'Don't let Aaron out of your sight. He'll run away shouting and screaming, just like yesterday.'

Aaron grinned to himself. *Not today, mate—I'll wipe that smirk off your face.*

Miles jumped to his feet, his face a bright scarlet. 'I must insist—'

Let it go. For once, Aaron agreed with Corey and his lawyer. The last thing he needed was Miles derailing his plan.

'Excuse us a moment,' Aaron said to Valerie. He grabbed Miles' arm and dragged him to a corner of the room. 'You need to back off, Miles. Leave it to me. The entire board are behind me on this.'

'Why wasn't I invited to the board meeting?' Miles protested. 'You had no right to go behind my back.'

'I didn't,' Aaron retaliated. 'If you'd bothered to check your email, you'd have found your invitation.'

Tony stood up and joined them. 'I got the email and a text message.' He glanced at Aaron. 'Good luck, mate. You've got balls, I'll give you that.'

Miles scowled. 'Am I the only one who doesn't know what the hell is going on?'

'Maybe that's for the best.' Aaron led them back to the table and addressed the mediator. 'Sorry for the interruption. We're ready to proceed now.'

'I'm glad to hear it,' Valerie said. 'Now, perhaps you could enlighten us about your impromptu board meeting.'

Aaron cleared his throat. 'The Parata Peak board agreed unanimously to go ahead with the joint venture—'

Corey jumped up and raised a hand in salute. 'Yes.'

'I was about to add,' Aaron continued, 'that we agreed to proceed on condition that Kaine is dismissed as vice president of Jensen Industries.'

'*What?*' Corey clenched his fist and glared at Aaron. 'No fucking way.'

Valerie rapped her hand on the table. 'I warned you about your language yesterday. Any more of that and I will have you removed from the building.' She turned to Aaron with her pencil poised above her notepad. 'Go on.'

'Parata Peak Power will not countenance any deal involving the Godzone Gorillas.' Aaron paused to enjoy the look of utter disbelief on both Corey and Kaine's faces. He was about to make their day even worse. 'My board has directed me to insist that Kaine leaves and takes no further part in the negotiations. We will require evidence of his resignation from his position with Jensen before progressing the deal. In addition, we insist on a written undertaking from Jensen that they have severed all ties to the Godzone Gorillas.'

Corey jabbed a finger in Aaron's face. 'You bastard!'

Valerie dropped her pencil. 'What have I just said about language? I really will have to ask you to leave.'

'Don't worry,' Corey hit back. 'If Kaine's being chucked out, I'm going too.'

'Wait!' Lance pulled Corey back into his chair. 'Do you want to lose everything?'

Corey's eyes bulged. 'I want to get even with that son of a bitch.'

'Calm down!' Lance shook his head and turned to Valerie with a nervous smile. 'Forgive my client's outburst. Kaine is a valued member of the Jensen team, and this has come as a shock.'

Valerie picked up her pencil. 'It seems you are the one who needs to confer with your client, Mr Everson. Please make this absolutely clear to Mr O'Connor—he's had his last warning. Any further swearing or threats and he will be escorted from the premises and excluded from the mediation.'

　　　　David Whittet

'Understood,' Lance said. 'Now, if we could have fifteen minutes, please.'

Valerie sighed. 'Very well. We will reconvene at eleven fifteen.'

Lance frogmarched Corey and Kaine out of the conference room. Corey stopped at the door. His nostrils flared, and he bared his teeth at Aaron.

Aaron relished the moment and discreetly gave Corey the finger. *Take that, loser!* Revenge had been a long time coming, but by God, it was worth the wait.

Valerie tidied her papers and stood up. 'I'm going for a coffee.'

Raised voices from the adjacent room confirmed Corey and Kaine were getting their just deserts. Aaron would have given his soul to listen in but instead had to deal with Miles interrogating him about the breakfast meeting.

'You're not messing me around, are you?' Miles demanded. 'Dame Cynthia and Margaret were both determined the deal would go through.'

'Perhaps they both have a conscience after all,' Aaron said with a grin. 'Mind you, it was only when I threatened to go public that they sat up and took notice. Imagine the headline: *Vice President of the Godzone Gorillas joins the Parata Peak Board.* Not a good look for Dame Cynthia or Margaret. Or the rest of us, for that matter.'

Miles shook his head. 'Look here, Aaron. If you're bullshitting—'

'No,' Tony interrupted. 'I was at the Zoom meeting, and it's all true.'

Miles eyeballed them in turn. 'Maybe you're both taking me for a ride. I talked to Dame Cynthia on the phone last night—'

'That was last night,' Tony shot back. 'I don't think she knew about Kaine and the involvement with Godzone Gorillas before the Zoom meeting this morning.'

Like hell! She knew alright. I'd love to know what the Gang's got on her. Aaron snorted. 'You're so naïve, Tony. How many times have you heard me warn Dame Cynthia and Margaret about getting into bed with the Godzone Gorillas?'

Tony lowered his head. 'I know. It's just—'

Aaron leant forward and finished the sentence for him. 'You don't want to think badly of anyone.'

Miles stood up and took his mobile phone out of his pocket. 'Excuse me. I need to talk to Dame Cynthia.'

The bastard doesn't believe me. Aaron shrugged. 'Suit yourself.'

Miles dialled the number and made for the door. 'Cynthia! What's this I hear about a board meeting this morning?'

Aaron rubbed his hands together. Miles and Lady Cynthia at loggerheads. This promised to be highly entertaining.

Miles stepped out into the corridor and shut the door behind him.

Damn! Aaron got up and put his ear to the door. He grinned as he listened to Miles and imagined Dame Cynthia's replies. The old lady had a sharp tongue when it suited her.

'I hope you realise,' Miles continued, 'you've landed me in an impossible situation, and made it look like we don't know what we're doing.'

Poor Miles. Dame Cynthia certainly wasn't making it easy for him.

'You want me to say that at the press conference? I couldn't possibly!'

Just as the conversation heated up, Miles' voice was drowned by Kaine bellowing in the next room.

'You think the Godzone Gorillas will stand for this? Just wait till I tell Reggie.'

Kaine's wrangling with Corey and Lance was just as juicy as Miles and Dame Cynthia's.

'Leave Reggie to me.' That was Corey's voice. 'I'll talk him round.'

'Your fancy words won't save you now.' Kaine again. 'Reggie will crucify you if this deal doesn't go through. And that's if he's in a good mood.'

'Cool it, both of you.' That was Lance. 'We need to work together on this … present a united front.'

Kaine obviously wasn't listening. 'Bollocks! We get back in there and let them see who's boss. Nobody messes with the Godzone Gorillas!'

'You want to get us all thrown out?' Lance was clearly struggling to keep the peace between them. 'You'll have to leave, Kaine. Valerie made that quite clear. Corey and I will have to fight this on our own.'

Aaron pictured Kaine foaming at the mouth as his explosive reply shook the building. 'Go fuck yourself, Lance. You too, Corey. I told Reggie it was a mistake putting a dumbass kid in charge of Jensen, but the son of a bitch wouldn't listen. This is your shit, Corey.'

'You're not pinning this on me.' Corey's voice this time. 'I warned Reggie it was a mistake you coming to the mediation and linking us to the Gang. But we haven't lost yet. Lance and I can still turn this around.'

'Shut it, retard.' Kaine again. 'We're screwed and you know it.'

     David Whittet

So there was no love lost between Corey and Kaine. It sounded like Corey would soon be out of favour with Reggie, too.

Aaron went back to his seat and winked at Tony. 'I wouldn't have missed this for the world.'

Valerie was back at the mediation table at eleven fifteen sharp with her pencil poised. Aaron couldn't decide who was most battle-worn when the rest of them filed back into the conference room. Corey's arms hung at his sides, and he stumbled into his chair. Kaine looked ready to erupt with his knuckledusters and his fists clenched. Was he going to hit somebody? Kaine's face was such a deep shade of purple that his tattoos were scarcely visible. Lance and Miles both looked as though they'd done half a dozen rounds with Mike Tyson.

Valerie cleared her throat. 'Before we recommence, I must ask Kaine to leave.' She eyed Kaine across the table. 'I made it clear yesterday that I was uncomfortable with your presence at the mediation.' She paused and fidgeted with her pencil. 'I should have acted more decisively yesterday. Today I have no choice. The board of Parata Peak Power has made it clear that they will not do business with anyone affiliated with a gang.'

Aaron smirked. *That means you should chuck Corey out, too.*

Kaine leapt to his feet and kicked his chair across the floor. 'I don't know why I bothered coming in the first place. The Godzone Gorillas don't mediate. They rule!' He glared at Aaron. 'You can take that look off your face, you little turd.'

Aaron resisted the urge to give him the finger.

'Leave now,' Valerie said. 'Or do I have to call security?'

Kaine stormed out of the room. 'Screw you! Nobody mocks the Godzone Gorillas and gets away with it.'

Aaron leant across the table to face Corey. 'Didn't you just say that you'd go too if Kaine got thrown out?'

'Shut it!' Corey hissed. 'You heard what Kaine said. You haven't won yet.'

I have. Aaron sank back into his chair, still eyeing Corey. 'Let's just wait and see, shall we?'

'Perhaps we could get back to the business in hand.' Valerie tapped her pencil on the table. 'So, provided Jensen Industries are prepared to sever all links with the Godzone Gorillas, are we all agreed that the deal goes ahead?'

Not so fast. Aaron sat up. 'I'm not signing anything until we have Kaine's resignation from Jensen Industries and an undertaking from Corey that he disassociates himself from the Gang.'

'I've thought about that,' Valerie said, 'and I drafted a proposed agreement during the break. My secretary is typing it up, and you'll have copies in a couple of minutes. You'll see that I have added safeguards about Kaine's removal and Jensen's involvement with the Godzone Gorillas.'

An hour later and the deal was finalised.

Aaron signed the contract with a flourish and thrust the papers across the table to Corey. 'Your turn.'

Corey grabbed the paper, his eyes blazing and his mouth open. Was he going to sign the agreement or spit on it?

'Don't be such a sore loser,' Aaron said.

'I'm no loser.' Corey gouged the paper with the force of his signature. 'I can still gobble you up and spit you out.'

'That's enough, Corey,' Lance said. 'Let's get out of here, and not a word to the reporters. Doubtless, the paparazzi will be lying in wait.'

And they were. Valerie read out a prepared statement on the steps outside the building.

'We are pleased to have reached a position acceptable to both parties and which brings stability to an industry essential to our economy.'

As Valerie droned on about the value of mediation, Aaron wondered when she had prepared her statement. It must have been before they reached an agreement. Was this just another step in her career pathway? Did she even care about the outcome as long as she got the kudos?

'The agreement reached today,' Valerie concluded, 'removes the threat of disruption to power distribution throughout New Zealand. I am proud to have brokered a deal so vital to our country.'

Cameras flashed like lightning. Aaron shielded his eyes as the paparazzi closed in.

'What's your take on the deal, Mr Casper?' a reporter shouted. 'You must be delighted to be one up on your old rival.'

Too bloody right. Aaron hesitated. There was so much he wanted to say, but both Miles and Tony had warned him about being cocky.

 David Whittet

'No comment, Mr Casper?' another reporter demanded, thrusting his microphone in Aaron's face. 'Can you guarantee there will be no gang interference in the power industry?'

'Absolutely,' Aaron said. 'The Godzone Gorillas or any other gang, come to that, have no place in the power industry. And it will stay that way while I am CEO of Parata Peak Power.'

'And how long will that be?' the reporter taunted.

'Is your position under threat?' another added.

'Of course it isn't,' Aaron shot back. *How dare they? I'm the winner here*. He was about to say more when Miles caught his eye. *Damn*. Aaron took a scrap of paper out of his pocket and read the brief statement Miles had scribbled out for him: 'This agreement signals a powerful alliance and confirms Parata Peak Power as the dominant force in hydroelectric power. The partnership with Jensen will enable us to expand our capacity and better serve the ever-growing energy demands of our country.'

Valerie stepped forward again. 'Thank you, Mr Casper.' She pulled Aaron aside. 'I'd like to get a photo of you and Corey shaking hands. That will show unity and cement the deal, so to speak.'

No bloody way. I'm not sharing this moment with that bastard. Aaron turned to face Valerie. 'We can't. He's buggered off.'

'No, he hasn't.' Lance pushed through the media scrum, dragging Corey with him. 'Mr O'Connor would be delighted for a photo opportunity with Mr Casper.'

So why is the bastard trying to get away? Aaron made sure he was on a higher step than Corey as they posed for the awkward photograph. Cameras flashed even more rapidly than before.

'That'll be perfect for tomorrow's front pages,' Valerie said, edging her way into the photograph.

Aaron locked eyes with Corey as their hands met in a firm grip, determined to savour the sweet revenge the moment brought him. What was his nemesis thinking? Corey certainly wasn't his usual cocky self. The fire in his eyes had dimmed, but that smug grin on his face hadn't vanished entirely. Had David finally defeated Goliath? Or did Goliath have another trick up his sleeve?

Tony patted Aaron on the back as the crowd dispersed. 'That was brilliant! How about a celebratory drink?'

'I'd love to,' Aaron said, 'but if you'll forgive me, there's somewhere else I need to be.' He took the box with the engagement ring out of his pocket and showed the ring to them. The opalescent, rose-tinted oval moonstone with its halo of iridescent diamonds sparkling in the sunlight. 'I'm hoping for a double celebration.'

Tony gasped in awe, dazzled by the magnificence of the ring. 'It's absolutely stunning. Can I take a closer look?' Tony's hand trembled as Aaron let him hold the ring. 'Wow! Just wow!'

'The moonstone is meant to represent a new beginning,' Aaron said. 'I only hope that holds true for Miriama and me.'

'I'm sure it will.' Tony handed the ring back to Aaron. 'Miriama is one lucky girl.'

Even Miles looked impressed. 'I never put you down as such a romantic, Aaron. Good luck with the proposal. I hope she says yes.'

Aaron held his breath for a moment. 'So do I.'

Tony grinned. 'What else could she say with such an exquisite ring?'

Aaron closed the jeweller's box and put the ring back in his pocket. 'Let's hope you're right. Now, if you'll excuse me.'

With a wave of his hand, Aaron started to walk towards the hotel.

'Okay, mate,' Tony called after him. 'But we're having an engagement party when we get back to Parata Peak.'

Aaron felt a chill run down his spine as he approached the hotel. He stopped dead, feeling a heavy presence looming over him. His legs shook as he slowly forced himself to look up. What Aaron saw made his heart sink—and his blood boil. Like a monster, Kaine's hulking body blocked the footpath.

Aaron steadied himself, struggling to keep his composure. His voice stammered. 'What the hell do you want?'

Kaine stood with his arms crossed and eyes blazing as if daring Aaron to move past him. 'You little turd. Thought you'd get one over on the Gang, did you?'

Don't let the bastard see you're scared shitless. Aaron forced himself to stand tall and meet Kaine's menacing eyes. 'Don't be such a sore loser. I won. You

     David Whittet

lost.' Aaron took a step forward, his heart racing and his palms sweating. 'Get out of my way.'

Kaine clenched his fists. 'Going to make me?'

A surge of adrenaline rushed through Aaron's body. For years he had fantasised about what he would do to this filthy scumbag if their paths ever crossed. Now they were standing face-to-face. Was this his chance to avenge his mother and finally get even?

'You son of a bitch!' Aaron edged closer and jabbed a finger in Kaine's face. 'I could kill you for what you did to my mother.'

'And I could kill you for the stunt you've just pulled off.' Kaine's eyes narrowed. 'Nobody messes with the Gang and gets away with it. If the Godzone Gorillas can't have Parata Peak Power, nobody will. We'll blow up your precious power station.'

Aaron's heart pounded. 'You wouldn't dare. We've got the best security in the country.'

'DLS Security, isn't it? With a little help from Jarrod O'Dell and the GRT Group.' Kaine smirked. 'They're no match for the Godzone Gorillas.'

Aaron gulped. *How the hell does he know about our security arrangements?* That was confidential information. None of it was mentioned in the mediation papers.

Kaine continued to taunt him. 'Your old man had the best security money could buy. Didn't do him much good, did it?'

'You bastard!' Aaron lunged at Kaine. 'I swear I'll kill you!'

Footsteps. Aaron glanced over his shoulder. It was Tony, running down the pavement towards him, with Miles a few paces behind.

'Don't be a fool,' Tony pleaded. 'He's not worth it.'

'Stay out of this, Tony,' Aaron shot back. 'This is my shit.'

Tony would never understand the burning rage that consumed Aaron. Thanks to Kaine, Aaron had grown up without a mother and without a father. Kaine had just all but admitted he'd played a part in Emir's death.

Aaron grabbed Kaine's gang-patched leather jacket. Now it was payback time.

Tony caught up and tried to pull Aaron away. 'Think about Miriama. You were going to propose to her tonight. Carry on like this, and you'll end up in hospital.'

'Tony's right,' Miles said. 'Think what it'll do to your reputation if this gets out. Your career will be finished.'

They were right—this could only end in disaster. Aaron could imagine the headline: *Parata Peak Power CEO in hospital after a public brawl with a notorious gangster*. Aaron sighed and let go of Kaine.

Tony grabbed Aaron's arm. 'Come on. Let's get you back to the hotel.'

Kaine snorted. 'You haven't got the guts, have you? You're a wimp. Just like your mother and father.'

For a moment, Aaron didn't give a damn about the consequences. He pushed Tony aside and landed Kaine a punch.

A sudden flash of light almost blinded Aaron. *What the hell was that?* He spun around to see a photographer poking a lens in his face.

Kaine grinned. 'Looks like you'll be tomorrow's headline after all.'

More photographers. More flashes. Aaron hid his face. Had Kaine set him up? How else did the paparazzi know to appear at that particular moment?

Tony pushed the photographers away. 'Clear off. Go on. Get out of here.'

A photographer sneered and gave Tony the finger. 'Shove off yourself.'

Miles pushed through the crowd. 'That's enough.' He bared his teeth at the paparazzi. 'Don't even think about publishing your grubby pictures. I'll sue the arse off you.'

Another photographer jerked his thumb at Miles. 'Piss off! We haven't had a scoop like this in ages.'

Miles stamped his foot. 'You won't be so cocky when you get the summons. I swear I'll screw the lot of you for every last cent you've got.'

The photographers backed off. Aaron could scarcely believe it. One by one, they packed up their cameras and left. And all because of Miles. Aaron had never had much time for Miles until now. But then he'd never seen the usually pedantic lawyer all fired up like this before. Today, Miles was a hero.

Miles pulled his mobile out of his pocket. 'I need to get an embargo on those photos fast. Otherwise, we're all in the shit.'

'Damn right you're in the shit!' Kaine reappeared, rubbing his hands together. 'You don't frighten the Godzone Gorillas that easily. We haven't even started.'

Miles sighed. 'Go home, Kaine, and let me make this call.'

     David Whittet

Kaine strode off, pumping his fist in the air. 'You'll regret the day you crossed the Godzone Gorillas. We'll destroy you. Blow your prized power station to bits. Smash it into smithereens. *Smithereens!*'

Aaron shuddered as Kaine disappeared into the distance, still ranting.

'Are you okay?' Tony asked, putting a hand on Aaron's shoulder. 'Would you like me to walk you back to the hotel?'

Aaron shook his head. 'I'm going for a walk. I need to get my head together before I can face Miriama.'

Tony frowned. 'You won't do anything silly, will you?'

'No.' Aaron shrugged. 'I just need to figure out how to tell Miriama that I'm going to be on the front page of tomorrow's newspapers, caught punching Kaine.'

The day had started with such promise. Aaron kicked a can down the street as he headed to the seafront. He watched the seagulls soaring into the sunset. If only Aaron were as free as them. He should be out on the town with Miriama, celebrating their engagement plus the success with the mediation. But, as usual, the Godzone Gorillas had ruined everything.

CHAPTER TWENTY-EIGHT

Would Miriama say yes if she knew about his brawl with Kaine? She'd warned him that the Gang would taunt him and urged him not to rise to the bait. Aaron put his hand in his pocket and clenched the jeweller's ring box. Perhaps he should delay the proposal until everything had blown over.

Aaron tossed a few coins into a busker's guitar case. The haunting song about lost opportunities made up Aaron's mind. He would go straight back to the hotel, explain everything to Miriama, and ask her to marry him.

'Darling!' Miriama flung her arms around Aaron the moment he entered her hotel room. 'I saw you on the television.'

What? Aaron's heart missed a beat. Had his altercation with Kaine hit the headlines already? 'I can explain …'

'No need,' Miriama said. 'You were brilliant at the press conference. I don't know how you got Dame Cynthia and the board on side.'

Aaron could breathe again. She'd only seen the impromptu stand-up media briefing outside the mediation offices. 'I let them have it straight. Threatened to go public about the company going into partnership with the Godzone Gorillas. Suggested that wouldn't be a good look for any of them.'

'You sneaky bastard.' Miriama kissed him. 'I love you.'

How could he tell her about the confrontation with Kaine after that? It would ruin the perfect moment for a proposal. Aaron had been waiting for this moment since he first met Miriama all those years ago at the *Gypsy Rose* and fallen captive to her mesmerising eyes. He'd read her palm that afternoon—and never dared hope he'd be proposing to her one day.

Aaron reached into his pocket and pulled out the ring box, slowly opening the lid to reveal the magnificent moonstone.

Miriama gasped, her breath catching in her throat as the light pulsed from the moonstone with its halo of diamonds. 'It's gorgeous,' she whispered, brushing away a tear. 'This is the most beautiful ring I've ever seen.'

'The moonstone symbolises a fresh start,' Aaron said, his eyes glistening with unshed tears. 'And that's what we both need.'

Perhaps he could have chosen a more romantic setting than the hotel room, but even if this wasn't the most elegant proposal, it was his one chance, and he wasn't going to miss it. Aaron took her hand and dropped down onto one knee. The radiance of the ring made up for the location, sparkling with a brilliance to match Miriama's admiring eyes.

'Miriama, will you marry me?'

Aaron mentally crossed his fingers as he spoke. Had Miles been successful and vetoed the paparazzi's damning pictures? Or would they destroy his reputation in the morning?

Miriama beamed. 'Yes, Aaron. Yes, yes, yes. A thousand times, yes.'

Aaron gulped. The common gang boy had won the heart of a beautiful princess. His hands trembled as he took the ring and slipped it onto her slender finger. Miriama's hand seemed to be made for the ring, which shone even brighter on her finger than it had in its box. It was almost like a ring from a fairy tale.

Aaron smiled and looked into Miriama's blissful eyes—could this be a sign of better things to come?

Miriama put her arm around him. 'We should celebrate. It's ages since we've had a night on the town. I'm going to get changed. I've got just the dress to go with the ring.'

Aaron shrugged as Miriama went to change. This should be the happiest moment of his life. Instead, he had a sinking feeling in the pit of his stomach. Would she change her mind tomorrow when she saw the headlines?

Miriama emerged from the bathroom. 'How do I look?'

Aaron stared at her. 'Stunning. Absolutely stunning.'

'Come on then.' Miriama picked up her handbag. 'Let's party!'

Celebrate. Party. Aaron clasped Miriama's hand as they left the hotel. *Live for tonight.* He intended to party like there was no tomorrow. Because if the paparazzi got their way, Aaron would have no tomorrow. At least, not one worth living.

It should have been perfect. A four-course gourmet meal at La Scala and dancing the night away at The Talk of the Town nightclub. And it would have been if Aaron hadn't spent the entire evening looking over his shoulder. Perhaps Kaine was stalking him and was about to pounce and create another scene. Dancing cheek to cheek with Miriama and surreptitiously squinting at the enormous television in the bar. His heart missed a beat at every commercial break. Would there be a newsflash with a closeup of him punching Kaine? Would their engagement be the shortest in history if Miriama saw it?

Miriama eyed him intently when they took a breather between dances. 'Not having second thoughts, are you?'

Aaron caught his breath. 'Of course not. What makes you think that?'

'Because you're looking at the bar more than me.' Miriama pointed to some voluptuous and scantily dressed girls on the dance floor. 'Perhaps you'd rather be dancing with one of them.'

Aaron shook his head. 'Don't be ridiculous. You're everything to me.'

Miriama frowned. 'Something's up. What is it?'

'Nothing.'

'I know you better than that.' Miriama kept her eyes fixed on him. 'You've been weird all night.'

What could he say? She'd seen through his pretence. Should he just come out with the truth? Aaron had never been a good liar. Trouble was, he'd never been much use at expressing how he felt either.

'Miriama, there's something I should have told you.'

'I'm listening.' Miriama took a sip of wine. 'Spill.'

Where to start? Aaron bit his lip. 'I was on a high after the mediation. I'd won. Saved Parata Peak Power from a dreadful mistake.'

'And finally got one over on Corey.' Miriama smiled. 'That photo of the two of you outside the mediation office was priceless. I saw it on TV.'

'I thought … I hoped …' Aaron hesitated. 'I'd set my heart on a double celebration. Success with the mediation and our engagement.'

'I said yes, and here we are. Celebrating.' Miriama took another slurp of wine. 'So why the long face?'

Aaron lowered his head. 'Something happened after that photo …'

Miriama rolled her eyes. 'Don't tell me you had a round of fisticuffs with Corey.'

     David Whittet

Aaron spluttered. 'No. I didn't see him after the photo, but while I was walking back to the hotel—'

Miriama cut him off. 'Talk of the devil! Isn't that Corey at the bar?'

Aaron followed her line of sight. He'd been paranoid that Kaine was still stalking him. But there was Corey with his cocky grin, surrounded by a bunch of adoring girls.

'Explain this,' Miriama said, her gaze shifting from Corey to Aaron. 'You thrash Corey at the mediation. Now he's on cloud nine, and you're in the doldrums. What aren't you telling me?'

Why couldn't he just spit it out? He would have done if Miriama hadn't interrupted him when she spotted Corey. Aaron closed his eyes and took a calming breath. 'I was trying to explain. On the way back from the mediation—'

Corey appeared, thumped Aaron on the back, and finished the sentence for him. 'Our hero of the day, the mighty Aaron Casper, started a punch-up in the street.'

Miriama glared at Aaron. 'Is this true?'

Aaron struggled to get the words out. 'No … at least … it wasn't like that …'

'So, what was it like?' Miriama put down her wine glass and tapped her fingers on the table. 'I'm waiting.'

Corey smirked. 'Hasn't he told you? Not content at manipulating the mediation, your precious Aaron assaulted a senior member of the Jensen board.'

Miriama shook her head. 'Aaron! What were you thinking?'

'It was Kaine,' Aaron stammered. 'The man who had my mother kidnapped and taken away.'

'Bullshit,' Corey scoffed. 'You made that up.'

Talk of his mother sent a fresh surge of adrenaline through Aaron's body. 'I did not, and I can prove it.' He glared at Corey. 'I hired a private detective—'

'Never mind all that,' Miriama interrupted. 'Did you or did you not attack Kaine on the street?'

'Go on, admit it,' Corey taunted. 'It'll be on the front page of all the newspapers in the morning.'

Aaron covered his face with his hands. Did Corey have inside information? The Gang had spies everywhere. Perhaps Corey already knew that Miles' attempt to block the story had failed.

Corey continued to mock. 'The news hacks will love this. *Business leader makes a vicious and unprovoked attack on an industry rival.* You couldn't have given them a better headline if you'd tried.'

'What crap!' Aaron stared at him in utter disbelief. 'It wasn't vicious or unprovoked. *Upstanding business leader defends himself against a ruthless gangster,* would be more like it.'

Corey snorted. 'In your dreams. We've had a word in the ear of our media contacts.'

'You stitched me up, you bastard!' Aaron clenched his fists. It was obvious now. He'd walked straight into a trap. 'Kaine was waiting for me, wasn't he? And you tipped off the paparazzi.'

Corey grinned. 'What if I did? Remind me what you said this afternoon about being a sore loser.'

Aaron jumped to his feet and raised his fist. 'You won't get away with this.'

'Calm down!' Miriama pulled him back to his seat. 'Everyone's looking at us.'

They were. Worse still, a bouncer headed toward them.

'Excuse me, sir,' the bouncer said, eyeballing Aaron, 'but you're disturbing our other guests. I must ask you to leave.'

Aaron froze. 'I'm sorry. I didn't mean to—'

Corey cut him off with a dismissive wave of the hand. 'It's okay. I'm going.' He winked at the bouncer. 'My friend's having a bad day. I don't want him getting into more trouble.'

Self-righteous prick! Aaron's fists remained clenched as Corey took off. How dare he take the high ground? Corey was the one tied to the Gang.

Miriama clutched her handbag. 'We're leaving too. Come on, Aaron.'

Aaron hung his head and followed Miriama out of the nightclub. The silence was unbearable as they trudged back to the hotel. What was she thinking? Was she mad at him? Should he get in first with his side of the story?

'Miriama!' Aaron took a deep breath. 'I'm sorry you had to see that. I was trying to explain about Kaine when Corey interrupted us.'

'Yes.' Miriama quickened her pace. 'But don't you think you should have told me *before* you proposed?'

Aaron caught up with her. 'I know. I wish I had.'

     David Whittet

Miriama gave him a sideways glance. 'I'd have understood. Of course I would, after what Kaine did to your mother. But to hear it from Corey.' She stopped and shook her head. 'And to be thrown out of a nightclub—'

'We weren't exactly thrown out.'

'Weren't we?' Miriama pulled a face. 'Well, it's the first time I've ever been asked to leave an establishment.'

And it'll be the last, I promise. Would she believe him if he said the words out loud?

Miriama took off down the street again before he had the chance to decide.

She turned back and stared at him. 'I'm disappointed in you, Aaron. What happened to the gutsy boy who took on the mob without a second thought?'

Aaron instinctively touched the scar on his chin. Okay, he'd stuffed up today, but he'd saved her from a vicious attack back then. Didn't that count for anything?

He ran after her. 'Miriama … we're still alright, aren't we? We're still …'

Miriama had disappeared into the distance before he could say the word 'engaged'.

❧

How had he managed to stuff things up so abysmally? Aaron collapsed on his hotel bed, still cursing himself for his stupidity. His heart stood still when his mobile rang. Was it Miriama? He fumbled and pulled the phone from his pocket. It was Miles. *Damn.* Miles was the last person Aaron wanted to talk to, and he declined the call.

Should he call Miriama? Aaron paused with his finger poised over her number. Maybe it would be better if he went round to her room and tried to make it up with her. Aaron sighed. He'd probably only make things worse. When they'd argued before, she'd calmed down by the following morning. Aaron resigned himself to a thoroughly miserable night alone.

Six in the morning. Aaron's mobile went off again. He rubbed the sleep from his eyes and glanced at the screen. Miles. *Go away.* Aaron put his phone on silent and tried to get back to sleep. He put his head under the pillow when his phone kept vibrating. *Damn you, Miles. Don't you ever give up?* Short of throwing his phone out of the window, Aaron wouldn't get any peace until he answered the call.

'What do you want, Miles?'

'Have you seen this morning's *Dominion Post*?'

'No.' Aaron sank back on the pillow. A phone call from Miles that early meant disaster. His picture would be on the front page, showing him punching Kaine. 'Give me a break, Miles. I don't want to know.'

'You need to see it. It's a tremendous splash.'

'I bet it is.'

'Get hold of a copy. As soon as you can. It's bound to be on breakfast TV.'

Miles' voice sounded excited. Had his lawyer turned on him, too? Perhaps Miles was in on yesterday's altercation, making sure he bumped into Kaine.

'Goodbye, Miles.'

Aaron's mind went into overdrive. What if Miles was under orders from Dame Cynthia or Margaret? He'd caught part of Miles' call to Dame Cynthia during the break at yesterday's mediation. Dame Cynthia and Margaret both wanted him out. What better way to disgrace him than goad him into a fight with Kaine?

Best get it over with. Aaron grabbed the remote and switched on the television. Sure enough, his picture was there as the presenter announced the headline news. What was she saying about him? Aaron reluctantly turned up the volume.

'Business leader Aaron Casper signed a crucial deal yesterday to prevent further gang interference in the power industry. A patched member of the Godzone Gorillas ambushed Mr Casper as he left the mediation offices. Mr Casper bravely fought off the disgruntled gangster's attempts to intimidate him.'

Aaron blinked again and again. Was he dreaming? Surely that couldn't be Dame Cynthia on the television news, praising him as a hero? But it was. However many times Aaron pinched himself, Dame Cynthia was still there, proclaiming him as the saviour of the power industry.

Why had he doubted Miles? Aaron raced out of the hotel to find a newsagent. The billboards said it all: *Power industry boss takes on the Gang and wins.* He stepped inside the shop, and his picture was on the *Dominion Post*'s front page, fighting off Kaine.

Aaron grabbed a copy and gazed at the headline:

          David Whittet

The forward-thinking of Parata Peak Power CEO Aaron Casper has thwarted a backdoor move by the Godzone Gorillas to take control of New Zealand's largest hydroelectric energy producer. With control of the power supply, the Godzone Gorillas would have held the country to ransom, with mass power cuts over winter.

Aaron's eyes shifted to the caption under the photograph: *No-nonsense industry leader Aaron Casper tells the Godzone Gorillas where to get off.*

The newsagent recognised him immediately. 'Mr Casper! Can I take a selfie with you? And the newspaper's on me.'

Aaron rushed back to the hotel and banged on Miriama's door. 'Miriama! You've got to see this!'

No reply. Perhaps she'd gone for an early morning walk to clear her head.

He waited in the hotel lobby. Nine o'clock and still no sign of her. Surely she wouldn't have checked out without saying goodbye. Aaron got up and spoke to the concierge.

'The young lady you were with yesterday?' the concierge said. 'She left first thing this morning. I called the taxi for her.'

Did that mean the engagement was off? Aaron tried to call her.

'The mobile number you have dialled is either turned off or out of range.'

Damn. She was probably on a flight home.

Slumped over the desk in his hotel room, Aaron berated himself for not being straight up with Miriama and for losing his temper with Corey at the nightclub. Would Miriama forgive him? Or was this the end? Aaron took another look at the newspaper and packed his case. Why was happiness always tinged with sadness and victory forever ensnared in defeat?

CHAPTER TWENTY-NINE

The Gypsy Rose *Caravan, Kaikōura Coast, a Fortnight Later*

Desperation drew Aaron back to the *Gypsy Rose*. Adulation from the media and industry leaders meant nothing without Miriama. She hadn't returned any of his calls. Her colleagues and friends made excuses. Would none of them tell him the truth?

Aaron hesitated on those rickety old steps outside the caravan. He hadn't seen Kāterina in years, but he was sure she was the only person who could help him. She opened the caravan door before he knocked.

'Nau mai, haere mai!' Kāterina embraced him and pressed their noses together in a hongi. 'I've been expecting you for days.'

'So, you've heard from Miriama?' Aaron asked. 'What did she say? Did she tell you why she ran away from me?'

'No,' Kāterina said. 'She hasn't been in touch.'

Aaron scratched his head. 'How did you know I was coming, then?'

Kāterina gestured for him to follow her into the caravan. 'I've felt a disturbance in the atmosphere. Between you and Miriama. And I've seen it in my crystal ball.'

Was he wasting his time? Aaron wanted facts, not cryptic crystal-ball gazing. He lowered his head as he stepped inside the caravan. 'Go on, Kāterina. What did you see?'

'Before we start,' Kāterina said, 'I'll make us some tea. My mouth's parched.'

Kāterina never imparted anything without a cup of tea. Aaron sat on the bench, watched her fill the old copper kettle and put it on the old stove. Being in the *Gypsy Rose* was like living in a time warp. Sure, the paintwork was fading, and there were a few more chips in the woodwork. But apart from that, nothing had changed since the time he'd read to Kāterina as a child. The same old ornaments and antiques crammed into every corner of the caravan. Trinkets hung from the ceiling. The crystal ball still perched on its plinth and the palmistry hands he had used to tell Miriama's fortune were still on the small circular table. Shelves

David Whittet

overflowing with stacks of leather-bound books. On top of the pile, a paperback copy of *Great Expectations* caught Aaron's eye. Kāterina must have bought it to replace the gilded volume she'd given him. Aaron mentally chided himself. He'd had the book all this time and still hadn't finished the story.

The kettle whistled when it neared the boil.

Kāterina muttered as she fetched the teapot. 'Fostering Miriama was an act of atonement. I'll never forget her face when I first saw her in the children's home. Those vacant eyes. A lost soul that I could save.'

Should he say something? Aaron wasn't sure if she was talking to him or to herself. It occurred to him he knew very little about Miriama's distant past. He shuffled back on the bench as Kāterina continued to mumble.

'She never played with the other kids, just sat in the corner on her own.' Kāterina poured the tea and turned to Aaron. 'You wouldn't think it now, would you?'

Aaron cleared his throat. 'How much does Miriama know about her past? Does she know who her birth parents are?'

Kāterina shook her head. 'Best she doesn't. Her father was a renegade lawyer and her mother one of his whores.'

Aaron gulped—that *would* destroy Miriama. Something else from Kāterina's rumblings troubled him. 'What did you mean when you said you fostered Miriama out of atonement?'

'Murua ahau! I wronged your mother and your grandmother.' Kāterina slurped her tea. 'Set off a chain reaction that destroyed so many lives.'

Aaron stared at her. 'What do you mean?'

'Your grandmother, Naomi, came to me in her hour of need. She was pregnant and desperate, and I turned her away.' Kāterina put down her teacup and wiped away a tear. 'Naomi ran away to a women's refuge and left your mother with Reggie.'

'That wasn't your fault,' Aaron said. 'Naomi left to get away from Reggie and the Gang.'

More tears rolled down Kāterina's cheeks. 'You don't understand. Thanks to me, Alicia lost her mother when she needed her most.'

'You're beating yourself up over nothing,' Aaron said. 'Aunt Helena told me she wouldn't be alive if you hadn't stopped Naomi from having an abortion.'

'That's true. I just wish …' Kāterina dried her eyes on an old handkerchief. 'I wish I'd been there for your mother.'

'But you were. When I was born.' Aaron looked down at the ragged rug on the wooden floorboards. 'You told me you delivered me here in the caravan. On this very floor.'

'I did. It was one of the proudest moments of my life. But …' Kāterina closed her eyes and whispered a prayer in Māori: 'Te Atua murua ahau. Kawea mai te rangimarie ki ahau.'

Aaron shook his head. 'What?'

'I asked God to forgive me and bring me peace.' She reached out to Aaron and rested a hand on his. 'I should have been there when they took your mother away. Done something to stop them.'

The memory of that night brought a tear to Aaron's eye. 'They were vicious thugs. There was nothing you could have done. They'd have beaten you to a pulp.'

'I could have got around Reggie. Forced him to set Alicia free. Ka pōuri ahau! Ka pōuri ahau!'

Despite Kāterina apologising, from everything Aaron had heard, nothing would've forced his grandfather Reggie into something he didn't want to do.

'I searched for her,' Kāterina continued. 'Dear God, how I searched for Alicia. I still had informants in the Gang, but I couldn't get a word out of them. "No way," they all said. "Are you trying to get us killed?"'

Aaron shrugged. *So how did you intend to find my mother once we had finished reading Great Expectations?* 'You did your best, Kāterina. Nobody could have done more.'

'Maybe not. But I had to redeem myself. Mind you, fostering Miriama wasn't easy, either. I had to call in every favour I could for that, too. The buggers at social services didn't think I could bring up a child in a caravan. Lucky, I still had some contacts in high places. And when they heard I was sending her to an elite school in Switzerland, they couldn't get it through the Family Court fast enough.' Kāterina rummaged in a drawer and pulled out a business magazine with Miriama's picture on the cover. 'Now, when I see Miriama making such a success of her life, I feel that at least I've done something worthwhile in my life.'

Aaron put his arm around her. 'You've done so much for me, too.'

'Not really.' Kāterina eyed him earnestly. 'I sometimes think I've just brought you a load of heartache.' She stuffed the magazine back into the drawer. 'Still, you didn't come here to listen to me rambling on about the past. You want to know what Miriama's playing at now.'

Damn right. Aaron caught his breath. 'Have you any idea where she is? Or why she left me without a word?'

'We'll soon find out.' Kāterina reached across for her crystal ball and caressed it with her fingers. 'Tell me, my precious, where is Miriama? Where is my headstrong girl?'

Aaron leant forward and gazed at the crystal ball. 'What can you see?'

Kāterina smiled. 'I see you and Miriama, back in each other arms.'

'Are you sure?'

'Certain.' Kāterina continued to run her fingers across the crystal ball. 'My precious never lies. You'll be together again in no time, and married, too. I promise.'

❧

Three weeks later, they *were* back together, planning their wedding at the picturesque Church of the Good Shepherd on the shores of Lake Tekapō. Perhaps Kāterina really did have magical powers after all.

They sat quietly on a pew in the church. Aaron's head had been all over the place during the past few days. He gazed through the panoramic window above the altar, spellbound by the magnificent view. The early evening sun glistened on the lake, with snow-clad mountains in the distance and a gentle breeze in the air. A moment of blissful tranquillity, a chance to take stock of his chaotic life and find new meaning.

Should he speak? Aaron had so many unanswered questions. His most recent night spent with Miriama had ended in disaster. Why had she run away? Where had she been these past few weeks? Aaron held her tight. However desperate he was for an explanation, he couldn't destroy such a divine moment in these exquisite surroundings.

Miriama broke the silence. 'So, you approve of my choice?'

'It's the most beautiful church I've ever seen,' Aaron said. 'I could sit here all night and soak up the atmosphere.'

Miriama nudged him gently. 'You'd better not. Don't forget you're taking me out for dinner tonight.'

Maybe he'd say something over dinner. They'd found a little restaurant overlooking the lake. Perfect. Fresh salmon and a glorious sunset. Aaron sipped his wine and sighed. No way would he spoil the ambience with ugly questions.

After dinner, they walked along the lakeside in the twilight. Arm in arm with the woman he loved in the crisp mountain air and the stars above—was it all too perfect?

Miriama squeezed his hand. 'I bet you're thinking about how you could turn this gorgeous lake into a hydroelectric power station.'

Was she serious? Aaron wasn't sure until he saw the grin on her face.

He smiled back. 'No, I was taking in the peace and tranquillity. Admiring the night sky and the twinkling stars. What could be more amazing than that? I could never build a power station here.'

'The poet versus the businessman, eh?' Miriama stopped and turned to face him. 'I know what's really on your mind. You're still trying to work out why I left you that morning in Wellington.'

Aaron felt a sudden chill in the night air. Did he really want to know? 'We're together now, and that's all that matters.'

'I'm sorry.' Miriama gripped his hand even tighter. 'I shouldn't have run away. But I was frightened.'

Aaron took a step back. 'Frightened of me?'

'No. Scared a life with you would be a constant battle against the Gang.' Miriama paused and took a deep breath. 'When I saw the headline in the newspaper, I panicked. I convinced myself there'd be Gang reprisals.'

Aaron shook his head. 'If only you'd talked to me before taking off. I'd have understood.'

'You'd have persuaded me to stay.'

'Of course I would.' Aaron put his arm around her. 'I can protect you. I saved you when we were kids, and I'll do it again.'

'You'll try. I know you will. It's just …' Miriama broke off and rubbed her eyes. 'Look what happened to your mother. Aren't you scared?'

'We have to be strong and stand up to the Gang.' Aaron stood tall. He couldn't let Miriama see he was quaking inside. 'The night those thugs took

David Whittet

my mother away … she'd just told me about David and Goliath, from the Old Testament. She said I had to be strong like David in the story. And I will be.'

Miriama shuddered. 'That's what I'm afraid of.'

'Why?'

'We're no match for the Godzone Gorillas.' Miriama turned to face him head-on. 'They have spies everywhere. These last few weeks, I've had loads of phone calls—'

Aaron waved a hand. 'That was me. I was desperate to talk to you.'

'I'm sorry, I should have taken your calls. That was mean of me.' Miriama shifted from one foot to the other. 'But it wasn't your calls that freaked me out. I keep getting calls from an unknown number at all hours of the day and night. I'm sure it was the Gang tracking me down.'

Aaron smiled. 'That was me, too. When you wouldn't answer my number, I got a batch of new SIM cards and kept trying.'

Miriama's jaw dropped. Was she mad at him?

'You're not making that up, are you?' she said. 'Just to make me feel better?'

'No way.'

Miriama shrugged. 'Well, you scared the shit out of me. I can tell you that.'

They both laughed and walked back to their accommodation.

'Anyway, Kāterina's coming to join us in a couple of days,' Aaron said. 'She wants to be here for Matariki.'

'She'll be stargazing as usual,' Miriama replied. 'That is if she gets here in that clapped-out caravan.'

Aaron chuckled. 'I tried my best to persuade her to buy a smart new motor home when I was a kid. She said that would be the end of everything.'

'Kāterina will never part with the *Gypsy Rose*. Or her precious crystal ball.' Miriama paused as they reached their accommodation, a small cottage they'd rented through Airbnb. 'Promise me one thing. You'll think about security for the wedding. Just in case.'

'I'm on it already,' Aaron said. 'I told you I'd keep you safe, and I meant it. I've hired a top-notch security company. The best in the land.'

Where had he heard those words before? Kāterina had told him about his parents' wedding. How his father had boasted about making the church as secure as Fort Knox. Aaron's stomach churned as he turned the key and opened the door of the cottage. The best protection in the world hadn't stopped his mother from getting gunned down at her wedding or saved his father from dying in an arson attack.

Aaron took off his coat while Miriama wandered into the kitchen. Was he scared? Maybe he was, but he would never let Miriama see it.

'Fancy a coffee?' Miriama asked. 'There's ground coffee and a plunger in here.'

'Brilliant, I'd love one.'

Was she right to be frightened? Could he really protect her? Aaron watched Miriama press down the plunger and pour the coffee. Would the Godzone Gorillas hunt them down?

Don't even think about it. No way would Aaron let the Gang get the better of him. Besides, he'd just shown he was far smarter than them. He sat down beside Miriama on the sofa and banished all negative thoughts from his head.

Miriama took a sip of coffee. 'The perfect end to the day. Fresh coffee and a night under the stars.'

'Now who's the poet?' Aaron grinned and snuggled up to her. 'I love you, Miriama. Never leave me again.'

❧

Aaron dreamt about his mother that night. He was five again and tucked up in bed, listening to one of his mother's bedtime stories. Such a warm and comforting dream. How safe he'd felt back then before the Gang violated their sanctuary and took her away from him. But wait—they weren't in his bedroom now. His mother was standing beside him in the Church of the Good Shepherd on his wedding day. What was she whispering in his ear?

'My darling boy, no power on earth could stop me from being here with you today.'

Aaron awoke with a start. 'Don't go! Mummy!' He reached out with his hands as if trying to hold on to the fading image. 'Stay with me … I've only just found you … and there's so much I want to tell you.'

It was too late. Aaron was wide awake. The dream was over, and his mother had disappeared. Now he'd never be able to tell her how he'd fought off his own

 David Whittet

Goliath and won. What would his mother have thought of Miriama? He felt sure they'd be best friends, but now he'd never know for certain.

Would Miriama notice he was distracted? Aaron struggled to concentrate when they met the vicar at the church to go through the order of service and choose the hymns for their marriage ceremony.

'"Amazing Grace" would be the perfect opening hymn,' Miriama said. 'What do you think, darling?'

'Great choice,' Aaron replied.

'You pick the next hymn,' Miriama said.

Aaron scanned the list of wedding hymns that the vicar had given them. 'How about "Lord of All Hopefulness"?'

'Splendid,' the vicar said. 'Both those hymns are popular with young couples. Why not close with "Lead Us, Heavenly Father, Lead Us"? That's another beautiful hymn.'

Aaron smiled nervously at the vicar. 'I chose my hymn because …'

Why *had* he chosen "Lord of All Hopefulness"? Aaron scratched his head. Was he subconsciously *hopeful* that his mother would be at the wedding like she was in his dream? Or was he just kidding himself? Perhaps it wasn't just a dream. Maybe it was one of those psychic experiences Kāterina was always on about. *Of course!* Kāterina could interpret dreams. Aaron couldn't wait for her to arrive so he could sound her out about his dream.

Aaron sat upright. Miriama and the vicar were still waiting for him to finish the sentence.

'I chose "Lord of All Hopefulness" because …' Aaron blinked back a tear. 'I know it's silly, but I was hoping my mother would make it to the wedding.'

Miriama put her arms around him. 'My darling! Are you okay?'

'I dreamt about my mother last night. In my dream she turned up at our wedding. Then I woke up.' Aaron gave up the struggle to hold back his tears. 'I just wish she could be here for the wedding.'

Miriama hugged him tighter. 'So do I.'

'I'm sure your mother will be with you in spirit,' the vicar said, gathering his papers. 'You two need some time alone together. We can carry on tomorrow.'

Aaron and Miriama walked from the church into town.

'I wish I could have met your mother,' Miriama said. 'Kāterina has told me so much about her. How the Gang stole her childhood and how she refused to let them claim the rest of her life. Alicia must have been one kick-arse woman.'

'She was.' Aaron paused. *But she did let the Godzone Gorillas take the rest of her life. She went back to Mickey, and that was her downfall.* 'If only she had got away when she had the chance. Then she'd be with us now.'

Miriama squeezed his hand. 'You heard what the vicar said. Alicia will be with us in spirit on our big day. That's what matters most.'

'Guess so.' Aaron shivered. *With us in spirit.* What did that mean? The vicar was a man of God. Maybe he had a hotline to the Almighty. Had a voice from above told the vicar Alicia was dead? That would explain why he said she would be there in spirit, watching the wedding from Heaven.

'You're miles away, aren't you, my darling?' Miriama turned to face him directly. 'I understand. I never knew my birth mother.'

That must have been hard. But Miriama had Kāterina. And could you really miss someone you'd never met?

As they walked along, Aaron was trying to work it out when a rumbling noise interrupted his train of thought. He turned his head towards the source, but a cloud of dust concealed the end of the street. There was something familiar about that creaking sound. Was it? Could it be? A horse's neigh confirmed everything.

'It's Cleo! I'd recognise that horse anywhere!' Aaron rubbed his eyes, the dust making them smart. 'Kāterina! Kāterina! I've been waiting for you!'

The dust cloud gradually dispersed. Battered and clanking and swaying from side to side, the *Gypsy Rose* rolled into town.

Miriama sighed. 'Trust Kāterina. Why does she have to make such a dramatic entrance wherever she goes?'

Never mind that. Aaron grabbed Miriama's hand, and they followed the caravan down the street. He waved his hands madly. 'Wait, Kāterina! We need to talk.'

Kāterina pulled on Cleo's reins. 'I know. You've had a dream! Give me an hour or two. I have to find a parking spot for the *Gypsy Rose*, and Cleo needs a feed.'

 David Whittet

How the hell did Kāterina know about his dream? Was she really psychic? Aaron shook his head as he watched the caravan lurch around the corner into a paddock.

Miriama must have guessed what he was thinking. 'Kāterina can't really see into the future,' she said as they walked back to their cottage. 'You understand that, don't you?'

Aaron eyed her quizzically. 'So how come she knew about my dream?'

Miriama shrugged. 'A clever guess, most likely.'

Aaron wasn't so sure. And he had to wait a couple of hours before he could interrogate Kāterina about his dream. Why did his heart tell him it would be the longest two hours of his life?

CHAPTER THIRTY

Maybe Miriama was right, and it was just guesswork, but Aaron had to be sure. Two hours later, he made his way to the paddock. Cleo gave him a welcoming neigh as he approached the *Gypsy Rose*. Tied up to the caravan with a rope to her halter, the poor horse could barely stand up.

Aaron stopped and stroked Cleo's mane. 'You look done for.' He picked up some hay from the ground and fed it to Cleo. 'I'm going to have words with Kāterina about you.'

Couldn't Kāterina see Cleo was getting older and past hauling the caravan on these long journeys? Why hadn't Kāterina bought a motor home like he'd told her all those years ago?

Aaron was about to go into the caravan when he heard Kāterina's voice. He peered through the window. Kāterina was talking to her crystal ball.

'You have been a good friend to me.' Kāterina pressed the crystal ball against her face as she spoke. 'Show me the future one last time.'

Aaron stepped back. *One last time?* What did she mean?

Kāterina's voice again. 'Please, my precious, let me see Aaron and Miriama married before I die. And help me find Alicia.'

Aaron burst into the caravan. 'You're not going to die. You can't! I won't let you.'

Kāterina put her crystal ball on its plinth and embraced Aaron. 'Taku tamaiti aroha! My dear boy. We are all passing figures in life's continuum. My earthly journey is all but complete. Yours is just starting.'

Aaron clung to Kāterina. 'I need you. Miriama needs you. Please don't leave us.'

'I'm here now,' Kāterina said. 'So sit down and tell me about this dream you've had.'

Aaron let go of her, and they huddled together on the bench.

'We were at the church,' Aaron began. 'Miriama and I were about to take our vows. My mother was standing behind me. I reached out to her—there was so much I wanted to say to her.'

     David Whittet

'So did you talk to her?' Kāterina asked.

'I tried to.' Aaron held out his hands. 'But she was gone in a flash. And then I woke up.'

Kāterina ran a finger through her grey hair. 'Did your mother say anything to you?'

'Yes.' Aaron's voice croaked as he struggled to get the words out. 'She said I was her darling boy and that no power on earth could stop her from being with me on my wedding day.'

Kāterina sat upright. 'Then I must find her and bring her to your wedding.'

Aaron lowered his head. 'If only you could.'

'I can and I will.' Kāterina jumped to her feet and paced up and down the caravan. 'I'll set out in the morning.'

Aaron stared at her. 'But you've only just got here. Besides, Cleo's absolutely exhausted.'

Kāterina continued pacing. 'My faithful steed won't let me down.'

Aaron shook his head. 'Cleo's getting old. You can't expect her to haul the caravan on another long journey so soon.'

'Maybe you're right.' Kāterina glanced at Cleo through the open door. 'Cleopatra and I are growing old together.'

Aaron stood up and gave Kāterina a gentle prod. 'You wouldn't be in this predicament if you'd listened to me all those years ago and bought a motor home.'

Kāterina glared at him. 'And I told you a traveller and their carriage can never be separated. A motor home would be the end of everything!'

Aaron waved a hand. 'Okay, okay. I'm sorry.'

'My time on this planet is running out, and the *Gypsy Rose* will be my home until I take my last breath.' Kāterina continued to eyeball him. 'That's why I must embark on this mission while I still can. Besides, there's not much time for me to find your mother before your wedding as it is.'

'But Kāterina—'

Kāterina reached for her coat. 'But nothing.'

'You're not going searching for my mother now, are you?'

'Good heavens, no.' Kāterina grabbed her ornately carved walking stick and made for the door. 'I'm off to the Tekapō observatory to see the Matariki stars. Why don't you come with me?'

Aaron followed her out. 'Miriama told me you're a keen astronomer.'

Kāterina smiled. 'Your grandmother Naomi nicknamed me Kōkā.'

'Why?'

'I couldn't sleep when I was a little girl. Still can't now.'

'So?'

Kāterina's eye glowed in the dark. 'I used to spend all night outside looking at the stars. My father called me a tohunga kōkōrangi. That's Māori for an astronomer. Your grandmother shortened it to Kōkā, and the name stuck.'

'So what are you going to see tonight?'

Kāterina gazed up at the heavens. 'The Matariki stars. The Pleiades star cluster that marks the start of the Māori New Year.' She turned to Aaron. 'You should get married on Matariki Day. Ka whai waimarie koe. It'll bring you luck.'

What? Bring the wedding forward? Aaron took a step back. That would give Kāterina even less time to find his mother before the big day.

'It's extra special this year,' Kāterina continued. 'It's the first time Matariki Day is a public holiday. I've campaigned to have the day recognised for as long as I can remember.'

In the caravan Aaron had seen fading black-and-white photos showing Kāterina marching on parliament. She often boasted about a hīkoi of protest she'd organised for a cause she'd believed in.

'I'd love to get married on Matariki Day,' Aaron said, picking up his pace to catch up with Kāterina. 'But that's impossible. It's next Friday. We couldn't possibly get everything arranged by then. Besides, the church is bound to be booked up for such a special day.'

'It isn't,' Katarina replied. 'I've checked with the vicar.'

Aaron shook his head. Was Kāterina for real? She had an answer for everything. Maybe she'd seen it all in her crystal ball.

'Okay,' he said. 'I'll talk it over with Miriama.'

Kāterina stopped and pointed to a hill. 'The observatory is up there.'

'Shouldn't I get Miriama?' Aaron asked. 'She won't want to miss out.'

Kāterina sighed. 'Miriama won't come.'

'Why not?'

'Miriama hates stargazing.' Kāterina cleared some shrubbery with her walking stick, and they climbed up the path to the observatory. 'It's my fault,

     David Whittet

really. I'd be out with my telescope in the middle of the night and see an exquisite constellation in the sky. I had to share its splendour, and I used to drag Miriama out of her bed to look through the telescope.

'"Isn't that magnificent?" I'd say to her.

'Miriama wasn't the least impressed. She'd stand there shivering and grumbling. I can still hear her moaning. "You've got me out of bed for this?"

'"But it's beautiful," I would insist.

'"My bed was beautiful," she'd retaliate.

'I could wax lyrical about the stars as much as I liked, but all she wanted was to get back into the warmth of her bed.'

That was *so* Miriama. Aaron smiled. 'Miriama never was much of a poet.'

'She doesn't know what she's missing,' Kāterina said as they reached the observatory. 'Prepare to be amazed.'

Aaron was beyond being amazed. The crystal-clear sky and the Matariki star cluster's brilliance illuminated the dark winter's night. The stars looked so close through the telescope that Aaron almost felt he could touch them.

Kāterina put a hand on his shoulder as he gazed through the telescope. 'Stunning, isn't it?'

'I wouldn't have missed this for the world,' Aaron replied, without taking his eye from the telescope.

'For Māori,' Kāterina continued, 'Matariki is a time of remembrance, joy, and peace. The stars herald another year and a new beginning. It's not just for Māori, either. It's for all New Zealanders.'

Aaron thought about Kāterina's words while they walked back from the observatory. Would the Māori New Year bring him luck and bless his relationship with Miriama? Perhaps they should forget all the invitations and arrangements for a lavish reception and get married on Matariki Day after all. But would that deny him the last faint possibility of his mother getting to the wedding? Aaron studied Kāterina, limping down the hill in the moonlight. Her gout must have been playing up again, and she was short of breath. Aaron sighed—such a frail, elderly lady would never find his mother in time.

'You go on ahead,' Kāterina said. 'Miriama will be waiting for you.'

'I'm walking you back to the *Gypsy Rose* first,' Aaron said. 'No arguments.'

'I can look after myself.'

Aaron took her arm. 'I know. But I'll sleep easier if I know you're safe. We can't have you falling over and breaking—' He broke off mid-sentence. A distressed, squealing noise echoed through the deserted street. It was coming from the paddock and becoming louder by the second. 'What the hell is that?'

Kāterina gasped. 'It's Cleo. She's in trouble.'

'Leave this to me.' Aaron let go of Kāterina's arm and raced down the street to the paddock.

A hooded man stood in front of the *Gypsy Rose*. Cleo reared up on her hind legs, desperately trying to fend him off.

'Piss off!' Aaron shouted. 'Can't you see you're frightening the horse?'

The man turned to face him, his head shrouded by the hood. All Aaron could see were his blazing eyes, piercing the darkness like laser beams.

'I said, piss off,' Aaron repeated. 'Get the hell out of here!'

The man didn't move. He just stared at Aaron without saying a word.

Aaron shielded his face from the man's incandescent eyes. Was the bastard trying to hypnotise him?

Kāterina stumbled into the paddock, gasping for breath. 'Don't you dare hurt my precious horse!' She staggered across to comfort Cleo. 'Cleo! My beloved steed. I won't let anyone harm you!'

The man waved a fist at Kāterina, his menacing eyes fixed on her. Aaron's heart missed a beat as Kāterina stepped forward to confront him.

'You don't scare me.' Kāterina glared at the man, her bulging eyes every bit as intense as his. 'Go now!'

The man didn't move. What was he going to do now?

Aaron pulled his mobile phone out of his pocket. 'I'm calling the police.'

'No!' Kāterina shouted. 'I don't want any trouble.'

Why didn't Kāterina want the police involved? Did she know this man? Or could it be just that she had parked illegally in the paddock and didn't want the police moving her on?

Kāterina continued to eyeball the man. 'Kanga koe! Haere atu!'

Was she putting a spell on him? Kāterina continued to curse in Māori and wave her arms at him.

'Kāore koe i te pōwhiri ki konei.'

     David Whittet

To Aaron's amazement, the man backed off. He paused for a moment at the paddock's edge, then ran off down the street.

Aaron put his arm around Kāterina. 'Are you alright? Who was that man? Have you seen him before?'

'Questions. Questions.' Kāterina bent down to pick up some hay. 'Too many questions.'

'What did you say to him?'

Kāterina fed Cleo the hay. 'I told him he wasn't welcome here.'

Aaron frowned. 'So you did know him?'

'It is of no consequence whether or not I know him.' Kāterina finished feeding Cleo and turned to Aaron. 'That man was an omen. Sent from on high to warn me.'

Aaron shook his head. This was no time for more of Kāterina's riddles. 'An omen? What are you on about? It was probably just a hobo out to steal your horse. Maybe your caravan too.'

Kāterina hobbled up the steps into the *Gypsy Rose*. 'Maybe he was just a tramp. But he was sent here for a purpose.'

Aaron followed her into the caravan. What *purpose* could some down-and-out vagrant have for her?

Kāterina took her crystal ball off its plinth and began caressing it. 'Tell me, my precious, what perils lurk ahead?' She sat on the bench and gazed into the ball. 'Murua ahau! I see Alicia … she's in danger … I must leave for Roaring Creek tonight!'

Aaron shook his head. 'You can't possibly. Cleo will never make it. She's worn out. So are you.'

Kāterina leapt up and put the crystal ball back on its plinth. 'Don't you want me to find your mother?'

'Of course I do.' Aaron swallowed hard. 'But I couldn't bear to lose you in a fatal accident because you and Cleo are both too tired to travel.'

'Didn't you hear me? Your mother is in danger.' Kāterina jumped out of the caravan to harness Cleo. 'You won't let me down, will you, Cleo?'

Aaron followed her out. 'If you must go tonight, I'll take you in the car.'

'No.' Kāterina turned to face him. 'This is a journey I must make alone.'

Aaron held up his hands. 'But Kāterina … please … if my mother's in danger, then I need to be there.'

Kāterina finished harnessing Cleo. 'You need to stay here for Miriama.'

Aaron knew it was useless arguing once Kāterina had made up her mind, but he had to try. 'Miriama can come with us. I'll go and wake her up.'

Kāterina glanced at the sky. 'The Matariki stars are with me. They will guide me to your mother.'

'Wait! Kāterina!'

Too late. Kāterina pulled on Cleo's reins, and the *Gypsy Rose* lurched forward.

'Giddy-up, Cleo!' Kāterina cried. 'Godspeed to Roaring Creek!'

Aaron stood transfixed. He watched Cleo pull the caravan out of the paddock and onto the road. Should he get the car and go after them? Kāterina would never forgive him if he did.

'Don't worry,' Kāterina shouted as the caravan disappeared into the darkness. 'I'll be back—with your mother!'

Would she? Could Kāterina possibly find his mother? With all their resources, the highest-paid private investigators in the land had drawn a blank. All Kāterina had was her crystal ball.

Aaron wandered back to their accommodation through the deserted streets. He shivered—not from the plummeting overnight temperature, but from the thought that he might never see Kāterina or his mother again.

     David Whittet

Two days passed, and still no word from Kāterina. Aaron sat alone at the breakfast table at their cottage. He'd bought Kāterina a mobile phone and had told her to keep it with her day and night. Why didn't she answer his calls? He'd spent long enough showing her how to use it. Had she met with an accident? Had the *Gypsy Rose* finally broken apart? Aaron shuddered. Maybe Kāterina was lying at the roadside on a remote country road.

Aaron pushed his bowl of muesli aside. Perhaps she was out of mobile range. Kāterina had promised to be back with his mother in time for the wedding. Had she ever let him down before? But the ceremony was tomorrow, on Matariki Day—the day Kāterina had assured would bring them good luck and a fresh start.

Why hadn't he gone after Kāterina in his car? Aaron asked himself the question for the thousandth time when Miriama burst into the room. She was always covered in perspiration when she came in from her morning run. Today, her tank top and track pants were saturated and her body shook.

'Whatever's the matter?' Aaron said. 'It's not … bad news about Kāterina, is it?'

Miriama shook her head. 'I was running along the shore when this weird man appeared—'

Aaron sat bolt upright. 'Did he have a hood covering his head?'

Miriama nodded. 'He was dressed in black, like some evil spirit. I tried not to look, but he blocked my way on the path.'

Aaron shot up from the table. 'I'm going to sort out this bastard once and for all.'

Miriama wiped the sweat off her forehead. 'You've seen this man before?'

'He was there when Kāterina left.' Aaron made for the door. 'I told him to piss off then. He obviously didn't get the message.'

'Be careful.' Miriama grabbed Aaron's arm. 'He's a monster. I caught a glimpse of his face. It was grotesque, covered in a hideous scar.'

'He freaked Cleo and Kāterina out, that's for sure. She thought he was a bad omen. That's why she took off so quickly.' Aaron paused on the doorstep. 'He'll just be a tramp, and the sooner he moves on, the better.'

Aaron marched to the lakeside. It was bad enough that the hobo had sent Kāterina out of town. Aaron would not let him terrorise his fiancée and upset their wedding plans. No way.

Where was the bastard? Aaron arrived to see the last of the joggers disappear into the distance. He scanned the deserted shoreline. No sign of the hooded man.

With a sigh, Aaron wandered back to their cottage. His thoughts turned once more to Kāterina. What if she had met with an accident? Should he call the police? He pulled his mobile phone out of his pocket. Would they take him seriously? After all, Kāterina was a recluse. The police would just say she'd gone back to her nomadic lifestyle. Perhaps he would be better off ringing around the hospitals to see if they had admitted her.

Footsteps interrupted Aaron's train of thought. Someone was following him. Perhaps the tramp hadn't legged it after all.

'Bugger off!' Aaron almost choked on his words as he turned to face not the tramp but an elderly woman. 'I'm sorry, I thought you were—'

'You were expecting the hooded man?' The woman pulled back her shawl to reveal her gnarled face. 'He's gone—for now, at any rate.'

Aaron shuddered. 'You think he'll come back? Have you any idea who he is?'

The woman tilted her head. 'Another lost soul striving to find his place in this troubled world.'

Who was this strange woman? Why did she talk in riddles? Aaron shrugged. She sounded just like Kāterina.

'You must be Aaron,' the woman continued. 'Kāterina told me I would find you here.'

'What?' Aaron took a step back. 'Kāterina sent you? Do you know where she is?'

The woman ran her fingers through her scraggly grey hair. 'Kāterina is a dear friend. We go back many years. But I fear—that wretched curse. I knew it would be her downfall.'

Aaron shook his head. 'Just tell me what you know. Is she in danger?'

'We are all in peril as we tread life's tortuous path.'

 David Whittet

'Yes, but what about Kāterina?'

The woman lowered her head. 'Dear Kāterina. Foolish Kāterina. I warned her about such an inauspicious mission.'

Aaron stamped his foot. 'Just tell me where she is.'

'All in good time. My mouth is dry and my legs are weary. Any chance of a cup of tea?'

Give me strength! Aaron raised his eyes to the heavens. The woman got more exasperating—and more like Kāterina—by the minute.

'Okay,' Aaron said. 'There's a café on the Main Street. But I want answers.'

Did this peculiar woman know anything? Aaron studied her face as they walked to the café. Was she just after a free breakfast? But she knew his name and Kāterina's, so she couldn't be a complete fraudster. Should he have taken her back to their accommodation? No, he didn't want to upset Miriama any further on the eve of their wedding. Not until he knew the woman was for real. He'd sound her out at the café.

Aaron ordered a full cooked breakfast for the woman and a double-shot espresso for himself.

'I don't even know your name,' he said as they sat down at a table by the window.

The woman gobbled her breakfast as though she hadn't eaten in a month. 'My name's Neina,' she said in between mouthfuls. 'Neina Ngatai.'

Aaron leant forward. 'Who are you, Neina? And how do you know Kāterina?'

'My friends call me an enchantress. My enemies call me a witch.'

'What about Kāterina?' Aaron asked. 'You said the two of you got back a long way.'

'Kāterina called me her friend.' Neina paused, almost choking on a sausage. 'But I fear I may have sent her to a watery grave.'

Aaron pulled back. 'You mean Kāterina's … dead?'

Neina put down her knife and fork and frowned. 'Kāterina came to me, desperate to revoke a curse. I told her she had to return to the waters of the Roaring Creek Falls.'

Aaron glared at her. 'What? A minute ago, you said you'd warned her about taking such a—what did you call it? An inauspicious journey.'

'I tried to stop her. Believe me, I did. A storm was breaking, and it would be cataclysmic. I felt it in my bones.' Neina paused again and blinked back a tear. 'You've no idea how I begged her to wait till the storm had passed.'

'But she didn't?'

Neina shook her head. 'Kāterina believed it was the only way to save your mother and bring her to your wedding.'

Aaron took a deep breath. 'Start at the beginning. I want the whole story. Kāterina, the curse, everything.' He drew closer, his eyes still fixed on Neina. 'Above all, anything about my mother.'

Neina shrugged. 'It's not a pretty story. Are you sure you want to hear it?'

Aaron nodded. 'Spill.'

'It was years ago, but I remember it clear as anything. The night Kāterina sought me out.' Neina wrapped her shawl around her shoulders and shivered. 'A storm raged that night, too. Kāterina had been on the road for days and was drenched when she arrived. Poor Kāterina. She looked like a drowned rat.'

Would this woman ever get to the point? Aaron toyed with the teaspoon in his coffee cup. 'Go on.'

'It was just after your mother met your father.' Neina lowered her head. 'Kāterina wanted my help to cast a spell.'

Aaron raised his eyes to the ceiling and then back to Neina. 'Did you help her?'

'For my sins—I did.' Neina cleared her throat. 'Kāterina had convinced herself that your father only married your mother to get a foothold in the Godzone Gorillas.'

'That's balls!' Aaron shot bolt upright. 'I'm sorry, Neina, but that's absolute nonsense.'

Neina rubbed her chin. 'Kāterina didn't think so. A good friend of hers, Alejandro Guerrero, was a director of your father's company. Alejandro told her how Emir boasted about marrying the Gang president's daughter. The board had threatened to abandon your father's long-cherished plan to build a water bottling factory at the Roaring Creek Falls for fear of gang reprisals. Your father claimed the Godzone Gorillas couldn't touch him once he'd married into the family.'

More lies! Aaron had heard of Alejandro Guerrero, but that didn't mean the story was true. 'You don't know what you're talking about!'

     David Whittet

'Don't I?' Neina pulled her chair closer and eyed Aaron. 'Your father was determined to build that water bottling plant, whatever the cost. The one thing standing in his way was a land claim held by the Godzone Gorillas. Now do you see why he was so keen to marry the daughter of the Gang's president?'

Aaron shook his head. 'Even if that's true—which it isn't—how come Kāterina never told me any of this?'

Neina shrugged. 'Didn't want to upset you, I guess.'

More like she knew I'd see through such bullshit. Aaron pinched his lips. 'A fat lot of good it did my father, anyway. The Godzone Gorillas murdered my father. Burnt him alive.'

'Aaron!' Neina shot him down with her eyes. 'I know it's hard for you to accept, but it wasn't the Godzone Gorillas who killed your father. It was a business rival who started the fire. Someone your father had double-crossed.'

Aaron returned her glare. 'It was Mickey.'

'Mickey had nothing to do with it.'

'The police caught him red-handed snooping around outside the house. Mickey started the fire.'

'You don't know that,' Neina said. 'You weren't there.'

'Nor were you.'

Neina sighed. 'I don't know what you've been told, but—'

'But nothing. It was Mickey. Callous bastard. He was there with the means and the motive.'

'Are you sure?' Neina ran her fingers through her grizzled hair. 'Kāterina says it was Mickey who rescued your mother from the fire.'

Aaron threw his arms in the air. 'Enough! I've had the best private detectives in the land investigate this.'

'But were they right? Kāterina was positive that Mickey saved your mother and that—'

Aaron cut her off again. 'No more.' He stood up and walked away. 'I don't have to listen to this.'

'You do,' Neina called after him. 'If you want to know what's happened to Kāterina.'

Should he keep walking? Aaron paused when he reached the door. He was desperate for news of Kāterina, but could he trust this freakish woman?

Neina followed him and put a hand on his shoulder. 'Maybe you're right. Perhaps it was the Godzone Gorillas who had it in for your father. I guess we'll never know the entire story.'

Aaron turned to face her. 'Where is Kāterina? Do you really know what's happened to her?'

'I do.' Neina led him back to the table. 'I'll tell you everything. But I'll need another cup of tea first.'

Was she taking him for a ride? Aaron stared at her bewitching eyes. 'Okay. On one condition. No more badmouthing my father.' Without waiting for her to answer, he ordered the tea at the counter and then sat down opposite Neina. 'Let's start again. You said Kāterina set out for the Roaring Creek Falls during a storm. What's become of her? Do you know where she is?'

The waitress arrived with a pot of tea.

Neina took a sip and pursed her lips. 'You may think the curse is just mumbo-jumbo, but Kāterina believed it. In cursing your father, she convinced herself she'd inadvertently cursed you and your mother too.'

Aaron took a deep breath. 'Neina, please. Just stick to the facts.'

Neina reached out across the table and clutched his hand. 'As God is my witness, I speak the truth.'

Perhaps Neina was telling the truth. A disturbing thought crossed Aaron's mind. Something Kāterina had told him still troubled him. Kāterina said she adopted Miriama as an atonement. When Aaron asked her what she meant, Kāterina said she'd wronged his mother. His grandmother too. And something about a chain reaction that had destroyed so many lives. Why had she told him that? Aaron shuddered. Had Kāterina sponsored his education because of a guilty conscience?

Neina continued her story. 'When Kāterina insisted on travelling back to the Roaring Creek Falls in that dreadful storm, I went with her on the *Gypsy Rose*.'

Aaron stared at her. 'You were there? So you *do* know what's happened to Kāterina?'

'I stayed with her as long as I dared,' Neina replied. 'I will never forget that night as long as I live. Rain lashed down, and the *Gypsy Rose* swayed from side to side. The storm was so violent I was afraid the axle would break and the wheels would fall off that rickety old caravan.

 David Whittet

'Kāterina cried out as we lurched down that winding track. "Faster, Cleo, faster. Get me to the Roaring Creek Falls. My life is ebbing away!"

'And it was,' Neina continued. 'I watched Kāterina's body disintegrate as we got closer to the falls. Her skin liquefied in front of my eyes. Her fingers turned to jelly as she pulled on Cleo's reins.'

Aaron scratched his head. How much of Neina's bizarre story was true? 'Go on.'

Neina's eyes sparkled as she related the story. 'A sudden flash of lightning lit up the landscape.

'"The Roaring Creek Falls!" Kāterina cried. "We've made it!"

'A deafening clap of thunder spooked Cleo, and she bucked against the ferocious wind. The *Gypsy Rose* crashed down the bank and landed right in front of the falls. A wooden bench fell on top of me and trapped me in the wreckage.

'I heard Kāterina wailing in Māori: "Na tata, heoi ano tawhiti!"'

'What does that mean?' Aaron asked.

'So near yet so far.'

Aaron frowned. 'So she didn't get to the falls?'

'By the time I freed myself from the rubble, Kāterina had gone. I looked up and saw her battling the elements to reach the falls.'

Aaron rolled his eyes. 'I thought you said her body was decomposing.'

'That's the extraordinary thing. It was as if nature had taken over, drawing her to the falls. A ferocious wind propelled her to her final destiny.' Neina paused and dabbed her eyes. 'I should have gone after her and shared her fate. But I was too scared to be dragged to my doom with Kāterina.'

'So you weren't with her at the end?'

'I heard her cry out.' Neina's voice broke as she repeated Kāterina's dying words: '"My beloved Miriama and Aaron! Live long! Be happy! Be at peace!"'

Aaron gripped his hands together. 'So you just heard her wailing. You didn't see her die. She may still be alive.'

'No.' Tears rolled down Neina's cheeks as she finished the story. 'I climbed to the top of the bank overlooking the falls and watched Kāterina's final moments. She held her crystal ball high above her head as she descended into the water below the falls. Fearless to the last, Kāterina's voice rang out across the valley:

"Kia te mana o te ra, me te pouri o te marama pupuri koutou haumaru mō te mure ore.""

Aaron felt his eyes well up too. Could these really be the dying words of the woman who had been his rock and his benefactor for so many years?

'Kāterina was quoting a Māori blessing,' Neina explained. 'May the sun's power and the moon's darkness keep you safe for eternity.' Neina paused and tipped her head back. 'Only the waters could silence Kāterina. She continued chanting words of wisdom until she was completely taken by the river. Once she disappeared from sight, I returned to help her beloved Cleo, trapped in the wreckage of the caravan. I set her free and she made for the forest.'

That dramatic ending was *so* Kāterina, Aaron thought, grasping the table for support. Had she sacrificed her life for him and Miriama? He closed his eyes for a moment. In his head, he could hear Kāterina's voice singing. Would the sun's power and the moon's darkness really keep him and Miriama safe forever?

'Tell me, Neina …' Aaron opened his eyes, but Neina had gone. He glanced through the window and saw her scurry down the street. 'Damn.'

Aaron hurriedly paid for the breakfasts and chased after her. But just like the hooded man, Neina had vanished. Who was this strange woman who had appeared out of nowhere and had left so unexpectedly? More to the point, could he believe a word she had said? So much of Neina's story didn't add up. If Kāterina's arms were disintegrating, how could she hold the crystal ball high over her head as she drowned? Was Neina just embellishing the story? Or was it all a load of bullshit?

One question troubled Aaron more than all the others. What should he tell Miriama? No sense in distressing her if Neina's story wasn't true. Still undecided when he got back to their cottage, Aaron paused on the doorstep before going in. The radio blared as usual—but this morning Miriama wasn't tuned in to her regular pop music station. Aaron's heart missed a beat. She was listening to the news on Radio New Zealand.

Aaron's fingers trembled as he opened the front door and staggered inside. 'Miriama … is everything alright?'

     David Whittet

Miriama turned to face him. 'I hope Kāterina's okay,' she said as their eyes met. 'There's been a terrible storm at Roaring Creek.'

'What?' Aaron flung off his coat and collapsed on the sofa beside Miriama. 'I've just been talking to some old woman who claimed—'

'Quiet,' Miriama interrupted. 'We're missing the update.'

Aaron held Miriama's hand as the newsreader announced that flash floods had struck Roaring Creek. Civil defence urged locals to stay in their homes and advised against any unnecessary travel to or from the area. Did this mean Neina's story was true? Aaron shuddered when the newsreader reported that police were searching for a family who'd been picnicking at the Roaring Creek Falls but hadn't returned. At least there was no mention of a gypsy caravan. But that didn't mean Kāterina hadn't—

The radio interrupted Aaron's train of thought. The newsflash ended, and a programme about the cultural significance of Matariki Day followed.

Miriama burst into tears. 'Matariki means so much to Kāterina. Her heart is set on seeing us married on Matariki Day. What if she doesn't make it?'

Aaron saw the pain in her eyes and jumped to his feet. 'We need to go to Roaring Creek and see what's going on for ourselves. If we set out now, we'll be there before nightfall.'

'No.' Miriama dabbed her eyes with her sleeve. 'Didn't you hear what they said on the radio? No unnecessary travel to or from the area.'

'Yes, but—'

'Kāterina wouldn't want us to put our lives at risk. Besides, we'd never get back in time for the wedding.'

Aaron bit his tongue. 'Maybe we have to postpone the wedding.' He felt a lump in his throat as he realised what he had just said. 'I mean, just for a week or two.'

'Kāterina wanted us to marry on Matariki Day, and we will.' Miriama drew herself up on the sofa and lifted her head to face Aaron. 'And who knows? Maybe Kāterina will show up for the wedding after all. She's surprised us before.'

'She sure has.' Aaron sat down again beside Miriama. Maybe it was for the best. If they didn't get married tomorrow, perhaps they never would. 'You're right. Kāterina will probably burst into the church in the middle of the service.'

But would she? Aaron sighed. And if she didn't, would Miriama regret not going straight to Roaring Creek? *Don't even think about it.* Aaron just held Miriama securely in his arms. He couldn't stop thinking about what Neina had said, nor could he erase a mental picture of the *Gypsy Rose* crashing over the Roaring Creek Falls. Kāterina had been there for him when his mother could not. The thought of Kāterina perishing in the ice-cold water, alone and friendless, was too much to bear. And with Kāterina's demise, all hope of her finding his mother had disappeared.

Miriama broke the silence. 'I wish …'

'What?'

Miriama's voice quivered. 'I was a difficult child. I pushed Kāterina to the limit. I wish … I wish I'd shown her more respect.'

'Kāterina brought us together. That made her happier than anything else.' Aaron brushed Miriama's hair away from her face. 'It can't have been easy for you. Being brought up in a caravan, then sent to school in a foreign country.'

'The Neuchâtel Academy for Young Ladies.' Miriama managed a half-smile. 'All that school taught me was how to be nasty to you.'

Aaron gave her hand a gentle squeeze. 'Just like Estella.'

Miriama tilted her head. 'Estella?'

Surely she hadn't forgotten. 'From *Great Expectations*.'

'Of course.' Miriama's eyes suddenly brightened. 'I remember now. We both read it to Kāterina one evening.'

'That's right,' Aaron said. 'I read Pip's lines, and you read Estella's.'

'It's all coming back to me.' Miriama's face reddened. 'Didn't Estella give Pip a hard time because he was a common labouring boy?'

Aaron grinned at her mischievously. 'She did. Same way you treated me for being a common gang boy.'

Miriama blushed some more. 'I'm guessing Pip forgave Estella. Are you sure you've forgiven me?'

'Of course I have.' Aaron gave her hand another squeeze. 'With all my heart.'

Miriama lowered her head. 'I don't deserve that.'

'You do. You're a different person now.'

Miriama looked up and dabbed her eyes. 'So how did the story end? Did Pip and Estella tie the knot?'

　　　David Whittet

'Not sure.' Aaron scratched his head. 'We didn't get that far. I cursed Dickens for writing such long books. Kāterina promised she would find my mother when we finished the book.'

'And you never did?'

Aaron shook his head. 'Kāterina gave me the book. I've often meant to finish it. But somehow … I just can't get back into it. It doesn't feel the same without Kāterina.'

Miriama sighed. 'We read Dickens at the academy. *David Copperfield*, *Bleak House*, *Little Dorrit*, but not *Great Expectations*.'

'Kāterina said Dickens wrote two endings for *Great Expectations*.' Aaron paused momentarily before continuing. 'One happy and one sad.'

'I'll stick with the happy ending.' Miriama glanced at her watch. 'We'd better get moving or we'll be late for the wedding rehearsal at the church.'

This should have been the happiest time in his life, but Aaron's head was still all over the place at the wedding rehearsal that afternoon. He had dreamt of marrying Miriama for so long. How cruel for their big day to be marred by such uncertainty. His thoughts returned to what he'd been told about his parents' wedding. That his mother was shot during the ceremony. Were all marriages doomed in his family?

Aaron shuddered as he practised his vows in front of the altar. He looked into Miriama's eyes and prayed that his wedding would be different.

PART FOUR

THE GOOD SHEPHERD

CHAPTER THIRTY-TWO

The Church of the Good Shepherd, Tekapō
Matariki Day, 24 June 2022

Was it a mistake to bring the wedding forward to Matariki Day? A sleepless night hadn't helped Aaron to come to terms with Kāterina's sudden disappearance and Neina's revelations. The original date for the wedding was a month away. If they'd stuck with that, then maybe Kāterina wouldn't have taken off so suddenly and ended up in the midst of a storm.

Perhaps an early morning walk might help clear his head. The usual joggers were out in force as Aaron wandered along the lakeside. No sign of Neina or the hooded man, though. Just as well. To make sure, Aaron had emailed a description of both of them to the security men last night. He'd also asked Errol Troy, who was in charge of security, to follow up.

Aaron flipped a stone across the water. He watched it glide across the still surface and then sink. *Pull yourself together, man. This WILL be the happiest day of your life.*

With that in mind, Aaron strode back to the cottage to deal with the vital questions any groom faced on their wedding morning. Would Tony arrive in time with the rings? Would his old mate embarrass him with some salacious stories during the best man's speech? What if Tony brought up that drunken party at Nigel's place or the night he lost big at the casino?

A taxi drew up as Aaron approached their accommodation. Talk of the devil—that must be Tony. *Hang on.* Aaron was halfway across the paddock to greet his friend when a sudden thought crossed his mind. *Tony said he would bring his own car.* So who was it in the back of the taxi? Wedding guests wouldn't arrive for another couple of hours and would go straight to the church. Aaron strained his eyes. Through the tinted glass he could just make out two women in the back seat. Could this be the answer to his prayers? Were they the two women he most wanted as guests at his wedding?

Aaron didn't wait to answer his own question. He stumbled in the mud as he rushed towards the car, his heart pumping. His mind told him not to get his hopes up, but his body wasn't listening. The two women in the taxi had to be Kāterina and his mother.

'Alicia … Mum … is that you?' Aaron flung the back door of the taxi open and froze. The woman he was about to embrace wasn't his mother. And it wasn't Kāterina sitting next to her. 'I'm so sorry. I thought you were someone else.'

The two young women sitting in the back seat of the taxi shared a confused glance.

'I hope we've come to the right place,' one of them said. 'We're here for the wedding. I'm Sabrina, and this is Laura. We're friends of Miriama's from Switzerland.'

Of course—Miriama had told him she'd invited two of her former classmates from the Neuchâtel Academy to be her bridesmaids.

Aaron didn't know where to look and stumbled with his words. 'Pleased to meet you. Welcome to New Zealand. Good of you to come such a long way for the wedding.'

'Thirty hours on an aeroplane,' Sabrina said, 'and believe me, it feels like we've been travelling our entire lives.'

'I didn't think we would make it in time,' Laura said. 'Trust Miriama to change the wedding day. We were damn lucky to get flights at such short notice.'

'Actually,' Aaron said, 'that wasn't Miriama's idea. It was Kāterina's, Miriama's foster mother. She wanted us to get married on Matariki Day. It's the Māori New Year.'

Laura grunted. 'A bit more notice would have been nice.'

'Well, we're here now,' Sabrina said. 'Don't take any notice of Laura. She's a grump when she's jetlagged. Now, Aaron, be a darling and help with the luggage. We'll need to get those bridesmaid dresses ironed pronto.'

Aaron got the cases out of the boot while Sabrina paid the taxi driver.

'Sabrina! Laura! So good to see you!' Miriama ran out in her dressing gown and flung her arms around the girls. 'Thank you so much for making the journey. Come inside. I'm about to put on my wedding dress.'

Aaron followed them in slowly, carrying the suitcases and berating himself for his disappointment. *Be happy for Miriama.* She was clearly overjoyed to see her best friends. He paused on the doorstep and listened to them giggling. It was so good to hear laughter again.

When Aaron took the cases into the bedroom, Miriama was changing into her wedding dress.

'Shut your eyes!' Miriama cried. 'It's bad luck for the groom to see the bride before the service.'

'Good luck with that,' Laura added. 'In a small cottage like this.'

Aaron put down the suitcases and took a step backwards. 'It's a bit late for that anyway, isn't it? I mean, we've been together all—'

Miriama laughed. 'I'm just kidding. Excuse me a moment, girls.' With her wedding dress still unzipped, Miriama took Aaron's hand and led him from the bedroom into the kitchen. 'The last twenty-four hours have been a nightmare for both of us. But when I woke up this morning, I felt a surprising sense of peace.'

'You did?'

Miriama rested an arm on Aaron's shoulder. 'I don't know if Kāterina is still here on Earth or up there amongst the stars she so loved, but I can feel her presence with us now, and she wants us to be happy.'

Aaron hesitated. 'I know.'

'Look!' Miriama pointed at the window. 'There's Tony. Why don't you go to the church with him? I've got to do my makeup, and we've loads of girl talk to catch up on.'

Aaron thought about what Miriama said while he walked to the church with Tony. Kāterina had often talked about her earthly journey as being part of a bigger picture. He looked up at the sky. Perhaps she would be happy up there with the stars, especially the Matariki cluster.

'What's up? Tony said. 'Not having second thoughts, are you?'

Aaron shifted his gaze from the heavens to Tony. 'Of course not.'

'Mate,' Tony said, 'you were miles away.'

'I'm sorry. It's just …' Aaron broke off. He didn't want to go through Neina's story and relive the past twenty-four hours with Tony. 'The last couple of days have been a bit stressful, that's all. Everything's okay now.'

Tony patted him on the back. 'Well, I'm here and I'm going to look after you. That's what a best man's for. Didn't Miriama look radiant in her wedding dress?'

Aaron felt a lump in his throat. 'She did.'

Maybe everything *was* okay now. Aaron hadn't seen his mother since he was five years old. He could barely remember what she looked like. But that morning he felt she was with him, leading him on from above, the way she'd always done since the day she disappeared.

Who was that woman sitting on a step outside the Church of the Good Shepherd? Aaron was sure he'd seen her before but couldn't think where.

'Aaron!' The woman stood up and embraced him. 'You don't recognise me, do you?'

Aaron shook his head.

'You were a little boy when I last saw you.' The woman beamed at Aaron. 'I'm Emir's sister. Your aunt Fonella.'

Aaron scratched his head. He and his mother had lived with Fonella when he was a small child, but they hadn't been in contact since then.

'It's fantastic to have you here,' Aaron said, 'but how did you find out about the wedding?'

'I read about you in the newspaper,' Fonella said. 'How you took on the Godzone Gorillas and won. Emir would have been so proud of you.'

Aaron felt a glow in his chest. 'Thank you. That means so much to me.' It did. Living up to his father's reputation was Aaron's driving force. But how did Fonella know the day and location of his wedding? That hadn't been in the newspapers. Had it? 'But I still don't understand how you—'

Fonella grinned. 'Remember, I'm a Casper too, and we thrive on a challenge. I tracked down your aunt Helena. When I turned up on her doorstep, she'd just received her invitation to your wedding. She persuaded me to come too. So here I am. Gatecrashing your big day.'

Aaron smiled back. 'I'm so glad you're here. I'd have invited you if I'd known where you were.'

'I nearly didn't come.' Fonella glanced at the church and shuddered. 'I was at your parents' wedding. I had to give your mother the kiss of life after she was shot.'

Aaron flinched. He wanted to know *everything* about that fateful day, and

 David Whittet

here was someone who could tell him so much about both his mother and his father. 'We need to talk.'

Tony stepped forward and whispered in Aaron's ear. 'Is this wise? This is your wedding day. Time to look to the future, not the past.'

Aaron scowled at Tony. Didn't Tony realise how much this meant to him? Aaron had spent his entire adult life trying to find out the truth about his parents' wedding, his father's death, and his mother's disappearance. And here was the one person who could give him some answers.

More guests arrived. Perhaps Tony had a point and this wasn't the right time.

Aaron eyed Fonella and took a deep breath. 'Can we talk later on? Maybe after the ceremony.'

'We could,' Fonella said, 'but you'll be busy with photographs after the service.'

'What about the reception, then?' Aaron said. 'We could find a private room at the hotel.'

Tony frowned. 'Miriama won't want you sneaking off during the reception.'

'Your friend is right,' Fonella said. 'Now, aren't you going to introduce us?'

'I'm sorry,' Aaron said. 'This is Tony, my best man.'

Aaron's mind was still racing while Fonella and Tony shook hands. Fonella could be his only chance to discover the truth about his parents. There was no way Aaron would let the opportunity pass.

A flash chauffeur-driven car drew up and Anton Le Squillier stepped out. Aaron shook his head and sighed. He'd idolised Le Squillier at first. The man who'd arrived at his aunt's house and told him of his good fortune. Initially, Aaron hadn't taken much notice of the rumours. Surely the man who had rescued him so gallantly couldn't be cheating his clients. Or could he? The heated arguments Aaron overheard while in the waiting room at Le Squillier's offices became harder to ignore. The more Aaron learnt about Le Squillier, the more uneasy he became. If Le Squillier had defrauded his other clients, was he ripping Kāterina off too? Was she paying for his expensive cars and lifestyle? That sinking feeling took away some of Aaron's excitement about going to business school. Why couldn't Kāterina have chosen a more trustworthy lawyer?

'Aaron!' Le Squillier extended a hand to Aaron. 'Congratulations on your special day.'

The force of Le Squillier's vice-like handshake always made Aaron wince.

'Thank you for coming, Anton.'

'Delighted to be here.' Le Squillier finally let go of Aaron's hand. 'I'm not just your lawyer, I'm your friend.'

Aaron stared at Le Squillier. *I choose my own friends.* A journalist had recently exposed Le Squillier for what he was—a cunning opportunist. And as usual, Le Squillier had brushed off the allegations and emerged almost unscathed. Why did the mud never stick? Take away the Savile Row suit, put him in a hoodie, and Le Squillier could have been the hooded man. Perhaps he was. The creep was devious enough.

'Why did you have to choose this pokey little church in the middle of winter?' Le Squillier continued. 'I could have arranged the cathedral in Wellington for you.'

How dare you? This is the most beautiful church in the world. Aaron bit his tongue before he said something he'd regret. 'It's what Miriama and I wanted.'

Another thought crossed Aaron's mind. If Kāterina *had* drowned at the Roaring Creek Falls, what did that mean for her estate? Had she appointed Le Squillier as executor of her will? Had she even made a will? Aaron couldn't make sense of it. Kāterina had lived like a pauper in that run-down caravan. Yet she must have had money to have put him through business school, and he was still receiving an allowance. Did this mean he would be dealing with Le Squillier for the rest of his days?

Le Squillier snorted when a taxi rolled up and a woman got out. 'I told you to have nothing more to do with your aunt Helena and her family. They won't help your image.'

Aaron ignored Le Squillier and ran towards his aunt.

'Aunt Helena!' Aaron flung his arms around her. 'You made it.'

'Nothing could stop me from being here for your wedding,' Aunt Helena said. 'Not even your uncle Ben.'

Aaron glanced around. Thank God she hadn't brought Ben and those hateful cousins with her. Aaron had kept up with Helena, but he hadn't seen Nancy, Tara or Lucy since the day Le Squillier had turned up at his aunt's house and announced the endowment.

'So, how is my uncle?' Aaron asked, biting his tongue. 'And what are my three cousins up to?'

 David Whittet

Helena shook her head. 'Don't ask.'

'I'll tell you about your cousins,' Le Squillier said, butting in. 'All three are in custody after terrorising the neighbourhood with a spate of ram-raids.'

Aaron watched his aunt lower her head. While there was poetic justice in the cousins getting their comeuppance, he felt for his aunt.

'I'm so sorry,' Aaron said. 'You must be devastated.'

Aunt Helena pulled herself up and shrugged. 'They got what they deserved. You, of all people, shouldn't feel sorry for them.'

'I don't feel sorry for *them*,' Aaron said. 'I feel sorry for *you*.'

'At least it's got Ben out of my hair for a while,' Helena said. 'He's busy with a bent lawyer, trying to get them off the charges.'

Le Squillier glared at Aaron. 'So you see, I was right all along. I told you continuing to associate with your aunt's family would tarnish your reputation.'

Aaron dismissed Le Squillier with a wave of the hand. Associating with a rogue like Le Squillier was far more likely to get him into trouble. For a moment, Aaron thought Le Squillier would leave with his nose in the air. *Good riddance.* Instead, without another word, Le Squillier rolled his eyes and marched into the church.

Aunt Helena shivered. 'That man always made me feel worthless. From the moment he first set foot in our house. Looking down his nose at me and sniggering. Making out I was holding you back.'

'Don't take any notice of Le Squillier,' Aaron said. 'I know you did your best for me.'

'But did I?' Aunt Helena looked at the ground. 'Remember when you told me you wanted to get a scholarship and go to university? And I put you down. Told you that you'd never make it.'

Aaron would never forget how long it had taken to summon the courage to talk to his aunt about his dreams. 'I'd been reading this book to Kāterina. I got it into my head that I had to become a gentleman to win Miriama's heart.'

'You came to me for support and encouragement.' Aunt Helena raised her head and met Aaron's eyes. 'And I shattered your dreams. Can you ever forgive me?'

Aaron paused before replying. Aunt Helena's dose of realism had almost destroyed him at the time. 'Nothing to forgive. You were right. There's no way

I would have got a scholarship. I only got to business school because Kāterina sponsored me.'

'Nonsense. They wouldn't have accepted you for business school if you hadn't got the qualifications.' Aunt Helena's expression brightened as she cast her eyes over Aaron. 'You would have succeeded with or without Kāterina or anyone else's help. Look at you today. You're the perfect gentleman.'

Aaron felt his cheeks flush. 'The church is filling up. We should find you a seat.' He took his aunt Helena's hand. 'Allow me to escort you to your pew.'

They stood at the entrance for a moment.

'Wow!' Aunt Helena gasped. 'Look at those flowers! And that view!' She pointed at the altar with its simple cross, the vast panoramic window, and the expansive vista over Lake Tekapō. 'I'd heard the church was attractive but never believed it could be this beautiful. It's … out of this world.'

Aaron grinned as his aunt struggled to find the words to describe the Church of the Good Shepherd. Lake Tekapō *was* stunning on the crisp winter morning, and the flowers that decked the church were magnificent. The intoxicating scent of the white lilies, red roses and orchids competed with the divine smell of incense. Could there possibly be a better setting to take his vows?

'I want you to sit here.' Aaron steered Aunt Helena to the front row and sat her next to Fonella. 'There—my two aunties together. What could be better?'

Aaron lost count of the number of times he asked Tony if he'd remembered the rings while they stood in front of the altar, waiting for Miriama.

'Cool it, mate,' Tony repeated. 'She'll be here in a minute.'

But would she? How could this humble gangland boy have won the heart of such an amazing woman? His life flashed before him. That first meeting with Miriama when he read her palm. He'd told her that one day she would meet a handsome prince and get married. She'd hit back, telling him she was spoilt for choice at the school in Switzerland. If she did get married, it would be to the son of a count or a president, not some miserable lowlife like Aaron.

Had she really changed? Did she truly love him?

 David Whittet

Aaron's questions were answered as Miriama walked down the aisle and their eyes met. Her adoring smile removed any lingering doubts he may have had.

'Dearly beloved,' the minister began, 'we have come together in the presence of Almighty God to witness and bless the joining together of this man and this woman in Holy Matrimony. Marriage is an honourable estate, and is therefore not to be entered into lightly, but reverently, advisedly, soberly, and with God's blessing.'

A noise at the back of the church. Aaron's heart missed a beat. He looked up to see Errol Troy arrive and squeeze into the back row. Trust Errol to be late.

'Aaron and Miriama,' the minister continued, 'the vows you are about to take are made in front of this congregation and before God, who is judge of all and knows all the secrets of our hearts; therefore, if either of you knows a reason why you may not lawfully marry, you must declare it now.'

Aaron's eyes remained fixed on Miriama as the minister began the marriage vows.

'Aaron, will you take Miriama to be your lawful wedded wife? Will you love her, comfort her, honour and protect her, and, forsaking all others, be faithful to her as long as you both shall live?'

Aaron's mouth was so dry he could barely get the words out. 'I will.'

The minister turned to Miriama. 'Miriama, will you take Aaron to be your lawful wedded husband? Will you love him, comfort him, honour and protect him, and, forsaking all others, be faithful to him as long as you both shall live?'

Miriama beamed, her cheeks glowing. 'I will.'

Aaron fumbled as he placed the wedding ring on Miriama's left ring-finger. 'I give you this ring as a symbol of my love, and with all that I am, and all that I have, I honour you, in the Name of the Father, and of the Son, and of the Holy Spirit.'

He could address the boardroom without hesitation and make a keynote speech without faltering. But here he was, trembling in front of an altar and the woman he loved. His palm was sweating as Miriama placed the ring on his finger.

The minister drew the service to a close. 'In the presence of God, and before this congregation, Aaron and Miriama have made their vows to each other. They have declared their marriage by the joining of hands and by the giving and receiving of rings. I, therefore, proclaim that they are husband and wife. Those whom God has joined, let no man put asunder.'

Aaron felt a distant rumble and shuddered. What was it? Was his mother trying to speak to him? He steadied himself on the altar. If it wasn't his mother, maybe it was Kāterina. Had she finally succeeded in lifting her curse?

The minister turned to Aaron. 'You may now kiss the bride.'

One look into Miriama's loving eyes, and the noise in Aaron's head disappeared. His lips touched hers and he was in heaven. Nothing else in the world mattered. If only that kiss could last forever.

The congregation applauded. Aaron caught Aunt Helena's eye. Yes, today he was a *true* gentleman.

Everyone stood for the closing hymn, "Lead Us, Heavenly Father, Lead Us". During the last verse, the minister gestured for Aaron and Miriama to follow him down the aisle.

> *Spirit of our God, descending,*
> *fill our hearts with heavenly joy,*
> *love with every passion blending,*
> *pleasure that can never cloy:*
> *thus provided, pardoned, guided,*
> *nothing can our peace destroy.*

Nothing can our peace destroy. Aaron felt that peace in his heart. With Miriama at his side, they were invincible. Nobody could destroy their happiness. Or could they?

Halfway down the aisle, Aaron couldn't shake the feeling that something was wrong. He felt that rumble again, and this time it wasn't in his head. It was coming from outside the church. He tried to ignore it at first, but it grew louder and louder.

Aaron wiped his forehead with the back of his hand. Why was he worried? Errol Troy had promised Aaron that the security arrangements would be impenetrable. Had there been a hitch? Is that why Errol had been late? Aaron shot him a sideways glance. Errol's self-important face gave nothing away.

Stay calm. Don't spoil Miriama's big day. Aaron gave Miriama a reassuring smile as they continued down the aisle.

 David Whittet

The heavy church door burst open with a deafening crash. Aaron froze, his mind racing and his heart thumping wildly. A menacing figure emerged from the shadows, silhouetted against the light like a mythical beast, breathing an icy chill over the congregation.

Miriama gasped and clenched Aaron's arm like a vice. 'What the … who the hell is it?'

Aaron knew who it was without a second look. It wasn't his mother or Kāterina. It was the hooded man. The man they'd seen lurking around the lakeshore before the wedding—the same man who had sent Kāterina fleeing in terror and likely to her grave.

'Leave this to me.' Aaron broke away from Miriama and confronted the hooded man. 'Show your face, you coward!'

Was it Corey? Aaron still believed it was Corey's father, Mickey, who had shot Alicia at her wedding. If it wasn't Corey under the hood, was it one of his minions from the Godzone Gorillas? Maybe it was Kaine, still out for revenge.

Aaron took a step closer. 'Come on. You don't frighten me. Show your face.'

The hooded man didn't budge. Aaron took another pace towards the man.

'No, Aaron.' Miriama rushed forward and grabbed his arm. 'Leave him. He might have a gun.'

'I can handle this.' Aaron calmly pulled the man's hood back to reveal his face. 'Oh, my God!'

Aaron stepped back, almost falling over in the aisle. Who was this grotesque man with his horrendously disfigured face? His coarse and hideously scarred skin virtually obliterated his features. Except for his eyes—they burned and remained focused on Aaron.

The congregation gasped, their eyes fixed on the towering intruder.

Miriama's eyes widened. 'That's the man I saw when I was out running,' she gasped, trembling all over. 'Oh, Aaron, I'm so scared!'

'Don't worry, my darling!' Aaron stood tall and took Miriama into his arms. 'I'll soon get rid of this lowlife.'

'Be careful.' Miriama's voice lowered to a whisper as she spoke. 'Who knows why he's here and what he's capable of.'

Aaron glared at the intruder. Was this really happening? 'Who do you think you are? How dare you barge in on our wedding ceremony?'

The man remained silent, his piercing eyes still blazing and fixed on Aaron.

Aunt Helena shot up. 'You've got some bloody nerve! Look what you've done. You've just ruined the most important day in Aaron and Miriama's life.'

Fonella also jumped to her feet. 'Just get out.'

The man extended an arm towards Aaron. 'What would a wedding be without the groom's father?'

What? Aaron's mouth fell open. He held on to Miriama with one hand and clasped a pew with the other. He'd dreamt his mother would show up at his wedding. But never his father. It was impossible anyway—Emir was killed in a fire. How dare this imposter pretend to be his father and mock his memory?

The man pushed forward and put a hand on Aaron's shoulder. 'It's me, son. Emir. I am your father.'

David Whittet

CHAPTER THIRTY-THREE

Aaron had long idolised the father he had never met. He refused to believe any of the reports he had heard about his father's shady business dealings. As far as Aaron was concerned, Mickey shot his mother at the wedding. Mickey started the fire that killed his father. Kāterina had insisted it was a hired assassin who did the shooting at the wedding, and Emir was the target. She claimed to have seen the assassin's face after he left the church. Aaron didn't buy that. Kāterina must have been mistaken. As for one of Emir's enemies being responsible for the fire, Mickey was there and had the means, motive and opportunity.

Likewise, there was no doubt in Aaron's mind that his father was dead. He'd read the fire officers' statements and police reports. The firefighters had been unable to reach his father. Investigators had found charred bones in the wreckage, and DNA testing had confirmed they were Emir's remains.

So who was the grotesque figure confronting Aaron in the church on his wedding day? Was it possible that his father had escaped the fire? With his hideously scarred face, the intruder looked like the survivor of a nuclear attack. Could this monster really be his father?

Aaron eyed Fonella. Surely she must know if this man was her brother. Fonella had shot up with Aunt Helena when the man first appeared and had ordered him to leave. Did that mean she didn't recognise him? Was she as much in the dark as everyone else?

'Fonella! Please!' Aaron called out. 'Is this man your brother?'

Fonella shook her head and burst into tears. 'I've never seen him before.'

She jumped up and fled down the aisle.

'Don't go!' Aaron shouted after her. 'If anyone can sort this out, it's you.'

The hooded man grabbed her arm as she ran past him. 'Fonella! It's me! Your brother, Emir.'

'Let go of me.' Fonella pulled away from him and ran out of the church.

Aaron glared at the man, even more certain he was an imposter. Fonella didn't believe him. And besides, the real Emir would never have allowed the Gang to kidnap Alicia. He would have been there for her, and if he had been alive all along, he'd have been there for Aaron, too. What father would have left him as a punchbag for Uncle Ben and an easy target for those hateful cousins? Even worse, allow Corey to victimise and beat him up when they were kids. As for hijacking his wedding ceremony, that was unforgivable.

'Get out!' Aaron spat the words at him. 'You are not my father!'

The man's piercing eyes drilled into Aaron's. 'Believe me! I know this is hard for you to understand, but I swear—I *am* your father!'

'If you are my father,' Aaron shot back, 'which I don't believe for a moment, where have you been all my life? Why have you just turned up now? So you could destroy the most precious day in my life?'

The man's eyes remained focused on Aaron. 'I have been there for you, son. Watching over you. Guiding you from afar. I've been your good shepherd.'

'My good shepherd? Bollocks!' Aaron gritted his teeth. 'My life was a misery before Kāterina rescued me. Kāterina is my guardian angel. Not you.'

The man's eyes narrowed. 'I have done more for you than that old witch ever did.'

'Enough! I want you to leave.' Aaron loosened his tie and undid the top button of his shirt. 'Now!'

Aaron turned to face Miriama. She had collapsed in a heap in front of the altar, with Sabrina and Laura kneeling beside her.

'Miriama!' Aaron cried out. 'My angel! Are you alright?'

'Of course she isn't,' Sabrina shot back, drying Miriama's tears with a handkerchief. 'Just get that man out of here.'

Aaron spun back to confront the man. 'Look what you've done to my wife. Get the hell out of here!' He glanced around at the congregation. Some guests hid their faces, but most were glued to the spectacle. 'What are you all staring at? The show's over.'

'No, it isn't,' the man said. 'It's only just begun.'

The wedding photographer put his head around the church door. 'Will you be coming out soon? Everything's set up for the photographs.'

Aaron wiped the perspiration off his forehead with his sleeve. 'Just give us five minutes and we'll be with you.'

    David Whittet

'No!' Miriama shrieked. Her makeup had run with her tears, and her dress was soiled with mascara. 'I don't want any pictures of me looking like this.'

Aaron stamped his foot and eyeballed the hooded man. 'If you're not out of here in the next sixty seconds, I'm getting security to throw you out.'

Errol Troy stood up, his face flushed. 'Actually, Aaron … about the security …!'

Aaron took a deep breath. 'What about the security?'

Errol's face grew even redder. 'Well … I thought … being as …'

Aaron cut Errol down with his eyes. 'You let him in, didn't you?'

Errol squirmed. 'I thought you would want your father to be here for your wedding.'

Aaron smacked his hand against a pew. 'This man is *not* my father.'

Anton Le Squillier got up and approached the man. 'Listen, Emir. Aaron's right. You shouldn't have just shown up like this at his wedding.'

Aaron glared at Le Squillier. 'You knew about this, too? Am I the only one who didn't know this monster was going to gatecrash my wedding?'

The man held out his hands towards Aaron. 'I'm not a monster. I'm your father.'

Aaron clenched a fist. 'Like hell you are.'

The minister stepped forward. 'May I remind you that we are still in the house of God? I must insist you leave the church and sort out your differences outside.'

Tony stopped Aaron as they filed out of the church. 'This is as big a shock to me as it is to you.'

Aaron eyed his old mate. 'Promise me you didn't know Errol and Le Squillier would pull this stunt?'

'I swear I didn't know,' Tony said, still hanging on to Aaron's arm. 'If I had, I'd have stopped it.'

Aaron hoped to find Fonella outside the church. She could quiz him. Ask him questions that only her brother could answer. But she was gone.

Why had she taken off? Did she know more than she was letting on? Aaron had read stories about people who seemingly came back from the dead. There was that famous French peasant. What was his name? Martin Guerre. Even his spouse had been unable to decide if the man who returned to their village was genuinely her husband.

Aaron pushed through the crowd to find Miriama. 'Darling!' He flung his arms around her. 'Don't let this fraudster ruin everything. I'll make it up to you. I promise.'

'Are you sure he's a fraud?' Miriama gestured towards the hooded man, who was in deep conversation with Errol and Le Squillier. 'Those two obviously think he's for real.'

'Fonella didn't,' Aaron said. 'Anyway, Errol and Le Squillier are a pair of rogues as well. I wouldn't trust either of them. I can't understand why Kāterina chose Le Squillier as her lawyer.'

Miriama shook her head. 'Old Barnaby McVeigh is her lawyer. Kāterina wouldn't trust anyone else to look after her affairs.'

Aaron frowned. 'Are you sure?'

'Pretty much.' Miriama paused for a moment. 'At least, it was Barnaby who sorted everything out and paid the bills when I went to boarding school.'

A police car drew up before Aaron could make sense of Miriama's revelation.

'Thank God for that!' Aaron let out a huge breath. 'They've come to arrest the imposter.'

But had they? Aaron rushed across to meet the two police officers as they got out of the car, but Tony got there first. What was Tony saying to them? And why weren't they handcuffing the imposter?

'That's the man you're after!' Aaron caught his breath and pointed to the hooded man. 'I don't know who he is, but he barged into the church during our wedding service pretending to be my dead father.'

Tony pulled Aaron aside. 'They're here for Miriama.'

'What?' Aaron took a step back. 'You mean they're not here to—'

Tony shook his head. 'It's nothing to do with your father.'

Aaron felt his blood pressure rising. 'That man is *not* my father.'

The two police officers approached Aaron.

'You must be Aaron Casper,' the first officer said, presenting her warrant card. 'My name is Senior Sergeant Judy Jefferson from the Greymouth Police. This is my colleague, Sergeant Terry Robbins.'

Aaron began to sweat. If the police weren't there to arrest the hooded man, then they must be bearing bad news. And it had to be about Kāterina.

'We're so sorry to disturb you on your wedding day,' Senior Sergeant Jefferson said, 'but we must talk to Miriama.'

     David Whittet

Miriama stepped forward and gripped Aaron's hand. 'It's my mother, isn't it?'

Senior Sergeant Jefferson looked around at the gossiping crowd. 'We need somewhere quiet to talk. Perhaps we could go into the church.'

Was this really happening? Aaron felt his chest tighten and his legs shake, but he had to stay strong for Miriama. Should he say something? But what could he possibly say that would help?

'Whatever happens,' he whispered in her ear as they followed the police officers back into the church, 'I'm here for you.'

The flowers didn't look nearly as stunning as they had a couple of hours ago. The sky had clouded over, casting a dim celestial light through the panoramic window.

Aaron thought he spotted a tear in the corner of the senior sergeant's eye as they sat down on a pew at the back of the church.

'There's no easy way to put this,' Senior Sergeant Jefferson began, 'and on your wedding day, too. But we have reason to believe that your foster mother, Kāterina Kururangi, has been involved in an accident at the Roaring Creek Falls. We had a search and rescue team at the falls looking for a family who'd been picnicking in the area.'

'Yes,' Aaron said. 'We heard that on the radio last night. But what about Kāterina?'

'When the rescue team located the family,' the senior sergeant continued, 'they reported seeing an old caravan crash into the water.'

Miriama held on to Aaron's hand. 'Kāterina's dead, isn't she?'

'We sent in a squad of police divers,' Senior Sergeant Jefferson said. 'They recovered a woman's body from the water.'

Miriama's fingernails dug deeper into Aaron's hand. 'It was Kāterina's body, wasn't it?'

Aaron felt that distant echo in his head again. He shifted his gaze from Miriama to the police officer. The answer to Miriama's question was written all over the officer's face, and Senior Sergeant Jefferson sounded as choked up as Aaron felt.

'We believe it is your foster mother,' Senior Sergeant Jefferson said. 'It seems you are Kāterina's closest relative, so we need you to ...'

Sergeant Robbins took over. 'We need you to identify the body, Miriama.'

Miriama opened her mouth to reply, but nothing came out. A little more than an hour ago, Aaron had promised to love her, comfort her, honour and protect her. He never imagined he would have to do so quite so soon.

'Where is the body?' Aaron asked.

'In the mortuary at Grey Hospital,' Sergeant Robbins said. 'We'll give you a police escort.'

Aaron used his free hand to embrace Miriama. 'It's going to be okay. I'll be with you. We'll face this together.'

Miriama released Aaron's hand, dabbed her eyes and sat up straight. 'No. You must stay here and find out if that man really is your father.'

Aaron flinched. 'He's not.'

'You don't know that.' Miriama closed her eyes for a moment and then focused on Aaron. 'At least, not for certain. I'm sure I've seen him somewhere before.'

Aaron's jaw tightened. 'I'll deal with him later.'

'He's not going away. What if he follows us to Greymouth.' Miriama turned to the police officers for support. 'We don't want him barging in at the hospital mortuary, do we?'

'Certainly not,' Senior Sergeant Jefferson said. 'But you'll be safe with us. We won't stand for any nonsense.'

Aaron tapped his fingers on the pew. 'I'm not letting you go alone.'

Miriama hesitated, then looked up. 'Sabrina and Laura will come with me.'

'I should be there, supporting you,' Aaron insisted. 'I'm your husband.'

'And you'll be with me in spirit.' Miriama took a deep breath and continued in a quiet and even voice, 'I know Kāterina meant almost as much to you as she did to me. You don't want to see her on a slab in the mortuary. I have no choice.'

Aaron hung his head. Miriama was facing personal tragedy, yet she was thinking of him and not herself. She was one incredible woman.

'Don't worry,' Miriama continued. 'Sabrina and Laura will look after me. Actually, I'm more concerned about you and that strange man.' She turned to the police officers. 'Can I nip over to our accommodation and change? I don't want to go to the hospital in my wedding dress.'

Sergeant Robbins took Aaron aside as they left the church. 'Have you really no idea who the man with the scarred face could be? Have you seen him before?'

 David Whittet

'I've no idea who he is,' Aaron replied. 'He turned up here a couple of days ago. In fact, he was the reason Kāterina took off. Then he turns up at our wedding claiming to be my father.'

Sergeant Robbins scribbled in his notebook. 'Well, if he causes you any trouble, call Constable Barrett at the Tekapō Police Station.'

'I will.' Aaron gazed across the empty car park. The last of the guests wandered away into the town. Aaron's heart sank as he scanned the horizon. The hooded man hadn't left. He was there on the shoreline with Errol and Le Squillier.

Aaron turned back to Sergeant Robbins. 'You should talk to those three. I'm sure they know something about Kāterina's death.'

'We won't know for certain if the deceased is Kāterina Kururangi until your wife identifies the body,' Sergeant Robbins replied. 'But yes, we will need a statement from your uninvited guest. I'll send Constable Barrett over to interview him.'

'You do that.' Aaron stomped his foot and began walking away. 'Now, if you'll excuse me, I want to see my bride before you take her away.'

An hour later and Miriama had gone. Aaron stood with his hands hanging by his side once her car with its police escort disappeared into the distance. His stomach churned and his heart bled. He should have been heading off on his honeymoon with his new bride.

Aaron would have remained there gazing at the horizon indefinitely if Errol Troy hadn't appeared and tapped him on the shoulder.

'Chin up,' Errol said. 'Your father's waiting for you. You've got a heap of catching up to do.'

Aaron kicked a stone down the road. 'Why do you keep calling him my father? The man's an imposter.'

Errol sighed. 'Don't be like that. I've known your father for a long time, and I can assure you, this man *is* your father.'

Since when did Errol Troy's word count for anything? Aaron wanted to berate him for going behind his back and letting the hooded man into the church. He must have known what consternation it would cause. But what was the point of arguing? Aaron followed Errol across a paddock to the shore of the lake.

'Don't be too hard on your old man,' Errol said as they walked. 'Smoke inhalation from the fire has caused brain damage.'

Could this be true? Aaron had read about the effects of smoke on the brain. No. Aaron dismissed the idea. Mickey had set fire to the house and had killed his father.

So many emotions in one day, and it wasn't over yet. Why was Aaron convinced there was even worse news to come?

CHAPTER THIRTY-FOUR

Raised voices broke the tranquillity of Lake Tekapō. Fists were raised. What were Le Squillier and the hooded man fighting about? Aaron looked away. Further down the shoreline, a family celebrated Matariki Day with a barbecue. A local kapa haka group performed a dance on the shore.

Aaron should have been celebrating too. They'd planned a Matariki-themed wedding reception, with singing, poi dancing and a traditional Māori hangi. Instead, with his bride gone, Aaron followed Errol Troy to an altercation that he knew in his heart wouldn't end well.

'Hear him out,' Errol said. 'That's all I ask.'

Hear him out? Aaron couldn't help but hear the hooded man yelling at Le Squillier as they got closer.

'Haven't you done enough damage for one day, Emir?' Le Squillier protested. 'I told you coming here today was a mistake.'

'If I wanted your opinion, Le Squillier,' the hooded man shot back, 'I would have asked for it. If you had done your job properly, none of this would have happened. Didn't I tell you to keep Aaron away from Kāterina and her poisonous daughter?'

What the hell? Aaron raced across the paddock to confront the hooded man. 'You bastard! How dare you? Kāterina has turned my life around. Everything I've achieved is thanks to her. And Miriama has brought me more happiness—'

'Bullshit!' The hooded man cut him off. 'Kāterina has done nothing for you. And as for Miriama—'

'You're the one talking bullshit,' Aaron hit back. 'Miriama has—'

The hooded man jumped in again before Aaron could finish his sentence. 'I knew Miriama was wrong for you from the first time I set eyes on her.'

More lies. The hooded man had never seen Miriama before. Or had he? Aaron's heart raced as the man continued with his story.

'I was forced into hiding. So I bought a castle on the Kaikōura Coast to escape my enemies. I was all but happy with my life, living in seclusion. Until that fateful day when I looked out and saw your sad eyes looking up at me.'

It was you? Aaron's legs turned to jelly, and he almost collapsed onto the ground. *You were the grotesque face at the window that almost scared us to death all those years ago?*

The hooded man bent down until he was at Aaron's level. 'My blood boiled when I saw the way that girl abused you. Treated you like a dog. Running you down. Denigrating you. I wanted to wring her neck. And I would have done if you hadn't scarpered.'

Aaron looked down at his feet. His mind returned to that awful day when he had gone with Miriama to the castle. What was it she'd said to him? *You're going nowhere, are you? You'll never be able to buy a girl a house like this place, will you?* She'd called him a loser. *A common gangland boy.* That had hurt more than anything.

That was all in the past. Aaron straightened. Besides, the man was watching them from the top-floor window. How could he possibly have heard what they were saying?

'You're guessing,' Aaron said. 'You have no idea what we were talking about.'

'I could see it in your faces,' the hooded man replied. 'She was all high and mighty. Pushing you away like you were an outcast. You looked so hurt. She destroyed you. I couldn't get your miserable face out of my mind.' He paused and looked Aaron straight in the eye. 'No son of mine will ever be disrespected like that again.'

'That was years ago,' Aaron said. 'Everything's different now. Miriama's changed.'

'Has she?' The hooded man edged closer to Aaron. 'Kāterina brought her up to torture men.'

'Bloody nonsense! Miriama has changed. She's my kindred spirit.' But as he spoke, something else Miriama had said that afternoon at the castle sprung into Aaron's mind: *Kāterina hopes I'll fall for you. Fat chance of that.*

'Why won't you believe me?' the hooded man asked. 'You know it's true.'

Aaron rapidly pulled himself together. He couldn't show any sign of weakness to this man. If any of his outlandish claims were true, he still had masses of explaining to do. 'Supposing you did escape the fire, which beggars belief, where

         David Whittet

have you been for the past twenty-eight years? It isn't just me you deserted. It's my mother too. You left her to the mercy of the Gang.'

'It's a miracle I got out of that fire alive. I was trapped under a fallen beam. I heard your mother crying for help, but I couldn't reach her.' A tear appeared in the corner of his eye. 'I would have saved her if I could. I swear.'

This was the first glimmer of genuine emotion Aaron had seen in this larger-than-life character. But it wasn't nearly enough to prove he was legitimate.

'Go on,' Aaron said. 'You were trapped under a beam.'

'The inferno blazed all around me. The house collapsed, and molten debris fell on top of me. When a fireball struck me, I was sure I would die.'

Aaron flapped his hands. 'You expect me to believe that you survived that?'

'That's the extraordinary thing. The fireball dislodged the beam and propelled me away. Adrenaline took over, and I crawled out of the back of the house. I rolled down a bank, spinning round and round to extinguish the flames, and then landed in a ditch. It's all a blur after that. I remember scrambling to a stream and the ice-cold water easing the pain of the burns.'

'How come you just disappeared off the face of the earth?' Aaron pointed at the man's scarred face. 'With burns like that, you'd have needed to go to hospital.'

'I had to lie low. I'd survived two assassination attempts, first at the church and then the house fire. Showing up at a hospital would have given my enemies another chance. I might not have been so lucky the next time.'

Aaron scratched the back of his neck. 'So, how did you manage the burns?'

Le Squillier stepped forward. 'Your father asked me to find a doctor who'd do the job and not ask any questions.'

Aaron scowled at Le Squillier. 'So you called in some backstreet quack?'

'No,' Le Squillier replied. 'A highly respectable surgeon who owed me a favour.'

Aaron turned back to the hooded man and snorted. 'You've had twenty-eight years to concoct a story, and this is the best you can come up with?'

'But it's true, son.' The hooded man reached out to Aaron with his hands. 'Every word of it. Why won't you believe it?'

'Because my father was an honourable man. He wouldn't have abandoned his wife and his son.' Aaron gestured at Le Squillier. 'And he definitely wouldn't have got a lackey to do his dirty work.'

Le Squillier drew himself up to full height. 'I'm no lackey. I'm a professional.'

Aaron squinted at Le Squillier. *A professional indeed. That's highly questionable.*

The hooded man ignored Le Squillier and continued to tackle Aaron. 'I had no choice but to act through a lawyer. Believe me. I was a sitting target for an assassin. Business adversaries wanted me dead. The Godzone Gorillas put a price on my head. But they all thought I was dead. I was safe as long as I kept it that way.'

Aaron drew back. 'Well, you've blown your cover now. A church full of people know you're alive.'

The hooded man put a hand on Aaron's shoulder. 'You're worth the sacrifice, son.'

Aaron pushed him away. 'Stop calling me that. I don't see how you could have survived in isolation all that time.'

'I had money. Lots of money in offshore accounts that I'd stashed away as a contingency fund.' The hooded man pinned Aaron with his eyes as he went on. 'That's how I could afford to buy that castle on the Kaikōura Coast. Somewhere safe where I could live in secret. Living like a hermit, with only myself for company, I thought about your mother. About Alicia. And about you, the son I'd never met.'

Aaron shook his head. 'I still don't buy it. If you cared about us that much, why have you left it until now to do something about it?'

The hooded man continued to eyeball Aaron. 'Oh, but I have. Long before I saw your sad face looking up at me at the castle, I had decided to set up a trust fund for you. I would send you to business school, see you excel, and make you a success.'

Aaron snorted. 'Liar! Kāterina paid for me to go to business school.'

'Really?' A knowing smile crept over the hooded man's distorted features. 'That's what she told you, is it?'

'Not exactly …' Aaron broke off. He thought back to what Miriama had said earlier that day. Kāterina's lawyer was Barnaby McVeigh, and she wouldn't have trusted anyone else to look after her affairs. 'I mean, I always believed Kāterina was my benefactor. She led me to believe it was her.'

'Did she indeed?' The hooded man's condescending grin made his face even more grotesque. 'Then she's the one making up stories.'

Aaron shuddered. Kāterina was a born storyteller, but she would never have knowingly deceived him on something so important. Would she? Perhaps he should have questioned how a hermit living in a run-down caravan could afford to pay for him to attend business school. But Kāterina had sent Miriama to boarding school in Switzerland. That must have cost a fortune. Perhaps that was why Kāterina had to live like a pauper—because she'd spent all her money on Miriama's education. No—thinking back, Aaron had heard Miriama talk about the large payouts Kāterina had received from her treaty work and the land settlements. Aunt Helena had also told him that Kāterina's nomadic existence was a lifestyle choice.

Errol Troy, who had remained quiet up to now, turned to the hooded man. 'Go easy on him, Emir. You've turned his life upside down. Remember what we agreed.'

Aaron flinched. He'd served with Errol on the Parata Peak board for years. In all that time, did Errol know someone was out there claiming to be his father? What exactly had they agreed?

'He needs to hear the truth.' The hooded man pushed Troy aside. 'Tell him, Le Squillier.'

Le Squillier cleared his throat. 'This man *is* your father. Everything he's said is correct.'

Aaron glared at Le Squillier. 'Why should I believe anything you say? You've never been straight with me.'

'I don't blame you for being suspicious.' Le Squillier edged closer to Aaron and addressed him directly. 'I was doubtful when Emir first summoned me to his castle. He ushered me into this palatial drawing room with portraits of warriors hanging on the wall. It felt like they were all looking down on me. Gave me a turn, I can tell you.'

The hooded man stamped his foot. 'Cut the crap. Just tell him what happened.'

'You had me track down Aaron to his aunt Helena's house,' Le Squillier continued. 'Then you sent me there to take him away from his aunt and set him up for business school.'

Aaron covered his face with his hands. 'I was so sure it was Kāterina.' He glanced up at Le Squillier. 'It *was* Kāterina, wasn't it? Tell me it was her!'

Le Squillier shook his head. 'I'm sorry, Aaron, but I've never had any dealings with Ms Kururangi.'

Aaron felt his eyes well up. 'She must have played some part in—'

'That witch had nothing to do with it,' the hooded man interrupted. 'It was all me. I had to see you succeed and take over where I left off in business.'

'She's not a witch.' Aaron fought back the tears. 'Kāterina was my friend.'

Now Kāterina was dead, and Aaron couldn't talk to her and find out if all this was true.

'Forget about Kāterina.' The hooded man opened his arms to Aaron. 'Come with me! We'll make an invincible team. With your exalted position and my financial backing, we will rule the power industry as father and son.'

'No!' Aaron pulled back. 'How do I know this isn't a scam?'

'I assure you,' Le Squillier said, 'I have had your best interests at heart all along. When Emir first instructed me to take you away from your aunt, I warned Emir it could be construed as child kidnapping if your aunt had legal custody of you.'

'Child kidnapping indeed!' The hooded man glared at Le Squillier. 'I told you he was my son, and I could do what I wanted with him.'

'Not any more,' Aaron said. 'I'm my own man now.'

Voices in the distance. Aaron turned to see Tony leading a uniformed police officer towards them.

'What's all this I hear about child kidnapping?' the police officer asked.

'This is Constable Barrett,' Tony said. 'He needs to interview our new friend.'

For a moment, Aaron thought the hooded man was going to make a run for it, but Le Squillier grabbed his arm.

Errol scowled at Tony. 'Did you really need to involve the police?'

'Aaron deserves certainty,' Tony replied. 'I'm sure that if our friend is who he says he is, he won't mind a chat with the police.'

That told him! Aaron couldn't help grinning as the hooded man glared at Tony and then Constable Barrett. *Thank God for Tony.* At least Aaron had someone on his side.

'I understand that you claim to be Emir Casper,' Constable Barrett said to the hooded man. 'Do you have any formal identification?'

     David Whittet

'What do you think?' the hooded man shot back. 'Everything I owned was destroyed in the fire.'

'I appreciate that,' Constable Barrett said. 'But you have had plenty of time to apply for replacement documents since then.'

'I chose to live in isolation,' the hooded man answered. 'Nothing illegal in that, is there?'

'Not as such.' Constable Barrett took a notebook out of his pocket. 'Police records show that Emir Casper's mortal remains were buried at St Andrew's Church in the Coromandel in 1994.'

The hooded man stared down at the constable. 'Then you buried someone else's remains, didn't you?'

'DNA evidence says otherwise.' Constable Barrett flicked through his notebook. 'So, if you're not Emir Casper, who are you? And I should warn you, identity theft *is* a crime.'

The hooded man kicked the ground. 'I don't have to listen to this.'

'I'm afraid you do.' Constable Barrett put away his notebook. 'I must ask you to accompany me to the police station for a formal interview.'

'Is my client under arrest?' Le Squillier asked.

'Not at this stage,' Constable Barrett answered. 'But we will interview him under caution. So it's fortunate we have his lawyer here. That'll save a lot of time.'

Le Squillier grunted. 'Come on, Emir. Let's get this over with. This apology for a cop won't know what's hit him.'

Aaron's mind was still racing and searching for answers as the hooded man left with Le Squillier and the constable.

The hooded man turned back and waved his fist in the air. 'You haven't seen the last of me, my son. I promise you we *will* rule the power industry as father and son. And he who controls power rules the world!'

'Whoever he is, the man's insane,' Aaron muttered.

'I told you, it's the smoke damage to his brain,' Errol said. 'It makes him super excitable. But deep down, he's the same Emir. I was hoping we could rehabilitate him and maybe find him a role at Parata Peak Power.'

No bloody way! Aaron took a step backwards. Had Errol taken leave of his senses too?

Errol turned to Tony. 'I only wish you hadn't gone running to the police. That'll make him even more paranoid.'

And even less able to return to business. Aaron shuddered as Errol left to follow Le Squillier and the hooded man to the police station. The hooded man continued to sound off as he disappeared into the distance. Would Aaron ever be free of him and get his life back? Could this madman truly be his father? Would Miriama understand? Would anything be the same again?

CHAPTER THIRTY-FIVE

Back at their accommodation, Aaron's head was still all over the place. How could Errol and Le Squillier have kept him in the dark for so long? *Bastards*. They were as bad as each other. For a moment, Aaron wished he could be a fly on the wall at the police station and hear what lies they were telling the constable. No. He had to distance himself from what had transpired that morning.

Tony helped him pack up his things at the cottage and load his car. Forever loyal and reliable, Tony was the best friend Aaron had ever had.

'You're a mate, Tony,' Aaron said. 'In fact, you're more than a mate. You're a lifesaver. I don't know what I'd have done if you hadn't turned up with the policeman.'

'It was the right thing to do,' Tony replied. 'Let's hope you get some answers.'

'I'm not sure I want to know.' Aaron paused while stuffing his clothes into a suitcase. 'Do you think that monster could be my father?'

Tony thought for a minute. 'I don't see how he could be. Not if they found DNA evidence of the real Emir Casper in the remains they buried.'

'DNA analysis was in its infancy back then,' Aaron said. 'They could easily have got it wrong. After all, they only found a few charred bones.'

Tony frowned. 'So you think he might really be your father?'

'I don't know.' Aaron closed the suitcase. 'He knows so much about me. It feels like he has been trying to micromanage me from a distance since I was a little kid.'

'Surely not.'

'All these years I thought Kāterina had paid for me to go to business school.' Aaron slumped onto the settee. 'But it couldn't have been. Le Squillier was never Kāterina's lawyer. And why would that man fork out a fortune for my education if he wasn't my father?'

Tony sat down beside him. 'None of it makes any sense, does it?'

'Sure doesn't.' Aaron put his head in his hands. 'Is it even possible to live incognito for twenty-eight years without being caught? And if he was so opposed to me marrying Miriama, why did he turn up at the church *after* we'd said our vows?'

'I wish I knew.' Tony put a hand on Aaron's shoulder. 'Do you know what he has against Miriama?'

'She could be nasty when we were kids. It came to a head when we were on a road trip in the *Gypsy Rose*. We stopped at a campsite on the Kaikōura Coast. There was this grand castle nearby. Kāterina forbade us to go near it as some mad recluse lived there.'

Tony raised an eyebrow. 'The mad recluse was our hooded man?'

Aaron nodded. 'Miriama insisted we explore the castle, and I went with her to prove I wasn't a coward. And yes, she was pretty mean to me.'

'So what happened?'

'The man came out and chased us away.' Aaron raised his head. 'Now he claims that he saw Miriama treating me like a dog. But he couldn't have heard what we were saying.'

Tony baulked. 'And that one event turned him against Miriama for life?'

'Kāterina and my father never got on. At least, that's what I've been told.' Aaron ran his fingers through his hair. 'It started with a wedding present, of all things. Kāterina had done up this old oil lamp as their gift, and my father took an instant dislike to it.'

Tony shook his head. 'There must have been more to it than that. Surely.'

'Kāterina told me Emir believed she had poisoned my mother against him. But it's all a load of crap.'

'Perhaps there's more to it than you think,' Tony said.

'Maybe.' Aaron fiddled with the wedding ring on his finger. 'Another thing, why did Kāterina take off when the hooded man showed up a couple of days before the wedding? She said his appearance was an omen. Did she know the man was my father? If she did, why didn't she tell me?' Aaron threw his head back. 'Now that Kāterina's dead, we'll never know.'

'Do you know for certain that it was Kāterina's body they pulled from the water? Have you heard from Miriama?'

Aaron sighed. 'I've tried calling her a few times, but her phone's turned off. I guess they don't want a phone ringing in the morgue.'

'What are you going to do now?' Tony asked.

    David Whittet

Aaron stood and picked up his suitcase. 'I'll drive to Roaring Creek and meet Miriama.'

'Will you be alright?' Tony grabbed another case. 'Would you like me to come with you?'

Aaron thought for a moment. 'Thanks for the offer. You're like a brother to me, but I need some time alone to get my head around all of this.'

Tony helped Aaron load the cases into the back of his car. 'As long as you're sure.'

Aaron closed the boot. 'Miriama and I should be driving to the airport. We were going to spend a few days in Melbourne for our honeymoon. We didn't have time to plan anything more extravagant once we decided to bring the wedding forward to Matariki Day. It would have been our first overseas trip after the pandemic.'

'You could still go,' Tony said.

'Maybe we will, after Kāterina's tangi,' Aaron said with a shrug. 'When all this has settled down. If it ever does settle down.'

Aaron was just a few kilometres down the road when a bright red Mercedes tailgated him with its horn blasting. *Bloody maniac!* Aaron pulled to the side of the road before the car rammed him into the ditch. *What the hell does he think he's playing at?* Aaron's heart pounded against his chest when the hooded man jumped out of the Mercedes.

'Are you trying to get us both killed?' Aaron yelled.

'No, son,' the hooded man said. 'I just want to talk to you.'

'We've talked already,' Aaron shot back. 'I've nothing more to say.'

The hooded man took a step closer to Aaron. 'But I have. We can't leave things like this.'

'So the police didn't arrest you?' Aaron said. 'I thought they would lock you up as an imposter.'

'Don't be like that.' The hooded man extended a hand to Aaron. 'All the years I lived in solitary confinement, I longed for the day I would reunite with my son. It was heartbreaking watching you from a distance. When I learnt you'd been successful at business school, all I wanted was to hug and congratulate you. Being unable to share the moment with you destroyed me. You've no idea what it's been like.'

Aaron glared back at him. 'And you have no idea what it's like to have someone barge in and hijack their wedding ceremony.'

'But I do,' the hooded man said. 'Your mother was shot at our wedding. I had to do the kiss of life before the altar while she almost bled to death.'

'Okay, I'm sorry.' Aaron kept his eyes pinned on the hooded man. 'But in a way that makes what you did even worse. You knew how it felt to have your wedding day ruined, yet you still did it to me.'

The hooded man stared back. 'I didn't come with a gun.'

'No.' Aaron slammed his car door shut. 'But if you really are my father, why didn't you get in touch sooner? You could have come to my graduation. I'm sure you could have managed a disguise with all that money you've got.'

The hooded man shook his head. 'I couldn't take a chance on someone recognising me. No amount of money can buy a disguise to hide these scars.'

Aaron scowled. 'Well, you turned up today. Scaring everyone to death with your grotesque face.'

'It was you that pulled off my hood.'

Aaron scratched his head. How could he make this man understand? 'Did you honestly imagine I would welcome you with open arms when you gatecrashed my wedding?'

'I thought …' The hooded man stared down at his feet. 'I thought you would be happy to see me.'

'Maybe I would have been if you'd gone about things properly.' Aaron stepped forward. 'It didn't have to be like this. You could have come as a wedding guest instead of making a scene at the church. We'd have gladly invited you to the wedding if only you'd asked.'

'I could *never* accept an invitation to see you marry that wretched girl. Why did you have to choose Miriama? You could have had any girl you wanted.'

'I chose Miriama because I love her.'

The hooded man snorted. 'You love the bitch who called you a loser and a common gang boy?'

Aaron flung his arms in the air. 'We've been through this before. That was a

 David Whittet

long time ago, and Miriama has changed. But yes, I loved her from the moment I first set eyes on her. Even when she called me all those horrible names.'

'Why can't you see? Miriama is a twisted child brought up by an evil witch.'

'What is it you have against Kāterina and Miriama? What have they ever done to you?'

'Kāterina tried to poison your mother against me.'

Would Aaron *ever* get a straight answer? 'Why? Because she gave you a wedding present you didn't like?'

'Of course not.' The hooded man shrank back. 'Kāterina told your mother I only married her to get leverage with the Godzone Gorillas. I was planning to build a water bottling plant at the Roaring Creek Falls, but the Gang claimed the land was theirs. That witch Kāterina insinuated that me marrying the president's daughter was the only way to get the Godzone Gorillas off my back.'

'And that's not true?'

'No. I loved your mother. I still do.'

Aaron told himself to calm down and think straight. 'Anyway, whatever Kāterina may or may not have said about you, none of this concerns Miriama. I love her. My life was a misery before I met Miriama.'

'And not much better afterwards, from what I've heard.' The hooded man jabbed a finger in Aaron's face. 'She's a man-hater who will bring you nothing but misery and blacken the family name. Dump her, son. Annul the marriage. Then you're free. Think about what we could achieve in partnership together.'

'If you're just going to slag off Miriama, you can piss off.'

The hooded man kicked the tyre of his Mercedes. 'I've risked everything, breaking my cover today. Please don't tell me it's all been for nothing.'

Aaron felt his fingernails digging into his palms. 'Whoever you are, if you want any part in my life, you will have to accept Miriama is the love of my life, and you will treat her with respect.'

The hooded man spat on the ground. 'Respect that vixen?'

'Stop calling her that.'

'Truth hurts, does it?' The hooded man rocked backwards and forwards. 'Perhaps I should have brought a gun to the wedding and shot the wretched girl.'

Something in the hooded man's blazing eyes told Aaron that he might just do it. 'You're mad. You should be locked up. I don't know why the police let you go.'

'Because I haven't done anything wrong—yet.' The hooded man's eyes grew even more incandescent with rage. 'Don't force me to do something I'll regret.'

Aaron raised a fist. 'If you do anything to harm Miriama, you won't have to worry about your enemies hiring an assassin because I'll do it for them.'

'You don't mean that.'

'Don't I?' Aaron moved slowly and deliberately towards the hooded man, his fist still clenched. 'All my life, I have longed for a father. When I was a kid, I used to think how different my life would have been if my father was still alive. It never crossed my mind that he was there all along, too much of a coward to come out of hiding and take care of my mother and me.'

'I was there for you, son. I paid for you to go to business school.'

'Some things count for more than money. No decent father would threaten to kill his son's bride on their wedding day. To think I defended you when people ran you down. Everyone blamed you for what happened to my mother. More fool me for sticking up for you.' Aaron eyeballed the hooded man. 'If you are my father, then prove it. We can do a DNA test.'

'We don't need a test.' The hooded man extended a hand to Aaron. 'We both know you're my son.'

Aaron shook his head. 'We don't.'

'I never thought a son of mine would doubt me like this.'

'So you refuse to take the test? Afraid of the truth?' Aaron turned away. 'Alright then. I want nothing more to do with you.'

'Don't you dare turn your back on me! Your future is with me! Me! Together we'll conquer the world.'

Aaron wasn't listening. He walked back to his car. 'If you won't take the DNA test, I guess I'll never know for certain if you're my father or not. But even if you are, I don't need you. I've managed the last twenty-eight years without you. I want you out of my life.'

'I'm warning you, Aaron. You're either with me or against me. I put you where you are. I can just as easily take you down.'

Aaron slammed the car door shut, started the engine and drove off at high speed.

     David Whittet

CHAPTER THIRTY-SIX

Aaron was halfway to Roaring Creek when he turned back. Miriama's phone was still turned off. She must still be busy with formalities. While he was desperate to reunite with Miriama, there was something Aaron had to do first.

The hooded man's final words still rang in Aaron's ears as he changed direction and headed for Parata Peak. *You're either with me or against me. I put you where you are. I can just as easily take you down.* There was a coldness in the man's voice when he made that final threat that set it apart from the rest of the man's ranting. With his cover broken, the hooded man was a loose cannon.

How seriously should Aaron take the man's threat? After Kaine's threatening behaviour during the mediation, Aaron had insisted on extra security, both personal and for the power station. But was that enough with the hooded man on the loose?

Had Aaron been too hard on him? Errol Troy said the man's volatility was due to brain damage from the fire. Was Aaron's failure to accept the man as his father and welcome him with open arms enough to send him over the top?

Aaron had to know if this man was his father. Such a pity Fonella had disappeared. More than anyone else, she could determine whether this man was her brother or an imposter. But there were other ways to unravel the mystery. The Parata Peak Power Station came into view on the horizon. Aaron hoped and prayed that a box locked away in his office might hold the answer.

Something wasn't quite right. Aaron sensed it immediately when he drew up at Parata Peak Power. He parked his car in his reserved space and opened the security app on his phone. Nothing unusual. The maintenance staff had checked in for their routine work. Matariki Day was a public holiday, so there was only a skeleton crew on site. Aaron disarmed the executive suite and made his way to his office.

Everything was just as he had left it. He picked up the framed photograph of his father off his desk, taken the day Emir had graduated with first-class honours at the University of Auckland. Aaron had kept this photograph beside him as a talisman throughout his career. Could that proud, smiling face in the picture possibly be the same man as the monster who had invaded their wedding?

Aaron took a folder out of the top drawer of his desk. A collection of carefully preserved press cuttings about his father. Aaron thumbed through the cuttings, reading the headlines: *Boy from the Wrong Side of the Tracks Signs Multi-Million Dollar Deal.* That was from *The New Zealand Herald. The Stuff of Legend.* That was *The Dominion* newspaper. Then there was the full page spread in *Business NZ* when his father had started his own company, Emir Casper and Associates.

It was time to open the safe. Aaron sighed and put the cuttings back in the drawer. He walked slowly and deliberately across his office to the secure storage room. Was he expecting too much? Could a police report and a box of his father's possessions, passed down to him through his mother and Aunt Helena, provide him with the certainty he needed?

Everything would have been so much easier if only the hooded man had agreed to provide a DNA sample. Perhaps there was another way. Aaron was sure the police report stated they had retained and stored DNA samples from the charred bones discovered in the burnt-down house. It was a long shot, but would sufficient DNA be left on his father's wristwatch, wedding ring or fountain pen for comparison with the sample held by the police? If so, and the samples matched, that would prove beyond doubt that the remains buried at the funeral belonged to his father and the hooded man was an imposter.

Aaron fumbled with the key to the secure storage room. His hand shook as he stepped inside and rotated the dial on the safe. The security app on his phone bleeped the moment the safe door swung open. He glanced at the phone's screen. Unauthorised access in zone four. That was the control room. *Damn it.* Aaron shut the safe door and locked the secure storage room. It was probably a false alarm, but he needed to investigate.

More bleeps sounded from his phone as Aaron hurried along the maze of corridors, each with their own Touch ID pad. Zones two and three now also showed unauthorised entries. Was someone trying to make a rapid escape?

     David Whittet

Aaron raced to the control room, but nothing happened when he put his finger on the touchpad. His security card didn't work either. What the hell was going on? Someone must have tampered with the sensors. Aaron kicked the door, but it still wouldn't open.

Could his day get any worse? His wedding was hijacked, and now security at his power plant was compromised. Aaron hammered on the door. Where the hell were the maintenance staff?

Aaron backtracked down the corridor. There was another way into the control room.

The Touch ID at the other end of the corridor also refused to let him through. Aaron was trapped with no way out. He reached for his phone. No cellular reception. No wi-fi. There was *always* cellular coverage and wi-fi at the power station. Someone had definitely sabotaged the infrastructure.

But who? Aaron immediately thought of the hooded man. Was that possible? Even allowing for Aaron's detour, there was scarcely time for the hooded man to have got here ahead of him. Although, with his seemingly limitless funds, the hooded man could have paid someone to infiltrate the plant. That seemed unlikely. To take over the power station's IT system would have taken months of planning and covert surveillance. If the hooded man was his father, why would he have gone to those lengths *before* Aaron had rejected him?

Aaron's focus turned to Kaine and the Godzone Gorillas. Kaine had promised revenge when they'd fought after the mediation. *We'll destroy you. Blow your prized power station to bits. Smash it into smithereens. Smithereens!* The Godzone Gorillas had the resources to mount an operation on this scale. Aaron had no doubt they were sufficiently vindictive to carry out the threat.

For an awful moment, Aaron even wondered if the hooded man could have been Corey in disguise. Corey and the hooded man were of similar stature, and you could do almost anything with makeup these days. Aaron told himself not to be so ridiculous.

Still, it looked increasingly likely that Corey would have the last laugh. Aaron was trapped in the power station with no means of escape. It was doubtful if anyone else would enter the plant before morning. What if the power station blew up before then? Would Aaron die on his wedding day?

Time passed slowly. Aaron kept checking his phone for cellular reception, but it remained blocked, and his phone's battery was running low. He repeatedly put his finger on the security pad, but what was the use? However many times he tried, it still wouldn't open the door. Aaron paced up and down the corridor. Maybe Tony or Miriama would notice he was missing. But they would never imagine he was at the power station. Aaron cursed himself. Why had he changed his mind and gone to Parata Peak? If only he'd gone straight to Roaring Creek to meet Miriama.

Exhausted by the day's events, Aaron huddled in a corner and tried to get some rest. A rumbling sound kept him awake, similar to the noise he'd experienced in the church. *Go away!* Aaron put his hands over his ears and tried to ignore it. It was just his mind playing tricks on him.

If only he could survive the night, the morning shift would rescue him when they reported for duty. Aaron looked at his watch and groaned. That was still eight hours away.

Aaron closed his eyes and tried to sleep. He began to drift off when the echo in his head became a deafening roar. The floor was giving way beneath him. Aaron gasped for breath. What the hell was happening? The control room door split in front of his eyes. The walls cracked as gigantic flames shot up to the ceiling. Aaron stumbled to his feet and stared as the blazing inferno engulfed the control room. His heart raced. He struggled to catch his breath amid the acrid smoke. Paralysed by fear, Aaron was powerless to stop all his professional hopes, ambitions and aspirations from imploding in a vortex of fire and molten destruction.

CHAPTER THIRTY-SEVEN

Aaron thought of his mother as he stood with his head in his hands, barely able to comprehend the devastation before him. She must have experienced the same blind terror when she fought for her life in the house fire. His skin turned black as it scorched in the intense heat. He choked on the toxic smoke while the control room equipment disintegrated.

If he survived, would Aaron suffer brain damage from smoke inhalation, just as his father had done? Aaron quickly corrected himself. As the hooded man had done.

The control room ceiling collapsed on top of him, catapulting him to the floor and trapping him under a mass of molten debris. Shards of liquified plastic landed on his head. He would die on his wedding day, burnt to death in a fiery cauldron.

Is this how his father—assuming the man was his father—felt when he was trapped under a beam?

With an almighty blast, the floor cracked and split into halves. Was this the end? Would he fall to his death in the giant chasm? At least the debris had shifted when the floor ruptured, and Aaron could crawl free. Wasn't this how the hooded man said he'd escaped from the fire?

Aaron's eyes streamed from the overpowering fumes. What was he going to do? Was there any way he could get out of this alive? He scrambled to his feet, urging himself to keep going. *If the hooded man could escape from an inferno, so can you.* Aaron struggled to find his way through the thick smoke and fumes. There should be an exit onto the parapet, if only he could get through the carnage in the control room. Aaron felt his body weaken and his concentration diminish in the searing heat. *Pull yourself together. Focus like you've never done before.* But as the smoke got thicker, Aaron's brain fog grew denser. His eyes were ablaze and his body spent. Aaron fell back to the floor amid the red-hot rubble. There was no way out for him. Better to die here than survive and end up as bitter and twisted as the hooded man.

Would the flames consume him, or would the smoke get to him first? As he lay curled up in the foetal position, Aaron thought about what Kāterina had taught him about karma. Had he brought this disaster on himself? Some months ago, community leaders in the Parata Peak township had raised concerns about the possibility of an accident at the power station. A fracture in the concrete of the giant spillway could flood the entire valley and decimate the township. Aaron had assured the leaders that fail-safe security processes at the plant ensured that could never happen. He'd spoken at public meetings and gone on local radio to reassure the community they were safe. And when some protestors camped on the site, he instructed security to remove them.

Perhaps dying in the explosion was his bad karma. Divine retribution for not listening when Tony had pleaded with him to take the risk seriously and implement measures to safeguard the community.

At least it was only him trapped in the inferno. Aaron would die alone. There was no sign of anyone else in the plant, so he prayed the maintenance crew had got out before the worst of the explosion. The board would be bound to enforce strict safeguards in the aftermath of the blast. At least some good would come out of the catastrophe. It wasn't the legacy Aaron had dreamt of, but at least his death wouldn't be entirely in vain.

Kāterina had also told him about near-death experiences and the afterlife. Aaron didn't see a bright light beckoning him down an endless celestial tunnel, nor did he feel a benevolent hand leading him towards a new and better world. Instead, a violent jolt roused him from his stupor. Was he entering the jaws of hell?

Aaron raised his head, his eyes still burning. A further explosion shook the remains of the power plant with the force of a massive earthquake. Shafts of daylight broke through the noxious fumes. Aaron crawled over the rubble and stared at the destruction. The blast had smashed the dam, and torrents of water from the reservoir cascaded into the valley. He *was* in the jaws of hell.

So much for his fail-safe security systems. This was the worst-case scenario the community had warned him about. Aaron covered his eyes. He couldn't bear to look at the relentless surge of water, a giant tsunami that submerged everything in its destructive path. The Parata Peak township would be wiped out. Was this his fault? Could he have prevented the tragedy if he hadn't been so pig-headed?

 David Whittet

No. Aaron scrambled to his feet. Nobody could have anticipated an explosion of this magnitude. The reinforcement of the concrete spillway that the community had demanded would not have made any difference to this seismic tidal wave.

Aaron climbed onto the parapet. Piercing sirens echoed through the valley. That meant civil defence had sprung into action. Police cars, fire engines, ambulances and recovery vehicles appeared in the distance. *Please, God, let them get the townsfolk out before they are underwater.*

Now that he was free of the molten debris, Aaron had a chance to escape. But he was the CEO of Parata Peak Power, which was akin to being the captain of the ship. Any ship's captain worthy of their position would stay on board to the bitter end.

Aaron paused for a moment. Staying behind would serve no purpose. It would make Miriama a widow on her wedding day. Aaron shuddered. He couldn't let that happen. Plus, he had to be there to oversee the reconstruction of the Parata Peak Power Station. The rebuild would be state of the art and demonstrate the future of hydroelectric power. Aaron was a survivor and he was back in survival mode. And not least, he was determined to find the perpetrators of this catastrophe and bring them to justice.

The flames continued to soar inside the plant. How to get out? Aaron made for the ventilation tunnels that ran under the power station. The dark subterranean passages all looked the same. Was he heading in the right direction? Aaron tried desperately to visualise the plan of the tunnels. He'd seen it so many times before but never took much interest in it. Now it was a matter of life and— Aaron couldn't bring himself to finish the sentence that ran through his head.

Deep in the bowels of the power station, the inferno became a distant rumble. Aaron could hear his heart pounding in the eerie quiet. Water spilt from the underground drains. He'd drown if the tsunami wave flooded the tunnels.

The near silence suddenly gave way to maniacal laughter, echoing through the labyrinthine passages. Was that the bomber escaping? Was it Kaine or one of his minions, or was it the hooded man? Perhaps one of his accomplices? Aaron ran down the tunnel in the direction of the laughter. He would catch the culprit red-handed.

The ground began to rock and Aaron lost his footing. The entire tunnel shook, and a resounding boom drowned the sound of the laughter. What the hell was it? *Please, God—not another bomb.*

Cracks began to appear in the reinforced concrete walls. Aaron glanced up. Above him, the tunnel was caving in even faster. If he didn't get out now, the tunnel would collapse on top of him.

Aaron ran for his life. He had no idea which way to go in the myriad of endless passages and concentrated on getting as far away as he could from the roar of the inferno. He paused to catch his breath and try to get his bearings. Thank God the compass on his smartwatch was still working. If he headed due east, that would take him out through the sewage pipe. He had only taken a few paces down the passage when a bright flash of light almost blinded him. Fire raged through the tunnels, and Aaron found himself chased by a ferocious fireball. *Keep going eastward. It's your only hope.*

The fireball was gaining on him. Aaron didn't dare look back, but the roar got closer. He didn't see the drainage shaft ahead of him until it was too late. Aaron fell down the abyss and plunged into a slimy mire. He'd never been so happy to find himself submerged in such foul and unsanitary sludge. The grunge told him he'd reached the sewer.

A bright light shone ahead, and it wasn't the fireball. It was daylight! Aaron swam through the sea of stinking excrement. *Not much further. You can do this.* The sewage got in his mouth and up his nose, but Aaron swam on undeterred. He'd come so close to death that he couldn't succumb at the last moment. *One final push, and you're there!*

The sunlight dazzled Aaron's already stinging eyes as he emerged from the sewage pipe. The stench of his soiled clothing and the human faeces that covered every inch of his body made him gag. He scrambled to the bank of the reservoir and attempted to clean himself up. The ice-cold water soothed his burning limbs, but it would take more than the crystal-clear water of the reservoir to get rid of the excrement that plastered his body and stuck to it like glue.

 David Whittet

Aaron squinted at the smouldering wreck of the power station. He would have wept if he hadn't been so physically and emotionally wiped out. Even more painful, he forced himself to turn and face the devastation in the Parata Peak township below. Emergency services continued to converge on the site. Molten debris still poured down onto the town, carried by the endless torrent from the reservoir. The blazing sirens competed with the cries of terror from the townsfolk as families evacuated their homes amid the rising flood water. The lucky ones managed to climb up the cliff to higher ground and safety. The less fortunate ones—

Aaron closed his eyes and covered his ears but could not blot out the children's crying. If the hooded man—his father—was responsible, was avenging his son's rejection worth the immense suffering and loss endured by so many innocent people? Of course, if it was the Godzone Gorillas, as Aaron suspected, they didn't care about anyone else's life.

Two police officers strode across the valley towards Aaron. Good. At last, he might get some answers. Had they caught the bomber already?

'Aaron Casper?' the first officer asked.

Aaron nodded.

'I am arresting you on suspicion of bombing the Parata Peak Power Station.'

What the hell? Before Aaron could take in what was happening, the second officer handcuffed him.

'You are not obliged to say anything, but anything you do say may be used in evidence against you.'

'You can't be serious,' Aaron stammered. 'This is outrageous!'

'Is it?' the first officer said. 'Well, you'll have the chance to tell your side of the story at the police station.'

The grim faces of both officers as they led Aaron away made it clear they *were* serious. Deadly serious.

CHAPTER THIRTY-EIGHT

The custody officer stepped back and surreptitiously held his nose.

'Excuse me a moment,' he said before he began processing Aaron.

Aaron watched him pull a mask out of a drawer and put it on.

'That's better,' the custody officer said. 'Now, I need your full name.'

Aaron knew full well the mask wasn't because he was worried about Covid-19.

'Why don't you let me take a shower?' Aaron asked. 'It would make things a lot pleasanter for everyone. At least, let me have some clean clothes.'

'All in good time,' the custody officer replied. 'Now empty your pockets. Your clothes will have to be bagged as evidence.'

Aaron put his wallet and his mobile phone on the benchtop.

'Your smartwatch too,' the custody officer said. 'And we'll need your passwords.'

'I'm allowed a phone call,' Aaron said. 'I need to speak to my wife.'

But what could he say to Miriama? Would she understand?

The custody officer went through Aaron's wallet. 'Fingerprints and photograph first. Then you can have your phone call.'

Aaron's shame should have been deeper as another officer inked his fingers for the fingerprints. But he'd run out of adrenaline, and his fight or flight response was spent. He slumped his shoulders as they took his mugshot and barely stirred when they swabbed his mouth for a DNA sample.

'I'm not saying anything until my lawyer gets here,' Aaron insisted when they had finished. 'Now, what about that phone call?'

Aaron's hand shook as he picked up the receiver and dialled Miriama's mobile number. *Please pick up. Please.* Aaron's heart missed a beat. Maybe she wouldn't take the call with it coming from an unknown number.

He'd almost given up hope when she answered.

'Hello. Who's there?'

     David Whittet

Aaron's mouth was so dry he could barely speak, let alone explain the dire situation he was in. 'Miriama! Thank God you picked up. You won't believe what's happened—'

'I know.' Miriama sounded as distraught as Aaron felt. 'Are you okay? I saw it all on the news.'

What? Aaron's shame felt immeasurably worse to learn that his arrest had been the lead story on the television news. Tears welled in his eyes as Miriama described the coverage, with shots of the smouldering power station and the decimation of the Parata Peak township. Culminating in a closeup of him being handcuffed. Miriama's voice faltered when she told Aaron that the news bulletin blamed him for the carnage.

Talk about trial by television! The adrenaline returned and Aaron blinked back his tears. 'How could they say that? I had nothing to do with the explosion. I was trapped in the plant. Almost burnt alive.'

'Hang in there,' Miriama said. 'The truth will come out. None of this is your fault.'

It wasn't—but that didn't stop Aaron from replaying the horrific scene in his mind, time after time. 'Women and children were running for their lives.' His voice choked and he struggled to continue. 'God knows how many of them drowned. Did they talk about loss of life on the TV coverage?'

'No,' Miriama said. 'They just went on about the number of people who'd lost their homes. Now listen, Aaron. We may not have long to talk. Have you asked the police to call Miles Mayhew?'

'Don't worry. I've told them I'm not saying anything without my lawyer present.'

'That's the spirit,' Miriama said. 'I'll drive to Christchurch and see you as soon as I can. Just remember, it's not your fault. And I love you.'

'I love you too.' Tears now rolled down Aaron's cheeks. Could mere words over a crackly phone line express how much Miriama's support meant to him? 'You're one in a million.'

'I know.'

'Miriama, before you go—'

The line clicked. Time was up, and Miriama had gone before he could ask her about Kāterina.

Dressed in an orange jumpsuit, Aaron sat in the dark cell. The police hadn't allowed him to shower or wash properly, and he wondered what smelt worse—him or the cell. Aaron gazed at the graffiti that covered every inch of the walls. The usual anti-police slogans full of expletives. *All cops are bastards. Fuck the pigs. Death to all narks.* They reminded Aaron of Uncle Ben. He'd have been perfectly at home in here. The inane slogans were just the sort of thing Ben would have scrawled on the wall during his many brushes with the law.

Miriama had insisted none of the carnage was his fault. But perhaps it was. If Aaron hadn't pursued the vendetta with Corey, the Godzone Gorillas wouldn't have been hell-bent on revenge. This was a double whammy for Corey. He'd destroyed Aaron's business and would now have him falsely imprisoned for the bombing.

Were the police still too scared to take on the Godzone Gorillas? Is that why they hadn't arrested Corey or Kaine? Was Aaron an easy target?

But he didn't know for certain that Corey and the Godzone Gorillas were responsible. What if it was the hooded man, and what if the hooded man was his father? Could Aaron have handled the entire situation better? The Tekapō constable had interviewed the hooded man and let him go. So the blame should be on the police, not Aaron.

Suppose Corey and the hooded man were in it together. Corey could easily have hired an out-of-work actor, made him up to look like a burns victim and have him turn up and disrupt the wedding. Aaron gasped. This was the one explanation that fitted all the facts. He couldn't wait to tell the detectives.

Aaron's confidence in his theory dwindled as he languished in the cell for what felt like hours. He tried to sleep. God knows he needed it. But his mind refused to shut down, and he continued to analyse every last detail of the day's events. He even thought about *Great Expectations*. A sad ending seemed even more likely now. No, that wasn't true. Aaron had Miriama behind him, and they would work this out. Still, Aaron wished he could change the narrative at a whim, the way Dickens had.

When an officer finally unlocked the cell door, Aaron's fingers were sore from biting his nails.

'I called Mr Mayhew as you requested,' the officer said. 'As Mr Mayhew

 David Whittet

is employed by Parata Peak Power, he sought clearance from the company to represent you.'

'Dammit!' Aaron shot up from his bunk. '*I* am the CEO of Parata Peak Power, and *I* authorise him.'

'Regrettably,' the officer continued, 'Dame Cynthia Forbes-Hamilton, the company president, has decided otherwise. Mr Mayhew is no longer able to act on your behalf.'

Aaron's mouth fell open. 'The bitch! She can't do this to me.'

'I'm afraid she can. She's the president.' The officer gave him a dismissive nod. 'Besides, with Mr Mayhew being counsel for the company, there would be a clear conflict of interest. So, unless you have another lawyer you wish us to call, I will ask the duty solicitor to represent you.'

Aaron spent another couple of hours alone in his cell, waiting for the duty solicitor. A plate of beef goulash that tasted worse than his school dinners was all he had for distraction. He was so desperate that he even considered asking the police to call Anton Le Squillier to defend him. Aaron shivered. He wasn't that desperate. Besides, Le Squillier was the hooded man's lawyer. Now that *was* a fundamental conflict of interest.

It was almost a relief when yet another officer came to escort Aaron to a dark, windowless interview room. He sat at the table, his eyes fixed on the video camera in the corner of the room and the tape recorder at the centre of the otherwise barren desk.

'Mr Williams is the duty solicitor,' the officer said. 'You'll have time with him on your own, then Detective Inspector Barnes and Detective Sergeant Campbell will interview you.'

Another long wait. Did they do this on purpose? Aaron looked over his shoulder. Sure enough, there was a mirror on the wall. Was it one of those one-way mirrors? Were they watching his every move? Would each twitch, blink or turn of the head be documented to use against him?

Half an hour spent thrashing out a strategy with the duty solicitor did not fill Aaron with confidence. Scott Williams, a neatly dressed and earnest young man, urged him not to make any comment. Aaron remained determined to test his theory that the hooded man was a stooge employed by Corey and the Godzone Gorillas. That made it obvious the Gang had masterminded the attack on the power station.

'It's up to the police to produce the evidence,' Mr Williams said. 'You have nothing to prove.'

'But I know what happened,' Aaron insisted.

'You *think* you do,' Mr Williams said.

Aaron tapped his fingers on the table. How could he make Williams understand? 'Kaine threatened to destroy me. He said the Godzone Gorillas would destroy me. He threatened to blow up the power station. Smash it to smithereens. Those were his exact words.'

Mr Williams scribbled something in his notebook. 'And who is Kaine?'

'Kaine is vice president of the Godzone Gorillas,' Aaron replied. 'He's also the vice president and Corey's right-hand man at Jensen Industries. Plus, he's the monster who kidnapped my mother.'

Mr Williams sucked the end of his pencil. 'It's still his word against yours.'

'No.' Aaron sat up straight. 'I've got witnesses. Tony and Miles.'

'Who?'

'Tony Roche. He's on the Parata Peak board. And Miles Mayhew is our company lawyer. They both heard what Kaine said.'

Mr Williams looked down at his papers and shrugged. 'That could be tricky. I understand Mr Mayhew has been instructed not to get involved—'

Aaron leant forward and pinned Williams with his eyes. 'We subpoena him. Put him under oath.'

'Maybe.' Mr Williams steepled his fingers. 'What about Mr Roche?'

'Tony's a mate. He'll stand up for me.'

'If he's your friend, he's hardly impartial.'

'Tony's the most honest man I've ever met.' Aaron fought the urge to stand up and scream. 'Can't you see? Corey has had it in for me since we were kids. He's been biding his time to get back at me. Especially since the mediation. This is his prime opportunity to frame me as the bomber.'

     David Whittet

'I strongly advise against bringing up your rivalry with Corey O'Connor.' Mr Williams frowned and jotted something else in his notebook. 'You will open up a can of worms that will leave you vulnerable.'

Aaron threw his arms in the air. 'But it's all true, and it's the vital clue to this madness.'

Mr Williams shook his head. 'The police will think you're paranoid.'

Aaron gave a heavy sigh. Did Williams think he was paranoid? 'I'm not crazy. But I have to tell the truth. Otherwise, Corey's won and I'll go down for this.' It occurred to Aaron as he was speaking that his spur-of-the-moment trip back to the power station had played into Corey's hands. 'Remember, I was found on site when the explosion happened.'

'I know that.' Mr Williams closed his notebook and stood up. 'I still think you should remain silent. If what you've told me is true, the police have no direct evidence against you. Start talking, and you'll only incriminate yourself.'

So you're advising me not to tell the truth? Aaron glared at Williams. 'The truth is the only way I can clear my name.'

Mr Williams opened the interview room door. 'I'll tell the detectives we're ready.'

❧

If getting through to Scott Williams had been difficult, explaining himself to detectives Matthew Barnes and Jessica Campbell proved impossible.

'You can't deny you were at the plant at the time of the explosion,' Inspector Barnes said. 'I put it to you that you had the opportunity and the means to commit the crime.'

Aaron stared at the detectives. 'Nonsense. I know nothing about explosives. And if I did, I definitely wouldn't have detonated the bomb while I was in the building. I'd have used a remote or a timer.'

'It sounds like you know a great deal about explosives,' Sergeant Campbell said. 'So you had means and opportunity. So what about motive?'

Mr Williams groaned.

Aaron kept his eyes fixed on the detectives. The last thing he needed was an *I told you so* moment from Williams.

'Motive?' Aaron rolled his eyes. 'Parata Peak Power has been my life over the past few years. I've built the company up into a world leader in renewable energy. I'm proud of what I've achieved. Why would I sabotage my entire livelihood?'

Inspector Barnes shrugged. 'People do the weirdest things.'

'When you've been in this job as long as we have,' Sergeant Campbell added, 'nothing surprises us any more.'

Aaron told himself to stay calm. 'If I was going to blow up the power station, do you think I would have chosen my wedding day to do it?'

'Like I said,' Sergeant Campbell replied, 'nothing surprises us.'

Were they for real? Aaron took a deep breath. 'It was Corey. He masterminded the whole thing. Why can't you see that?'

'We will be interviewing Mr O'Connor,' Inspector Barnes said. 'We'll be speaking to Kaine, too.'

Speaking to them? You need to arrest them, not me. Aaron met the detective's eyes. 'You'll need a lie detector with that pair. Kaine will deny threatening me.'

'Will he?' Inspector Barnes raised an eyebrow. 'Perhaps we need to use a lie detector on you, Mr Casper. I believe you had an altercation with Kaine after the mediation. Fighting in the street. Are you usually a violent man, Mr Casper?'

'Only when someone threatens to blow up my power station.' Aaron paused as a thought rushed into his head. 'What about the CCTV? That will prove it wasn't me.'

Sergeant Campbell shook her head. 'That will all have been destroyed in the explosion.'

'Hang on a minute,' Aaron exclaimed. 'There's a black box in a fireproof vault in the foundations of the plant. It will have recorded the stream from all the security cameras until the explosion destroyed them. Retrieve the black box and you'll have your proof.'

'We'll send a team out to find it straight away,' Inspector Barnes said. 'You'll need to give us detailed instructions on where to find it.'

'Why don't you let Aaron go with your team?' Mr Williams said. 'It would save a lot of time, and my client is hardly a flight risk.'

Aaron couldn't stop himself from smirking. He'd won round one and put Williams and the detectives in their place.

 David Whittet

Inspector Barnes stood up. 'You will have to wait in your cell until we get a team together.' He paused when he reached the door. 'I should tell you. We've brought your hooded man in for questioning. The man who claims to be your father. He's in the next cell.'

CHAPTER THIRTY-NINE

How can they do this to me? Are they trying to drive me insane? Aaron felt his chest tighten as the officers led him back to his cell. He didn't want to see the hooded man so looked down at his feet while he walked. But as they got closer, he couldn't stop himself squinting at the adjacent cell.

'Son! Is that you?' the hooded man cried out.

How should Aaron address the hooded man? He refused to call him 'Emir' or 'Dad' until he was certain the man was his father.

'It's Aaron. But I'm still far from convinced I'm your son.'

Aaron caught a glimpse of the man's face. Without the now infamous hood and dressed in an orange jumpsuit, the burns definitely looked real. It was one hell of an amazing makeup job if they weren't.

Back in his cell, Aaron squatted on the bunk. How long would it take the police to get a team together? More to the point, how long would he have to endure this intolerable situation?

'Speak to me!' the man shouted from his cell. 'Is there anything I can do to prove I'm your father?'

Aaron's instinct was to ignore this weird and irascible man. The truth would come out when the black box was found. Well, at least it would show if he was involved in the explosion. But that still wouldn't answer the most pressing question—was this freakish man really his father?

The man's voice again. 'I get you're mad at me. Maybe I was wrong to turn up at your wedding—'

Damn right. Aaron put his head in his hands and refused to listen to the rest of the man's unctuous rambling.

Silence once more. Aaron got up and paced up and down the cell. An inner voice told him to use the opportunity and challenge the man to come clean.

'Here's what I think,' Aaron began. Why did it feel so unnatural to be holding a conversation and not be able to see the other person? After all, that's how it was on the telephone. 'I think you're an imposter. Maybe you're an out-of-work

 David Whittet

actor. Whatever. Corey employed you to barge into my wedding and ruin my day. I haven't made up my mind about the bombing. Maybe Corey engaged you to do that too. Or perhaps that was one of his other stooges.'

'No, son!' There was desperation in the man's voice. 'You've got it all wrong.'

'You successfully sabotaged my wedding day,' Aaron shot back. 'I didn't get that wrong.'

'I was so worried about you wasting your life with that girl. Miriama is not right for you.'

Aaron banged the cell wall with his fist. What was the use? They'd been through all this before. 'Miriama is my wife and I love her. If you were my father, you'd accept that. And if you don't, I want nothing more to do with you.'

Another tense silence.

Aaron continued to stride around the tiny cell in circles. 'You've no idea how much I wanted a father when I was a kid. Convinced myself my dad had been a great man. A visionary. I idolised his memory. Now—if you're my old man, I got it all wrong.'

'Don't say that—'

'Why not?' Aaron kicked the floor. 'It's true, isn't it?'

'I did have a vision,' the man said, his voice trembling. 'I wanted to build a water bottling plant at the Roaring Creek Falls. Make the unique healing properties of the minerals available to everyone. Bring health to all. And I would have done if the Gang hadn't got in the way.'

If the man was an imposter, he had certainly done his homework. But then again, if he was working for the Godzone Gorillas, they would have given him the background on the water bottling development.

Aaron sat down again on the bunk. 'That doesn't prove anything.'

'I told you how I saw you all those years ago when you came to my castle with that girl. If I recognised you back then, surely you can't believe I'm some unemployed actor recently recruited by the Godzone Gorillas.'

Aaron frowned. The man had a point. 'If it was you we saw that day, and you were so worried about me, why didn't you come forward then? That was when I really needed a father.'

'I wish to God I had.' The man's voice croaked. Was he crying? 'I was a wanted man. There was a price on my head. I wanted to break cover, but Le Squillier talked me out of it.'

Could anyone talk this single-minded and self-centred man out of anything he'd set his mind on? Aaron thought about it for a moment. If anyone could persuade him to change his mind, it was the obsequious Le Squillier.

Aaron took a deep breath. 'Go on.'

'I figured the one thing I could do for you was to set you up for business school. Le Squillier tracked you down to your aunt's house. How I longed for the day I could come out of hiding and meet you. I wanted us to work together and build a business empire as father and son. Not this mess. Both of us locked up in the slammer, dressed like convicts. Everything I do ends up in disaster. I did everything I could to find your mother. Alicia, the love of my life. I failed her, too.'

The man was sobbing now. Aaron felt empathy for him for the first time and would have jumped up and hugged him if there wasn't a cell wall between them.

'I was just five when they took my mother away.' Aaron brushed away a tear of his own. 'I don't think I'll ever get over that day. Once I had some money, I searched for her. Employed loads of private detectives. They all promised the earth, and each was as useless as the last. One of them, Sullivan was his name, found an ex-gangster called Gerry, who'd belonged to the Godzone Gorillas. He was one of the bastards who kidnapped my mother. But he'd no idea where she was.'

'You hired Rodney Sullivan?' the man exclaimed. 'I used him, too, and didn't get any further.'

He knows Sullivan's first name. Aaron's mouth fell open, and he sat on the edge of the bunk as the man continued.

'None of the local private detectives were any use. I flew in an expert from the USA. Dean Dickerson. He claimed to be a specialist in kidnappings and said he had solved numerous cold cases that the police had abandoned.'

'And was he any help?' Aaron asked.

'He found this ten-year-old boy called Donny. He was the son of one of Alicia's guards when she was held in captivity by the Gang. Donny had been good to Alicia, smuggling in food and treats for her. He promised he'd take us to Alicia. That was the first time I broke my cover. The plan was for Donny to

　　　David Whittet

lead us to the hideout where they held Alicia. We went in the dead of night with some heavies of our own. But when we arrived, the hideout was empty. The Gang must have got wind we were onto them and moved her to another hideout. Or else they—'

Aaron finished the sentence for him. 'You think they killed her, don't you?'

No reply. Just a sob from the next-door cell.

Aaron bit his lip. Why had he brought up the possibility of his mother being murdered? 'We don't know she's dead.'

'I couldn't face life alone any longer. If Alicia was dead, I wanted to die with her. I went back to the Roaring Creek Falls. The place where I first met her. I decided the falls would be my final resting place.

'I climbed to the top of the falls and looked down over the edge. One more step, and I'd be gone. The falls should have been the scene of my greatest triumph with the water bottling factory. The centre of my business empire. Alicia should have been by my side in my moment of victory. And she would have been if it wasn't for those bastards in the Godzone Gorillas gang. I cursed the lot of them.'

Aaron sniffled and wiped his nose on the sleeve of his jumpsuit. 'You were going to jump? What stopped you?'

'I was about to jump to a certain death when this strange old woman suddenly appeared beside me. She called herself Neina.'

Aaron almost fell off the bunk. *Of course!* So much had happened in the last couple of days that he'd virtually forgotten his encounter with Neina. She'd called the hooded man *another lost soul striving to find his place in this troubled world.* 'So, what did Neina say to you?'

'She told me I could jump if I wanted to, but my soul wouldn't rest if I did. I was right on the edge of the falls, and I was so shocked I nearly lost my footing and went over. She even knew my name.'

Aaron shuffled towards the wall that separated them. 'Neina and Kāterina were friends. That'll be how she knew your name. But how did she know you'd be at the falls at that moment?'

The man snorted noisily. 'Perhaps Kāterina saw it in her crystal ball.'

'Maybe.'

'Don't get me started on that wretched crystal ball,' the man said. 'More like she'd been lying in wait and pounced when she saw me. I asked her who she was and what she wanted with me.

'"Look on me as your guardian angel," she said. "I'm here to help you find inner peace and fulfilment."

'"Fat chance of that," I said and told her to bugger off unless she could bring Alicia back from the dead.

'"I can't do that," she said, "but I can help you to make peace with your son."

'I stepped back from the edge of the falls and asked her what she knew about my son. She told me you were getting married, and I should be at the wedding.'

I bet she didn't tell you to barge in and slag off the bride. Aaron opened his mouth to say the words out loud but stopped himself. Errol Troy had said brain damage from the fire had made the man more irascible and diminished his self-control. Better let the man finish his story first.

'Then she rambled on about a curse Kāterina had placed on me,' the man continued. 'Neina said it would pass on to my descendants, which put you in danger. She urged me to seek out Kāterina and get the curse lifted.'

Aaron sat up straight. 'So that's why you turned up at the *Gypsy Rose* in Tekapō that night and spooked Cleo and Kāterina. But you didn't say a word.'

'I didn't need to. She knew why I was there.'

Aaron scratched the back of his neck. 'She sure took off suddenly after you left. What was it she said? Something about your being sent for a purpose. But I thought she meant she would find my mother and bring her to the wedding.'

The man grunted. 'Well, she definitely failed at that, didn't she? And judging from the trouble we're both in now, she didn't have much more success lifting the curse.'

A police officer arrived and unlocked Aaron's cell.

'Inspector Barnes has got the search team together,' the officer said. 'He wants you to get cleaned up for the operation.'

The officer let him out and led him away from the cells. Aaron held back and took another hard look at the man in the next cell.

'What about him?' Aaron said. 'Aren't you going to release him?'

'Inspector Barnes isn't finished with Emir Casper yet,' the officer said. 'If that is his real name.'

Aaron eyeballed the officer. 'It is.'

Before the explosion, Aaron sought DNA evidence to determine whether the hooded man was his father or a fraud. Aaron didn't need the DNA test now. This man was his father.

CHAPTER FORTY

Aaron felt almost human again after being allowed a shower. And if the change of clothes the police had provided weren't the height of fashion, they certainly beat the orange jumpsuit.

'A quick heads-up,' Inspector Barnes said as they prepared to leave the police station. 'There's a media scrum outside. We'll go out the back way, and I'll shield you as best I can. But some of these journalists are vultures when they sniff a scandal.'

A mass of camera lenses and pulsating flashlights greeted Aaron as he stepped out into the yard at the back of the police station.

'Were you in league with your father?' a reporter shouted. 'Was it a conspiracy between you to bomb the Parata Peak Power Station?'

'I hope you're proud of yourself,' another reporter yelled. 'Women and children drowned in the flood water.'

'It wasn't me or my father,' Aaron shot back as Inspector Barnes hustled him into the patrol car. 'It was the Godzone Gorillas.'

'Then why are you under arrest?' a third reporter screamed.

The barrage didn't let up as the police driver started the engine and hooted at the crowd to let them through. Cameras continued to flash, and some angry bystanders banged on the car's windows.

'Have you any idea how many innocent lives you've destroyed?' a woman shouted.

'It's a bloody disgrace,' another added. 'I hope the cops aren't letting you go.'

'With the media, it's guilty until proven innocent,' Inspector Barnes said as they drove off. 'Not like us.'

'I'm not so sure,' Aaron said. 'Some of the questions you fired at me weren't much different from the slurs the reporters were shouting.'

'Don't push your luck,' Inspector Barnes replied with a wry smile. 'I'm giving you a chance to prove your innocence, aren't I?'

Aaron leant back in the seat. Would they find the black box, and would it prove his innocence? He'd been supremely confident a few hours ago. Now he wasn't so sure. What if the security system had malfunctioned and there were no video backups? Aaron shuddered as another thought entered his head. Suppose the Godzone Gorillas had tampered with the equipment. The Gang were masters of sabotage. They could have dismantled the CCTV cameras or overridden the system. Worse still, they might have found the black box and destroyed it.

Aaron wiped the perspiration off his forehead with the back of his hand. He couldn't let the detectives notice he was worried. They would see it as an admission of guilt.

The closer they got to Parata Peak, the faster Aaron's heart thumped. His mind replayed the public meeting when he denigrated the locals' concerns about an accident at the power station. A woman elder had stood up and berated him. What was it she said? *That's bullshit and you know it. There's no way you can guarantee our safety.* Another woman waved her fist at him. *I will hold you personally responsible if anything happens to our beloved community.*

Kāterina would have agreed with the townsfolk. She had told him that she'd organised protest marches against the development of a bottling plant at the Roaring Creek Falls. No wonder there was such animosity between Kāterina and his father.

Aaron wished Kāterina was here today. If ever he needed that wise woman's guidance, it was now.

Surface water covered the road as they drove further up the valley. The driver slowed down to negotiate the flood water and the numerous potholes, on alert for fallen rocks. Aaron forced himself to keep his eyes open when they drove past the Parata Peak township. People swam back to their houses to recover their possessions. Children made makeshift rafts from broken wooden doors to rescue their pet animals. Aaron caught sight of two elderly women wading through water that came up to their waists. Were these the women who had challenged him at the public meeting?

The power station was still smouldering when they arrived. A burnt-out shell was all that remained of Aaron's vision to create a model of sustainability for the future. There were fragments of shattered concrete everywhere he looked. The spillway was smashed from top to bottom, leaving a giant chasm between the two halves, the sight of which tore Aaron's heart apart.

Sergeant Campbell helped Aaron out of the police car.

'Are you okay?' she asked.

'No,' Aaron replied. 'But this has to be done. We have to get the black box. I want to find the bastard who caused this disaster as much as you do.'

'Here, put this on.' Sergeant Campbell handed him a protective overall and headgear.

Aaron spotted the charred remains of his car in what was once the vehicle bay. He sighed. That didn't matter. It was only a machine.

The team put on their helmets and zipped up their overalls. They looked like astronauts about to embark on a mission to a far-off planet. Reality struck once more as Aaron led them through the smoking rubble. He could no longer hold it together when each step forward confronted him with further devastation. Deep breaths, he told himself. *You can do this*. But he couldn't. Aaron broke down and cried.

Sergeant Campbell gave him a handkerchief.

Aaron dried his eyes and blew his nose. 'I'm sorry. It's just …'

'All too much for you, isn't it?' Sergeant Campbell said.

Aaron nodded. 'Give me a minute and I'll be okay.'

'That's fine,' Sergeant Campbell said. 'This can't be easy for you.'

Aaron took a deep breath and tried to find his bearings amongst the wreckage. 'The vault was directly under the control room, so it will be somewhere under this heap of rubble.'

The team was equipped with excavation equipment and started clearing layer after layer of molten metal and mangled machinery.

Inspector Barnes and Sergeant Campbell stood back as the team worked. At first, Aaron couldn't hear what they were saying over the noise of the excavation. But he caught their conversation when the drilling stopped.

'Aaron is innocent,' Sergeant Campbell said. 'I can see it in his eyes.'

'I'm not as certain as you are,' Inspector Barnes replied. 'He could be putting on an act.'

'He's genuine,' Sergeant Campbell said. 'You can't fake distress like that.'

'I'm not so sure.' Inspector Barnes took a step back and stared across at Aaron. 'Let's wait and see what the evidence shows, shall we?'

After several hours of digging and drilling, the team unearthed the vault.

 David Whittet

Would the black box still be there? Would it still be intact? Aaron's heart should have been racing, but he'd run out of adrenaline. His hand shook as he went through the numerous combinations of numbers in sequence to open the vault. And there it was inside. A device no bigger than a shoe box that would prove his innocence.

⁂

What would happen now? Desperate for an answer, Aaron attempted to engage with the detectives on the drive back to Christchurch Central Police Station.

'You've got your evidence now,' Aaron said. 'So am I free to go?'

'We'll talk about that when we get back to the station,' Inspector Barnes replied. 'We've still got a long way to go in this investigation.'

Aaron sighed. Was he no nearer an end to the nightmare? As they passed the Parata Peak township, he closed his eyes and spent the rest of the drive in silence.

Answers were no more forthcoming when they arrived at the station. The custody officer returned him to his cell. *What the hell?* That was *not* what Aaron expected.

The adjacent cell was empty.

'What have you done with my father?' Aaron asked.

'He's still helping us with our inquiries.'

The stern look on the officer's face told Aaron he wouldn't get any further answers about his father's whereabouts.

Aaron sat brooding in his cell for the next couple of hours. What were the detectives doing? Shouldn't he be up there with them, helping to decipher the encrypted data on the black box?

At last, the custody officer returned with Scott Williams.

'Good news,' Mr Williams said. 'I've negotiated bail for you provided you cooperate with police to get the data off the black box.'

We could have started that hours ago. Aaron wanted to say the words out loud. But what good would that do? Detectives clearly worked at their own pace. Instead, Aaron had a more pressing question as they walked down the corridor.

'Have you any idea where they've taken my father?'

'No,' Mr Williams replied. 'I'm not acting on his behalf. He has his own lawyer. What was his name? Ah, yes. Le Squillier.'

Inspector Barnes met them in reception. 'We're all exhausted,' he said. 'Let's call it a day. We can start work deciphering the black box in the morning.'

What? Aaron flinched. Another night of uncertainty? 'Can't we—'

Sergeant Campbell walked past and interrupted him. 'Aaron, you need to get a good night's sleep and come back in the morning.'

Aaron doubted if he'd ever sleep well again. But he had to admit his brain was positively scrambled.

'We'll meet here at nine in the morning,' Inspector Barnes said. 'Aaron, you will need to work alongside our forensic IT team and provide the necessary passwords for them to access the data in the box. Now, you need to sign the bail papers and you are free to go.'

The custody sergeant handed Aaron's possessions back to him. Fifty missed calls on his mobile. Twenty of them from Dame Cynthia Forbes-Hamilton.

'So, I'll see you in the morning,' Mr Williams said, shaking Aaron's hand. 'Take the sergeant's advice and have a good rest.'

Aaron froze. How would he get home without a car? He was about to ask Williams for a ride when he spotted Tony sitting in the waiting room.

'Mate!' Tony jumped up and embraced Aaron. 'I heard you were in here. We've all been so worried about you.'

Why wasn't Miriama here? 'You're a true friend.' Aaron did his best to hide his disappointment that it was Tony, not Miriama, who came to collect him. 'I don't know what I'd do without you.'

Tony smiled. 'You'd survive whatever life throws at you. Now let's get you home. You look shattered.'

Would he survive? Aaron wasn't so sure as he got into Tony's car.

'I guess Dame Cynthia is after my scalp,' Aaron said, fastening his seat belt. 'There's a ton of missed calls from her and the rest of the board on my phone.'

'They're pretty mad,' Tony said, 'but there's something else.'

Aaron knew instinctively it was about Miriama. His mind went into overdrive. Was something wrong? Had she taken the news of Kāterina's passing badly? He should never have let her go back to Roaring Creek without him. If he had gone with her, things would have been different. The power station

     David Whittet

might still have been blown up, but he wouldn't have been arrested, and he wouldn't be out on bail now.

'What is it, Tony?' Aaron said. 'Spill. I need to know.'

'There's no easy way to say this.' Tony stalled the engine as he reversed out of the car park. 'It's about Sabrina and Laura.'

What was Tony on about? 'I'm not interested in Sabrina and Laura. I want to know why Miriama isn't here.'

Tony hesitated. 'Sabrina and Laura have been talking to her … saying things about you … Sabrina in particular …'

Aaron sat up so suddenly that he locked his seat belt. 'What? They don't know anything about me. We met for the first time just before the wedding.'

'Sabrina's saying you must have known about your father. That you orchestrated the whole thing. His appearance at the wedding—'

'Bloody nonsense!' Aaron thought his head would explode. How dare someone he didn't know badmouth him to the woman he loved? The adrenaline was back, pumping through his body. 'Surely Miriama didn't take any notice of such bullshit? She could see I was as shocked as everyone else.'

'Sabrina claims that when she arrived in a taxi with Laura, you mistook them for someone else. She says you were expecting it to be your father.'

'Bollocks!' Aaron fumed. 'When I saw two women in the back of the taxi, for a split second, I dreamt it might be Kāterina, bringing my mother to the wedding. But that's all it was. A fantasy. And definitely not about my father.'

'Sabrina insists that because Errol and Le Squillier both knew he was coming to the wedding, you must have known too.' Tony pulled up at traffic lights. 'Crazy, I know. But Miriama's vulnerable at the moment.'

'I'd be the last to know what Errol and Le Squillier were up to.' Aaron paused to think. 'I was allowed one telephone call from the police station when they arrested me. I used it to call Miriama. She said she would drive straight back from Roaring Creek to support me.'

'I'm sure she would have done if Sabrina hadn't taken advantage of Miriama's grief. Sabrina has persuaded Miriama to go back with her to Switzerland.'

'I don't believe it. Miriama would never leave without giving me a chance to explain.' Aaron pulled his mobile out of his pocket and called Miriama. 'Damn.' The call went straight to voicemail.

'Maybe it's for the best.' Tony gave Aaron a sideways glance. 'It'll give Miriama a chance to get her head straight while you concentrate on clearing your name.'

What planet was Tony on? 'Miriama will never get her head straight with Sabrina poisoning her mind.'

They spent the rest of the drive in silence. Aaron couldn't understand why Sabrina had it in for him. Miriama had mentioned Sabrina's jealousy and over-dependence on her friends. Maybe that should have been a red flag. Sabrina had been upset when Miriama chose to spend her vacations with Aaron rather than at Sabrina's parents' château on the banks of Lake Lucerne. But surely Aaron deserved an explanation before Miriama left the country. They were newly married. Did those vows mean nothing to her?

Four days of intense work with the police's forensic IT team and Aaron no longer cared who was responsible for the bombing. He called Miriama repeatedly, but she never picked up. His heart missed a beat whenever his mobile rang, but it was invariably Dame Cynthia and never Miriama. Aaron wasn't ready to talk to Dame Cynthia. Was his job on the line? What did it matter if it was? If he'd lost Miriama, Kāterina and his mother, they might as well incarcerate him and throw away the key.

Aaron's eyes were still sore from the fire. Eight hours of staring at a computer screen each day and trawling through the CCTV footage made them even more blurred. But one image stood out.

'That's Kaine!' Aaron pointed to the screen. 'I told you it was the Godzone Gorillas.'

The forensic team enlarged the image of the shadowy figure.

Aaron jumped up and down. 'Look, I can just make out his tattoo. That's the Godzone Gorillas' gang patch.'

'There's someone behind him,' the lead forensic officer said, zooming in on the image. 'Look.'

Aaron stared at the screen. 'It's Corey! I swear it is! See that tattoo on his neck?'

     David Whittet

Working late into the night, the team found more footage showing the two figures acting suspiciously below the control room. In addition, the CCTV record showed that Aaron had entered the power station on the day of the bombing exactly as he had said. Further, there was no CCTV evidence of any abnormal activity or wrongdoing on Aaron's part.

Does this mean I'm free? Aaron had to tell Miriama. What if she'd already left? In that case, Aaron would be on the next flight to Switzerland once he got his passport back from the police.

❁

Aaron had to wait for the debriefing interview the next day for his answer. The same stark, windowless room. But today, the table was covered with printouts of the screenshots from the CCTV footage.

'Thank you for cooperating with the investigation,' Inspector Barnes said. 'We are now satisfied that you were not responsible for bombing the Parata Peak Power Station.'

Sergeant Campbell picked up one of the printouts. 'We are fortunate that the CCTV caught the suspects' tattoos. It could have been difficult to identify them otherwise.'

'So, what happens next?' Aaron asked.

'There's an arrest warrant out for both Kaine and Corey,' Inspector Bernes replied.

Aaron fiddled with the wedding ring on his finger. 'So where does this leave me? Am I allowed to travel? I have to make an urgent overseas trip.'

Inspector Barnes sat up straight. 'You're not going after your father, are you?'

Aaron tensed. 'No. Why do you ask?'

'We released your father on bail at the beginning of the week,' Inspector Barnes said. 'He failed to show at the agreed time.'

Aaron leant closer. 'Why is my father still on bail?'

'If he genuinely is your father,' Sergeant Campbell prompted.

'We still suspect he may have had a role in the bombing,' Inspector Barnes said. 'And there's another matter we need to talk to him about.'

Aaron sighed. What else had his father been up to? 'Maybe he broke his bail conditions because he was confused. He suffers from brain damage due to smoke inhalation during that awful fire all those years ago.'

'We planned to organise a full psychological and neurological assessment,' Inspector Barnes said. 'Perhaps that's why he took off.'

'He has a castle on the Kaikōura Coast,' Aaron said. 'He could be hiding out there.'

'We've already visited. Looks like it's all been shut up for some months. We think he's fled the country.' Inspector Barnes eyed Aaron suspiciously. 'Are you sure you're not planning to follow him overseas?'

Aaron shook his head. 'Definitely not. I'm going to find my wife. This whole business has been too much for Miriama, and she's gone off with her two bridesmaids to Switzerland.'

'Okay.' Inspector Barnes collected his papers together. 'As long as you keep in touch and let us know where you are. We will need you as a witness.'

'Good luck, Aaron,' Sergeant Campbell said as they got up. 'I hope everything works out for you.'

'So do I,' Aaron said.

Surely Miriama had to believe him now—provided he could find her. Well, his father had disappeared again. That was a distraction Aaron could have done without. Would it be another twenty-nine years before his old man reappeared?

Aaron followed the detectives into reception.

'Just a couple of papers to sign and you're free to go,' Inspector Barnes said. 'Remember what I said about staying in contact.'

The officer behind the front desk handed Aaron a pen and indicated where he should sign.

What the hell was that noise? Aaron recognised the voice, and the threatening language that followed, laced with expletives.

'Fuck you! Get your hands off me. You'll regret messing with me, you motherfuckers.'

Aaron looked up. Two uniformed officers escorted Corey into reception.

Corey clenched his fists and fought against his handcuffs. 'What's that little shit doing here?' He glared at Aaron. 'What's the bastard been saying about me?'

     David Whittet

The officers struggled to restrain him. 'Calm down, Corey. Don't make things worse for yourself.'

Corey broke free and spat in Aaron's face. 'Take that, you son of a bitch.'

Aaron wiped the spit off his face and watched the officers drag Corey away to a cell. While Aaron's life was still in turmoil, tonight he was free and Corey was behind bars. Aaron allowed himself to forget his troubles for a few glorious moments. David had finally defeated Goliath.

CHAPTER FORTY-ONE

If only Miriama were there to share his moment of triumph. Corey and Kaine were both facing prosecution. Now Aaron could prove to her that he was innocent of the bombing. He had to get to Switzerland fast before Sabrina and Laura told Miriama even more lies.

Tony said the right things when he drove Aaron home from the police station. 'Fantastic news. I'd give anything to have seen the expression on Corey's face. They've arrested Kaine too? You must be stoked.'

'I am,' Aaron said, 'and I can't wait to tell Miriama.'

'She'll be thrilled too, especially after all that's happened in the past couple of weeks.'

There was an edge to Tony's enthusiasm. Tony was a true friend. He had dropped everything to drive Aaron to and from the police station each day during the investigation. But Tony kept reminding him that he couldn't continue to ignore Dame Cynthia's calls and shirk his responsibility to the company.

'Are you still planning to fly to Switzerland?' Tony asked. 'You can't leave without fronting up to the board. It's not just Dame Cynthia. It's everyone. The staff, our contractors and customers. They need an explanation and a recovery plan. You're the CEO. We're all looking to you for leadership.'

'I've been a bit busy this week, in case you hadn't noticed.' Aaron bit his lip. He hadn't meant to be flippant, and Tony had been so good to him. 'I'm sorry. You're right. Of course you are. I'll call Dame Cynthia tonight.'

'Be careful when you speak to her,' Tony urged. 'Stay calm. No sarcasm. I know your head's still all over the place. Mine would be too. But Dame Cynthia is an old lady. This has been a terrible shock to her, and it will take her a long time to recover.'

At least she wasn't arrested and dragged away into a police cell. 'Don't worry. I'll be good and keep my cool.'

❧

Keeping it together when talking to Dame Cynthia Forbes-Hamilton didn't come easily to Aaron, and tonight it was more difficult than ever.

Aaron held his phone away from his ear as Dame Cynthia blasted him.

'So you've finally deigned to speak to me, have you? You've single-handedly destroyed our company, and you don't have the guts to face up to it.'

Aaron felt his blood pressure rise. Keeping his promise to Tony would be a struggle.

'I've been to hell and back in the past week.' Aaron counted to ten before continuing. 'I appreciate how stressful this has been for you, but imagine what it's been like for me. I've lost everything. And all on my wedding day.'

'You're young,' Dame Cynthia said. 'You have your life ahead of you and time to build a new career. I don't.'

Didn't Dame Cynthia understand how much of himself Aaron had invested in developing the business? 'My heart and soul are in Parata Peak. You know that. And I'm proud of what we've achieved.'

'You've left us in one hell of a mess,' Dame Cynthia shot back, 'and I hear you're abandoning us for Switzerland. Is this true?'

'Yes.' Aaron took a deep breath. How could he make Dame Cynthia understand without getting worked up? 'Miriama has left for Switzerland without saying goodbye or giving me a chance to explain. Her two bridesmaids have fed her a pack of lies. I have to go after her.'

'Well, you'll have the chance to explain yourself to the Parata Peak board tomorrow morning,' Dame Cynthia said. 'I've called an emergency meeting at the Parata Peak community hall. The one building in the valley that's still standing. I should warn you, too. We will table a vote of no confidence in you as CEO of the company.'

Had Dame Cynthia no heart? She'd been trying to get rid of him for ages, but did she have to kick him so hard when he was down? Aaron sat motionless for what felt like hours after the phone call ended. Dame Cynthia had seized her golden opportunity. Would the board vote him out? What did it matter anyway? Right now, he only cared about getting Miriama back.

Tony arrived early the following morning. 'Things may get out of hand. The paparazzi have been camped outside the community hall since dawn, and the locals have surrounded it.'

'I've had a skirmish with the media already,' Aaron said. 'When the police took me back to the site to recover the black box. I guess everyone's baying for my blood.'

Tony opened his briefcase. 'I think we should write a short, prepared statement for you to read to the reporters. We'll make it clear that you won't make any further comments. I'll be standing right beside you.'

'You're a mate,' Aaron said. 'Last week, you were my chauffeur. Now you're my minder.'

'I care about you.' Tony put a hand on Aaron's shoulder. 'Miriama, too. You're going to get through this.'

Aaron sighed. 'Am I? It doesn't feel like that at the moment.'

'It will, and you'll be stronger than before.' Tony started his laptop. 'Now let's get your statement written. I've also got a counter motion to the no-confidence vote.'

Would anyone listen to his statement? The media circus was out in force, and locals surrounded Tony's car when they approached the community hall. Tony sounded the horn to disperse them. The crowd responded by throwing mud and debris at the vehicle.

Tony wound down his window and shouted at the crowd. 'There's no need for that. Mr Casper will make a statement shortly. None of this is his fault. Now, will you please let us through?'

While Tony sounded confident, Aaron spotted the beads of sweat on his friend's forehead. It was so unfair. Tony didn't deserve this aggravation.

Aaron was sweating too. Were they going to be lynched? Why had Dame Cynthia chosen the community hall for their meeting? It would have been far safer to hold the meeting away from the site or, better still, via Zoom. But perhaps

     David Whittet

this was all part of Dame Cynthia's plan to discredit him. Get him mobbed by the crowd, and then fire him.

Tony pulled up as close to the hall as he could and gave Aaron a reassuring look. 'Remember what I said. Be contrite. Show empathy and let them see how much you care about their loss.'

Aaron undid his seat belt and clutched his prepared statement. 'I do care about their loss. I've scarcely slept for a week thinking about it.'

'I know that,' Tony said. 'You've got to convince them. Don't let them provoke you. And above all, don't lose your rag.'

Aaron shielded his eyes as Tony helped him out of the car. Shutters clicked incessantly. The paparazzi's camera flashlights felt even brighter than they had a week ago, and the reporters were far more aggressive.

'Are you going to resign, Mr Casper?' a reporter shouted. 'Or are they going to fire you?'

'How many innocent Kiwis' pension funds have you robbed?' another reporter jeered. 'Were you in on your father's Ponzi schemes? Are you planning to pay back the millions of dollars your father embezzled?'

Ponzi schemes? Embezzlement? The police had told Aaron they needed to question Emir on another matter. Aaron never dreamt they were investigating anything so serious and far-reaching. No wonder his father could afford that massive castle on the Kaikōura Coast.

'I have no knowledge whatsoever of my father's business dealings,' Aaron said, trying to make himself heard over the heckling. 'I didn't know he was alive until a week ago—'

'You expect us to believe that?' a reporter interrupted. 'Don't you feel any responsibility for the "mum and dad" investors who've lost everything in your father's scams?'

'Of course I care about them,' Aaron said. 'I believe the police are investigating—'

The reporter interrupted him again. 'We understand your father has broken his bail conditions. Do you know where he is hiding?'

Tony grabbed Aaron's arm. 'Stick to your statement. You don't need to answer any questions about embezzlement.'

A woman pushed forward through the crowd. 'You won't remember me.'

Aaron did, and he couldn't bear to look at her.

'Four months ago, in this very hall,' the woman said, 'you told us we were safe. The dam would never split in two. Well, now it has. My home is wrecked, and my granddaughter is in hospital.'

'And when we protested outside the plant,' another woman said, 'you had your security men cart us off.'

Aaron wanted to explain. Tell them that no amount of safety measures could prevent a disaster in the event of a bomb of this magnitude exploding. This was the Godzone Gorillas doing. Why wasn't the crowd mad at the Gang?

A stern look from Tony told Aaron to keep his mouth shut.

'Aaron Casper will now make a statement,' Tony said, leading Aaron through the barricade of reporters. 'After that, we will have a private meeting with the Parata Peak Power board. Mr Casper will not be making any further comment.'

Aaron cleared his throat. He glanced at his prepared speech and then up at the people. The speech seemed all wrong amidst such suffering. He couldn't read it. Tony would probably curse him for it, but Aaron had to speak from the heart.

'I came to read a statement to you.' Aaron waved the papers in the air. 'Seeing firsthand the devastation the explosion has caused you, no pre-written statement is adequate to express the depth of my feelings and my sorrow at the grief you are all suffering. To those of you who have lost loved ones—I was trapped in that explosion, and it was a miracle that I escaped. I shall forever feel guilty that I survived, while others did not. If I could change places with them, I would, with all my heart.

'To those who have lost their homes—I promise we will rebuild this community. The Parata Peak community is resilient, and it will thrive again.'

'And will you listen to our concerns about safety in the future?' a woman shouted.

'I will.' Aaron heard Tony groan, but he couldn't stop now. 'When the power station is rebuilt, I believe we should move it further up the valley. God forbid there should ever be another catastrophe like we've just experienced. But if there were, the township would be safe. I will propose the change of location to the board this morning.

'Finally, I know you are all angry with me, and rightly so. But the bombing was the work of the Godzone Gorillas alone. I commend the police for the

　　　　　David Whittet

arrest of the ringleaders and trust that this will cripple the Gang's operations and reduce the risk of further atrocities.'

The crowd gave him a muted applause.

Tony patted him on the back. 'Well done. You've probably opened us up to a load of compensation claims, but it was certainly brave.'

'And probably equally foolhardy,' Aaron replied. 'But it had to be said. They'd never have accepted our prepared statement.'

Aaron felt his muscles relax as he followed Tony inside the community hall. Addressing the crowd was far scarier than confronting Dame Cynthia and the board.

⁂

They were all in there, ready and waiting. Dame Cynthia, Margaret, Errol, Daniel, Steven and the rest of them. How had they escaped the media scrum? Had they been camping out in the hall all night? Errol looked mighty smug. Was he in on Emir's Ponzi schemes?

'Good morning, Aaron,' Dame Cynthia said. 'I must say, it is rather unusual to make a public statement before rather than after the board meeting. Perhaps you are afraid of the outcome?'

'It was Tony's idea,' Aaron replied.

'I thought we should be upfront and honest with everyone from the outset,' Tony said.

'Well anyway,' Dame Cynthia said in her haughtiest voice, 'that means we get the last word. I'll make my statement *after* we conclude this morning's business.'

Aaron was about to reply when Tony caught his eye and mouthed, *Don't rise to the bait.*

'This shouldn't take long,' Dame Cynthia said. 'There is just one item on our agenda. A vote of no confidence in our chief executive officer, Aaron Casper.'

'Shouldn't we be talking about what we can do for the townsfolk?' Aaron said. 'They're far more important than I am. Many have lost loved ones and their homes. I've just promised the local people—'

'You had no right to do so,' Dame Cynthia shot back. 'God knows, the rebuild is going to cost us enough.'

'It's covered by our insurance policy,' Tony said. 'I've talked to our insurers. They're sending a loss adjuster down in the morning.'

'When it comes to the rebuild,' Aaron said, 'we need to consider a different location for the plant so that in the unlikely event of a further accident, the flood water will flow away from the township.'

'You've changed your tune, haven't you?' Daniel said. 'You were the one who banged on about the safety of the current site.'

'I know.' Aaron lowered his head. 'I was wrong. It's a mistake I will regret to my dying day.'

Dame Cynthia glared at Aaron over her bifocals. 'It seems your career has been riddled with bad decisions. And thanks to you, we can no longer meet our contractual obligations and will have to lay off staff. Even if we do rebuild, we'll have lost a vast portion of our business and market share by the time we're up and running again.'

Tony tapped his fingers on the table. 'That's not fair. None of this is Aaron's fault. The Godzone Gorillas bombed the site. The police have arrested Corey and Kaine. No amount of preparedness on our part could possibly have made any difference to the outcome.'

'That's as may be,' Dame Cynthia said. 'Aaron is still to blame. Why did the Godzone Gorillas bomb us? Because of that ill-advised takeover bid for Jensen Industries that Aaron talked us into. And all because Aaron had a vendetta with Corey O'Connor.'

Aaron sunk his head even lower. Everything Dame Cynthia said was true.

Tony rose to his feet. 'I have a counterproposal to make, Dame Cynthia. We cannot underestimate the personal and professional disaster Aaron has faced this week. We owe him our support. A man claiming to be his father hijacked his wedding. Aaron believed his father was dead, and we're still uncertain of the man's true identity.'

'He is Aaron's father,' Errol interrupted. 'I can vouch for that.'

Aaron raised his head and stared at Errol. *If you knew all along, why the hell didn't you tell me? Were you party to his Ponzi schemes?*

Tony must have been thinking the same thing. 'I guess you'd know, Errol. I'm sure we'd all love to hear about your dealings with Emir, but that's a story for another day.' Tony turned back to face Dame Cynthia. 'Not only was his

          David Whittet

wedding ruined, but Aaron narrowly escaped dying in the explosion. And Miriama, his new wife, is so distressed by everything that she's taken off to Switzerland with two of her friends.'

'I appreciate that Aaron is your friend, Tony,' Dame Cynthia said, 'but we must put personal feelings aside. We've heard enough. You must leave the room while we take the vote, Aaron.'

Tony remained on his feet. 'I will speak, and I will put my counterproposal forward. We mustn't lose sight of what Aaron has brought to our company.'

Aaron felt his eyes well up. Why was Tony being so good to him? He didn't deserve such a loyal friend.

'May I remind you,' Tony continued, 'that Parata Peak was facing closure under government ownership. Thanks to Aaron's leadership, we were able to get the investment to establish ourselves as a private company.'

'Tony's got a point,' Steven said. 'Before Aaron came on the scene, we were a small company without a future.'

'And that's what we are now,' Dame Cynthia muttered.

'We need Aaron more than he needs us,' Tony resumed. 'In these troubled times, we must have someone of Aaron's calibre to see us through. If we let him go, he'll be headhunted and take his talents elsewhere, and that will be our loss.'

Aaron shut his eyes. He'd never felt so humbled. Or so contrite. Had he always acted in the company's best interest? Or was Dame Cynthia right? The takeover bid was an act of vengeance against Corey. The Godzone Gorillas too. And the explosion was undoubtedly the Gang's retaliation.

Dame Cynthia glanced at the clock. 'Have you finished, Tony? Can we get on with the vote?'

'I was about to table my counterproposal,' Tony said. 'I propose we grant Aaron an extended leave of absence. We owe him this much. Extended leave will allow him to get his head together, travel to Switzerland and resolve matters with Miriama.'

Margaret raised an eyebrow. 'I agree we must come together if we are to rebuild the company and our reputation. Tony's solution makes sense.'

Aaron raised his head and stared at Margaret. She was the last person he expected to support him.

'Margaret!' Dame Cynthia snapped her fingers. 'You can't be serious. Remember what we agreed?'

'We've had enough bad publicity already,' Margaret said. 'If we sack our CEO, we're admitting it was our fault. The scandal will only escalate.'

'That makes sense,' Errol said. 'I'll second that.'

'Me too,' Steven said.

'I propose Tony as interim CEO while Aaron is on leave,' Margaret added.

Aaron glanced around the room. Everyone nodded except for Dame Cynthia.

'It seems you have all made up your minds,' Dame Cynthia said. 'Personally, I think it's short-sighted. Aaron and Tony, kindly leave the room while we vote on the counterproposal.'

Aaron could barely look at Tony as they waited in the foyer. While they were writing the prepared statement earlier that morning, Aaron had been secretly planning his resignation letter. Now he had another chance—thanks to his best mate.

'You didn't need to do this, Tony. But I'm glad and grateful you did. Even if all those things you said about me weren't deserved.'

'Nonsense,' Tony said. 'I meant every word I said.' A grin appeared across his face. 'Even Margaret agreed with me.'

Aaron smiled back. 'Yes, but for the wrong reasons.'

Errol burst out of the hall and gave Aaron a hearty pat on the back. 'Congratulations! You are still our leader!' Errol turned to Tony. 'Congratulations to you too, Tony. Our new interim CEO.'

The locals had dispersed when Aaron and Tony eventually left the hall, but the press remained in force. Aaron caught the tail end of Dame Cynthia's press briefing.

'At today's meeting, we affirmed our support for Aaron Casper as CEO of Parata Peak Power. We have granted Mr Casper a leave of absence to settle some personal issues. We look forward to his return and support his vision to rebuild our company.'

Dame Cynthia spoke without a hint of shame. The hypocrite. Aaron had half a mind to tell the reporters what she said inside during the meeting.

Tony tapped Aaron on the shoulder. 'Come on. Let's get you home.'

Aaron overheard a reporter phoning in her report as they walked to Tony's car.

     David Whittet

'This is Rosa Murphy for Radio New Zealand News, reporting from the Parata Peak community hall, where the board of Parata Peak Power have just concluded their emergency meeting. We understand Aaron Casper is leaving the devastation behind and flying to Switzerland. Doubtless to live off the ill-gotten gains his father has sequestered in unnamed Swiss bank accounts.'

Aaron was about to berate the reporter when he heard a familiar voice from behind.

'Perhaps he won't need to go to Switzerland now.'

Aaron spun around. 'Miriama! You've come back!'

'I never left,' Miriama said. 'I've been such a fool. My head was all over the place. Sabrina and Laura kept on at me. They almost drove me insane.' Miriama brushed away tears with her hand. 'I wasn't here when you needed me. Can you ever forgive me?'

'Forgive you?' Aaron flung his arms around Miriama. 'There's nothing to forgive. You're here now. Nothing else in the world matters.'

The paparazzi were packing up but got their cameras out again to capture the dramatic and emotional reunion.

Would that mean better headlines in tomorrow's newspapers?

'So what will you do now, Aaron?' a reporter shouted. 'I assume this means you're not going to Switzerland.'

Aaron whispered in Miriama's ear. 'Honeymoon?'

Miriama nodded.

Aaron turned back to the reporter. 'We're going on our honeymoon, and I'm not telling any of you our destination.'

Aaron and Miriama spent two glorious weeks in Melbourne. Fine dining, theatre, opera, concerts, art galleries, museums and sightseeing. All the things they never had time for in their chaotic lives.

'I don't want to go back,' Aaron said at breakfast on their last day.

Miriama's eyes gleamed. 'We don't have to. You've got extended leave. I can do some freelance work remotely. Where do you want to go? Fiji, Tahiti, Honolulu? The world's your oyster.'

Aaron grinned. 'Anywhere but Switzerland. But seriously, we must go back sometime and face up to everything.' He eyed Miriama intently. 'I'm not sure I am the right person to rebuild Parata Peak Power. Perhaps I should resign.'

'That's nonsense.' Miriama reached across the breakfast table and squeezed Aaron's hand. 'It'll be a battle, but that's your strength. You thrive under pressure. I'll be at your side, I promise.' She leant back and finished her coffee. 'Though, I've always wanted to go to Tahiti.'

Aaron had dreamt of visiting Tahiti too. Maybe he was at his best when the heat was on, but for the next few weeks he would forget about Parata Peak Power, the Godzone Gorillas and everything else. Except for Miriama.

   David Whittet

EPILOGUE

Roaring Creek Domain, One Year Later

Aaron was late for his sugar fix that day. Nothing had been quite the same since the explosion at Parata Peak. He wasn't sure he would ever know the whole truth about the bombing. Objections from corrupt Gang lawyers resulted in countless delays, and the case still hadn't come to trial. Kaine remained in custody, but Corey was released on bail.

Then there were the conspiracy theories about his father. The storm that arose when this mercurial character finally resurfaced still brought Aaron out in a cold sweat.

The Donut Caravan became Aaron's happy place. Each afternoon the caravan parked on the Roaring Creek domain and he would buy a doughnut. Sometimes two or three if he'd had a particularly stressful day.

As he strolled across the domain that afternoon, he didn't recognise the woman sitting on a park bench, staring at him. Surely it wasn't another wretched reporter who had tracked him down. She wasn't dressed like one, a bit drab and dowdy looking, but then reporters would do anything to get a story.

It was a three-doughnut day. Aaron purchased them from the caravan, chatted with the doughnut lady, and wandered back over the domain.

'Best doughnuts ever,' he said to the woman on the park bench, who was still eyeing him.

'I've never tried one,' the woman said, 'but they do look nice.'

As Aaron walked away down the path, the woman called after him. 'You always had a sweet tooth. Even as a little boy.'

Aaron stopped dead in his tracks. He turned to face the woman.

'Aaron!' the woman cried out. 'My beloved son!'

Their eyes met, and Aaron dropped all three doughnuts to the ground.

'My mummy!' Aaron ran up to her and flung his arms around her. 'My mummy!'

With tears streaming down her face, she cuddled him so tightly that he could scarcely breathe. 'I have waited twenty-five years for this moment. Twenty-five long, hard years. I can't believe I've found you.'

'I can't believe it either!' Aaron rubbed his face against hers, and their tears intermingled. 'I never thought I'd see you again. I've missed you so much. I've tried to find you. You've no idea how many private detectives I've hired.'

'I'm here now and that's all that matters.' Alicia dried her eyes and pointed across to the Donut Caravan. 'Look. We're embarrassing those folk.'

Aaron turned his head. Everything was a blur through his tear-filled eyes, but he could make out a couple at the caravan getting their doughnuts. He waved at them and gave them a thumbs-up sign. They reciprocated by blowing a kiss.

'They're not embarrassed,' Aaron said. 'They're happy for us.'

'And so they should be,' Alicia said. 'I love you, my little Aaron. I've wanted to say that to you again every day for the past twenty-five years!'

Aaron ran his fingers through his mother's grey hair. She was so thin that he felt her bare bones when he hugged her. That and the lines on her face told him how much his mother had suffered. She needed pampering, and he was going to make sure she got it.

'You're coming home with me,' he said. 'There's so much to talk about. Twenty-five years of catching up. And I'm going to look after you.'

'Yes! *Yes!*' Alicia wiped away a fresh flood of tears. 'My darling boy, that means more to me than you'll ever know. I want to come home.'

 David Whittet

AUTHOR'S NOTE AND ACKNOWLEDGEMENTS

My debut novel *Gang Girl* occupied me for more than a decade. Like most first-time authors, I felt immense satisfaction when the final round of editing was completed and the book was ready for publication. Despite my elation, I knew in my heart that Alicia's story was far from over.

So what was next for Alicia? An idea came to me while working on the final draft of *Gang Girl*, and I added an epilogue. Would Alicia's recently rekindled relationship with Mickey withstand the news that she was expecting a child by his arch-enemy, Emir?

Early in the planning, I decided that the second book had to be Aaron's story, Alicia's beloved son. Many readers of *Gang Girl* have taken Alicia's struggles to their hearts. I apologise to them that we lose Alicia so early in *Goliath and the Gang*. However, I promise Alicia will be back in the final novel of the trilogy, where her struggle to escape the Godzone Gorillas will reach a dramatic conclusion.

Mickey's many admirers will be pleased to know that he will also return in the next book. While demoralised following his brutal de-patching from the Godzone Gorillas, his spirit remains alive. His mischievousness is still there too, and Mickey plays a vital role in the denouement.

Gang Girl was born of the twenty-plus years I spent working as a rural doctor in a remote New Zealand community. *Goliath and the Gang* takes inspiration from my move south to the beautiful Waitaki District, with its magnificent lakes and hydroelectric power stations. Privatisation of the power industry remains a contentious issue in New Zealand. It was headline news when I first drafted the story in the early 2010s, with the government selling shares in Mighty River Power, as it was called back then.

My mind went into overdrive. Imagine two deadly rivals. Both have gang connections and become leaders of competing power companies. What if they are intent on destroying each other? The scene was set for an almighty war between Aaron and his nemesis, Corey.

Many residents in Kurow, a small town in the Waitaki Valley, dread a tsunami-like wave should there be an accident at the nearby Waitaki Dam. Suppose Corey and the Godzone Gorillas, or the crazed man who claims to be Aaron's father, decided to blow up the fictional Parata Peak Power Station as an act of vengeance against Aaron?

I have lived and breathed with these characters for the past fifteen years and am indebted to those who have shared the journey with me. This book is dedicated to Joyce Cocchi, whose unrelenting enthusiasm and support for the project have sustained my creative efforts throughout this writing marathon.

I am also thankful to my fantastic beta readers, who have provided invaluable feedback and encouragement. Especially to Nicky Sinclair and Dave Buckerage for your encouragement and insights into the characters and story.

For me, the greatest joy of being an indie author is the ability to choose my own publishing partners. Editing can make or break a book—and an author's career. Finding the right editor is essential for every writer. It is their most important professional relationship. I'm glad I found Renell Judais at Proof Perfect NZ. Renell used her expertise and meticulous attention to detail to perfect the manuscript.

Likewise, I am indebted to my proofreader, Stephanie McConchie, at Focus Proofreading & Editing. Stephanie has shown a remarkable commitment to the project beyond simply proofreading.

A special shout out to Holly Dunn for designing the stunning book cover. Holly has also created a new cover for *Gang Girl*, which we are relaunching alongside *Goliath and the Gang*. I can't wait to see her concepts for *Godzone and the Gorillas*, the final book in the trilogy. You are an extraordinary talent, Holly. I am honoured to have your work on my book cover once more.

I'm deeply grateful to Dave MacManus and the brilliant team at CP Books for making the publishing experience stress-free and enjoyable.

Thanks to Karen McKenzie, my publicist at Lighthouse PR, for again expertly guiding me through the book launch and the myriad of interviews.

You have all played a vital part in helping me to realise my dream.

My incredible family deserves my most profound appreciation. I can never thank Siriporn, Mark and Rebecca enough for standing by me through the countless drafts and revisions.

I have been genuinely heartened by the number of readers who have told me

　　　　　David Whittet

that they relate to Alicia and her struggle to escape from her gang upbringing. While *Goliath and the Gang*, like *Gang Girl*, is a work of fiction, the characters are drawn from my experiences living and working in rural and provincial New Zealand. I have been privileged to meet many brave women, like Alicia, and countless conflicted characters, like Aaron, all trying to find their way in the world. Kāterina is another character close to my heart. She reflects the many wise Māori women I have been honoured to know.

These wonderful people are my inspiration and the life and soul of my writing.

ABOUT THE AUTHOR

David Whittet is a family doctor, a multi-award-winning independent filmmaker, and an author.

Storytelling has been in David's DNA for as long as he can remember. As a child, the serialisations of classic literature on television each Sunday at teatime were the highlight of his week. A dramatisation of *Oliver Twist* had a profound effect on him. In its day, Dickens' novel reformed the UK's Poor Law, which convinced David of the written word's potential to change the world.

He decided then that he wanted to be a writer. Subsequently, A J Cronin's novels inspired David to become a doctor, especially *The Citadel* (1937), which pre-empted the National Health Service's foundation in the UK and beyond. Further proof that books change lives.

David's work as a GP brings authenticity and gritty realism to his writing. His twenty-plus years of practice in rural New Zealand inspired his debut novel. *Gang Girl* is the story of a notorious gang leader's daughter and her lifelong struggle to escape the gang and forge her own destiny.

Medicine is a constant source of inspiration for David's writing. Like writing, general practice is about being interested in people's stories. His second novel, *The Road to Madhapur*, draws on David's personal experience of family medicine in both New Zealand and India. The colourful cast of characters David has met throughout his career—colleagues and patients alike—breathe life into his writing.

IndieReader described *The Road to Madhapur* as a 'beautiful, heartbreaking coming-of-age story where the characters' lives are beset by strife and hardship. The cultural setting of Madhapur, beautifully evoked with breathtaking imagery and remarkable attention to detail, serves as the perfect backdrop where Theo and Elisha's paths collide and they find love, meaning and purpose.'

Enjoyed *Goliath and the Gang*? Please consider leaving a review or a rating on Goodreads and Amazon:

https://www.goodreads.com/author/show/21574252.David_Whittet
https://www.amazon.com/stores/author/B0BHPW9NW6

Learn more about the inspiration behind the book at David's website:

https://davidwhittet.com

For the latest news on David's work, exclusive previews, events, short stories and advance reader copies, sign up for his newsletter:

https://david-whittet.ck.page/subscribe